ATTENDING DAEDALUS
GENE WOLFE, ARTIFICE
AND THE READER

Liverpool Science Fiction Texts and Studies
General Editor DAVID SEED

Series Advisers: I. F. Clarke, Edward James, Patrick Parrinder and Brian Stableford

ATTENDING DAEDALUS

GENE WOLFE, ARTIFICE
AND THE READER

PETER WRIGHT

LIVERPOOL UNIVERSITY PRESS

First published 2003 by
LIVERPOOL UNIVERSITY PRESS
4 Cambridge Street
Liverpool L69 7ZU

British Library Cataloguing-in-Publication Data
A British Library CIP record is available.

ISBN 0 85323 818 9 cased
ISBN 0 85323 828 6 paperback

Typeset in Meridien by
Koinonia, Bury, Lancashire
Printed and bound in the European Union by
Bell and Bain Ltd, Glasgow

To my parents,
who taught me to read

Contents

Acknowledgements

No work of this kind is ever completed without incurring significant debts to many generous individuals. *Attending Daedalus* is certainly no exception. I am chiefly indebted to Gene Wolfe, who has graciously given interviews, corresponded with me on matters professional and personal, and who, with his charming wife, Rosemary, welcomed me into his home. Between 1992 and 1997, Wolfe put aside time in his busy schedule to answer my letters and provide me with first editions of his work as they were published, often at considerable cost to himself. Without the Wolfes's generosity and hospitality, I would not have been able to attend the Science Fiction Research Association (SFRA) conference in 1994 to test my theories, nor spend an illuminating week as their houseguest.

Since this book began as my doctoral thesis, I am particularly grateful to Tony Barley, my supervisor at the University of Liverpool, who knew when to leave me alone, and to my examiners, Professors David Seed and Edward James, who have continued to encourage me in my academic career.

I should like to express my gratitude to Brian Attebery, Joan Gordon, Gary K. Wolfe, and other delegates at the SFRA–25 conference in Chicago who challenged my stance and thereby helped me to consolidate my argument; to John Clute, Colin Greenland and Joan Gordon, who provided me with copies of their reviews on request; to Pat McMurray who entrusted me with his Cheap Street Editions of Wolfe's *The Old Woman Whose Rolling Pin is in the Sun* and *At the Point of Capricorn*; and to Amy Sisson, formerly an editor of the *SFRA Review*, who sent me copies of all the Wolfe-related material published in that periodical. I also wish to acknowledge the kindness of Bruce Pennington, who agreed to provide one of his wonderfully evocative paintings for the cover.

While I am thankful to the staff of the Sidney Jones Library at the University of Liverpool, all of whom have been most helpful, particular gratitude is due to Andy Sawyer, Administrator of the Science Fiction Foundation Collection at Liverpool, who has obliged my requests tirelessly. Equally, I should like to thank Alex March for her invaluable assistance in researching 25 years of science fiction magazines, journals and fanzines during the early stages of this project. Special thanks must also go to Jenni Woodward, who helped me to conclude vital research in a flurry of searches through the Science Fiction Foundation archive and whose unrelenting enthusiasm and support kept me sane in the closing and difficult months of preparing *Attending Daedalus* for publication.

For their patience, endurance, and unstinting support—which has occasionally gone unacknowledged—I am deeply thankful to, and for, my parents, Muriel and Ron Wright, who remain my first and best critics.

Preface

Gene Wolfe has written a distinguished body of science fiction, fantasy and science fantasy that has been widely reviewed and admired. To date, he has published 20 novels, a collection of wartime letters, a volume of poetry and over 100 short stories. In view of his critical success, his reputation, and his considerable canon, it may seem remarkable that this is only the second book-length study of his fiction and the first to address any material published after 1983.

However, as the majority of critics and reviewers who have approached his oeuvre would admit, Gene Wolfe is a complex and wily writer, ambiguous, subtle and playful. His fiction is intricately wrought, densely allusive, and conceptually elusive; it encourages misreadings, demands thoughtful reflection, and is able to involve the reader in labyrinthine possibilities for interpretation. The elaborate and puzzling nature of Wolfe's writing, together with the fact that Wolfe works in a popular cultural form, seems to explain his critical neglect.

Confronted, then, with the magnitude and range of Wolfe's output and the paucity of detailed analyses available, it seemed critically advantageous to concentrate the focus of the present volume on the conceptual and thematic centre of Wolfe's corpus, the four-volume *The Book of the New Sun* and its coda, *The Urth of the New Sun*. For a variety of reasons, *Attending Daedalus* has taken an unusually long time from submission to publication. The manuscript was delivered in 1999, before Tor published *On Blue's Waters*, the first volume of Wolfe's *The Book of the Short Sun*. When I was sent proofs in June 2003, it was tempting to rewrite the concluding chapter to include a discussion of *The Book of the Short Sun*. I resisted that temptation, primarily because I felt I had little to add to my treatment of *The Book of the New Sun* and its sequel. Any consideration of *The Book of the Short Sun* would certainly have lengthened my argument, but I doubted that it would have developed or deepened it to any meaningful extent. Secondly, *Attending Daedalus* was always intended to encourage others to write about Gene Wolfe, whose work deserves more attention than it has yet received, despite the efforts of many perceptive, dedicated and enthusiastic Wolfe scholars to foster dialogue and debate. It seemed appropriate, therefore, to leave *The Book of the Short Sun* as comparatively virgin territory for other writers to explore. And thirdly, if I had succumbed to the temptation to revise the concluding chapter, how could I have stood firm against the possibility of reworking the one before it—and the one before that? Hence, *Attending Daedalus* concludes with an analysis of *The Book of the Long Sun* in relation to Wolfe's Urth Cycle and the sincere hope that others will follow Joan Gordon, Michael Andre-Driussi and myself in publishing books that attempt to do justice to one of science fiction's most notable literary figures—indeed, to one of the most important writers of the twentieth, and possibly twenty-first, century.

In terms of its approach, this study addresses a hitherto largely ignored aspect of Wolfe's fiction: its effect on the reader. Accordingly, *Attending Daedalus* is devoted to exploring how Wolfe's preoccupations and idiosyncrasies as a creative artist may influence, manipulate and finally illuminate that reader.

A Note on Editions

In most cases, the editions of Gene Wolfe's works cited throughout *Attending Daedalus* are either first editions or share their pagination with the first editions. Notable exceptions include:

1. *Operation Ares* (London: Fontana Books, 1978).
   The only UK paperback edition to date.
2. *The Fifth Head of Cerberus* (London: Quartet Books, 1975).
   The first UK paperback edition.
3. *Peace* (London: New English Library, 1989).
   The most recent UK edition of the text.
4. *The Devil in a Forest* (London: Grafton, 1985).
   The only UK paperback edition to date.
5. *Gene Wolfe's Book of Days* (London: Arrow Books, 1985).
   The only UK paperback edition to date.
6. *Free Live Free* (London: Legend (Arrow Books), 1989).
   The pagination of the Legend edition corresponds to the mass-market hardback edition published by Gollancz and Tor Books in 1989. The first edition of *Free Live Free*, published by Ziesing, is a limited edition and contains a number of textual variations from the subsequent mass-market hardback and paperback editions.

Abbreviations

The following abbreviations are employed throughout for frequently cited texts. They are introduced only after the initial full citation, however, and, unless otherwise stated, always refer to the editions listed below. The list is arranged chronologically, with the date of first publication given in parentheses immediately after the title where the referenced text is not the first edition.

Novels and Anthologies by Gene Wolfe

Island	*The Island of Doctor Death and Other Stories and Other Stories* (1980) (London: Arrow Books, 1981).
Shadow	*The Shadow of the Torturer: Volume One of The Book of the New Sun* (1980) (London: Arrow Books, 1981).
GW Days	*Gene Wolfe's Book of Days* (1981) (London: Arrow Books, 1981).
Claw	*The Claw of the Conciliator: Volume Two of The Book of the New Sun* (1981) (London: Arrow Books, 1982).
Sword	*The Sword of the Lictor: Volume Three of The Book of the New Sun* (1981) (London: Arrow Books, 1982).
Citadel	*The Citadel of the Autarch: Volume Four of The Book of the New Sun* (1983) (London: Arrow Books, 1983).
S. Mist	*Soldier of the Mist* (1986) (London: Orbit, 1988).
Urth	*The Urth of the New Sun* (1987) (London: Orbit, 1988).
Storeys	*Storeys from the Old Hotel* (Worcester Park, Surrey: Kerosina Publications, 1988).
Species	*Endangered Species* (1989) (London: Orbit, 1990).
S. Arete	*Soldier of Arete* (1989) (London: New English Library, 1990).
Pandora	*Pandora by Holly Hollander* (1990) (London: New English Library, 1991).
Nightside	*Nightside the Long Sun: Volume One of The Book of the Long Sun* (New York: Tor, 1993).
Lake	*Lake of the Long Sun: Volume Two of The Book of the Long Sun* (New York: Tor, 1994).
Caldé	*Caldé of the Long Sun: Volume Three of The Book of the Long Sun* (New York: Tor, 1994).
Exodus	*Exodus from the Long Sun: Volume Four of The Book of the Long Sun* (New York: Tor, 1996).

Works by Other Authors

Guide   Joan Gordon, *Starmont Reader's Guide 29: Gene Wolfe* (Washington: Starmont House, 1986).

Strokes   John Clute, *Strokes: Essays and Reviews 1966–1986* (Seattle: Serconia Press, 1988).

Part I
Initiations

The same critics who spend hundreds of pages discussing various peculiarities of the author's supposed nature often devote none to that much more significant person, the reader for whom he wrote.
— Gene Wolfe, 'Introduction' to *Endangered Species* (1989)

1. 'Silhouette': An Introduction
to Gene Wolfe

In the revised edition of *The Encyclopedia of Science Fiction*, John Clute describes Gene Wolfe as 'quite possibly the most important writer' working in the science fiction (SF) field.[1] From Clute's assured tone, the reader could be forgiven for accepting this comment as the conclusion of a dynamic critical debate. It is, however, nothing of the sort. While Wolfe has received considerable acclaim for his stylistic versatility, his ability to produce detailed and credible fictional worlds, and his skill at characterisation, he remains one of the most neglected and misunderstood writers of contemporary science fiction and fantasy.

As this bio-bibliographical introduction reveals, Wolfe's work has provoked little academic interest (possibly because of its complexity), except for a number of reviews and articles that have disregarded perhaps the most crucial factor in understanding his writing: the effects on the reader of his literary techniques and strategies. If Wolfe's fiction is to receive the analytical attention it deserves, there is a need therefore to argue why he should be considered as one of the 'most important' writers of SF. *Attending Daedalus* seeks to provide that argument by progressing from an overview of Wolfe's career to a detailed examination of his magnum opus: *The Book of the New Sun* (1980–83) and its sequel, *The Urth of the New Sun* (1987).

The style, subtlety, range and intricacy of Wolfe's stories and novels belie his non-literary background. Born an only child on 7 May 1931 in Brooklyn, New York, Wolfe spent the first 10 years of his life moving from state to state before his family finally settled in Houston, Texas. Wolfe's love of books was inherited from his parents and fostered further by his mother, who read to him throughout his childhood.

It was in Houston that Wolfe first read pulp magazines, the influence of which can be seen, on one level or another, in many of his tales, but most notably in 'The Island of Doctor Death and Other Stories' (1970). He continued to read SF at every possible opportunity, especially those stories featuring Buck Rogers and Flash Gordon. Providentially, Wolfe was enrolled at the Edgar Allan Poe Elementary School, an institution he found entirely conducive to his burgeoning interest in science- and supernatural fiction.[2] After graduating from Lamar High School he attended Texas Agricultural & Mechanical where he studied mechanical engineering and began writing short fiction for *The Commentator*, a college magazine. Two of these early stories, 'The Case of the Vanishing Ghost' (1951) and 'The Grave Secret' (1952), have subsequently been reprinted in *Young Wolfe* (U. M. Press, 1992).

Wolfe's contributions to *The Commentator* ceased in 1952 when he left college halfway through his junior year with poor grades. No longer protected by his student deferment, he was drafted into the army where he recorded his experiences in the USA and Korea in a series of letters to his mother (now published by U. M. Press as *Letters Home* [1992]). His recollections of training and of the slow, inexorable journey to the front lines were highly influential in the writing of Severian's passage towards the conflict threatening the Commonwealth in *The Book of the New Sun*, itself a version of Stephen Crane's *The Red Badge of Courage* (1895).[3]

After being discharged, the G. I. Bill enabled Wolfe to attend the University of Houston, where he graduated as a Bachelor of Science in 1956. He married Rosemary Dietsch, with whom he would have four children, moved to Cincinnati to start a career as an engineer with Procter & Gamble, and began writing seriously in an effort to earn money for furniture.[4]

Wolfe's persistence eventually brought him success in October 1965, when the skin magazine *Sir!* published 'The Dead Man', a modest ghost story set in India. 'The Dead Man' is, in essence, an alternative and more polished version of the story Wolfe tells in 'The Grave Secret', in which a dead man discovers his own deathly state. In this way, 'The Dead Man' reveals itself to be a seminal text, anticipating Wolfe's particular interest in subjectivism and altered states of consciousness. Although a second publication, 'Mountains Like Mice', followed in 1966, Wolfe's writing career could not be said to have begun properly until Lloyd Biggle invited him to join the Science Fiction Writers of America (SFWA). The SFWA's list of markets included the *Orbit* series of anthologies edited by SF writer Damon Knight. In 1966, Knight purchased 'Trip, Trap'—with revisions— for *Orbit 2* (1967). Wolfe openly acknowledges his debt to Knight in the dedication to *The Fifth Head of Cerberus: Three Novellas* (1972), in interviews and in conversation:

> When I sent 'Trip, Trap' to Damon Knight I set it out in two columns, one showing how each of the characters saw things from their perspective. He couldn't produce it as two columns so he sent it back to me marked with the breaks he thought would be the best places for the Earthman to speak and for the alien to speak. I spent an evening going through it and trying to improve on what he had

done, and found out that I couldn't. He had gotten the whole thing right. All the breaks were right. When I got through that evening I felt I had learned a great deal just by going over his work and seeing why it was right and why it worked to break it in those places.[5]

'Trip, Trap', which used an epistolary form to relate an ironic anthropological tale that confirmed Wolfe's interest in the subjective nature of perception, was the first of 18 sales that Wolfe made to Knight, whose *Orbit* collections contain some of Wolfe's most accomplished short fiction. These memorable stories include 'The Changeling' (*Orbit 3*, 1968), 'The Island of Doctor Death and Other Stories' (*Orbit 7*, 1970) (which earned Wolfe his first Nebula Award Nomination), 'The Fifth Head of Cerberus' (*Orbit 10*, 1972), 'Forlesen' (*Orbit 14*, 1974) and 'Seven American Nights' (*Orbit 20*, 1978).

In 1970, Wolfe published his first novel, *Operation Ares*. Written in 1967 and heavily cut by Wolfe and Don Benson, editor of Berkley Books, *Operation Ares* was dismissed by Joanna Russ as 'a failure, shadowy and inconclusive'.[6] Despite the negative reviews it received, and a conservative politicisation atypical of Wolfe, *Operation Ares* is a competent first novel describing a dystopian North America administered by pacifists and threatened by a resurgent nationalist rebellion. The plot is made more complex by an invasion from Mars, mounted by Earth's abandoned colonies, a pacifist deal with the Russians and Chinese military and financial aid for the rebellion. Stylistically, *Operation Ares* is not so much 'an aberration' in Wolfe's canon, as Joan Gordon would have the reader believe,[7] but a text published at a time when Wolfe's narrative skill had already surpassed what he had been capable of in 1967. Like 'The Dead Man' and 'Trip, Trap', *Operation Ares* is a seminal text, indicating Wolfe's burgeoning fascination with the motivating power of engineered myths and with hierarchical systems of manipulation and deception.

Whatever disappointment Wolfe may have felt at the reception of his first novel was compensated by the praise he received in 1972, a year that marked a turning point in his career. Quitting Procter & Gamble, Wolfe accepted an editorial post at *Plant Engineering*, a large US trade magazine, moved to Barrington, Illinois, and published *The Fifth Head of Cerberus: Three Novellas*. Located on the French-settled twin planets of Sainte Anne and Sainte Croix, these three stories unite a number of the principal themes of Wolfe's oeuvre.

The first novella, 'The Fifth Head of Cerberus', describes a young man's quest for identity on Sainte Croix in a society populated by clones of himself and his father, who are, essentially, one and the same biological person. '"A Story" by John V. Marsch' could either be an artificial myth reconstructed by anthropologist Marsch from observations made on

Sainte Anne, or else a genuine myth retold, depending on whether its author was Marsch or Victor Trenchard, the shape-shifting aborigine who accompanies and eventually replaces him during his expedition. The final piece, 'V.R.T.', describes Marsch/Trenchard's exploration of Sainte Anne, his return to Sainte Croix, and his subsequent imprisonment for unspecified crimes in a cut and paste series of diary entries and transcribed recordings read by one of the prison officials.

Seductive, ambiguous and altogether fascinating, *The Fifth Head of Cerberus* was widely reviewed in periodicals as diverse as *Analog Science Fiction/Science Fact*, *The New York Times* and *The Times Literary Supplement*. The book was praised for its subtlety, depth and elaborate structure; its vividness and thematic coherence; and, less effectively, for the way in which it examined the issues of colonisation and suppression.

More important at this point, perhaps, were those reviews that contributed to establishing a conflicting image of Wolfe. Where Michael Bishop and Pamela Sargent highlight the stylistic excellence and ambiguity of the book and P. Schuyler-Miller uncovers its subtexts,[8] Thomas Monteleone and George Turner concentrate on the effects on the reader of the text's perplexing density. Monteleone observes how the fragmentary nature of 'V.R.T' 'forces the reader to patiently piece together all the separate incidents' of the story, arguing 'that Wolfe is making implications of considerable significance; but at times the prose turns inward and becomes so circular that the meaning is lost'.[9] 'The entire book is a great open-ended experiment that forces the reader to extrapolate', Monteleone remarks, and draws attention to the apparently writerly qualities of the book by noting that 'the conclusions are left up to individual readers'.[10]

George Turner also recognises the book as 'one of the more complex products of SF, open to a deal of opinion and interpretation',[11] but he sees this openness as subordinate to the 'slow revelation of the real state of anthropological affairs on the twin planets'.[12] Deciding what has actually occurred, and what is occurring, on Sainte Anne and Sainte Croix is, according to Turner,

> one of the major charms of the book. The answers are there, but Wolfe does not throw them at you; the book must be read with care and attention because sometimes the clues lie in a word or a phrase buried in a sentence ostensibly about something else. He has not offered a baffling, exhausting puzzle, but rather has laid his trail with marvellous care so that there is an exhilaration in keeping up with the pace he sets.[13]

The reader is left with contradictory visions of Wolfe as a writer. On the one hand, Monteleone sees him as the originator of an open text that confuses the reader until its meaning is lost, whereupon the reader is abandoned; on the other, Turner presents him as a writer who guides the reader through his alien worlds to the actual state of affairs existing at the heart of the text.

Turner's view is the more accurate. *The Fifth Head of Cerberus* is a conundrum, but it is one in which sufficient clues exist for the reader to determine a large proportion of what has happened on Sainte Anne and Sainte Croix. Those ambiguities that remain serve, as Albert Wendland suggests, to extend speculations raised by the narrative's thematic pre-occupations

> into their ... contemporary relevance; the lack of answers is like that today found in our search for morality and understanding ..., the frightening and yet growing realisation that harming a supposedly separate object will lead to harming the subject too, to harming one's self.[14]

Accordingly, *The Fifth Head of Cerberus* can be read as a subtle indictment of the exploitation of 'foreign' or 'alien' cultures that reveals how the exploiters, through their actions, may lose their own identity, their 'humanity'. As such, it is one of science fiction's most intricate anti-colonial novels.

In 1973, Wolfe won the Nebula Award for his novella 'The Death of Doctor Island', the tale of a mentally disturbed youth imprisoned in, and manipulated by, an artificial but sentient satellite. The following year, *Locus: The Newspaper of the Science Fiction Field* also conferred its award for Best Novella on the story.

Between 1973 and the publication of his second novel, *Peace*, in 1975, Wolfe produced a variety of stories with subject matter ranging from humanity's abuse of the environment ('An Article About Hunting', 'Beautyland' [1973]) to alien contact ('Alien Stones' [1973]) and subjectivism ('Feather Tigers' [1973] and 'Cues' [1974]).

Wolfe's initial 'mid-western' novel, *Peace*, which received the Chicago Foundation for Literature Award in 1977, was the first long work to reflect Wolfe's interest in the nature and mechanics of memory and of memory systems, something to which he would later return in *The Book of the New Sun* and *Soldier of Arete* (1989). In *Peace*, a ghost (Alden Dennis Weer) haunts the memory places of his life, now collected beneath the roof of a symbolic house, after being freed from the grave by a falling tree. The title is, of course, ironic. Rather than suggesting a condition (that of resting in peace), it alludes to Weer's quest for peace as he revisits his memories in the hope of finding a meaning to his former life.

When no reviewer recognised Weer's deathly state, *Peace* was labelled as a mainstream novel and the ghost's story quickly became Wolfe's first misinterpreted narrative. Martin Last, for example, believes Weer to be 'an aging small-town man'; Richard Lupoff accepts him as an 'elderly middle-western businessman who's worried about his health, and down at the doctor's office does a few recollections-of-things-past'; and to Colin Greenland, Weer is 'an old man, withdrawn into a circle of firelight where he lies, half-paralysed, listening to the ticking of his life'.[15]

Steve Carper finds himself in difficulty when he attempts to reconcile his literal reading of the book with its fantastic shifts in time and place:

> Weer is a middle-aged man suffering from the effects of a stroke he knows (imagines?) he will receive twenty years in the future. He putters through a huge, rambling house that is a metaphor for the book, and as he wanders the story picks up the actions that took place in whatever room he is in or thinking of. Reminiscences. Or else the story he is writing in several of these rooms is this book as a piece of fiction. Or else he is telling it in pieces to his doctor in the form of stories made up around the pictures of Thematic Application [sic] Test cards. Or else ... The book is suffused with the same gently enigmatic quality that distinguishes Wolfe's best science fiction.[16]

By appealing to the ambiguity of Wolfe's other work, Carper excuses himself for not making a commitment to any of his readings and, inevitably, his review lapses into confusion.

George Turner avoids analysing *Peace* by appealing to the sanctity of art: 'I prefer not to insult a minor masterpiece and a genuine literary experience by dissecting it', he remarks, attempting to justify the inconclusiveness of his reading.[17] Although Turner insists that *Peace* is an 'utterly realistic novel', he does make several useful points about the narrative.[18] He identifies its tapestry-like qualities, the warp and weft of its embedded tales, its structural dependency on recurring objects and the contribution that these elements make to what he understands as 'an examination of the complexity of existence, of its interaction and connectivity'.[19] However, rather than being 'an examination' of existence, it is more accurate to describe *Peace* as a representation of the interconnectedness of human existence.

In the longest study of the book published to date, Joan Gordon observes how '*Peace* unites Wolfe's most common themes of memory, isolation, and rejection with another theme, the nature of time, which will become more and more important in his later work' (*Guide*, p. 30). While Gordon, like George Turner, misinterprets Weer's condition and categorises *Peace* as a mainstream novel, her oversight does not diminish the acuteness of her observations. For Gordon, *Peace* is a memoir-novel in which Weer's admission of the unreliability of his memories serves to inform the reader of 'the connection between reality and fiction' (*Guide*, p. 36). It is, she argues,

> a metafiction: a story about stories ... It is a self-conscious artifact which, through its artificiality, tells us something of the truth about reality. Trapped within our own minds, we can understand the world only as it is mediated by our minds and memories. (*Guide*, pp. 36–37)

Peace is, in effect, a treatise on subjectivism in which Wolfe explores the fabric of experiences, mysteries, stories, deceits and encounters contextualising the individual in time and space.[20]

Somewhat prophetically, Steve Carper suggests that *Peace* is 'a forerunner of the works that will satisfy all'.[21] This prediction was fulfilled four years after the publication of Wolfe's third novel, *The Devil in a Forest* (1976), a story describing the maturation of its adolescent protagonist, Mark, as his community struggles for survival against lordly oppression and brigandry in medieval Europe.

Marketed as a juvenile novel, and a fantasy, *The Devil in a Forest* was not widely reviewed. Nevertheless, those who did encounter it remarked on its content with enthusiasm. Beverly Friend, for example, highlights the ambiguous morality of its characters and Wolfe's ability to manipulate his readers' emotions by constantly re-presenting its murderous villain Wat (whose name emblematises his equivocal nature) as both a Robin Hood figure and a homicidal outlaw. Friend goes on to note how the text's convoluted plot structure reflects Wolfe's oblique characterisation and maintains the tension that the reader experiences as Mark vacillates between good and evil.[22]

In the course of her review, Friend indicates that '*Nothing* [in the text] is as it originally appears to be!' 'Nothing', in this instance, refers to the text's supernatural events which, while creating the ambience of the fantastic, are subject to rational explanation, to the multifarious guises of Wat, and to the chicanery of Mother Cloot, an old woman who plays on the villagers' superstitions and believes herself, in her drug-addicted state, to be a witch. These aspects of the novel provide a foretaste of the more elaborate generic and thematic deceptions Wolfe would later work in *The Book of the New Sun*, to which Friend's maxim is equally pertinent.

Although Darrell Schweitzer dismisses *The Devil in a Forest* for lacking depth, the late Susan Wood sees in its simplicity 'a timeless basic story: about human evil, which creates a world in which everything seems corrupt and "slippery", and about human faith, redeeming that world'.[23] Rather than lacking depth, as Schweitzer suggests, the deeper concerns of the book identified by Wood exist as subtexts or undercurrents to be glimpsed through the development of Mark.

Joan Gordon expresses her awareness of these issues and reports how the novel forms

> a vehicle for two lessons which Wolfe suggests rather than pro-
> nounces. Through Mark's experiences with Wat, charming yet
> cruel, and the Abbé, reserved yet kind, he learns that it is unwise to
> follow thoughtlessly those people or notions most attractive or
> popular. Instead, he learns to rely on his own reason to determine
> that which is good and follow it, though good and evil are often
> intertwined. Neither Mark nor the reader is told about these lessons.
> The actions of the novel lead Mark to incorporate them in his
> behaviour and the reader is led to agree with Mark's decisions.
> (*Guide*, p. 46)

Gordon's commentary isolates the text's concerns and indirectly overturns Schweitzer's opinion that *The Devil in a Forest* is a simple book. Neither Mark's progression towards a rational, moral standpoint, nor the world that shapes that progress, is handled in a simplistic way; indeed, both are constructed with the same subtlety and attention to detail found in Wolfe's other fiction.

The texture of the medieval setting is woven to create a world poised between the declining pagan religions and the expansion of Christianity. It is clear that Wolfe favours Christianity, but the superiority of its compassion and reason do not emerge until Mark has matured sufficiently to recognise the moral differences between the old faiths and the new, and choose between them (see *Guide*, pp. 47–49).

The Devil in a Forest is, then, comparatively conspicuous among Wolfe's work for addressing the themes of religious faith and moral choice directly and unambiguously. Wolfe's interest in these themes, which recur throughout his career but most notably in *The Book of the New Sun* and the four-volume *The Book of the Long Sun* (1993–96), has led several critics to cite Wolfe's Roman Catholicism as a key element in his composition as a writer. However, while it is true to say that Wolfe has written at least one Catholic story, 'The Detective of Dreams' (1980)—a pastiche of Poe—it is unwise to accept Wolfe's incorporation of religious themes, symbols and narrative patterns at face value.[24] As Wolfe himself explains:

> I am a Catholic in the real communion-taking sense, which tells you
> a lot less than you think about my religious beliefs ... I believe in
> God, in the divinity of Christ and in the survival of the person ...
> Like every thinking person, I am still working out my beliefs.[25]

Wolfe's self-portrait is typically evasive, yielding little definitive information about someone who understands that there are no easy or unequivocal

answers to any of the questions that may be asked, of him, of ourselves, or of the world at large. Importantly, though, the fact that Wolfe is still 'working out' his beliefs should alert the reader to the danger of any preconceived notions of how Wolfe will treat religious material. Just as it is imperative to read in context the allusions, intertexts and references that inform and suffuse Wolfe's fiction, so it is vital to recognise how Wolfe appropriates and recontextualises elements of religious practice, symbolism and belief in his fiction, especially in *The Book of the New Sun*.

Gordon sees *The Devil in a Forest*, with its orphaned, apprenticed protagonist, its stratified medieval society, its rationalisation of apparently supernatural events, and its sense of transformation, as a 'trial run' for *The Book of the New Sun* (see *Guide*, pp. 49–50). It would, however, be more precise to argue that Wolfe's entire writing career from 1965 to 1976, when he began work on *The Book of the New Sun*, had been a 'trial run' for a text that assembles many of his recurrent themes and techniques.

Divided into four volumes, *The Shadow of the Torturer* (1980), *The Claw of the Conciliator* (1981), *The Sword of the Lictor* (1981), and *The Citadel of the Autarch* (1983), *The Book of the New Sun* recounts the rise of its mnemonist narrator, Severian, from obscurity as an apprentice torturer to political and universal significance as the ruler of the Commonwealth. Set on the richly textured far-future world of Urth, a denuded and technologically exhausted planet that languishes under the baleful glare of a dying sun, the novel appears to be a narrative of moral and spiritual growth similar in nature to *The Devil in a Forest*.

Between the publication of *The Devil in a Forest* and *The Shadow of the Torturer*, Wolfe's output of short fiction declined as he drafted and redrafted his tetralogy. Although he won a Rhysling Award for Science Fiction Poetry for 'The Computer Iterates the Greater Trumps' in 1978, this could hardly have prepared him for the international attention he received when Timescape published *The Book of the New Sun*.

Widely and effusively praised, each volume of the tetralogy won at least one of SF's most coveted awards: *The Shadow of the Torturer* took the Howard Memorial Award and the World Fantasy Award in 1981, and the British Science Fiction Association Award in 1982; *The Claw of the Conciliator* brought Wolfe his second Nebula in 1981, while *Locus* honoured the novel with its Best Fantasy Novel Award in 1982; *The Sword of the Lictor* received the British Fantasy Award for Best Novel in 1983; and *The Citadel of the Autarch* took the John W. Campbell Memorial Award in 1984.

With the success of *The Shadow of the Torturer*, Wolfe became a commercially viable writer. His work, which, as Martin Last observes, had been 'mostly unheralded—except by a "cult" class of readers',[26] was suddenly marketable and two anthologies, *The Island of Doctor Death and*

Other Stories and Other Stories (1980) and *Gene Wolfe's Book of Days* (1981), which collected Wolfe's best short fiction, were published to exploit his popularity.

The Book of the New Sun was applauded in a variety of periodicals ranging from *The Magazine of Fantasy and Science Fiction* to *The Library Journal* and *The New York Times*. It was acclaimed for its imaginative fertility, its controlled and meticulous style, the craftsmanship of its construction and, most surprisingly in the light of subsequent commentaries, for its straightforwardness.[27] Michael Bishop, for example, sees *The Shadow of the Torturer* as

> an immediately accessible book for anyone with moderate intelligence and the ability to read. (Certainly it does not present some of the problems of interpretation that *The Fifth Head of Cerberus* ... has posed for the wary and unwary alike.)[28]

Richard E. Geis concurs, arguing that it is 'not an obscure novel, not ambiguous, not in the least (so far) a New Wave saga'.[29]

This faith in the tetralogy's clarity persisted, almost uninterrupted, through the publication of *The Claw of the Conciliator* (which led Colin Greenland to observe how *The Book of the New Sun* was already being considered as 'the next classic SF sequence, on a par with *Earthsea*, the Titus Groan books or even ... the *Foundation Trilogy*'[30]) and *The Sword of the Lictor*.

Among all the extravagant praise, writer and reviewer Algis Budrys, who agreed that the publication of *The Book of the New Sun* was indeed 'a seminal event' in the history of SF, gave voice to his growing suspicion that the narrative might not be as straightforward as it first appeared:

> I am in the presence of a practitioner whose moves I cannot follow; I see only the same illusions that are seen by those outside the guild [of writers]. I know the cards are up the sleeves somewhere, but there are clearly extra arms to this person.[31]

The image of Wolfe as illusionist and cardsharp is accurate and one that critics would later adopt as they began to share Budrys's sense of deception.

Most reviewers experienced a feeling of having been duped two years after Budrys, when Wolfe concluded his tetralogy. In his review of *The Citadel of the Autarch*, Baird Searles suggests the origins of this critical discomfort and poses a provocative question:

> *The Book of the New Sun* is too complex and oblique a work to evaluate on one reading. It will undoubtedly be considered a landmark in the field, one that perhaps marks the turning point of science fiction from content to style, from matter to manner. Mannered it certainly is, and stylish; [but] under that glittering edifice of surprising words

and more surprising events and characters, is there a story or concept of any stature?'[32]

Searles's understanding of how the text's complexity and obliqueness oppose efforts towards evaluation was echoed by other reviewers, including Colin Greenland, who, in his tellingly entitled article 'Wolfe in Sheep's Clothing', observes:

> Wolfe is subtle as well as bold, lavish with sly puzzles, mysteries and revelations that have had more than one reader suddenly waking up in the middle of the night saying, 'My God, it can't be!' But it is. Second and third readings are indicated.[33]

Like Searles, Greenland recognises how the mysterious and revelatory nature of the text poses problems for the reader, who is required to return to the text again and again if he or she wishes to solve its 'sly puzzles' and formulate an interpretation.

While reviewers realised that *The Book of the New Sun* 'conceals more than is initially apparent',[34] none could discover what it was the text concealed. Eventually, it became clear that, despite their approval of the narrative's fluidity of style, the conception of its enigmatic, alien Earth and the depth of its characterisation, many critics had no more idea of the subject matter or the relevance of the tetralogy now it was complete than they did at the beginning of *The Shadow of the Torturer*.

Indeed, although Searles prophesied that *The Book of the New Sun* was 'certainly the sort of novel that will provide a field day for critics, essayists, people who make lists, analysers, and academics', his prophesy has gone largely unfulfilled.[35] A notable exception is Michael Andre-Driussi, whose *Lexicon Urthus: A Dictionary for the Urth Cycle* (1994) forms an erudite glossary of the obscure and archaic words and pronouns found within *The Book of the New Sun* and its sequel.

Few analysts have examined Wolfe's tetralogy as a literary construct, however, and those who did preferred to study its more accessible qualities or else debate endlessly minor details of plot in often ill-conceived exegetical frenzies. Prime examples of extravagant exposition are Robert Borski's 'Thinking About the Mandragora in Wolfe's *Citadel*' and 'Masks of the Father: Paternity in Gene Wolfe's *Book of the New Sun*'. Borski—who administers 'Cave Canem', a website dedicated to *The Fifth Head of Cerberus* —is one of Wolfe's more imaginative and idiosyncratic analysts. However, although 'Thinking About the Mandragora' is a rather nebulous and inconclusive reading of a minor episode in *The Citadel of the Autarch*, 'Masks of the Father' is a series of speculations regarding the nature and relationships of the father figures that appear in the tetralogy. Often more conjectural than erudite, Borski's ruminations are nevertheless fascinating for suggesting the importance of an undisclosed conspiracy driving the main narrative.[36] Unfortunately for Borski, this conspiracy is only a minor part of the more extensive transtemporal mythopoeic intrigue, discussed in Chapter 5, that underlies *The Book of the New Sun* and *The Urth of the New Sun* (1987).

In an early study of the tetralogy, C. N. Manlove chooses to offer an extended synopsis of the book in which he identifies Wolfe's debt to William Hope Hodgson, Mervyn Peake and Robert Graves, the text's motif of reversal, and its metaphorical boundlessness. He draws no conclusions.[37] Peter Malekin, on the other hand, arrives at a very distinct conclusion from his examination of the themes of perception, reality and time in his article, 'Remembering the Future: Gene Wolfe's *The Book of the New Sun*':

> The reader is given an imaginative inkling not only of a different world, but of a different mode of experiencing the fact of world as such, of any world. In this respect, *The Book of the New Sun* is a very substantial literary achievement.[38]

For Malekin, the novel's strength lies not only in its presentation of an alien world but also in its employment of an equally alien set of social and psychological norms through which that world is viewed. Importantly, he sees among its characters 'a subordination of reason … in favour of an … acceptance of symbols',[39] a trait that he does not explore but which has far-reaching implications for an interpretation of the text as a mythogenetic masquerade (see Chapter 5).

Further investigations of the peripheral concerns of *The Book of the New Sun* also appeared in review journals and fan magazines where their often contradictory arguments reflected the critical confusion that the narrative aroused. From out of this jumble of interpretations two critics, John Clute and Joan Gordon, emerged as the definitive voices in Wolfe criticism. Together, Clute's review articles and Gordon's *Starmont Reader's Guide* are the only fully reasoned analyses of *The Book of the New Sun*, and their arguments are discussed in Chapter 4.

The tentative conclusions that did emerge were, however, largely invalidated in 1987, when Wolfe published *The Urth of the New Sun*, a coda to *The Book of the New Sun* that undermined many of the conceptions that critics had of the earlier work. It was, perhaps, for this reason that reactions to *The Urth of the New Sun* were mixed. Critical opinion was split dramatically between those reviewers, including Colin Greenland and Peter Nicholls, who considered the book as a seamless extension of Wolfe's earlier masterpiece, and those who felt it to be a lesser achievement than the original tetralogy.[40]

The commercial success of *The Book of the New Sun* enabled Wolfe to resign from his editorial post at *Plant Engineering* and devote himself to full-time writing in 1983. Wolfe was highly productive the following year, publishing three small-press collections: *The Wolfe Archipelago*, the punningly titled *Plan[e]t Engineering* and *Bibliomen: Twenty Characters Waiting for a Book*, a series of fictional biographies. His novel, *Free Live Free*, appeared as a limited edition in 1984. This intriguing and ironic tale follows the lives of four members of the USA's homeless underclass as they are caught up in a series of conspiracies. Although the text seems to be a mainstream work at first, Wolfe manipulates its apparent generic identity constantly, imitating the conventions of the realistic novel, the paraliterary fantasy and the detective story (with brief descents into farce). The book is finally revealed to be straight SF when the main characters uncover a plot involving a time travel device developed by the US military.

When *Free Live Free* received its mass-market US edition in 1985, 'the book was cut by about 4000 words … The order of chapters was changed slightly, and a chronology was added as end matter. The British edition [published by Legend] lacks the chronology.'[41] In the Tor edition, Wolfe explains that the chronology was added after a request from the editor of the US trade edition, but does not suggest a reason for its inclusion.[42] It seems likely, however, that Tor felt a chronology necessary to explain the book's convolutions by accentuating the elusive clues and temporal anomalies that Wolfe provides as indicators of the book's dependency on time travel.

Free Live Free is a complex novel. Its trans-temporal plotting makes considerable demands and the reader must pay close attention if he or she is to follow the events unfolding around the characters. The book succeeds not only because it is possible to deduce what has occurred (with or without the Tor chronology) but also because Wolfe's characters are believable, his prose accessible and his juxtaposing of action and dialogue, mystery and revelation, so finely balanced that the reader is driven towards the conclusion by amusement, bemusement and curiosity.

Although John Clute hailed *Free Live Free* as 'an exemplary fable',[43] it failed to arouse much critical interest, unlike *Soldier of the Mist*, published in 1986. Bringing Wolfe renewed attention and his third Best Fantasy Novel Award from *Locus*, *Soldier of the Mist* is a historical fantasy set in ancient Greece. Narrated in the first person by Latro, its amnesiac Roman protagonist, the novel describes the closing months of the Persian War and Latro's recruitment as a pawn in a feud between Demeter and the Huntress, Artemis.

Soldier of the Mist and its sequel, *Soldier of Arete*, were both well received, not least because of Wolfe's ability to recreate the Classical world in vivid economical detail.[44] More interestingly, reviewers recognised how Latro's amnesia, and the ancient world locale, transposed Severian's almost faultless memory and the far future setting of Urth. Accordingly, they concluded that the *Soldier* novels were a self-conscious inversion of *The Book of the New Sun*.[45]

While appearing entirely credible, this deduction overlooks the important thematic and conceptual similarities existing between the two series which suggest that, rather than being a simple inversion of Severian's odyssey across Urth, Latro's dazed wanderings serve as an elliptical exegesis of *The Book of the New Sun* and its sequel. In this sense, they mark the beginning of a revisionist phase in Wolfe's career as the author initiates a process of 'metafictional cartography', using later novels to 'map', that is, to guide the interpretation of, his *magnum opus*.

If the contrast between *Free Live Free* and *Soldier of the Mist* testifies to Wolfe's versatility, then *There Are Doors* (1988), Wolfe's third 'mid-western' novel, confirms his imaginative dexterity and reveals his ability to assimilate a variety of intertextual material. *There Are Doors* unites elements from Kafka's *The Castle* (1926) with the myth of Atys and Cybele to tell a story of obsessive love in a world where men die (a literalised pun, perhaps?) after orgasm. The ruler of this world, the multiplex Goddess, travels through the Doors of the title into parallel worlds (including, the reader assumes, that of Kafka's novel), where she seduces men who do not expire after sex. These men, entranced by her beauty, often follow her back to her world where they are usually incarcerated in mental institutions. Mr Green, the novel's mentally disturbed protagonist, is one such lover, and his quest for a reunion forms the plot of the book.

Heavily atmospheric, *There Are Doors* is Wolfe's most successful novel on an emotional level. The reader experiences the protagonist's suffering, his sense of loss, joy, confusion and hope as the book concludes with Green still searching for his lover. Any charge of sentimentality is mitigated by the harshness of the Goddess's sinister, winter-wrapped city and by allusions to AIDS.

Part of the novel's success lies in the fact that, as Gordon observes, 'it allows an immediate sense of understanding instead of our usual sense of dislocation and ambiguity on entering one of [Wolfe's] worlds'. Gordon is not deceived by such accessibility, however, and argues convincingly that the ambiguity typical of Wolfe's fiction is ever present:

> Underneath the novel's surface traction it remains as slippery as ever. Our determination of Mr. Green's state of mind determines the nature of the story and the likelihood is that all the alternate stories—the man and his elusive lover, the man and his goddess, the man seeking true relationships, the hallucinating man—are simultaneously true. Well, if there are alternate worlds, why not alternate stories?[46]

This writerliness, which Clute also observes,[47] forms an integral part of the novel, and is instrumental in deepening the text's emotional impact. As Green realises he cannot be certain of what is happening to him, the reader begins to sympathise with his confused mental state. Sympathy becomes empathy when the reader recognises that the ambiguous nature of the narrative has fostered a similar sense of uncertainty in his or her own mind. Character and reader are united: neither can have confidence in their interpretations and both must seek clarification from the Goddess, a quest that continues beyond the novel's final page and remains unresolved.

Whereas *There Are Doors* attracted little critical attention, *Storeys from the Old Hotel*, an uneven British anthology of Wolfe's short fiction also published in 1988, brought Wolfe the World Fantasy Award in 1989. *Storeys from the Old Hotel* collects a number of pieces, ranging from the early and seminal 'Trip, Trap' (1967), to 'Parkroads: *A Review*' (1987), a whimsical Borgesian examination of a fictional film, to the restrained prose poem, 'In the Mountains' (1983), to two paraliterary fantasies, 'The Green Rabbit of S'Rian' (1985) and 'The Choice of the Black Goddess' (1986).

Wolfe's fourth mass-marketed anthology, *Endangered Species*, followed in 1989, reprinting some of his more writerly narratives, including the 'Thag' sequence ('The Dark of the June', 'The Death of Hyle', 'From the Notebook of Dr Stein' and 'Thag' [1974–75]), 'Silhouette' (1975) and 'Lukora' (1988). Although 1989 also saw the publication of *Soldier of Arete*, the year was significant for bringing Wolfe the Skylark Award for Contributions to Science Fiction. Ironically, it was after gaining this accolade that he published *Castleview* (1990), his fourth 'mid-western' novel and his most poorly received work since *Operation Ares*.

Castleview is set in the fictional mid-western town of Castleview, which takes its name from the mysterious castle-like mirage that appears occasionally beyond its suburbs. Here, the newly arrived Shields family is embroiled in a series of frenetic encounters with characters from folklore and Arthurian legend. As Clute observes, 'the book is not about finding Arthur, but about enlisting one' of the many Arthurs, or Arthur-figures, populating the text:

> *Castleview* is a tale of *recruitment*. The time for an expiatory final battle is once again nigh, and Morgan le Fay must find a hero to oppose. She must find one who will take up with chivalrous abandon the immortal role. It must be her brother, the once and future king.[48]

With his usual consummate dexterity, Wolfe transforms what could have been a clichéd fantasy, in which a human hero is recruited to save a fantastic realm by opposing the forces of evil, into a series of anarchic incidents that whirl the reader along at breakneck speed. Drake Asbury III argues that this pace has a detrimental effect on characterisation:

> The characters are a curious lot but lack substance. Many are intro-
> duced but none are fully developed. They are so caught up in the
> mysteries around them that they fail to react in believable ways. They
> accept too easily unexplained shootings, deaths, and the disappear-
> ances of family members. They are simply stand-ins needed to react
> to the weird situations the writer throws at them.[49]

The two-dimensional characters and their acceptance of the staccato
events unfolding around them confers a sense of unreality on the text, an
unreality that Wolfe exploits with references to cinema and television, to
Calamity Jane, *King Kong*, *True Grit* and the *Indiana Jones* films. 'On TV that
would be a whole season', comments Anne Schindler-Shields as she reflects
on the events of the previous two hours of her life.[50] This remark, together
with Wolfe's other allusions to the visual media, literature (especially
Malory's *Le Morte D'Arthur* and Tennyson's *Idylls of the King*), myth and
fairy tale, prompted the editor of the *SFRA Review* to provide a footnote to
Asbury's review: 'An alternative, comedic way to read *Castleview* is to view
it as an ironic parody of contemporary mainstream, SF, or fantasy fiction
as well as film and TV plots, characters, themes and techniques.'[51]

Although this theory is not developed, the notion is convincing in
accounting for why Wolfe, a writer known for his strong characterisation,
balanced plots and paced revelations, should create a novel with comparatively shallow characters, kaleidoscopic action and an unexceptional style.
The reader, it seems, is in the realm of parody as well as faery, and can
appreciate *Castleview* better as a witty indictment of mass-market entertainment achieved through imitation (the book itself is a burlesque of
recruitment fantasies and soap opera characterisation), exaggeration (it
compounds soap opera plotting and pacing) and ironic example (it shows
how myth can be debased through its appropriation by the popular
media). The novel can be regarded, therefore, as a form of meta-media
that condemns implicitly the commercialisation of literature and myth
through its own ironic commercialisation of literary and mythic material.
On a more serious level, *Castleview* is an oppressive recruitment fantasy
that exposes Wolfe's understanding of how the individual can be subject
to, and subjugated by, mythic systems alien to that individual.

In *Pandora by Holly Hollander*, his second novel of 1989 and his last 'mid-
western' novel to date, Wolfe turned his attention from parody to pastiche.
This light, humorous detective story, whose protagonist is the daughter of
a corrupt upper-class Chandleresque family rather than the usual gumshoe,
was almost wholly ignored by reviewers and yet is not an insignificant
work in Wolfe's canon. Progressing as a series of ruminations on the

possible perpetrator of a bomb attack on a school summer fête, and on a subsequent murder, the book can be read as a metafictional disclosure of the deceptive authorial techniques employed by that 'wily sleight of hand artist Wolfe'.[52]

However, to read the book solely in this manner would be to do Wolfe a severe injustice. *Pandora by Holly Hollander* is not only significant for its metafictional qualities but also for its characterisation. Its narrator, the eponymous Holly Hollander, a pretty high-school girl, candid, wry, and all-American, is probably one of Wolfe's most remarkable creations. There is no point in the novel at which the reader is conscious of the then 59-year-old male author's presence behind the narrating voice. Holly is irrepressible, charming, and seems to possess more life and independence than many actual people. She is a tribute to Wolfe's powers of characterisation and his skill in assuming distinct narrative voices.

In the years following the publication of *Pandora by Holly Hollander*, Wolfe compiled *Castle of Days* (1992), an anthology edition of *Gene Wolfe's Book of Days*, *Castle of the Otter* (1983) (a discursive account of the writing and publication of *The Book of the New Sun*) and additional material, and produced a series of short stories while he composed his second tetralogy, *The Book of the Long Sun* (1993–96).

The Book of the Long Sun (*Nightside the Long Sun* [1993], *Lake of the Long Sun* [1994], *Caldé of the Long Sun* [1994] and *Exodus from the Long Sun* [1996—the year Wolfe won the Lifetime Achievement Award at the World Fantasy Convention]) is located in the same fictional universe as *The Book of the New Sun*. The narrative is set inside *The Whorl*, a generation starship containing an immense cylindrical chamber whose inner walls are landscaped with mountain ranges, rivers, lakes, forests and cities. Illuminating this huge, artificial chamber is the 'long sun' of the title, a plasma stream fixed at the axis of the cylinder and orbited by a 'shade' that regulates the diurnal pattern aboard ship. The vessel itself has been launched on its mission by Typhon the First, the two-headed dictator Severian kills in *The Sword of the Lictor* and meets again, in the past, in *The Urth of the New Sun*.

Typhon's murderous family is present aboard the ship in the form of sentient computer programs which are considered as gods and goddesses by the vessel's passengers, with whom they interact. Acting through the 'sacred windows'—essentially computer monitors—they enlist various factions in their conspiracies against one another from their realm of 'Mainframe'. Mediating between the 'gods' and humanity are the Pateras, *The Whorl*'s priests, and the Mayteras, or nuns. When the tetralogy opens, however, these A. I. 'deities' are manifesting themselves less and less as *The Whorl*, like Urth, succumbs to entropy. Advanced technology is rare aboard ship and chemico-mechanical people, 'chems', are becoming increasingly scarce as their systems fail and spare parts are consumed.

Wolfe creates the diverse cultures of *The Whorl* with his characteristic painstaking attention to detail, carefully evoking the ambience of South America, particularly Mexico, under Spanish rule. While this flavour indicates *The Whorl*'s origin among the far future South American societies of *The Book of the New Sun*, it also rationalises the presence of aspects of Wolfe's Roman Catholicism in the ship's bizarre religion, itself a conflation of mathematics, Catholicism and the Roman custom of augury.

Like *The Book of the New Sun*, *The Book of the Long Sun* charts the rise of a young man, in this case Patera Silk, an augur from the city of Viron, from obscurity to political significance in a society characterised by plotting and mysteries of Byzantine complexity. After Silk apparently receives a 'revelation' from 'The Outsider', a god whose dominion extends beyond *The Whorl* and who possibly represents Jehovah, Allah and the Christian Trinity, the devout augur rises through blood and fire to become caldé of his city, having helped to depose the corrupt city council, the Ayunta-miento. The final volume, *Exodus from the Long Sun*, shows that *The Whorl* has actually arrived at its destination, a twin-planet system which forms the setting for *The Book of the Short Sun* (*On Blue's Waters* [1999], *In Green's Jungles* [2000] and *Return to the Whorl* [2001]).

Explicitly identified with *The Book of the New Sun* through its four-volume structure, its plot, and the location of its action within the same fictional universe, *The Book of the Long Sun* continues the elliptical metafictional exegesis of the earlier tetralogy that Wolfe began in the *Soldier* novels. Through a series of carefully developed parallels in plot, characterisation and xenography, or world building, Wolfe exposes many of the subtextual features of the earlier text, including its preoccupation with the effects of engineered myths and messiahs, with false gods, and with the nature of revelation and deception. The intensely compact time frame of the narrative, in which the entire action of the tetralogy covers less than 14 days, only serves to emblematise the status of *The Book of the Long Sun* as an intensification of the more elusive aspects of *The Book of the New Sun*.

To read Silk's story from this perspective alone is, of course, to deny the text independent status, an action unwarranted by a book distinguished by the individuality of its peoples (both artificial and humanoid), its settings, which are exquisitely realised throughout, and its captivating narrative. It would also neglect the significant literary sources resounding through the text. Where *The Book of the New Sun* featured a panoply of intertextual references, *The Book of the Long Sun* acknowledges a distinct debt to two of Wolfe's most significant sources: Jack Vance (whose influence on *The Book of the New Sun* Wolfe has already acknowledged) and G. K. Chesterton. Silk is Father Brown, sleuthing his way through an environment as vivid as anything Vance has produced.[53]

Once again, critics have seized on Wolfe's ability to create credible fictional worlds, on his smoothness of style and on his strong characterisation as sources of comment.[54] In so doing, they have ensured that the criticism of Wolfe's work has largely stagnated rather than progressed.

Given that much Wolfe criticism has its attention fixed on the author's stylistic versatility, his imaginative range, and his skills at characterisation and structuring, *Attending Daedalus* addresses alternative issues to suggest fresh reasons for considering Wolfe as 'possibly the most important writer of contemporary science fiction'. It takes as its focus *The Book of the New Sun* and *The Urth of the New Sun*, works that represent the thematic, formal and stylistic centre of Wolfe's oeuvre, to provide new insights into the characteristics of Wolfe's fiction.

In concentrating on *The Book of the New Sun* and *The Urth of the New Sun* (which have come to be known collectively, with associated short stories, as 'The Urth Cycle'), it is essential to produce a credible interpretation of the work from which further investigations can proceed. However, considering the well-documented equivocality of the text under discussion, producing such a reading is difficult.

To help obviate whatever obstacles may arise, the first section of *Attending Daedalus* continues with three preliminary examinations of Wolfe's work. 'Trip, Trap' isolates the thematic preoccupations of Wolfe's fiction from 1966 to 1984 to provide evidence to substantiate later claims that challenge current critical opinions of The Urth Cycle. Chapter 3, 'In the House of Gingerbread', describes the interpretative game that Wolfe plays with the reader and highlights the potential difficulties that this game may pose for the critic. The fourth and final chapter of this section, 'The God and his Man', provides a synopsis of The Urth Cycle (to help contextualise issues raised in later chapters) before addressing the critical response to the pentalogy and observing how reviewers have fallen victim to Wolfe's literary games-playing.

In the light of observations made in 'Initiations', the second section, 'Investigations', offers a detailed analysis of The Urth Cycle. Chapter 5, 'The Toy Theatre', reveals the pentalogy's hitherto undiscovered story, establishing a foundation for the following five chapters, each of which identifies one of Wolfe's strategies for concealing this story. 'The Last Thrilling Wonder Story?' demonstrates how Wolfe disguises a work of science fiction as fantasy by recontextualising genre conventions to foster critical misreadings. Expanding on this study of recontextualisation, Chapter 7 examines how Wolfe's subversion of the literary traditions of the autobiographical form and the quest narrative may also serve as a method for encouraging misinterpretation. Chapter 8, 'Cues', considers the effects that Wolfe's use of eclectic and archaic diction can have on the reader while noting the contribution such language makes to the sequence's thematic coherence. In Chapter 9, Wolfe's linguistic, literary and extraliterary eclecticism is read as part of the textual memory system that encompasses the entire structure of *The Book of the New Sun*. It also reveals how this structure enables the reader to recall with ease the progression, if not the details, of the narrative from memory. Adopting the idea of text-as-system, Chapter 10 investigates how the sequence's labyrinthine microstructure, and its inter- and intratextual echoes, may oppose analysis, paying particular attention to Wolfe's unconventional use of conventional metafictional techniques.

While such an approach may seem arbitrary, it arises as a consequence of the convoluted nature of the text itself. By dividing Wolfe's narrative into its constituent parts, and examining each element separately, yet in relation to the others, the reader can appreciate better a text apparently constructed to obfuscate its own concerns.

The final section, 'Conclusions', argues that Wolfe's *Soldier* novels and *The Book of the Long Sun* offer a metafictional commentary on The Urth Cycle. Read in this light, Wolfe's pentalogy can be seen to overturn the anti-intentionalist position adopted by many contemporary literary critics in favour of the more traditionalist stance, despite appearing to enact the reverse. The conclusion also examines *Pandora by Holly Hollander,* which offers an adequate metaphor for interpreting Wolfe's work. A joyous, liberated metafiction, *Pandora* draws attention to Wolfe's preoccupation with the solution of mysteries using the iconography of the lock and the key. In so doing, it re-emphasises the model of interpretation that shapes almost all of Wolfe's fiction, that of author as encoder and reader as decoder of elliptical yet elegantly labyrinthine conundrums.

2. 'Trip, Trap': Psychology and Thematic Coherence

From the beginning of his professional writing career, Gene Wolfe has expressed a fascination for a number of interrelated psychological phenomena that are significant to an understanding of his oeuvre. These phenomena include the subjective perception of ontological reality; the reconstruction of perceived reality from memory; the psychological manipulation of the individual within economic, political and spiritual systems; the relationship between internal fantasy and external reality; and the psychological potency of myth, faith and symbolism.

Michael Bishop observes that, as a consequence of this 'persistent interest' in psychology, Wolfe

> often produces stories with open-ended conclusions, characters who are neither wholly heroic nor unremittingly villainous, and plot lines as dependent on the ebb and flow of the protagonist's mental state as on the tides and tumults of physical action.[1]

The ambiguity found in Wolfe's fiction, in his characterisation and in his plotting, is an essential strategy in the production of what Wolfe believes to be 'good writing'. He argues that 'good writing' should be 'multileveled, like a club sandwich. Savants talk of writing being linear—one thing at a time. But a good writer is often saying two things at once, and sometimes three or even four.'[2] In Wolfe's opinion, 'good writing' also requires the author to deal with 'major themes', and his deployment of ambiguity enables him to synthesise and develop 'three or even four' 'major [psychological] themes' simultaneously.[3]

Wolfe's habitual concern with one such theme, the subjective nature of perception, is apparent from the publication of his first short story, 'The Dead Man', to *Exodus from the Long Sun*. 'The Dead Man' draws its principal conceit, the notion of a dead man, unaware of his demise, being alerted to his condition, from Wolfe's earlier story, 'The Grave Secret', which appeared in the Texas A&M magazine *The Commentator* in 1951.[4] Throughout his career, Wolfe has returned to this simple narrative idea to produce 'The Packerhous Method' (1970), 'Checking Out' (1986), and the self-consciously titled 'The Other Dead Man' (1987).[5]

Although these stories explore subjectivity at an elementary level, they demonstrate Wolfe's awareness of how the psychology of character can govern reader response. The utilisation of the third person narrative form throughout these tales, rather than implying the existence of an omniscient narrator, works to emphasise the protagonist's subjective perception of consensus reality. By restricting his point of view to that of his protagonist in each story, Wolfe controls how much information the reader receives and only allows that reader to become aware of the leading character's true state through an external source. In 'The Grave Secret', 'The Dead Man', 'Checking Out' and 'The Other Dead Man', secondary characters comment on the protagonist's zombie or ghostly state; in 'The Packerhous Method', the characters remain unaware of their embalmed, automated status as Wolfe shares the irony of their subjectivity with the reader by repeating the beginning of the story at its end: the characters are locked in a temporal loop defined by their embalmer's programming.

Wolfe developed the theme of subjectivity in 'Trip, Trap' (1967) (*Storeys*, pp. 214–39), a short story that relates the adventures of Dr Morton Melville Finch, PhD, an extraterrestrial anthropologist working among the natives of Carson III. The narrative is presented in an epistolary form that alternates Finch's letters to his university with reports sent by a Carsonian, Garth, to his sovereign, the Protector of the West Lands. Although both men experience the same events, each describes them from a different perspective. Their often contrary observations contribute to a vivid (and humorous) representation of the human mind's inability to perceive the 'reality of reality'. This theme becomes explicit when Finch and Garth encounter a *traki*, which Finch recognises as an alien shape-shifter, but which Garth believes to be a troll. The *traki* explains: 'YOU CAN NEVER SEE ME OBJECTIVELY, YOUR RACE BEING WITHOUT OBJECTIVE PERCEPTION. THE SHAPE YOU SEE NOW IS SUBJECTIVELY CORRECT, WHICH IS THE WAY YOU DEFINE REALITY' (*Storeys*, pp. 230–31).

The *traki*'s idealist view of human perception is partly Platonic, inasmuch as Plato perceived the body, 'that which brings us in touch with the world of external reality ... as a distorting medium, causing us to see through a glass darkly'.[6] For the Platonic Wolfe, the senses form a barrier that prevents the comprehension of a larger, external reality.

The *traki*'s suggestion of an objective reality beyond the subjective vision framed for the human mind by the senses draws Wolfe back from the brink of solipsism. Wolfe is not arguing that everything the mind perceives is a product of that mind. Rather, he is emphasising his belief in an objective universe that cannot be perceived accurately through the senses because an individual codifies and quantifies that universe according to his or her expectations and experiences. For example, Finch can only perceive the *traki* analogously (as a four-armed ape or a manifestation of Professor Beatty from his university): the creature's actual nature is impossible for him to determine.

The notion of an objective universe existing beyond the senses recalls Hegel's suggestion that 'nothing ... is ultimately and completely real except the whole'.[7] Hegel conceived of the notion of the whole as

> a complex system of the sort that we should call an organism. The apparently separate things of which the world seems to be composed are not simply an illusion; each has a greater or lesser degree of reality, and its reality consists in an aspect of the whole, which is what it is seen to be when viewed truly.[8]

The *traki* is part of one such complex system, a system of which Finch and the reader remain unaware. Its existence is a manifestation of a 'lesser degree of reality' and a part of a larger 'whole'. Its reality, that is, its precise characteristics and function, cannot be deduced unless its relationship to, and purpose within, the whole can be determined. As a vision of the whole is not provided in the story, the *traki* remains an enigma and its own subjectivity—of which it is unaware—becomes a source of irony.

Hegel's distinction between the appearance of 'the apparently separate things of which the world seems composed' and its reality as 'an aspect of the whole' is a sustained theme in Wolfe's fiction. His protagonists, because of their reception of information through the senses and their specific spatio-temporal locations, are incapable of perceiving the whole and often misconceive the nature of what they experience.

Like the psychologist, Hermann Helmholtz, Wolfe understands that

> sensory signals only have significance as the result of associations built up by learning. We are essentially separate from the world of objects, and isolated from external physical events, except for neural signals which, somewhat like language, must be learned and read according to various assumptions, which may or may not be appropriate.[9]

Helmholtz's observations are useful in approaching Wolfe's work as they introduce two notions relevant to a wider understanding of his fiction: the concept of association, which features in Finch's misconception of the *traki*'s appearance and is intrinsically important to the structure, characterisation and deflective qualities found in The Urth Cycle; and the incidence of visual illusions. Helmholtz suggests that

> We usually refer to incorrect inductive inferences concerning the meaning of our perceptions as illusions of the senses. For the most part they are the result of incomplete inductive inferences. Their

occurrence is largely related to the fact that we tend to favour certain ways of using our sense organs—those ways which provide us with the most reliable and consistent judgement about the forms, spatial relations and properties of the objects we observe.[10]

'Incorrect inductive inferences' abound in Wolfe's first-person narratives. For example, when confronted by the *traki*, Finch is, ironically, too preoccupied with *listening* for the creature's movements to *understand* its words and gain an adequate inference of its nature:

> 'WE WHO BROUGHT YOU HERE HOLD ALL THIS WORLD AND YOU CANNOT CROSS THE SEAS OF EMPTINESS AGAIN WITHOUT OUR AID.'
> I was too busy at the moment to digest that rather cryptic statement. I managed to open the pocket at last and was getting out my paralyzer and illuminator. As soon as I was able to fumble off the safety catch on the paralyzer, I lit up the cavern. (*Storeys*, p. 230)

Through his desire for vision, Finch fails to apprehend the significance that the creature's words have for suggesting its origin and the history of its species; he is an unreliable narrator because of his inherent, unavoidable subjectivity and his emotional response to sense stimuli.

Although the late Thomas D. Clareson suggests that 'Trip, Trap' shows that 'one of Wolfe's primary concerns has been with man's perception and comprehension of the universe',[11] it is more accurate to observe that Wolfe shows a greater fascination for humanity's incapacity to apprehend and understand that universe because it cannot free itself from the trap of its own mental processes and the incorrect interpretations that result from those processes.

By presenting the contrasting epistolic narratives of Finch and Garth alternately, Wolfe draws attention to the ambiguity of their accounts. They are both unreliable narrators in so far as the text is focalised through them. However, through the juxtaposing of their limited perspectives the reader may become aware of the partiality of their judgement and, hence, their subjectivity. Katie Wales defines focalisation as

> the 'angle of vision' through which the story is focussed, but in a sense which includes not only the angle of physical perception (e.g. close or distant, panoramic or limited) but also cognitive orientation (complete or restricted knowledge of the world described) and emotive orientation (subjective or objective).[12]

Wolfe's fiction is densely populated with such unreliable narrators and, although their employment is described in the following chapter, it is perhaps valuable to note, at this point, that these narrators constitute one of the key elements in the interpretative game that Wolfe plays with his reader.

In 'Trip, Trap', the dual perspectives of Finch and Garth allow the reader to become privy to the characters' unreliability but leave the precise history of, and socio-political situation on, Carson III a mystery, since neither Garth nor Finch possesses adequate knowledge of the universe's objective whole. Each man exists in a subjective state induced by his inability to share what others perceive with any degree of accuracy. Accordingly, in Wolfe's fiction, first-person narratives represent a form of textually focused fantasy and constitute a signal to the reader to question the veracity of what is described.

Wolfe reuses the associated themes of subjectivity and the distinction between the apparent and the real variously to examine the human penchant for therapeutic fantasies in the dangerously abstracting role play of 'Beech Hill' (1972) (*Species*, pp. 32–38); to investigate the effects of the environment on a fertile, alien imagination in the whimsical 'Feather Tigers' (1973);[13] and to address the effects of the perpetuation of a lie, a fantasy, long after the inspiring reality is unattainable in 'The Marvellous Brass Chess-Playing Automaton' (*Storeys*, pp. 113–30) and 'Kevin Malone' (1977) (*Storeys*, pp. 37–49). It is also an inherent part of 'The Toy Theatre' (1971) (*Island*, pp. 237–43), 'Alien Stones' (1972) (*Island*, pp. 18–49); 'Continuing Westward' (1973) (*Storeys*, pp. 43–49) and, most notably, The Urth Cycle.

Intimately associated with Wolfe's interest in perception is his fascination with memory. Wolfe understands that

> Memory is all we have. The present is a knife edge, and the future doesn't really exist … So memory's ability to reconnect us with the past, or some version of the past, is all we have. I'm including racial memory and instinct here ('instinct' is really just a kind of racial memory) … This whole business about memory is very complicated because we not only remember events but we also remember earlier memories.[14]

This remembrance, open to interpretation and misinterpretation, forms the basis of 'the unreliability of memory' which, as Wolfe admits, is the 'root idea' underpinning his interest in subjectivity and the ensuing distinction between the apparent and the real. These three themes are so closely collocated in Wolfe's fiction that they function as an indivisible thematic monad, often dictating the style and the content of his texts.

Wolfe argues, rather convincingly, that if our experiences or our memories disagree with the rationally constructed, Western conception of the world, we deny them to make sense of existence:

> The universe is far larger, far stranger, than we are ever going to be able to recognise. We live our lives mostly by deliberately disfiguring the bits we don't understand. We say, 'Well, this isn't a piece of the puzzle at all.' Well, it is a piece of the puzzle—it's just that the puzzle is a lot more comfortable to work with when it's simple, if we push the things we don't understand to one side ...[15]

It is this disfigurement of memory that leads to its unreliability, to the possibility that an individual may remember something that actually occurred but which proved so inconsistent with that individual's certainty of what is probable that it is suppressed or else reinterpreted as another species of incorrect inductive inference. Given Wolfe's recognition of this tendency to re-code experiences according to prior assumptions, it is unsurprising that his fiction frequently involves characters endeavouring to make sense of events inconsistent with their previous understanding of the world. Number Five from 'The Fifth Head of Cerberus', Mark, the protagonist of *The Devil in a Forest*, Nadan Jaffarzadeh from 'Seven American Nights' (1978), Latro and Patera Silk are perhaps the most obvious examples, although the protagonists of 'The Grave Secret' and its early derivatives are conspicuous seminal characters.

The relationship of perception to memory and self-validation is also important in Wolfe's oeuvre:

> The question is: are you going to trust your eyes? ... Moses can't go back to Egypt and show them the burning bush. He can't do that. It's not there any more. All he can say is, 'I saw this bush and it was on fire and an angel of the Lord spoke to me out of the bush.' And he knows it happened. At least, he's pretty sure it happened, but he can't prove it.[16]

Accordingly, Wolfe's fiction is populated by characters attempting to decipher their experiences through memory, to disentangle fact from fantasy, event from dream or nightmare. Dennis Alden Weer from *Peace*, Latro, the *Soldier of the Mist*, and Mr Green of *There Are Doors* are prime examples.

Wolfe readily acknowledges the formative influence that Proust's *A la recherche du temps perdu* (1913–27) had on his own explorations of memory,[17] which include 'The Fifth Head of Cerberus' and 'The Island of Doctor Death and Other Stories' (1970) (*Island*, pp. 1–17), 'Eyebem' (1972) (*Species*, pp. 225–36), *Peace*, 'Suzanne Delage' (1980) (*Species*, pp. 361–67), The Urth Cycle, and the *Soldier* novels.

With the exception of 'Eyebem', which introduces the cyclical motif common to much of Wolfe's fiction in a quirky, ironic tale of human endurance surpassing that of robots, and the enigmatic 'Suzanne Delage', which describes an old man's melancholy—and possibly futile—quest to discover something extraordinary in his mundane life, all of these stories employ the theme of memory to explore the nature of identity.

Mary Warnock states that, 'There is no sense at all in the identity-question, or the answer to it, unless we think of persistence through time, the past and present being separate',[18] a concept to which Wolfe draws attention when he suggests that 'memory's ability to reconnect us with the past, or some version of it, is all we have'. For Wolfe

> We have no means of identifying [an object] as the same [object] without the notion of temporal duration, surviving many changes of place. The notion of identity or non-identity is meaningless ... unless it means identity or multiplicity over ... time ... All that is necessary for us to be able to claim that it is the same [object], is a continuous story that can be told of how the [object] as it was last year came to be where it is now, in the shape it is now in ... The case of people does not differ very much.[19]

An individual's continuity over time, apprehended through the medium of memory, and the sense of identity gained from that continuity (explored by Locke, William James and Sartre[20]) is examined by Wolfe in a variety of ways to illustrate a number of different functions served by memory.

'The Changeling', for example (which, as Joan Gordon observes, pre-figures several aspects of *Peace*,[21] and is allocated 'Homecoming Day' in *Gene Wolfe's Book of Days* [1981]) describes the return of Peter Palmer, a Korean War veteran convicted of desertion, to his home town. Presented as a first-person narrative, Palmer's story recounts the mystery he discovers on his arrival back in Cassionsville (also the setting for *Peace*). Once in town, Palmer can find no record of his life there: his picture is missing from school photographs and whatever reports existed about him in the local newspaper have been destroyed by fire.

The story is a puzzle typical of Wolfe, which requires careful reading to solve. On his return, Peter Palmer encounters a childhood friend, Peter Palmieri, who is only three or four years older than he was when Palmer left town approximately 20 years earlier. In two decades Palmieri has aged barely four years. His adopted father appreciates that Palmieri is not ageing according to real time, but this observation alerts the reader not simply to the fact 'that this is a work of speculative fiction' as Joan Gordon suggests (*Guide*, p. 59), but to the coexistence of Peter Palmer and Peter Palmieri *in Palmer's memory*. Palmieri is the little boy Palmer was when he left Cassionsville with his father after his mother died. Gordon pieces the story together and concludes:

> He [Palmer] uses memory to escape into a time when he still has his
> mother, when he felt that he had a hometown. Peter Palmieri, his
> alter ego, never grows beyond the age at which Palmer lost his
> mother ... Palmer's adult isolation, beginning with his father's death
> ('he was the last family I had, and many things changed for me
> then' (GWBD., p. 192)), compounded in a Korean prison camp and
> later a U.S. military prison, might drive him back to a childhood
> which, however sad, would nevertheless be surrounded by an
> idyllic haze of recollection. (*Guide*, pp. 59–60)

Recontextualising the Peter Pan myth of the eternal child, Wolfe
demonstrates how memory can construct a therapeutic fantasy world into
which psychologically scarred individuals can withdraw to find a kind of
mental security. The story concludes with Palmer alone on an island (a
recurrent image of isolation in Wolfe's writing[22]), visited by childhood
friends in a metaphorical representation of what may be his incarceration
in a US military prison. Palmer revives his past self and the world of his
childhood to find an otherwise unattainable freedom.

The concept of an individual retiring into memory either to protect his
or her sanity or to make sense of existence recurs in 'The Fifth Head of
Cerberus' and 'The Island of Doctor Death and Other Stories'. In 'The
Island of Doctor Death and Other Stories' comic book cruelty contrasts
starkly with the emotional abandonment of a lonely boy, Tackie Babcock,
by his drug-addicted mother. Fantasy and reality merge as characters from
Tackie's pulp novel, *The Island of Doctor Death* (a lurid reworking of H. G.
Wells's *The Island of Doctor Moreau* [1896], whose protagonist, Ransom,
may derive from C. S. Lewis's Cosmic Trilogy [1938–45][23])—Dr Death,
Captain Ransom, the beastmen Golo and Bruno, and the beautiful Talar of
the Long Eyes—appear and befriend Tackie. The melodramatic elements
of the book Tackie reads, with its scenes of human experimentation and
violence, act as a counterpoint to, and thereby reinforce, the more
mundane horror of his isolation and neglect. As the fictional characters
cross into Tackie's life through his imagination, their presence facilitates
the reader's recognition of his solitude. As Joan Gordon suggests, the adult
Tackie

> will know the difference between the realities and fantasies of his
> childhood and ... he will ... know that it was the fantasies which
> gave him the most companionship and the most intense vitality, not
> his mother who lived in her own dream world of drugs ... and we
> know that the narrator of this story [which is told in the second
> person] is the adult Babcock recreating his puzzling childhood so he
> can deal with it. (*Guide*, pp. 61–62)

Unlike Palmer, who withdraws into the Neverland of memory, Tackie uses his recall of fantasy and reality to understand his experiences as a boy and recognise his ability to conquer loneliness through the power of his imagination. At the conclusion of the story, Dr Death informs Tackie that, just as he can re-read the book he does not want to end, so he can 're-read' his own life in order to make sense of its events. The fact that, as an adult, Tackie is still returning to his hybrid fantasy world of childhood does, however, suggest that he is still struggling to come to terms with the neglect he suffered as a child.

Like Palmer's mental version of Cassionsville, or Settler's Island and The House of 31 February in 'The Island of Doctor Death and Other Stories', Weer's home in *Peace* is a memory construct. The rooms through which Weer wanders, and the objects that inspire his reminiscences, seem to derive from the Classical art of memory, 'which ... seeks to [allow individuals to] memorise through a technique of impressing "places" and "images" on memory [and which] has ... been classed as mnemotechnics'.[24] Weer's house provides locations for the associational images that trigger its owner/builder's recollections of his life and demonstrates Wolfe's familiarity with the mnemonic techniques that he would later use subtextually in The Urth Cycle and overtly in *Soldier of Arete*.

Consistently non-sequential, full of incomplete tales and complex sentences in which parenthetical commentaries and embedded clauses imitate the fabric of the text's interwoven reflections, *Peace* ends as it begins, with its protagonist still searching for the elusive factor that will unite his fragmented memories into a coherent and significant whole. This inconclusiveness exerts a powerful influence over the reader, who becomes increasingly intrigued by Weer's reminiscences. The first-person narrative form encourages the reader to follow the protagonist's quest for meaning and, when the novel ends (it does not conclude), that reader is left with an overwhelming desire to return to the beginning of the book and continue his or her efforts to solve the mystery of Weer's life.[25]

Wolfe readily admits that *Peace* is semi-autobiographical since he and Weer, as only children, have 'similar souls'. Being an only child, Wolfe sees his situation as

> a wonderful and terrible thing—terrible because one ends up being the last of the line, the only one who remembers the customs and teachings of the now sunken land of Home. I remember how we used to sit in the living room, my mother, and my father and I and my dog, Boots. The couch and the floor lamps are all gone; the house is sold; I am the only thing left; if I had to, I could not prove it was not all a dream.[26]

'I'm Ishmael at the end of *Moby Dick*, who quotes the line from *Job*: "Only I am left to tell you"',[27] says Wolfe, emphasising how the only child is acutely aware of how memory can exist as a paradox of individual validation and internalised fantasy. In Wolfe's introspection lies a possible explanation for his interest in memory, identity and the ambiguous nature of reality: if only one individual (and many of his characters are solitary offspring or else are raised away from siblings) retains a memory image, how can that individual verify that its origin lies in a remembered experience rather than a dream?

This question is never answered directly by Wolfe (not least because it can have no answer!), but the stories that originate from such speculations suggest that Wolfe believes that self-knowledge can only be sought, although it may never be found, in a revision of the experiences that have contributed to the formation of an individual's personality and sense of identity.

Wolfe's preoccupation with the psychology of individuals reappears in 'The Blue Mouse' (1971), in which servicemen judged incapable of combat prove to be the most savage troops of all;[28] in 'The HORARS of War' (1970) (*Species*, pp. 237–57), where Wolfe's characteristic ambiguity raises the question, posed throughout *The Fifth Head of Cerberus*, of how an individual can determine his or her own biological nature if he or she imitates another psychological form so completely that no difference can be distinguished; in 'The Death of Doctor Island' (1973) (*Island*, pp. 77–131), in 'Silhouette' (1975) (*Species*, pp. 445–506), in which alien entities play with human consciousness to render even subjective reality indeterminate; and in several studies of obsession, including the short story 'My Book' (1982) (*Species*, pp. 374–76), and *There Are Doors*. Wolfe's concern with the mind and mental states is emblematised by the recurrence of mental institutions or facilities in 'The Doctor of Death Island' (1978) (*Island*, pp. 244–93), 'The Death of Doctor Island', *Free Live Free*, *There Are Doors* and in *Pandora by Holly Hollander*.

Wolfe's interest in psychological processes is not restricted to explorations of those mechanisms found within the individual psyche, however; indeed, a proportion of his work examines what he seems to perceive as recurrent psychological traits in the human species. Paramount among these, and expressed in 'How the Whip Came Back' (1970) (*GW Days*, pp. 13–31), is his recognition of the inherent human desire to be 'master over someone else' (*GW Days*, p. 25). In 'How the Whip Came Back' Wolfe describes a declining USA in which 79 per cent of the population favour the lease of federal and state prisoners as workers; in effect, a return to slavery. The protagonist, Miss Bushnan, and the Pope, are the only major figures who might oppose the government's move, but Miss Bushnan agrees to the motion, aroused by the notion of owning her own husband (who is already serving a prison sentence), while the Pope accepts the ruling as he sees an opportunity for the rebirth of his dwindling Catholic Church among the new slave class.

The story is important for its attention to two forms of interconnected manipulation: while it implicitly condemns the human tendency to subjugate others, it also recognises the potential of organised religion to recruit and operate among a people in need of emotional or spiritual comfort. Both the government and the Roman Catholic Church are shown as accretive authorities prepared to exploit the individual. For the bureaucratic hierarchy the loaned prisoners are cheap labour; for the Catholic Church they represent the opportunity for a return to the Apostolic Era when Christianity grew from the ranks of the Roman slave classes. It is perhaps worth noting that Wolfe, himself a Catholic, seems to perceive the Church's refusal to oppose the slavery motion in order to increase its congregation to be just as outrageous as the leasing of convicts.

'How the Whip Came Back' contains two principal features that are central to an understanding of Wolfe's fiction and of the multi-volume novels in particular: his recognition of the existence of systems of control and constraint, and the mitigating effects of religious faith.

Manipulative systems recur throughout Wolfe's work, where they are frequently explored through the use of microcosms: in 'Thou Spark of Blood' (1970),[29] three astronauts are hypnotised and confined in a capsule to determine their psychological responses only to murder one another before the test is complete; in 'Straw' (1975) (*Storeys*, pp. 105–12), airborne mercenaries in an alternative medieval Europe are denied the straw they need for refuelling their hot air balloon in order to force them to defend the castle where they have landed; and in 'When I was Ming the Merciless' (1976) (*Species*, pp. 194–202), a campus sociological experiment by a political science major goes wrong and the student groups involved revert to savage tribalism.

Wolfe's explorations of manipulation are, in most cases, a restatement of his 'distrust of concentrations of power', his fear that individuals

> swallowed by Procter and Gamble [for example], become just a cog in its innards or so much a company man that we'll be just a voice coming out of its mouth. Its beastliness is what people don't like to recognise when they look in the mirror.[30]

Wolfe's recognition of the dehumanising effect of working for a large corporation led to the writing of 'Forlesen' (1974) (*GW Days*, pp. 120–77), a fantasised semi-autobiographical account of life as an employee of a US conglomerate. Emmanuel Forlesen (or Manny Forlesen, as he prefers to be called, a name that reinforces the allegorical cast to the narrative when translated as 'man for lesson') discovers his entire life compressed into a single day in a symbolic rendering of the numbing, repetitive nature of corporate existence. Wolfe's penchant for equivocality provides an ending more chilling for its inconclusiveness. When he returns home from work, Forlesen discovers a small man with a coffin waiting for him:

> 'I want to know if it's meant anything,' Forlesen said. 'If what I suffered—if it's been worth it.'
> 'No,' the little man said. 'Yes. No. Yes. Yes. No. Yes. Yes. Maybe.'
> (*GW Days*, p. 177)

The ambiguity with which 'Forlesen' concludes emphasises not only the impossibility of knowing whether life has or had any definitive meaning, but also the unsatisfactory feeling that Wolfe assumes is felt by individuals working within a corporate business system. The uncertainty that the little man expresses externalises and reflects Forlesen's own confusion at the end of his dehumanising career.

While the horror of Kafka-esque bureaucracy and capitalist manipulation is suggested by the mundane end to Forlesen's surreal lifelong day, the brutalising qualities of a totalitarian future are present with cold efficiency in Wolfe's novelette, 'The Death of Doctor Island'. In this story, emotionally or mentally damaged persons are used by a faceless administration as victims or companions for those who have suffered similar breakdowns but whose convalescence is judged to be more important to society.

Throughout these fictions, Wolfe rarely shows any hope for the survival of freedom or the possibility of rebellion. His authority figures are implacable and recognise the effectiveness of employing lies, masquerades and myths to secure the cooperation of the individual. In 'Kevin Malone', for example, a young married couple facing financial difficulties are employed to stay in a mansion where they receive a generous living allowance. The master of the house is apparently absent until, one night, after weeks of entertaining, the couple's marriage breaks down. In a fit of temper, they demand to see the owner and Kevin Malone appears to explain that he had grown up in the house as the son of servants. Placed in an orphanage at the age of 12, Malone reached maturity and made his fortune. He bought back the house and lived in the rooms above its stables as he had as a boy.

Although Malone needed to rediscover home, or at least an approximation of it, he could not simply apply for a job at The Pines because he 'had to have control. That's something I learned in business', he explains (*Species*, p. 47). Accordingly, he hired the couple as 'stage properties', to live as the master and mistress of the house. While their presence provided him with the impression that he was still a servant, Malone was, paradoxically, their master. His forced revelation shatters his carefully orchestrated illusion and the couple are forced to leave, knowing the reality that exists behind the drama.

'Kevin Malone' unites many of Wolfe's themes but is especially relevant to an understanding of The Urth Cycle, the *Soldier* novels and *The Book of the Long Sun* for demonstrating how a manipulative ploy can be 'dressed up' to give the impression of free will and self-determination. Malone creates a fantasy for Marcella and her husband to sublimate their anxiety as they live out a scheme designed for Malone's own psychological benefit.

Wolfe's awareness of the manipulative power of such masquerades became observable first in *Operation Ares*. In this novel, Martian colonies (abandoned when the US administration deemed scientific work and experimentation an unnecessary waste of resources) construct the myth of ARES, an organisation dedicated to returning the USA to its scientific and commercial supremacy. ARES is a fiction:

> ARES never had anything near the size and power we've liked to pretend. Our Chinese friends would call it a paper tiger; there has never been an indigenous pro-Martian movement on Earth. We faked the broadcasts and the books ARES was supposed to have printed were actually done in Portugal by a publisher who was happy to keep quiet if he was well paid.[31]

This deception works to galvanise the US population into action against the repressive administration of the pacifists governing the country. The manipulation of the US citizens is subsequently reflected in their manipulation of the Russian and Chinese forces, which are struggling to secure their own interests. ARES, Wolfe's phantom organisation, encapsulates his recognition of the motivating potential possessed by 'paper tigers', of how faith can be exploited to gain the compliance of an important majority. In *Operation Ares*, fiction reshapes consensus reality by fostering a sense of purpose, an idea that is central to the story of The Urth Cycle (see Chapter 5).

When asked from where this preoccupation with manipulation is derived, Wolfe explains:

> I suppose it comes from the idea that we are in fact manipulated—and we all are. Some of us are willing to acknowledge God as the god-like power in our lives. Even those who are not—are manipulated, not only by God but a whole host of subsidiary powers, political, economic, and so on. We tend to think that we have free will ... In the mass we're very predictable. There's very little difference between

traffic flowing on a highway and a liquid flowing through a pipe. They act in about the same way. [That predictability] is the basis for exploitation.[32]

Hence, the married couple who fall victim to Kevin Malone, the rebels of *Operation Ares*, and characters like Mark, Severian, Latro and Patera Silk are successfully manipulated because they are predictable. This predictability is intrinsic in the people of Urth and allows for their complete deception by the Hierogrammates (see Chapter 5).

Wolfe's recognition and consistent employment of the delusory power of the illusion and the fabricated lie are an extension of his epistemological idealism. Just as Garth and Finch cannot perceive the *traki*'s objective reality, so the rebels of *Operation Ares* cannot distinguish what is perceived as real and what is, in fact, occurring as a result of having their subjectivity exploited.

From his treatment of such themes, it is clear that, to Wolfe, life is an ambiguous round of perceptions and misperceptions in which the individual must struggle, and ultimately fail, to apprehend the precise nature of existence. The senses form a barrier to understanding; the memory an unreliable recording device to which the individual can return for clues to the conundrum of life; the world a system of manipulation wherein people must live as best they can according to their physical, psychological and social restrictions. While it could be argued that the literary importance of Wolfe's fiction derives from the thematic integrity by which this vision is conveyed, it is, perhaps, more pertinent to argue that the real strength of Wolfe's work arises from his ability to make the reader experience this conception of existence through the reading process. It is the techniques by which Wolfe achieves this extension that form the subject of the next chapter.

3. 'In the House of Gingerbread': Interpretative Games and the Psychology of Reader Response

Wolfe's concern with psychology is not solely restricted to the thematic exploration of subjectivity, memory, manipulation and deception through the experiences of his fictional characters. He is also mindful of the psychology of the reader, and makes a concerted effort to establish parallels between the reader's reception of his work and the trials of his sensuously misguided, externally controlled protagonists.[1] In order to compel the reader to endure his particular perception of life, Wolfe utilises, either singly or in combination, four artful strategies: the employment of unreliable first-person narrators, the introduction of ambiguity and ellipsis, the inclusion of intertextual references, and the subversion or hybridisation of familiar generic conventions.

The adhibition of unreliable narrators (including Finch and Garth in 'Trip, Trap', 887332/Eyebem in 'Eyebem', John V. Marsch/Victor Trenchard in 'V.R.T.', the unnamed narrator of 'The Toy Theatre' and Nadan Jaffar-zadeh in 'Seven American Nights' [*Island*, pp. 358–410]) enables Wolfe to bind his protagonists' psychological processes closely to those of the reader, and hence impose his characters' subjectivity on that reader. By uniting the fictional 'I' with the actual 'I', Wolfe encourages the reader to identify with his unreliable narrators and to accept their restricted view of the world as trustworthy. In this way, Wolfe is able to blind the reader to the possibility of making judgements independent of the narrator and can thereby disarm efforts towards penetrative enquiry.

Clearly, by opposing the reader's interpretative autonomy, Wolfe is able to lay a series of traps for the unwary reader, some of which may lead to widely inaccurate assumptions regarding what is occurring in the narrative. If the reader wishes to avoid the potential interpretative pitfalls that the author prepares, he or she must refuse to be manipulated in this way and strive continually to see through the veils of subjectivity woven by such narrators.

Wolfe himself often aids this avoidance by disclosing the unreliability of his narrators in one of two ways. In his less intricate narratives, including 'Trip, Trap' and 'The Toy Theatre', he reveals his characters' subjective standpoints directly, either by juxtaposing conflicting viewpoints or, more commonly, by exposing a hitherto undisclosed fact of the Hegelian 'complex system', which dictates and contains the dramatic action of the text.

Alternatively, in his more complicated fiction, he discloses the narrator's focalisation indirectly by providing often elusive clues to what '[Henry] James called [the narrator's] *inconscience*; the narrator is mistaken or believes himself to have qualities which the author denies him'.[2] In such cases, Wolfe merely alludes to certain aspects of the fictional 'whole' and leaves the reader to deduce its precise nature from the (often elliptical) information provided.

Whenever Wolfe employs a first-person narrator, therefore, there is always either an explicit or an implicit appeal to the reader's sense of irony. In *The Rhetoric of Fiction*, Wayne Booth suggests that

> If a master puzzle maker had set out to give us the greatest possible difficulty, he could not have done more than has been done in some modern works in which this effect of deep involvement [achieved through the agency of a first-person narrator] is combined with the implicit demand that we maintain our capacity for ironic judgement.[3]

In those narratives where Wolfe reveals the unreliability of his narrator openly, the invitation to form an 'ironic judgement' is explicit and less complex than it is in texts where such unreliability is hidden surreptitiously, where the petition to the reader's notions of irony is largely implicit, and where the unsuspecting reader is likely to fall foul of the author's strategies.

In 'Seven American Nights', which chronicles the adventures of a young Iranian tourist, Nadan Jaffarzadeh, in a post-catastrophic USA, Wolfe's appeal to the reader's 'capacity for ironic judgement' is explicit. On his arrival in the USA, Jaffarzadeh buys what he believes to be a hallucinogenic drug in which he soaks one of six candy eggs, resolving to eat one sweet on each of the remaining nights of his stay.

Recorded as a first-person narrative, the story abounds with uncertainties as the reader, like Jaffarzadeh, is unsure when, or if, the drug is effective. As a consequence, the veracity of all Jaffardazeh's experiences after he ingests the first egg becomes suspect. Which of his many strange encounters are hallucinations? Are any of them hallucinations, or are his ghastly visions of a decaying USA actually a phantasmagoric odyssey in which his subjectivity is no more intense than usual? These questions cannot be answered as the authenticity of the events recounted in Jaffarzadeh's notebook remains in doubt. George Aichele observes:

> The uncertainties of identity within each of these three parts of the story [Jaffarzadeh's journal, a letter from a detective hired by his family to locate him and the concluding paragraph describing two

women reading his book] and the ambiguities created by their apparent interrelationships to one another, make the identity of the story impossible to determine.[4]

While the reader could argue that Jaffarzadeh's story is a conundrum designed to ensnare the reader in a series of interminable puzzles, Michael Bishop remarks that 'Gene Wolfe plays an unorthodox variety of hardball, but he always plays fair',[5] and this sense of fair play manifests itself in Wolfe's direct disclosure of Jaffarzadeh's unreliability. By emphasising early in the narrative that the mysteries of the story cannot be resolved, Wolfe indicates that the text is an insoluble self-referential puzzle about the conundrum of perception rather than an enigma for the reader to solve by detection.

In forcing Jaffarzadeh's psychological processes on the reader, Wolfe destabilises that reader's assumptions concerning the trustworthiness of observation and writing (as he does in '"A Story", by John V. Marsch' and 'V. R. T.' in *The Fifth Head of Cerberus*) and conveys economically the fragility of what an individual accepts as ontological fact. Accordingly, the reader appreciates the irony of his or her own incapacity to overcome a sensuously based understanding of the world through Jaffarzadeh's inability to recognise his (possibly intensified) subjectivity.

In texts where Wolfe suppresses the unreliability of his narrators, the reader enters into an interpretative game with the author, a game in which obfuscation and revelation are finely balanced to provide clues that indicate the narrator's untrustworthiness. Such games, as Booth suggests, are intellectual in nature:

> Whenever an author conveys an … unspoken point, he creates a sense of collusion against all those, whether in the story or out of it, who do not get that point. Irony is always thus in part a device for excluding as well as including, and those who are included, those who happen to have the necessary information to grasp the irony, cannot but derive at least part of their pleasure from a sense that others are excluded.[6]

If the reader is sufficiently sagacious, he or she discovers the focalisation of Wolfe's covertly unreliable narrators and apprehends how the author extends his thematic concerns with subjectivity into the relationship between the interpreter and the text. As a result of his or her temporary delusion by the apparent veracity of the first-person narrative form, the reader not only observes the narrator's 'inconscience' but also appreciates the fallibility of his or her own perceptions.

On reflection, the reader understands that it was not until Wolfe indicated a narrator's unreliability (usually by alluding to his or her inconscience), that he or she began to question the trustworthiness of that narrator's account. Accordingly, the reader learns how easily he or she can be duped and begins to question his or her reactions to the text: to become, in effect, a self-conscious reader.

Once the reader comprehends Wolfe's skill at deluding the unwary, he or she is enrolled in a group of initiates who perceive the traps that the author lays 'for his narrator and those readers who will not catch the allusion'. The reader begins to collude with Wolfe 'behind the speaker's back [and behind the backs of those readers who accept the observations of his unreliable narrators as entirely trustworthy] agreeing on the standard by which he [and they are] found wanting'.[7]

Games-playing of this kind is often so perplexing in Wolfe's fiction that many reviewers and critics resign from attempting analyses and declare their frustration. Bruce Gillespie, for example, remarks that: 'Anybody who can see definitely what Gene Wolfe's fiction is all about is a liar or a fool or Gene Wolfe.'[8] This somewhat bald comment was elicited by *The Fifth Head of Cerberus*. Considered by Michael Bishop as a text worthy of a place beside 'Faulkner and Pynchon', the three novellas comprising *The Fifth Head of Cerberus* 'echo, reflect, ramify, and illuminate one another so thoroughly and mysteriously that a reader is pursued by resonances long after he puts the book aside'.[9]

Through the employment of clones, shape-shifting aliens and twins, Wolfe creates in *The Fifth Head of Cerberus* a disorienting equivocality dependent on a sustained attention to doubling. This duplication is emblematised by the duality of the twin-planet system of Sainte Anne and Sainte Croix and by the repetition of the title *The Fifth Head of Cerberus* in the first novella, 'The Fifth Head of Cerberus'. The reader, like the various characters, Sandwalker, the Old Wise One, John V. Marsch and Victor Trenchard, cannot be confident that he or she can determine the exact biological nature of the planet's inhabitants. (Indeed, the title 'V.R.T.' not only alludes to Victor Trenchard but may also represent the way VeRaciTy or VeRiTy is broken up throughout the book.) Only diligent re-reading in the light of each successive novella, pursuing the clues that Wolfe weaves into the text, will help to solve the puzzle.

Although Gillespie finds 'such devotion to sleight of hand ... daunting', he also understands its importance in sustaining the reader's interest. He admits that 'Only the urge to find out what the hell was going on kept me reading'.[10] In so doing, he identifies the principal effect of the text's ambiguity: the seduction of the reader, who is baffled by puzzles of identity and who must, therefore, adopt the role of a detective if he or she wishes to determine what is actually occurring in the fictional environment. Faced with this prospect, Gillespie declares his exasperation: 'Hints, hints, damnable hints and clues! That's all there is in Gene Wolfe's stories: little pieces of the jigsaw and one is never quite sure that there is a pattern to the jigsaw.'[11]

The uncertainty that Gillespie expresses after struggling through *The Fifth Head of Cerberus* illustrates an important effect of the text's initial equivocality. As Wolfe believes that 'Ambiguity is absolutely essential to any story that seeks to counterfeit life, which is filled with them',[12] it seems probable that the equivocation found in *The Fifth Head of Cerberus*, and in his oeuvre as a whole, is intended to simulate a part of Wolfe's own vision of 'life'. By encouraging the reader to vacillate between interpretations, the author awakens the reader to the knowledge that the so-called facts or norms of existence may not possess veracity independent of the individual.

While this observation suggests, initially, that Wolfe's fiction exhibits an unrelenting, convoluted writerliness, such textual openness is frequently transient or artificial. Rather than being unassailably obscure, Wolfe's stories and novels often contain an unambiguous element that contextualises, or reforms, the ambiguous elements in the text. The indeterminate aspects constitute, therefore, a means by which the reader 'can be made to have … strong intellectual curiosity about "the facts", the true interpretation, the true reasons, the true origins, the true motives, or the truth about life itself'.[13] They tease the reader, fostering an 'intellectual curiosity' that may encourage him or her to seek 'the truth' about the complex systems existing beyond what is readily apparent in Wolfe's writing.

Through an examination of Wolfe's employment of ambiguity, the reader is led to appreciate the paradox at the heart of much of Wolfe's fiction. On the one hand, the author wants his reader to experience an exaggerated sense of his or her own subjectivity; and on the other, he has a desire to 'play fair' with that reader, to offer a reward for any effort he or she might invest towards discovering 'the facts, the true interpretation' of a story or novel. Wolfe provides remuneration in the form of clues that explain, or account for, the dramatic events and socio-political situations in his stories. When these clues are uncovered, much of the ambiguity is dispelled and the text is brought into sharper focus.

Incorporating allusions, however elliptical, to 'the true interpretation' of a given fiction, satisfies Wolfe's sense of fair play but prevents all but his most writerly texts, including *Peace* and 'Silhouette', from imitating completely his view of existence. By positioning a reality or an interpretation or a truth, deducible by the reader but indistinguishable to the narrator, behind his ambiguous tales, Wolfe seems to betray his own efforts to 'counterfeit life', becoming the originator of intricate, but solvable, puzzles. Wolfe does not disagree. Instead, he draws attention to the intellectual and political purpose underpinning his construction of decipherable mysteries:

> I think that what I'm saying to the reader is that this is how life is
> and if we were to think about it more than we do, we would all see
> deeper into it than we do. We would have a better grasp of what
> you call 'the contextualising reality' of our own lives, of our own
> society. The problem is we don't look at things that we take for
> granted and as a result we generally don't look very deeply at the
> facts. The best way, I think, to get people to look more deeply into
> them is to show them some other reality, some other system, other
> kinds of lives, so that they can see into theirs to some extent.[14]

In other words, Wolfe is employing science fiction and science fantasy in a
traditional manner, as literatures of Suvin's cognitive estrangement.[15] By
presenting the reader with 'some other reality, some other system, other
kinds of lives', Wolfe estranges the reader from the realm of mundane
reality. However, Wolfe intends that the process of decoding those other
systems, of discovering the extractable 'truth' embedded in the convoluted
narratives that describe them, should feed back into the reader's cognitive
consideration of his or her socio-cultural environment. As a consequence,
Wolfe seeks to encourage his readers to challenge the 'things that we take
for granted' and see more perceptively into their own realities.

Nevertheless, attempts to obtain this heightened awareness by unravel-
ling Wolfe's complex textual riddles are complicated by the knowledge
that Wolfe constructs both unresolvably open texts, which in his opinion
do 'counterfeit life', and those fictions that contain an intended actuality or
interpretation, and therefore do not. In those narratives that do not possess
a solution—'Seven American Nights', for example—Wolfe's emphasis is on
making the reader conscious of his or her inconscience; that is, on fostering
an increased sense of personal limitations. On those occasions when he
provides a deducible resolution, no matter how difficult it is to apprehend,
his intention is to alert the reader to the possibility of understanding
more—about the text and about 'life'—through diligent and sceptical
reflection. As a result, the reader is required to determine which texts
possess directions to 'true interpretations' before attempting to uncover
what those interpretations might be. The interconnectedness of these two
directions of enquiry results in Wolfe's conundrums becoming wrapped in
enigmas that the reader must penetrate before attempting to solve.

It seems likely, then, that Wolfe's fiction is designed, at least in part, to
raise the intellectual and critical awareness of his readers. Booth notes:

> In his early *Atlantic Monthly* review [Henry James's] whole emphasis
> is on this one aspect: 'When he makes him well, that is makes him
> interested, then the reader does quite half the labour.' James is not
> thinking here simply of giving the reader a sense of his own

cleverness. He is making his readers by forcing them onto a level of awareness that would allow for his most subtle effects.'[16]

In other words, it should be argued that Wolfe's narratives are constructed to educate the reader until he or she appreciates the subtlety of the author's techniques, experiences the sense of collusion described above, and becomes self-consciously aware of how his or her reactions to the text have been elicited. By extension, that reader is also more conscious of individual fallibility and the machinations of the real world.

Having made the reader sensitive to his or her own subjectivity through the deployment of unreliable narrators and ambiguity, Wolfe uses inter-textual references to impress on that reader how he or she can become the manipulated pawn of a controlling author(ity) figure. Michael Worton and Judith Still observe: 'Both axes of intertextuality, texts entering via authors (who are, at first, readers) and texts entering via the readers (co-producers), are, we would argue, emotionally and politically charged; the object of an act of influence.'[17] This influence can be used to elicit a required response effected when

> The reader inescapably strives to incorporate the quotation [allusion or reference] into the unified textuality which makes of the text a semiotic unit. The reader thus seeks to read the borrowing not only for its semantic content but also for its tropological and metaphor-ical function and significance.[18]

The reader's inescapable striving to assimilate an allusion into a text to confer coherence on the work 'inevitably engages the reader in a speculative activity'.[19] This activity is directed towards discovering what the 'metaphorical function and significance of the intertext' might be.

In extreme cases, Wolfe's allusions permeate a text so thoroughly that it is impossible to appreciate the narrative fully without having recourse to cross-referencing. For example, it is unlikely that the reader will apprehend the literary and mythic nuances of *There Are Doors* without referring to Kafka's *The Castle* and the myth of Atys and Cybele. Similarly, *Castleview* can be considered as an incomplete novel inasmuch as an understanding of the story depends on knowledge of Malory's *La Morte D'Arthur*, Tennyson's *Idylls of the Kings* and the Watergate conspiracy.

In the case of *Castleview*, at least one reviewer—Wendy Bradley—has dismissed the novel as an intellectually exclusive text. After researching '*The Arthurian Encyclopedia* and ... consulting a handy world authority on Malory', Bradley discovered that 'Wolfe is not playing games solely with the *Morte D'Arthur*', and admitted that the book made her feel 'dumb'.[20] Accordingly, Bradley feels compelled to run Wolfe's maze of allusions as a result of her limited knowledge and a desire to understand.

By creating such a heavily intertextual fiction, Wolfe presents himself as an arch-manipulator, capable of driving the reader to seek solutions to the text's obvious incompleteness in works beyond that text. The sense of incompleteness that the reader experiences when encountering an inter-text derives from what Michael Riffaterre terms intertextual 'signposts', or 'connectives'. Riffaterre defines these signposts as 'words and phrases indicating on the one hand, a difficulty—an obscure or incomplete utter-ance in the text—that only an intertext can remedy; and, on the other hand, pointing the way to where the solution must be sought'.[21] Wolfe uses these connectives to impel 'the reader to search for its [the inter-text's] reason' for being in the text. 'Since textual justification is lacking, readers turn to outside associations for an answer.'[22] By turning to these outside associations, the reader is directed away from the narrative to sources that have either a revelatory effect, bringing Wolfe's text into sharper focus, as in the case of *Castleview*, or an obfuscatory function, entangling the reader in webs of digressive and decorative intertextuality.[23]

Regardless of what function the intertext serves within a given narrative, the compulsion that the reader feels to resolve 'a difficulty ... in the text' removes a part of his or her freedom. If the reader desires to comprehend a narrative more completely, he or she is stimulated into active research by an intertext's ambiguous significance. Wolfe's intertextuality therefore enslaves the reader by coercing him or her into exploring a system of connectives.

Clearly, in *Castleview*, this process of deflection can have an educational effect. By tracing Wolfe's sources, Bradley discovers that the text is more than a simple recontextualisation of Arthurian motifs and recognises the gap between her original knowledge and that of the author. However, rather than feeling heartened at the indirect education she received as she strove to establish a collusion with Wolfe, and thereby understand the book, she experiences only a feeling of inadequacy. Instead of recognising her inclusion into Wolfe's group of informed readers (whether she desires such membership or not), Bradley expresses a sense of exclusion that derives not from her newly enlightened stance but, oddly, from her original, bewildered standpoint. While the critic could appreciate Bradley objecting to the interpretative somersaults that the text's incompleteness compels her to perform, it is difficult to understand why, after all her research, she still feels 'dumb', and does not derive satisfaction from the extension of her knowledge and 'the sense that others are excluded' from a fuller comprehension of the text.

As a bibliophile, Wolfe has read widely, endowing himself with a wealth of material on which he can draw to manipulate the reader. While his love of books may be attributable to a sickly childhood, his eclecticism is partly the result of his profession. When asked to name the three works that influenced him most, he replied wryly: *'The Lord of the Rings ...*, *The Napoleon of Notting Hill* and *Marks' Mechanical Engineer's Handbook'*.[24] This diverse combination suggests the unity between the fantastic, the contemporary and the scientific found in much of Wolfe's work. For example, 'In the House of Gingerbread' (1987) (*Species*, pp. 91–110) translates the Grimm Brothers' fairy tale 'Hansel and Gretel' into a twentieth-century urban setting with close attention paid to the workings, and potential lethality, of microwave ovens.

To these three formative texts Wolfe adds:

> [Chesterton's] *The Man Who Was Thursday*, [Koestler's] *Darkness at Noon*, [Kafka's] *The Trial, The Castle*, [Proust's] *Remembrance of Things Past*, [Peake's] *Gormenghast Trilogy*, [Thomas Wolfe's] *Look Homeward Angel* ...[25]

'the Oz books, and the two Alice books ... Borges, who was also influenced by Chesterton ... Dickens, H. G. Wells ... and Bram Stoker ...'[26]

To this extensive reading list could be added Wolfe's childhood reading of *Buck Rogers* and *Flash Gordon*; Edgar Allan Poe; and a host of writers, including Robert E. Howard and H. P. Lovecraft, whose work was published in *'Planet Stories, Thrilling Wonder Stories, Weird Tales, Famous Fantastic Mysteries*, and *Amazing Stories'*.[27] The influence of these pulp magazines on Wolfe's fiction appears in a number of his tales, but most notably in 'The Island of Doctor Death and Other Stories' and 'The Last Thrilling Wonder Story' (1982) (*Species*, pp. 119–49).

Wolfe works like an alchemical editor, splicing, synthesising, transforming the material at his disposal to produce, if not gold from lead, then something that is certainly dazzling from a host of precious and non-precious, literary and paraliterary sources. His elaborate eclecticism is readily apparent even on a cursory inspection of his oeuvre. The world of the *Superman* comics and Shakespeare's *King Lear* are combined with an allusion to Browning in 'To the Dark Tower Came' (1977) (*Storeys*, pp. 131–36), a paradoxical, Borgesian tale of human corruption and decline; the cartoon inventions of Walt Disney are subverted to explore the ethics of the capitalist appropriation of animal forms in 'Three Fingers' (1976) (*Island*, pp. 71–76); and the events of the Second World War are re-presented as a wargame and a German economic invasion of Europe to amuse the reader before Wolfe offers a chillingly casual suggestion of the inevitability of a nuclear holocaust in 'How I Lost the Second World War and Helped Turn Back the German Invasion' (1973) (*GW Days*, pp. 89–108).

Wolfe's use of intertexts is a strategy that not only alerts the reader to the existence of manipulatory forces at work on the individual but which also demonstrates the misleading effect that memory may have on an accurate perception of new (reading) experiences. Whenever a familiar intertextual allusion is encountered, the reader's memory is engaged, and associations are established between the text currently under scrutiny and those read on previous occasions. In this way, Wolfe ensures that the reading process mimics the associational process of memory that he explores so effectively in the structuring of *Peace*, which depends largely on the vagaries of a Thematic Apperception Test (in which a patient is shown various picture cards that evoke strings of memory images). This appeal to memory enables Wolfe to exploit the reader's knowledge and encourage misreadings of the text at hand.

Part of the adumbratory power of an intertext lies in its capacity to foster one kind of reading at the expense of another. Riffaterre observes that: 'Facts of reading suggest that, when it activates or mobilises the intertext, the text leaves little leeway to readers and controls closely their response.'[28] Wolfe often exploits this controlling effect by using an intertextual allusion as the foundation for the subversion or the recontextualisation of a familiar literary form.

For example, in 'Suzanne Delage'—which has provoked significant discussion on the Internet[29]—Wolfe leads the reader to believe that the text is an uncanny tale by imitating the initial narrative stages of such stories. If the reader is acquainted with supernatural fiction, he or she recalls its conventions and may begin to accept Wolfe's text as an example of the genre when, in fact, the story actually subverts rather than reproduces the form. Riffaterre remarks that, 'In a response rendered compulsive, and facilitated by the familiar model, as soon as the reader notices a possible substitutability, he or she automatically yields to the temptation to actualise it.'[30] In the case of 'Suzanne Delage', the 'familiar model' is the weird tale. The reader accepts the story as such because he or she sees 'a possible substitutability' and subsequently actualises that substitution only to discover his or her expectations undercut.

Like Jonathan Culler, Wolfe understands that, 'To read a text as literature is not to make one's mind a *tabula rasa* and approach it without preconceptions; one must bring to it an implicit understanding of the operations of literary discourse which tell one what to look for.'[31] Recognising that his reader is not a blank slate, Wolfe manipulates existing reading protocols to encourage the reception of a specific text as one form of fiction when in fact it may be something altogether different. To overcome this ploy, the reader must always be aware of his or her own pre-existing reading strategies and should resist the 'temptation to actualise' the familiar models to which Wolfe's intertextuality appeals.

Refusing to be seduced by the allusive mimicry of Wolfe's fiction amounts to withstanding the invitation to form the 'incorrect inductive inferences' described by Helmholtz.[32] In order to avoid such inaccurate readings, the reader is required to discover what E. D. Hirsch terms 'the intrinsic genre' of a narrative, 'that sense of the whole [text] by means of which an interpreter can correctly understand any part'.[33] Uncovering the intrinsic genres of Wolfe's fiction is often ineffably difficult because his writing appears, initially, to be unrelentingly intergeneric.

At the extreme end of this intergenericism is the conflation of song and prose. The carol 'Good King Wenceslas', for example, forms part of the inspiration for *The Devil in a Forest*, whose title imitates the syllabic structure and rhythm of the second and fourth lines of each verse of the song. *The Fifth Head of Cerberus* blends science fiction with myth; *Peace* unites the mainstream with the fantastic; and The Urth Cycle synthesises SF, fantasy, myth and eschatology.

Wolfe's intergenericism is, however, often explosive, designed to conceal a text's intrinsic genre by manipulating the reader into fostering 'extrinsic genres', or 'wrong guess[es]' that derive from a previous reading experience.[34] (It should be noted that Wolfe himself may be alluding to this quality of his work in *Free Live Free* which, although it activates the reader's memory of mainstream, fantasy and detective fiction, eventually discloses its own intrinsic genre as science fiction.) The movement from an extrinsic to an intrinsic reading is, as Stanley Fish describes, 'not a rupture but a modification' of the reader's understanding, a reorientation of past literary experiences that results in the overturning of the text's apparent generic qualities in favour of its actual generic nature.[35]

Reader response critic Wolfgang Iser notes:

> The efficacy of a literary text is brought about by the evocation and subsequent negation of the familiar. What at first seemed to be an affirmation of our assumptions leads us to our own rejection of them, thus tending to prepare us for a reorientation. And it is only when we have outstripped our preconceptions and left the shelter of the familiar that we are in a position to gather new experiences.[36]

By evoking and negating the familiar, Wolfe illustrates how the memory can form a barrier to understanding because of its dependence on association and how established reading protocols can be manipulated to deprive the reader, at least temporarily, of his or her interpretative freedom.

Consequently, coming to understand Wolfe's fiction is like learning the rules of a game. If the reader succeeds in perceiving the rules of Wolfe's literary game, then the experience of reading his fiction becomes an educational one. By stimulating the reader to reject primary assumptions and existing preconceptions, Wolfe not only lifts the reader onto a level of alertness that will allow for subtle effects, but also reveals to those more cautious readers how they ascribe meaning to a text—and, by implication, to their own social contexts. In fostering this scepticism, Wolfe is, in effect, acting analogously to

> the narrator at the end of *A la recherche du temps perdu*, [who observes: My readers] will become '*les propres lecteurs d'eaux-mêmes*': in my book will read themselves and their own limits.[37]

For the prudent, reflective reader, reading Wolfe's fiction not only results in a progression towards an understanding of the author's ideation of existence but also in a growth towards what Jonathan Culler describes as 'literary competence'. This development arouses in the reader a burgeoning awareness of his or her 'condition as *homo significans*, maker and reader of signs'[38] both within and beyond the immediate text.

Wolfe's 'playful, allusive and often downright sly literary awareness, dense with ideas and changed signs',[39] means that the reader is always, metaphorically, 'In the House of Gingerbread', reading constructions where codes are changed and snares set. If the reader remains unaware of Wolfe's deceptive literary games-playing, he or she will, inevitably, foster misreadings of the text under consideration by failing to apprehend the narrative's intrinsic genre and the contextualising reality that substantiates it.

The production of misreadings has been a defining feature of much Wolfe criticism to date, especially regarding his most conceptually significant and intellectually challenging texts, *The Book of the New Sun* and *The Urth of the New Sun*. It is time now to reconsider these novels bearing in mind both the recurrent themes that define Wolfe's oeuvre and the techniques that influence and shape the reading process. In this way, Wolfe's body of fiction can be reassessed according to the insights gained into works that stand at the thematic and aesthetic heart of his canon.

4. 'The God and His Man': Critical Responses to The Urth Cycle

Currently the most complex work in Wolfe's oeuvre, The Urth Cycle is located on the immensely ancient world of Urth. Millions upon millions of years of human civilisation have left the planet one vast relic, its geology having long succumbed to layer after layer of archaeological remains. Commercial mines sunk into these strata yield fragments of mysterious, lost ages: ruins, bones, obscure relics with forgotten purposes, and count-less indeterminate artefacts. Languishing beneath a sun grown old and red and massive, Urth is dying: its winters are becoming protracted, the stars remain visible throughout the day, and its peoples live among the accretions of cultures barely remembered.

Urth is a world divided by conflict. In a far future South America, the Commonwealth is engaged in a protracted war of attrition with trans-equatorial Ascia, whose armies assail the Commonwealth's mountainous northern border. These invaders are, however, only the servants of powerful Lovecraftian monstrosities which have travelled across space to conquer Urth and enslave its peoples.

Hope is kept alive in the Commonwealth by popular faith in its ruler, the Autarch, and in the legendary, Christ-like Conciliator who came to Urth long ago to prophesy that a New Sun would bloom and rejuvenate the denuded land. The prophet and his prophecy are believed and the populace trusts that the Conciliator's Second Coming will herald the arrival of the New Sun.

The reader is guided through this bizarre world by Wolfe's narrator/protagonist Severian, who is blessed, or cursed, with a perfect memory. *The Book of the New Sun* is Severian's memoir, written 10 years after he becomes Autarch, when his apparently faultless recall enables him to record and comment on his youthful experiences with a beguiling clarity.

The Shadow of the Torturer begins with Severian, ignorant of his true parentage, apprenticed to the feared guild of torturers. He has lived all his short life in the guild, learning the 'art' of dispensing pain within the confines of the Matachin Tower. Severian's life of drudgery and study is relieved briefly when he secretly saves the life of the rebel warrior Vodalus, rescues the injured fighting dog Triskele, and falls hopelessly in

love with Thecla, a 'client' condemned to death by torture. After his elevation to the rank of Journeyman, Severian witnesses Thecla's 'excruciation'
on 'the Revolutionary', and resolves to spare her further torment. He
steals a knife from the guild's kitchen and smuggles it to her cell, where
she commits suicide. Severian confesses his crime to his Masters and is
exiled to northern Thrax, the City of Windowless Rooms, where he must
serve as lictor to the Archon. On this journey he takes with him the
executioner's sword, *Terminus Est*, and the Brown Book, a collection of
fables that he has removed from Thecla's empty cell.

After leaving the Matachin Tower, Severian finds himself in the vast
city of Nessus, where his phantasmagoric journey to the throne of the
Commonwealth truly begins. Approaching the city gate, Severian encounters
the travelling players, Dr Talos and Baldanders, and becomes embroiled in
a plot masterminded by the twins Agilus and Agia, who covet his valuable
sword. The lusty Agia leads him through a series of kaleidoscopic misadven-
tures, all pregnant with undisclosed significance. In her company, he comes
into possession of a seemingly mystical gem, the Claw of the Conciliator,
and befriends the amnesiac child-woman Dorcas, who rescues him from
drowning in the nightmarish Garden of Endless Sleep in Nessus' Botanical
Gardens. At The Inn of Lost Loves he intercepts an intriguing note
intended for Dorcas which warns her against both him and Agia, and
informs her that she is the unknown writer's mother 'come again'.[1]

Agia's desire for Severian, which she almost consummates at the inn, is
later replaced by a bitter enmity after he executes her brother. As Severian
leaves the city bound for Thrax in the hope of restoring the Claw to its
guardians, the Pelerine priestesses, Agia follows him, accompanied by
Hethor, an aged sailor infatuated by her smouldering sexuality who
summons extraterrestrial horrors to plague Severian at her behest.

Once at the city gate, Severian is separated from Dorcas but meets
Jonas, a man with a metal hand. With Jonas, Severian continues his colourful and episodic journey north in *The Claw of the Conciliator*. En route, he
narrowly avoids death at the hands of the vengeful Agia, becoming
ensnared in Vodalus's revolutionary plans, and achieves a 'transcendent'
union with Thecla. The lovers' reunion constitutes one of the most
dream-like sequences of the novel as Vodalus's stewards serve portions of
Thecla's cooked corpse to his outlaws in a ghastly parody of the com-
munion service. Through the agency of the analeptic alzabo—an exotic
drug—the memories preserved in Thecla's cannibalised flesh are brought
to life in the rebels' minds, but only Severian recalls her experiences and
personality in detail.

Charged with taking a secret missive to one of Vodalus's co-conspirators,
Severian barely survives a perilous ride to the Autarch's palace, the House

Absolute. Here, he and Jonas are incarcerated briefly before Jonas, now known to be a robot with a human hand and torso, departs from Urth using trans-spatial mirrors. Severian delivers Vodalus's message to his spy and discovers him to be none other than the Autarch himself. The Autarch then instructs his servant, Father Inire, to return Severian to the palace gardens where he rejoins Dorcas, Dr Talos, Baldanders and the actress Jolenta. Together, they perform Dr Talos's dizzyingly allusive allegorical play, 'Eschatology and Genesis', before Talos and Baldanders depart for Lake Diuturna, where they plan to rebuild their home.

Declining the invitation from a seductive and voluptuous undine to join her and Abaia (one of the huge aliens besieging Urth) in sexual abandon beneath the waves, Severian leads Dorcas and the increasingly feverish Jolenta across the pampas towards Thrax. Seeking shelter, they enter a strange stone town where they find Vodalus's servant, Hildegrin, a witch and the alien Cumaean intent on raising the spirit of Apu Punchau. With the help of Severian and Dorcas, the Cumaean summons a shade who bears an uncanny resemblance to Severian and to the funeral bronze in the mausoleum where he played as a child. Almost hypnotised, Severian and Hildegrin rush the ghost but an unearthly force repels them. When Severian recovers, Jolenta is dead, and he resumes his journey northwards with Dorcas.

Severian is already lictor at Thrax when *The Sword of the Lictor* begins. However, he does not remain in office long. Although his stay is punctuated by a series of cryptic events, it is his departure from Dorcas that forms one of the most astonishing scenes of the book. Their relationship is already in crisis when Dorcas explains that she can no longer stay with him. A bout of sickness has caused her to vomit lead weights and she now realises that until Severian fell into the lake in the Garden of Endless Sleep, she had lain dead and preserved by its waters for many years. Now she feels she must return to Nessus to seek her past.

Severian is similarly unable to stay in Thrax since he refused to murder a faithless wife for the Archon. Compelled to part by circumstance, their separation is one of the few poignant moments in the narrative as Severian understands that the innocence, wisdom and love with which Dorcas shielded him from the darker side of himself are now gone and he must travel alone. Leaving Dorcas, Severian flees into the mountains above Thrax. There he finds temporary succour with a peasant family before the treachery of Agia and the predations of the chillingly deceitful alien alzabo force him to resume his flight.

His route takes him through mountains carved into statues of previous Autarchs (and reminiscent of a gigantic Mount Rushmore) where he falls foul of the two-headed tyrant Typhon. Wolfe replays the Temptation of

Christ in the wilderness when Typhon offers Severian mastery over Urth if he submits to his will. Sensing a trap, Severian refuses, provoking Typhon into an attempt to destroy him. Severian evades his clutches, however, deduces his weakness and kills him.

Although he escapes Typhon's malice, Severian's descent from the mountains to Lake Diuturna places him in unexpected danger from Baldanders and Dr Talos. Brought to their castle as a prisoner, Severian is greeted as an old friend by three alien Hierodules who explain that they and their kind seek to foster a renaissance in humanity. One of these aliens, Famulimus, secretly reveals to Severian that the ghastly faces they hide behind the masks they wear are merely other masks designed to frighten the people of the Commonwealth into maintaining the Autarchy.

When the Hierodules leave aboard their spaceship, Baldanders destroys the Claw as a symbol of the superstitiousness he despises in humanity. Furious, Severian launches an attack on the giant. They fight back and forth through the castle until *Terminus Est* shatters under a blow from Baldanders's energy mace. Severian is stunned and can only watch as a mob of oppressed islanders storms the keep, forces the rampaging giant into the lake, and ransacks his home.

In the aftermath of the battle, Severian mourns his ruined sword while he searches for the broken fragments of the Claw along the lake side. A flash of light attracts his eye and he spies a glittering thorn wedged among the rocks. In a moment he realises that the real Claw of the Conciliator was not the blue stone he carried from Nessus, but what he assumed was a thorn-shaped fault at its heart. With the Claw in his possession once more, his spirits rise and he travels onwards with fresh resolve.

Severian's new sense of purpose does not sustain him for long, and *Citadel of the Autarch* begins with him scavenging for food near the northern battlefields. During one of his forays, he 'resurrects' the amnesiac soldier, Miles, who then helps him to a lazarette administered by the Pelerines. He learns that the restored Miles is also, in some obscure way, Jonas, who has returned to Urth to seek Jolenta, whom he loves. Severian explains her death but Miles/Jonas will not listen and leaves him alone once more. Severian takes this opportunity to return the Claw to its rightful guardians by concealing it in the altar of their temple where Mannea, mistress of the postulants, requests his aid in rescuing a hermit from the path of the war. When he fails in his mission, he returns to the lazarette but finds it ravaged by cannon fire. The Pelerines and their patients are dead; the Claw lost.

Now aware of the danger of being arrested as a deserter, Severian joins a force of irregular cavalry. He soon arrives on one of the many battlefields where the Commonwealth and Ascia clash in their perpetual war. In one of the most vivid and ambitious set pieces of the narrative, the opposing armies engage in a thunderous military exchange involving energy weapons and the deployment of cavalry and air power. Genetically engineered soldiers and animals are committed to the carnage; lasers scythe through ranks of infantry and a multitude of troops hurtle to destruction as their commanders probe the enemy defences. In the chaos of one such attack, Severian suffers a leg wound and loses consciousness.

In the final third of the novel, the pace of the narrative accelerates as Wolfe brings the disparate elements of his story to a conclusion in a sequence of startling, staccato disclosures.

The battle over, the Autarch plucks Severian from the corpse-littered field only to plunge him into more intense danger when the flier he is piloting is shot down en route to the House Absolute. Vodalus reappears as their captor but his ignorance of the Autarch's true identity saves them both from immediate execution. Instead, they are force-marched through a mosquito-infested jungle to an Ascian encampment. Here, the dying Autarch explains 'the abomination ... the eating of the dead', a ceremony by which the rulers of the Commonwealth preserve a sense of continuity in the seemingly random process of Autarchial succession.[2] Following the Autarch's terrible instructions, Severian ingests parts of the monarch's forebrain with a compound even more powerful than the drug that reunited him with Thecla. In the minutes that follow, the personalities of the Autarch and of each of his predecessors crowd in on Severian's consciousness and blind him to his surroundings.

Lost in the autarchs' labyrinthine existences, Severian is barely aware of his status as the new ruler of the Commonwealth when the aquastors— the animated memories—of Master Malrubius and Triskele snatch him to safety. As they fly north, Malrubius explains the incredible voyage that Severian is destined to make in order to face judgement on Yesod. There, the omniscient Hierogrammates will debate his worthiness as the Epitome of Urth and decide from his example whether the human race deserves the boon of a new sun. If he fails in this test he will, like the Autarch before him, suffer emasculation and thus may condemn Urth to oblivion.

Malrubius goes on to recount the history of Severian's universe, providing the reader with an opportunity to apprehend the story of The Urth Cycle. However, the reader is given little time to appreciate the significance of Malrubius's account as Wolfe moves the text quickly into its final phase.

Left on the shore of the world-sea, Ocean, far to the south of Nessus, Severian ponders his destiny before beginning his trek back to the Citadel to claim his throne. As he quits the beach, he snags his arm on a thorn bush. Examining the wound, he removes a blood-soaked thorn from his flesh and, somewhat incredulously, believes it to be nothing less than the Claw of the Conciliator itself.

Subsequent revelations come thick and fast as the novel approaches its conclusion. On his return to the Citadel, Severian discovers the identities of his father and, in one of the more surprising divulgences of the book, his paternal grandmother, who is none other than his one-time lover, Dorcas. While Severian determines that the boatman he saw in the Garden of Endless Sleep was his grandfather, the identity of his mother, known only as Catherine, remains an enigma, and has been perceived by John Clute as the book's most important mystery.[3]

The Book of the New Sun ends as Severian seeks out Valeria, a girl he met as an apprentice, for his bride, and awaits his day of judgement. He rules for 10 years before the Hierogrammates finally summon him to Yesod to realise his ultimate destiny.

The Urth of the New Sun begins with Severian bound for Yesod aboard a vast spaceship powered by the suns' photonic winds striking its thousands of miles of night-black sail. During the voyage, he explores the mazy vessel, helps to defeat a mutiny mounted by crewmen opposed to the destruction that the New Sun will bring, and masquerades as a sailor to learn more about the workings of the ship. It is while he is fulfilling his duties as a crewman that he slips and plunges to his death in one of the ship's enormous holds. His subsequent 'resurrection' is conveyed so elliptically that the reader begins to suspect that if any sense is to be made of Wolfe's text then very careful attention must be paid to even the most apparently innocent of the narrator's signs.

After the restored Severian's arrival on the calm and beautiful water-world of Yesod, he is taken to the examination chamber where his trial proves to be anti-climactic. When he is brought before Tzadkiel, the Hierogrammate appointed to his case, Severian hears how he has been observed throughout his journey to Yesod. Tzadkiel has already concluded that Severian is worthy of taking a new sun back to Urth and his appearance before the seat of judgement is merely a formality.

In the single most important chapter of the entire pentalogy, Apheta, a Hierogrammate 'larva', explains that the Hierogrammates are playing a cosmic game against entropy in the hope of securing their own evolution by manipulating various human species. In less than two short paragraphs Wolfe subverts the sense of transcendence and religiosity which permeates his text. This subversion is played down, however, as the Hierogrammates return Severian to Urth millennia before his own birth. Here he fulfils the role of the legendary Conciliator, using power drawn from the New Sun that now travels through space from Yesod to Urth.

After Severian cures a young girl's withered arm, smoothes away an old man's malignant tumour and resurrects a drowned sailor, reports of his powers spread; he attracts disciples and is inevitably betrayed to the authorities in an act reminiscent of Judas's betrayal of Christ. Captured and beaten, he is taken to the Matachin Tower, where he recounts his life story to a fellow inmate and meets Ymar, a boy destined to become the first Autarch to face, and fail, testing on Yesod.

The book begins its final phase as Severian is taken north to meet Typhon who, at this time, is Autarch over both Urth and its interstellar empire. During their brief conversation, the reader comes to understand why the tyrant was so eager to win Severian (whom Typhon recognised as the Conciliator) over to his cause in *The Sword of the Lictor*. When Severian displeases Typhon, the Autarch condemns him to death. Before the sentence can be carried out, Severian entrusts the Claw to one of Typhon's disgraced officers and, with Tzadkiel's help, travels forward in time to arrive in his own empty tomb in the gardens of the House Absolute. He rolls away its stone in a manner obviously recalling the events at Christ's tomb, and rushes to the palace for a brief reunion with Valeria before the New Sun explodes overhead.

As the old sun erupts with new life, violent disturbances in the balance of the solar system buffet Urth. Ocean heaves restlessly, gathers itself and consumes Nessus and the Commonwealth in a monstrous tidal wave that bursts through the doors of Severian's audience chamber, floods the palace, and leaves the survivors adrift on the uneasy sea.

Although servants from the House Absolute, and later a passing sailor, save Severian from drowning, he becomes suicidal in the face of the destruction he has wrought and throws himself back into the ocean. His attempt to drown himself comes to nothing, however, when he discovers that he can breathe underwater. More confused than ever, he withdraws into the past.

In the penultimate movement of the novel, Severian travels into an ancient period of Urth's history where the natives revere him as the solar deity Apu Punchau. When he tries to leave their stone town (which is destined to become the ruin he enters in *The Claw of the Conciliator*) the natives are terrified that this departure will prevent the sunrise. In panic, they pursue and garrotte him. Severian is 'resurrected' once more by the three Hierodules he met in Baldanders' castle. Between them, they explain to Severian that he is an aquastor originally reanimated by Tzadkiel aboard the ship bound for Yesod and now restored by their intervention. From the Hierodules Severian learns that aspects of himself are spread throughout time, as Apu Punchau, as Severian, and as the unknown nobleman buried in the necropolis that surrounds the Matachin Tower. Linking each of these aspects together is the trans-temporal power of the

New Sun and Severian's own personal anima, a phrase Wolfe uses (in the Jungian sense) to indicate the life essence or spirit. If two forms of the same individual come too close, as Severian and Apu Punchau do in *The Claw of the Conciliator*, a violent reaction may destroy both manifestations.

With this knowledge, Severian returns to the post-diluvian Urth, now called Ushas, and takes residence in an emergent shore-culture, which recognises him as its most powerful deity, the Sleeper. *The Urth of the New Sun* ends rather than concludes with an image of Severian as part of yet another mythological system.

Wolfe brings The Urth Cycle to a close with an appendix to *The Urth of the New Sun* in which he remarks that 'The thoughtful reader will find little difficulty in advancing at least one plausible speculation' to account for one of the many mysteries present in the text.[4] Located as it is in the final line of the novel, Wolfe's parting challenge ensures that the reader is aware of the presence of puzzles within the text, puzzles that have determinable, though often indistinct, solutions. The text is, quite unashamedly, a conundrum, and one that entices the reader into attempting a decoding of its riddles by its very opacity.

The enigmatic nature of The Urth Cycle has resulted in a critical response that has been disappointing, with contradictory assertions, unresolved conjectures and inconclusive arguments standing as testimony to the bewildering effects of Wolfe's games-playing.

The confusion experienced by critics and reviewers is especially clear in the commentaries concerning the question of the generic identity of the text. Much critical opinion is divided into two mutually exclusive camps: one advocating the text as fantasy, the other perceiving it as science fiction.[5] Leaving aside the multivalency of the terms 'fantasy' and 'science fiction', the existence of contradictory generic readings indicates that Wolfe is undertaking specific operations with the genre conventions of fantasy and SF.

Paul Kincaid observes:

> Those who are not particularly enamoured with fantasy … may find the first chapter of *The Shadow of the Torturer* disconcerting as they wend their way through the traditional paraphernalia of strange names and mysterious meetings loaded with dark significance. Fans of fantasy, on the other hand, may find the rest of the novel disconcerting as they discover that it bears no more than a superficial resemblance to their beloved genre.[6]

Kincaid recognises the generic duplicity occurring within the book. He understands that while Wolfe has loaded his text with the trappings of paraliterary fantasy, this 'traditional paraphernalia' disguises a curious hybrid of fantasy and science fiction that Wolfe terms 'science fantasy'.[7] Although this hybridisation is examined in Chapter 6, it is pertinent to note at this point that such intergenericism is partly responsible for the contradictory arguments concerning the plotting of The Urth Cycle.

Joan Gordon suggests that, 'The plot (the story) of The Book of the New Sun is straightforward and at first glance, unexceptional' and sees the tetralogy as a heterogeneous union of 'a coming-of-age story, a quest story, an adventure story, a success story, and a save-the-world story' (Guide, p. 74). Her standpoint corresponds broadly to that of a number of other critics who believe the text to be a picaresque adventure, 'quite weak on plot', with a direction that 'seems arbitrary'.[8] This standpoint is opposed by Frank Catalano who, like Budrys, sees the tetralogy's plot as 'quite complex'.[9]

The difference between Gordon's perception of The Book of the New Sun and the opinions of Catalano and Budrys arises from a confusion between the definitions of plot and story. 'Plot' describes 'the pattern of events and situations in a narrative or dramatic work, as selected and arranged both to emphasise the relationships between … incidents and to elicit a particular kind of interest from the reader or audience'. Conversely, 'story' denotes 'the sequence of imagined events that we reconstruct from the actual arrangement of a narrative (or dramatic) plot'.[10] Where Gordon treats plot as synonymous with story, she means plot specifically; Catalano, on the other hand, seems to be referring to story.

The resolution of plot with story is achieved when the reader recognises that the seemingly arbitrary incidents that occur around Severian are the products of a subtextual story concerning the Hierogrammates's struggle against entropy. The late Susan Wood alludes to this connection when she remarks, 'The plot is a thread: the quest is for nothing less than the nature of reality itself, under all the dreams and illusions of life.'[11] The quest is not, however, one that is undertaken by Severian: it is a search to be pursued by the reader if the book's story is ever to be extracted from its digressive and discursive 'dreams and illusions'. The reader's quest is for clues that will allow the complex science fictional story to be deduced from the conventional rite-of-passage fantasy structure it imitates.

By locating the story on a subtextual level and then obscuring it within an apparently conventional heroic adventure, Wolfe offers his readers two opportunities for making incorrect analyses. If the reader perceives the subtextual story without understanding why it remains within the subtext, the purpose of Severian's odyssey across Urth and the effect it has on both the character and the reader are unlikely to be identified. Conversely, if the reader uncovers the story, and apprehends why that story exists at a subtextual level, the narrative comes into focus more fully. If, on the other hand, the reader accepts Severian's phantasmagoric trek as the story of the novel, and remains satisfied that The Urth Cycle is picaresque fantasy, then the actual story may never be uncovered. In this case, the narrative may be classed as an imaginatively and stylistically superior paraliterary fantasy of the kind practised by writers such as David Eddings, Terry Brooks and Robert Jordan.

This element of choice is Wolfe's principal device for confounding the reader. Not only does he enable the critic to read his text as intricately plotted or comparatively plotless, he also seems to provide sufficient textual evidence to sustain either argument by rendering his story barely determinable. Of course, the paradoxical appeals of the text should be sufficient to make any cautious reader suspicious, locating him or her in a suitably sceptical position.

By not detecting the relationship between the plot of The Urth Cycle and its underlying story, several (insufficiently sceptical) critics have accepted Severian's pseudo-philosophical digressions and the text's symbolism as indicative of *The Book of the New Sun* being some imprecise form of quasi-Christian parable.[12] Kincaid, for example, believes that

> *The Book of the New Sun* has a clear underlying Christian theme. It was subtly done but evident in small ways, such as the 'Hierogrammates' (sacred scribes) and the 'Hierodules' (sacred slaves), both of which turn out to be creations of an earlier breed of man. But now [in *The Urth of the New Sun*] the Christianity comes much more blatantly to the fore. It is impossible to miss the identification of Severian with Christ ... the way he dies and rises again, his identification as the Conciliator, his judgement before Tzadkiel whose appearance is angelic ...[13]

Kincaid does not identify the 'clear underlying Christian theme', however, and his review overlooks how *The Urth of the New Sun* explodes much of the quasi-religiosity of *The Book of the New Sun* by disclosing the Hierogrammates's evolutionary strategies and revealing the Conciliator to be a time-travelling Severian, revelations that move the text away from the sacred towards the secular.

When Kincaid perceives 'Hierogrammate' and 'Hierodule' as indicative of a latent religious element, he overlooks the fact that Wolfe's diction invariably functions allusively. These nouns are meant to be 'suggestive rather than definitive' (*Shadow*, p. 302) and, although they imply that the Hierodules and Hierogrammates possess divine intent, they do not indicate any actual divinity within the aliens or their highly evolved human masters. Kincaid recognises that the Hierodules and the Hierogrammates are 'the creations of an earlier breed of man', but does not follow the thought through to state that they are not, therefore, part of any angelic hierarchy.

When Kincaid accepts the symbolism and incidents that Wolfe appropriates from orthodox Christianity as analogous to their biblical counterparts he, like Gordon, does not apprehend the role that such features play in the context of the novel.[14] The biblical allusions that reappear throughout The Urth Cycle are no more, and no less, significant to Wolfe's characters than the multitude of similar allusions to pagan mythologies: rather, they exist to foster misreadings.

Wolfe's success in encouraging misinterpretations through such allusiveness can be observed in the writings of those critics who have noted that 'Severian is inescapably a Christ-figure'.[15] Wolfe invites this identification by drawing distinct parallels between his protagonist and Christ on a number of occasions.[16] For example, by having Severian raise the dead (including Dorcas and Miles), Wolfe prompts the reader into assuming that Severian is a Christ-like messiah. However, within the fictional environment, the resemblance is merely coincidental: Severian is actually no more than a tool used by the Hierogrammates to further their own mythogenetic strategies (see Chapter 5).

The reader should not be deceived into accepting Wolfe's allusions as evidence of the themes and concerns of the text. In The Shadow of the Torturer, Severian argues: 'We believe we invent symbols. The truth is they invent us, we are their creatures, shaped by their hard, defining edges' (p. 17) and Wolfe constructs his entire narrative to prove this maxim. In substantiating its veracity, he establishes an interrelated two-tier mythogenesis in which the myths manufactured by the Hierogrammates correspond to the series of myths, or misreadings, resulting from the strategies he employs in his games with the reader.

There is, however, an inescapable religious aspect to The Urth Cycle. This quality does not depend on Wolfe's Roman Catholicism, as some critics have suggested,[17] but on his recognition of the power of myth to shape humanity's secular and spiritual life (see Chapter 7). Wolfe's oblique means of conveying his recognition of humanity's dependence on myth has led Paul Brazier to dismiss The Book of the New Sun as 'perverse'. Brazier's 'disencryptic' analysis finally challenges those critics who find literary merit in the text's opacity:

> For me, great literature says something profound about the moral/ ethical/political experience of being alive. According to friends who admire it, The Book [of the New Sun] is a highly complex and very polished puzzle. Well, so is the Sunday Times Crossword puzzle and no-one claims that to be great literature.[18]

Although Brazier's confrontational attitude invigorates the debate over whether the tetralogy is anything more than a clever conundrum, it prevents him from perceiving Wolfe's thoughtful examination—and enactment—of faith and delusion which ensures that the text is not simply 'a highly complex and very polished puzzle'.

Brazier suggests that Wolfe's narrative technique encompasses Rabkin's Transformation (named after Eric Rabkin, the US scholar), a phrase that describes instances in which a grammatical or graphical structure contains, 'at either end ... an interpretation which precludes the obvious interpretation at the other end'.[19] To illustrate his argument, Brazier quotes the sentence: 'I feel more like I did when I came in than I do now', and provides a sketch of *Mad* magazine's *piyout*, a diagram of a three-dimensional object whose confused lines prevent it from being realised in three dimensions—as in the graphics of M. C. Escher.[20] As Brazier remarks, from the evidence of the Introduction to *Gene Wolfe's Book of Days*, which begins as an introduction but concludes as a short story, Wolfe is familiar with the conceit.

Extending the analogy, Brazier quotes a passage from *The Shadow of the Torturer* to illustrate its relevance for a reading of *The Book of the New Sun*: 'A fiacre drawn by a pair of onegars was dodging towards us ... The fiacre drew up to her [Agia] with the skittish animals dancing to one side as though she were a thyacine' (*Shadow*, p. 162). Brazier notes how

> Wolfe engages our trust with the first term [*fiacre*, which the reader recognises as a carriage from an earlier description], extends it onto the bridge of the second [*onegar*, which, from its context, the reader understands to be a draft animal], and betrays it with the third [*thyacine*, whose meaning is indeterminable from evidence in the text]; and this three-stage mystification is a paradigm of how Wolfe generates his misdirection.[21]

While Brazier's comments help to reveal how Wolfe's text works in its appropriation and subversion of generic and literary forms, including the quest pattern and the autobiographical form (see Chapter 7), his conclusion is erroneous:

> If Rabkin's Transformation is used *behind* the text, then we must realise this implies that there is also a solution behind the text. This is why I have called this section 'disencryption' rather than 'decoding' or 'solution'; the encryption, the presenting of the story as a puzzle, is a deliberate ploy to mark Wolfe's change of the rules. Which in turns means, finally, that the puzzle itself is meaningless.[22]

Although it is likely that Wolfe does create his conundrum in part to obfuscate the changes he works on traditional literary codes, there is no reason to assume that the presence of this conundrum signifies a lack of 'moral/ethical/political' significance in the text. Wolfe's artful puzzle, as complex as it is, is far from 'meaningless', although its complexity may have the self-defeating effect of suggesting such nonsensicality.

The intricacy of the text has resulted in many critics withdrawing from considering Wolfe's narrative techniques in favour of more traditional sources of comment, supporting claims for the tetralogy's value by examining its style, setting, characterisation and themes.[23] More importantly, Gordon notes how the prodigiousness of Wolfe's esoteric language reflects the prodigiousness of Severian's memory (see *Guide*, pp. 77–78). Like Jorge Luis Borges's eponymous character Funes the Memorious, Severian has a copious memory and its contents not only create the memory system described in Chapter 9 but also constitute a series of inter- and intratextual echoes that may mystify the reader (see Chapter 10).

Gordon observes how Wolfe's textual maze is constructed initially from interconnected 'words, images and ideas' and extended by the incorporation of embedded stories (see *Guide*, p. 79). Several such tales occur within *The Book of the New Sun*, including 'The Tale of the Student and His Son' and the drama 'Eschatology and Genesis' in *The Claw of the Conciliator*; 'The Story of a Boy Called Frog' in *The Sword of the Lictor*; and the cluster of narratives related by the hospitalised soldiers in *The Citadel of the Autarch*. A number of critics have argued that these embedded tales suspend the progression of Severian's memoir unnecessarily.[24] Others have accepted them as culturally specific, meaning more to their fictional auditors than they do to the reader.[25]

Conversely, Gordon suggests that these stories move the reader towards the centre of Wolfe's textual maze and, therefore, towards meaning (*Guide*, p. 80). However, rather than leading the reader towards the focus of the novel (Severian's manipulation by the Hierogrammates), the tales that Severian recounts direct the reader onto discursive and peripheral self-reflexive pathways (see Chapter 10).

Wolfe's embedded stories have provided critics with countless opportunities for establishing links between *The Book of the New Sun* and its source material.[26] Yet, as Michael Bishop observes, while 'Wolfe's work appears to flow from such heterogeneous fonts as Poe, Dickens, Melville, Twain, Chesterton, and Borges', it employs these sources 'in such rigorously transmuted proportions that he [Wolfe] could easily deny, and with utter credibility, any or all of these ostensible influences'.[27] Bishop appreciates that Wolfe has transformed his intertextual allusions until they serve a specific, and independent, function within the narrative. It is unnecessary to determine their sources to enjoy and understand The Urth Cycle.

Roz Kaveney disagrees: 'It is of course logical when dealing with a novel so concerned with texts within texts that one should have to go for an understanding of it to texts outside it.'[28] However, there is no logical reason for assuming that the resolution of Wolfe's narrative conundrum lies in the work of earlier authors simply because he alludes to it. Indeed, if the reader attempts to identify these references, he or she will fall victim to Wolfe's deflective strategy. Kaveney's position is precisely the stance that Wolfe wishes the reader to adopt on an initial reading as he encourages that reader to uncover the sources of his intertexts.

As Clute observes, *The Book of the New Sun* is

> A text which embroils its readers in a fever of interpretation and which seems designed to unpeel its layers of possible meaning more or less indefinitely until the reader begins to feel that his exegetical dance is somehow isomorphic with the true *Book* [*of the New Sun*] itself ... (*Strokes*, pp. 152–53)

The isomorphism that Clute finds between the reader's response to the tetralogy and the text itself lies in the relationship between Wolfe's narrator and the reader, both of whom are experiencing a world they do not fully comprehend.

It is this world that confronts the reader with multiple opportunities for (mis-)interpretation. These opportunities arise not only from Wolfe's characters, who are 'archetypes [that] carry a powerful and symbolic emotional freight from our Greco-Roman and Judeo-Christian traditions' (*Guide*, p. 86), but also from the aggregation of allusions that open the text still further to a 'fever of interpretation'.

Initially, Clute believed that an understanding of *The Book of the New Sun* could only be achieved through the recovery of textual clues: 'Making sense of Gene Wolfe, it seems to me, is initially a job of decipherment. Interpretation of the text must follow its decipherment, must subtend some consensus about the raw configurations of the story itself' (*Strokes*, p. 163). While Clute is correct to stress the need to discover what is occurring within Wolfe's fictional universe, his early efforts towards 'decipherment' were directed towards revealing the identity of Severian's family, particularly his mother. As a consequence, his preliminary conclusions are a combination of the perspicacious and the eccentric.

In 1986, Clute revised his 1983 *Washington Post Book World* review of *The Citadel of the Autarch* and observed that Severian 'writes *The Book of the New Sun* (and this may be the key to much of its disingenuousness about explosive material like the question of Severian's parentage) to prompt us' (*Strokes*, p. 152). Although Clute believes the work's 'disingenuousness' to arise from Severian's character rather than from its actual author, his augmented observations mark a substantial shift in his reasoning. Clute now understands that the 'explosive material' contained within *The Book of the New Sun* is deployed to elicit a response from the reader. While Clute does not suggest what the reader is prompted to do, it seems likely that such material is introduced to deflect the reader's attention from the story and thereby maintain the narrative's overall opacity.

The discursive power of The Urth Cycle has been exposed indirectly by Michael Andre-Driussi who, in 1994, published his *Lexicon Urthus: A Dictionary for the Urth Cycle*. The lexicon is a laudable and scholarly attempt to trace the symbolic, mythical and historical resonances of Wolfe's pentalogy and represents a significant contribution to the decipherment that Clute once considered so important. With the lexicon now published, there is a need to uncover the story of The Urth Cycle and describe how, and why, Wolfe conceals it so thoroughly. What is required, as Clute realises, is 'the kind of close critical reading of text that serious critics of the Modernist and Post-Modernist novel assume to be absolutely mandatory for starters, with understanding to come later, after some work has been done' (*Strokes*, p. 159).

Wolfe himself helps to formulate this 'close critical reading' by providing clues as to how The Urth Cycle should be read in two short stories, 'The God and His Man' (1980) and 'A Solar Labyrinth' (1983), and in several novels published after *The Citadel of the Autarch*. While 'A Solar Labyrinth' has implications for an understanding of how the structure of The Urth Cycle helps obscure its story (see Chapter 10), 'The God and His Man' alludes to how Severian's memoir encourages the reader to foster misapprehensions of its subject matter, story and content.

In 'The God and His Man', 'the mighty and powerful god Isid Iooo IoooE' comes to the world of Zed in his spacecraft.[29] He summons Man from Urth and sends him among the tribes of Zed. Man wanders with the people of the high, hot lands before he becomes a chief in the steaming jungles. When he indulges in an orgy of sex, Isid Iooo IoooE drives him south into the cold lands where he labours as a ditch digger. Eventually, Man abandons his life as a labourer and becomes an orator who angers the ruling party with his rhetoric. He avoids arrest for dissent and Isid Iooo IoooE summons him back to the ship where the god asks him which of the three peoples, those of the high, hot lands, the jungles or the cold lands he loved the most, and why. Man explains that he loved 'The people of the steaming lands [since they were] innocent of justice and injustice alike. They followed their hearts, and while I dwelt among them I followed mine ...' Isid Iooo IoooE replies: 'You have much to learn, Man ... For the people of the cold lands are much nearer to me [with their sense of justice]' (*Species*, p. 208). Man argues for the firm character of the people of the high, hot lands, but the god confronts him with a maxim: 'It is better that a man should die than he should be a slave' (*Species*, p. 208). Man recognises the truth of this and destroys the god, but his fate aboard the orbiting ship remains undisclosed.

'The God and His Man' can be read as a metaphor for the relationship between the writer (Isid Iooo IoooE), the text (the world of Zed) and the reader/critic (Man) who comes from Earth/Urth. Man's extendable maser-weapon, 'whose blade is as long as the wielder wishes (though it weighs nothing)' (*Species*, p. 204), symbolises the critic's 'pen', which may go to great lengths but, as Wolfe believes, may carry little metaphorical weight.[30]

The identification of Wolfe with Isid Iooo IoooE is suggested by the composition of the god's name. 'Is' is conjugated with 'id', the Freudian term denoting 'the unconscious reservoir of primitive instincts from which spring the forces of behaviour'[31] and thereby implies that the god 'is' a manifestation of Wolfe's 'id', or authorial persona. The repetition of 'I' in Iooo and IoooE seems to confirm this suggestion.

Like Isid Iooo IoooE, Wolfe arrives at, or creates, a fictional world to which he brings, or attracts, the reader. Immersed in the author's hetero-cosm, the reader, like Man on Zed, is offered various analytical choices. There are opportunities to determine what the narrative's themes might be, which are more significant, and what metaphorical or cognitive function is served by the story. This process of selection is analogous to the choices that Man must make when he decides which tribe is the most 'lovable'.

When the author clouds the evidence on which such a decision is based with an unreliable narrator, ambiguity and intertextuality, the narrative may be misinterpreted, just as Man misinterprets which tribe the god expects him to favour. Like Man, the reader may produce a (mis-)reading in keeping with his or her own reading/life experiences rather than deducing the god's/author's intentions. The people of the cold lands symbolise 'the true interpretation' that Wolfe wishes the reader finally to extract from The Urth Cycle, while the peoples of the jungle and the high, hot lands emblematise the alternative, and inaccurate, readings that are available.

If Man had chosen the people of the cold lands, he would have experienced all the choices that Isid Iooo IoooE offered and formulated the 'reading' that the god intended. He would have attained a new level of awareness from his experience of life on Zed which, in turn, would have enabled him to deduce the god's intentions. Similarly, if the reader of The Urth Cycle extracts the intended interpretation of the text from the multifarious readings available, this new sensitivity may lead to an understanding of Wolfe's authorial motives and to a more critical or cognitive reflection on the world.

The destruction of the god at the conclusion of the story marks the metaphorical death of the author as Man, the reader-figure, fails to acknowledge the god's/author's intent. The god's/author's purpose has no relevance in Man's/the reader's misinterpretation of the world/text and he is, therefore, consigned to oblivion. Man's fate, adrift in an empty starship, is possibly a representation of the insular ground that the reader/critic occupies when he or she fails to apprehend the writer's purposes.

Isid Iooo IoooE's death arises from his failure to observe that he is as much an enslaver of Man as Man was of the people of the high, hot lands. By testing Man's intellect and judgement, the god deprives him of his freedom, just as Wolfe enslaves the reader in chains of interpretative possibilities. Taken metaphorically, Wolfe seems to be suggesting that his death, which occurs whenever a reader misapprehends his intentions, may be the consequence of his overestimation of the reasoning capacity of his readers. The ambiguity of the text may become a pathway to a kind of professional suicide where Wolfe's penchant for ellipsis, rather than prompting the reader's intellectual growth, may, paradoxically, overthrow efforts towards understanding. If the reader does apprehend the narrative's story, however, Wolfe's techniques are revealed as successful methods for educating the reader in the reading process through the reading process.

Once the story of The Urth Cycle is determined, it is possible to construct a suitable strategy for interpretation. Wolfe seems to aid his reader here by proposing one possible method of analysis in *The Shadow of the Torturer*, when Severian explains to Dorcas:

> Whatever happens has three meanings. The first is its practical meaning ... 'the thing the plowman sees'. The cow has taken a mouthful of grass, and it is real grass and a real cow ... The second is the reflection of the world about it. Every object is in contact with all others, and thus the wise can learn of the other by observing the first. This might be called the soothsayers' meaning because it is the one which such people use when they prophesy ... The third meaning is the transsubstantial meaning. Since all objects have their ultimate origin in the Pancreator, and all were set in motion by him, so all must express his will—which is the higher reality ... Everything is a sign. (*Shadow*, p. 272)

Joan Gordon takes this passage to indicate that:

> The tetralogy is not to be taken strictly at face value ... Our world, Severian's memoir, and Wolfe's fiction all demand such threefold interpretation. It is a notion very close to the medieval one of quadruplex allegory. There, each thing, each story, has a literal meaning ('what the plowman sees'), a metaphorical one, an analogical one (these two are combined in the 'soothsayers' meaning'), and an anagogical one (which corresponds to its 'transubstantial meaning'). (*Guide*, pp. 91–92)

Gordon's triadic interpretative method, prescribed by Wolfe himself, is unsatisfactory as it favours an unrestrained exegetical exercise employing a variety of analytical approaches.

With an author as self-conscious as Wolfe, it seems likely that the three choices for interpretation described by Severian form a deliberate parallel with the three tribes that Man must choose between in 'The God and His Man'. This intertextual association appears to indicate that if the reader employs all three strategies (that is, 'lives' with all three 'peoples'), without considering their effects on him or her, as a reader, the conclusions reached will fail to equate to the author's intended reading.

However, the connection between 'The God and His Man' and The Urth Cycle also suggests, albeit obliquely, that one of the interpretative procedures proposed by Severian is more valuable for directing the reader to the interpretation that Wolfe intends. Selecting the most appropriate strategy is not easy but it seems probable that, by following Severian's instructions for such multifarious exposition, Wolfe wants the prudent reader to observe how the manipulation of archetype and symbol can support largely extraneous or artificial 'soothsayers' and 'transubstantial' readings. Since neither of these approaches brings the reader any closer to determining the motive of the extraterrestrial forces guiding the development of Urth's humanity, or to recognising the moves in Wolfe's literary game, only the 'practical' approach retains any real critical validity.

The writing of any criticism relating to The Urth Cycle will, therefore, be a partly autobiographical exercise. The conclusions reached should indicate that understanding proceeds from earlier misinterpretations which led to a more complete comprehension of the text. When the reader gains an awareness of the inaccuracy of his or her preliminary readings through a greater familiarity with the pentalogy, those misreadings become invaluable for demonstrating how Wolfe shapes reader response.

In order to uncover Wolfe's manipulative strategies, it is imperative to deduce the story of The Urth Cycle and then self-consciously reflect on the obstacles that opposed this deduction. Chapter 5 begins this process by disclosing the text's concealed story.

Part II
Investigations: The Urth Cycle

An enigma. There it is before you—smiling, frowning, inviting, grand, mean, insipid or savage, and always mute with an air of whispering, Come and find out.

—Joseph Conrad, *Heart of Darkness* (1901)

5. 'The Toy Theatre': Uncovering the Story of The Urth Cycle[1]

Uniting Wolfe's recurrent interests in manipulation and psychology, the story of The Urth Cycle describes a human race caught in two complex processes: that of an external cosmological conspiracy masterminded by the Hierogrammates, and that of its own psychological need for lenitive myths.

Wolfe directs the reader to this conclusion through the adhibition of theatrical metaphors. As Joe Sanders remarks, 'the relation of audience ... to performance is a recurring motif in Wolfe's fiction'[2] (appearing in texts as diverse as 'The Toy Theatre' [1971], 'The Eyeflash Miracles' [1976], 'Seven American Nights' [1978], *Free Live Free* [1986] and *The Book of the Long Sun* [1993–96]), and invariably indicates the presence of a disjunction between what is apparent from a narrative's plot and what is occurring at the level of its story.

For example, in 'The Toy Theatre' an aspiring and talented marionettist travels to the planet Sarg to study under the master puppeteer, Stromboli. Throughout the story, the narrator learns his art until, at the spaceport, the reader begins to suspect that what he or she has accepted as a human commentator is, in fact, a mechanised marionette, endeavouring to deny its artificiality. What the narrator has observed is an example of Joruri, 'The Japanese puppet theatre. The operators stand in full view of the audience, but the audience pretends not to see them.'[3] The narrator, like Columbine, Lucinda, Julia, Lili and Zanni the Butler, is Stromboli's puppet but, in order to sustain the illusion under which he lives, he 'pretends not to see' his operator.

Similarly, the dramatic action of The Urth Cycle constitutes a contrived performance populated with marionettes. Throughout the pentalogy, costumes are donned (Severian wears the robes of a pilgrim, Agia disguises herself as a soldier), masks worn (Agilus appears first wearing a death's-head, Severian has his torturer's mask), masques attended (in *The Sword of the Lictor*), plays performed (in *The Shadow of the Torturer* and *The Claw of the Conciliator*) and roles adopted until the reader begins to perceive the incidents unfolding around Severian as merely the spectacle beyond the proscenium arch. By implication, there is a playwright for this drama (excluding Wolfe, the literal author, for a moment), a director and machinery, none of which is readily apparent.

Above and beyond the 'stage' of the narrative's plot are the Hierogrammates, who orchestrate its mythogenetic drama (the outline of which is given in the play 'Eschatology and Genesis') that is played out on Urth. The world-as-stage scenario becomes explicit in *The Citadel of the Autarch* when Master Malrubius's aquastor explains:

> We are ... powers from above the stage ... some supernatural force, personified and brought onto the stage in the last act in order that the play might end well. None but poor playwrights do it, they say, but those who say so forget that it is better to have a power lowered on a rope, and a play that ends well, than to have nothing, and a play that ends badly. (*Citadel*, p. 243)

Although Malrubius's words allude to the text's own fictiveness and Wolfe's self-consciousness at 'employing powers from above the stage', or a deus ex machina, the aquastor's presence demonstrates that Severian's experiences are being coordinated by such powers (which include both the author and the Hierogrammates). Wolfe's challenge to the reader is to step beyond the stage, to see through the play, and to discover the motivation of those who direct and regulate the performance by removing the masks they wear.

Behind the dramatic action of The Urth Cycle is a narrative of survival, not transcendence or spiritual growth, but a representation of the Darwinian principle which dictates that only those most able to adapt to a specific environment will survive. The reader is, therefore, confronted with a vision of cosmological natural selection which, because it is masterminded and consciously controlled by an alien race for its own evolutionary gain, becomes a revelation of authoritarianism.

To understand this subtext fully, the reader must appreciate the cosmology of Wolfe's universe. According to legends introduced into Commonwealth society by the Hierodules, a race of beings 'cognate with' (akin or related to) *Homo sapiens* once colonised the galaxies. These creatures, the Hieros, or Holy Ones, discovered other intelligent species which they reshaped into companions for themselves. This reshaping was an act of torture, and 'uncountable billions suffered and died under their guiding hands' before they succeeded in creating a 'race such as humanity wished its own to be: united, compassionate, just'. When that cycle of creation ended, those who had been formed, and who would come to be known as the Hierogrammates, escaped to Yesod, 'the universe higher than our own' (*Citadel*, p. 279). From there, like Janus, they looked forward and back through time until they discovered Urth, whose humans they shape as they themselves were shaped in a previous creation.

The relationship between human and Hierogrammate is finally disclosed on Yesod by Apheta as she explains the Hierogrammates' motives to Gunnie, one of the sailors aboard Tzadkiel's ship in *The Urth of the New Sun*:

> 'The Hierarchs and their Hierodules—and the Hierogrammates too—have been trying to let us [*Homo sapiens*] become what we were [the Hieros]. What we can be … That's their justice, their whole reason for being. They bring us through the pain we brought them through. …' Apheta said, 'You in turn will make us go through what you did. … Your race and ours are, perhaps, no more than each other's reproductive mechanisms. You are a woman, and so you say you produce your ovum so that someday there will be another woman. But your ovum would say it produces that woman so that someday there will be another ovum. We have wanted the New Sun to succeed as badly as he [Severian] has himself. More urgently, in all truth. In saving your race he has saved ours; as we have saved ours of the future by saving yours.'[4]

The Hierogrammates and humanity are intimately connected in a feedback mechanism made tangible by the Hierogrammates' ability to perceive all epochs of time. Apheta's analogy between their relationship and that of a woman to her ova is, itself, analogous to Richard Dawkins's Selfish Gene hypothesis.[5]

Dawkins's thesis argues that the individual is a complex 'survival machine built by a short-lived confederation of long-lived genes'. The survival machine is the human body with its 'confederation' of gene types which endure through the agencies of the spermatozoa and the ova. Dawkins observes that

> A gene can live for a million years … The few [which do survive do so] because they have what it takes, and that means they are good at making survival machines. … Any gene that behaves in such a way as to increase its own survival chances in the gene pool at the expense of its alleles [genes responsible for similar physical characteristics like eye colour which are in physical competition for the same location on a chromosome] will, by definition, tautologously, tend to survive. The gene is the basic unit of selfishness …[6]

Dawkins defines biological selfishness thus:

> An entity, such as a baboon, is said to be altruistic if it behaves in such a way as to increase another such entity's welfare [or chances of survival] at the expense of its own. Selfish behaviour has exactly the opposite effect … My own definition is concerned with whether the effect of an act is to lower or raise the survival prospects of the

presumed altruist and the survival prospects of the presumed
beneficiary.[7]

While appearing as an act of altruistic beneficence, the Hierogrammates'
salvation of Urth is a selfish undertaking; and selfishness masquerading as
altruism is entirely in keeping with Dawkins's theory, which recognises
that 'there are special circumstances in which a gene can achieve its own
selfish goals best by fostering a limited form of altruism ...'[8]

The Hierogrammates are acting to conserve their development. Urth is
important to them because the Hieros, the species who created them,
evolved from human stock before the end of the old creation. Their
apparently altruistic actions towards humanity, their granting of the boon
of the New Sun, must be recognised as a Hierogrammate means to a
Hierogrammate end; the (comparatively) short-term benefits conferred
on *Homo sapiens* who, in all probability, will be destroyed together with the
old universe, are merely the by-products of the Hierogrammates' determination to ensure their own biological ascent.

Throughout The Urth Cycle, Wolfe is exercising his palpable belief in
Typhon's statement that 'All life acts to preserve its life—that is what we
call the Law of existence.'[9] In order to help guarantee their evolution, the
Hierogrammates accept Severian as the Epitome of Urth and transport
him to Yesod to determine the fitness (biologically speaking, his breeding
potential, but in this case suggestive of the human capacity for creating
the Hierogrammates by 'torturing' alien species) of humanity.

The system of trials on Yesod, in which the fitness of representatives
from Urth's colonised worlds is determined, can therefore be seen as
analogous to the environment to which organisms must adapt or die. On
Yesod, the fittest species are selected to receive new suns to ensure that
genes favourable to the evolution of the Hierogrammates' manipulators
will be preserved. As a consequence, the whole pseudo-spiritual mystical
system of Yesod begins to appear as a symbolic rendering of the selection
pressures that govern the survival or extinction of entire species.

Apheta states, 'your race is important to us. It would be far less
laborious if we could deal with it all at once, but you are sown over tens of
thousands of worlds, and we cannot. ... The worlds are very far apart'
(*Urth*, p. 135). The species examined on Yesod are, collectively, the gene
pool of the Hierogrammates' progenitors. Those species whose genes are
judged favourable to Hiero evolution are permitted to survive; those that
express no potential for such development are consigned to oblivion. The
Hierogrammates' ruthlessness (arguably, they have the technical prowess
to save all the diverse species of humanity) is a direct result of their genes
'instructing' them to be merciless in their trans-temporal breeding pro-
gramme, to act in their own self-interest.

Wolfe is happy to acknowledge that he has read several reviews of the Selfish Gene hypothesis and related articles in *Scientific American* and other journals. It seems likely, then, that when he began his story of 'god-like forces exploring and influencing various probability lines until they found one in which Urth did not die', Dawkins's theory helped to crystallise the Hierogrammates' motives for 'exploring and influencing' the 'probability lines' of Urth's potential future history.[10]

Given his reputation as a punster, it seems probable that Wolfe's employment of the Selfish Gene hypothesis also forms a gross pun on his own name. Gene's/Wolfe's selfishness is manifest in the notion that the text seems contrived, primarily, to satisfy the author's love of games-playing rather than to gratify the reader's need for entertainment.[11] However, given Wolfe's determination to foster scepticism in his reader, to use his own form of cognitive estrangement to heighten the reader's sensitivity to the distinction between the apparent and the real, it seems likely that such games-playing is instructive—if the reader is sufficiently sagacious.

Both Wolfe and Dawkins present human beings as tools: for Dawkins, they are 'survival machines [like] great lumbering robots';[12] in Wolfe's universe they are unwitting pawns in the Hierogrammates' game against universal dissolution. The difference between Dawkins's thesis and the trans-temporal interspecies system formulated by Wolfe is a matter of degree. Where Dawkins is deducing biological principles that govern behaviour, Wolfe is presenting a fascist celestial order in which the authoritarian Hierogrammates deny humanity what are perceived as basic human rights: justice, freedom and compassion.

The concept of injustice masquerading as justice is central to the text. For example, in endeavouring to vindicate the existence and role of his guild in *The Sword of the Lictor* (pp. 25–27), Severian makes an appeal to an obscure celestial system of judgement. He concludes, rather lamely, with a recognition that torturers are 'devils … But we are necessary. Even the powers of Heaven find it necessary to employ devils' (*Sword*, p. 27). Severian's attempt to justify his actions by invoking a mythic parallel fails ultimately because the reader is denied a glimpse of Heaven and an encounter with its demons; the cruelty of the torturers remains an entirely secular form of punishment analogous only to the equally secular cruelty of the Hierogrammates.

Beguiled by the Hierogrammates' show-trial, Severian repeatedly informs the reader that Tzadkiel (the Hierogrammate presiding over his judgement) is just, yet Tzadkiel admits he/she cannot be just and leaves Apheta struggling to explain why:

> It is easy for those who need not judge, or judging need not toil for justice, to complain of inequality and talk of impartiality. When one

must actually judge, as Tzadkiel does, he finds he cannot be just to one without being unjust to another. In fairness to those on Urth who will die, and especially to the poor and ignorant people who will never understand what it is they die for, he summoned their representatives [the shipmen] and gave you, Autarch, those who had reason to hate you for your defenders. That was fair to the shipmen but not to you. (*Urth*, pp. 160–61)

Apheta conceals the racial selfishness that motivates the Hierogrammates behind an implication of higher purposes. However, Tzadkiel is not seeking justice, he/she is *judging*, that is, determining, whether the humans on Urth are likely to evolve into the Hierogrammates' precursors.

Within this controlled, manipulative system of governance, freedom is vigorously excluded and an emphasis on servitude sustained. After the apocalyptic flood consumes Urth, the faceless survivors are represented by Odilo, Pega, Thais, Eata and Severian. Of these, Odilo, Pega and Severian are all servants of one form or another, and Thais is likely to have been a minor noble serving in the Autarch's court. Only Eata is a free man, and his submission to sleep before Severian can recount his experiences on Yesod marks his comparative independence from the mythogenesis initiated by the Hierogrammates.

As survivors, Severian, Odilo, Pega and Thais represent those individuals best suited to life on the post-deluge world, and their now-defunct social status emphasises humanity's standing as a servant race. Although numerous reasons are offered to account for why Severian was selected, 'a torturer to save the world' (*Urth*, p. 161), the most significant remains undisclosed. However, from clues within the narrative it is possible to argue that he is chosen for his willingness to act compliantly. He does not judge; as a torturer he merely obeys: 'We are trained from childhood not to judge, but only carry out the sentences handed down by the courts of the Commonwealth' (*Sword*, p. 59). Severian has been indoctrinated into accepting the instructions and authority of the hierarchies above him without question. Such obedience is taken to the extreme by the Ascians, who 'obey because they could not conceive of any other action' (*Citadel*, p. 230).

Although Severian sees the Ascians as an alien culture, they are, in their unthinking obedience, analogous to the torturers. Severian realises that, 'In all the lofty order of the body politic ... we [the torturers] are the only sound stone. No one truly obeys unless he will do the unthinkable in obedience; no one will do the unthinkable save we' (*Sword*, p. 252). For his willingness to obey the instigators of the unthinkable, he is co-opted into the Hierogrammates' schemes.

Like the Ascians, Severian, too, lacks the power of independent action when he is told that he 'must serve Tzadkiel' (*Urth*, p. 35); he readily admits to Apheta that 'I am my lady's slave' (*Urth*, p. 121); and when he abases himself before Tzadkiel, he states: 'Mighty Hierogrammate, I am the least of your slaves' (*Urth*, p. 283). Tzadkiel replies, 'If they [Severian's enemies] had been wise, they would have known you for our servant and not fought against you at all' (*Urth*, p. 284).

Wolfe suggests the pervasiveness of such hierarchical power structures at the conclusion of *The Urth of the New Sun* when Odilo, Pega, Thais and Severian attain the status of mythical gods attended by numerous servants. In this way, he emphasises that the pattern of hierarchical obedience established in the relationship between the Autarch, who serves the Hierodules, and the Hierodules, who serve the Hierogrammates, all of whom apparently serve the Increate, is a recurrent, universal pattern.

In *The Shadow of the Torturer*, Severian observes that, 'I have always found that the pattern of our guild [with its masters, journeymen and apprentices] is repeated mindlessly in the societies of every trade, so that they are all of them torturers, just as we' (*Shadow*, pp. 41–42). Clearly, analogies can be drawn between the torturers' guild and the Hierogrammates' organisation. The Hierogrammates represent the master torturers, the errant Hierodules their journeymen, and humanity the apprenticed species whose service to the future has barely begun. The 'mindlessness' of this repetition arises from the lack of purpose for the human species beyond its assigned role in the Hierogrammates' machinations.

Recognising the implication that *Homo sapiens* is a servant species whose sole significance rests in its future genetic development answers some of the most fundamental questions concerning the purpose of human existence. Since humanity will create the Hierogrammates, it no longer has to

> resort to superstition when faced with the deep problems: is there a meaning to life? What are we for? What is man? After posing the last of these questions the eminent zoologist G. G. Simpson put it thus: 'The point I want to make now is that all attempts to answer that question before 1859 [when Darwin's *On The Origin of Species* was published] are worthless and that we will be better off if we ignore them completely.[13]

For many people, a purely biological explanation for human existence is untenable, as Dawkins discovered when he first published his thesis.[14] There appears to be a profound psychological need among *Homo sapiens* for something more than a merely scientific account of the purposes of life.[15] Humanity requires a spiritual dimension to existence that transcends time and mortality. This need is satisfied by the creation of mythic or religious belief systems that mitigate the harshness of the universe by bestowing (a possibly artificial) order on it. As psychoanalyst Rollo May remarks, myth 'is a way of making sense in a senseless world. ... Myths are like the beams in a house: not exposed to outside view, they are the structure which holds the house together so people can live in it.'[16]

The Urth Cycle defines this condition of humanity and how it can be exploited when the Hierogrammates conceal their conspiracy by constructing the legend of the Conciliator. Within the text, Wolfe is implying that his universe is such a void of spirituality and human purpose that *Homo sapiens* requires myth structures to protect its collective sanity. He is, therefore, advocating C. G. Jung's theory that 'The religious myth is one of man's greatest and most significant achievements, giving him the security and inner strength not to be crushed by the monstrousness of the universe.'[17] Wolfe provokes this reading by showing how his fictional humanity develops an *Umwelt*, a subjective racial reality, aided by the Hierogrammates' subtle mythopoesis, and gains a sense of purpose through its faith in the Conciliator's apparent divinity.

Wolfe alludes to humanity's susceptibility to mythic explanations for existence in the same passage that encourages the reader to adopt several interpretative methods. This becomes clear when the reader reconsiders the point at which Severian and Dorcas reflect on the nature of their universe. Severian explains that everything has three interconnected meanings:

> Whatever happens has three meanings. The first is its practical meaning ... 'the thing the plowman sees'. The cow has taken a mouthful of grass, and it is real grass and a real cow ... The second is the reflection of the world about it. Every object is in contact with all others, and thus the wise can learn of the others by observing the first. This might be called the soothsayers' meaning because it is the one which such people use when they prophesy ... The third meaning is the transsubstantial meaning. Since all objects have their ultimate origin in the Pancreator, and all were set in motion by him, so all must express his will—which is the higher reality ... (*Shadow*, p. 272)

Dorcas responds by observing that 'it seems to me that ... the third meaning is very clear ... But the second is harder to find and the first, which should be the easiest, is impossible' (*Shadow*, p. 272).

Dorcas's perspicacity emphasises the process of adumbration at work within the human psyche. The people of the Commonwealth are so distanced from the reality of their universe by their need for a transcendental relevance that they cannot apprehend straightforward biological relationships through the imposed veils of superstition, personified by the soothsayers, and organised religious dogma, represented by a belief in the Pancreator.

Dorcas's acknowledgement of this condition reveals that the inhabitants of Urth, represented by Severian, are prevented from recognising their precise place in the cosmos, initially by the volume of mythic material they have inherited from previous ages and, second, by the myths promulgated by the Hierogrammates. Clearly, it seems probable that the reader will undergo the same degree of abstraction from the fictive reality as a consequence of his or her corresponding sensitivity to mythic accounts of existence.

The creation of the Conciliator myth, and earlier solar legends (including that of Apu Punchau), enables the Hierogrammates to mitigate any anxiety that the population of the Commonwealth might feel concerning the destructive rebirth of the sun by suggesting that the universe is unfolding according to some obscure plan known only to the Increate. In this way, they are not only capable of diffusing, or undermining, the kind of rebellion that occurs on board Tzadkiel's ship in *The Urth of the New Sun*, but are also able to maintain a formative control over human development.

As the Hierogrammates can construct entire solar systems, it is unlikely that Severian is required to introduce the White Fountain into Urth's failing star. Rather, it is for the purpose of convincing humanity that the arrival of the New Sun is somehow linked to the Increate's mystical and obscure designs that the Hierogrammates recruit Severian as the agent of their deception. As their pawn, he serves to initiate and maintain their influence over Urth. Throughout the narrative, he remains an unconscious puppet in their mythogenetic charade, a status to which Wolfe alludes in a key sequence in *The Shadow of the Torturer*. Sharing a bed with Baldanders at an inn in Nessus, Severian dreams of the undines, the monstrous water-women who serve the alien serpent, Abaia. 'Who am I?' he asks them and, laughing, they reply by showing him what he is. In his sleep, he sees

> a little stage and curtain, such as are used for children's entertainments ...
>
> [The curtain] rippled and swayed, and began to draw back as though teased by an unseen hand. At once there appeared the tiny figure of a man of sticks. ... He carried a club (which he brandished at us) and moved as if he were alive. When the wooden man had jumped for us, and struck the little stage with his weapon to show us his ferocity, there appeared the figure of a boy armed with a sword. This marionette was as finely finished as the other was crude ...
>
> After both had bowed to us, the tiny figures fought. The wooden man performed prodigious leaps and seemed to fill the stage with the blows of his cudgel; the boy danced like a dust mote in a sunbeam to avoid it, darting at the wooden man to slash with his pin-sized blade.

At last the wooden figure collapsed. The boy strode over as if to set his foot on its chest; but before he could do so, the wooden figure floated from the stage, and turning limply and lazily rose until it vanished from sight, leaving behind the boy, and the cudgel and the sword—both broken. I seemed to hear (no doubt it was really the squeaking of cartwheels on the street outside) a flourish of toy trumpets. (*Shadow*, pp. 141–42)

This dream vision, which results from the undines' powers to travel through time and (presumably) to communicate telepathically, alludes to the battle that Severian ('a boy armed with a sword') will fight with Baldanders ('the wooden man') at the conclusion of *The Sword of the Lictor*, in which both the giant's energy mace and Severian's executioner's blade are destroyed (see *Sword*, pp. 282–92). More importantly, however, it confirms that the narrative action of the novel is a drama occurring within a toy theatre, directed by 'the unseen hand' of the 'God-like forces'.

As the Hierogrammates' marionette, Severian is powerless to oppose their schemes, even if he understood them fully, and his relative impotence is suggested by the description of his puppet counterpart as a 'dust mote in a sunbeam'. Severian is just such a speck, caught in the swirling events that bring the White Fountain, like a sunbeam, into the heart of the old sun. His inability to gauge his role in the Hierogrammates' strategies, and his own self-importance, are mocked at the conclusion of the puppets' battle when his analogue's empty victory over 'the man of sticks' is celebrated with a derisive 'flourish of toy trumpets'.

The Hierogrammates employ Severian as their puppet to overcome an aspect of human nature remarked on by Thecla during her political philosophising in *The Shadow of the Torturer*. Reading from the book of fables that Severian later steals from her empty cell, Thecla explains:

'It was thought of Thaleleus the Great that the Democracy'—that means the people—'desired to be ruled by some power superior to itself, and of Yrierix the sage that the commonality would never permit one different from themselves to hold high office.' (*Shadow*, p. 97)

While this observation alludes to the nature of the Autarch, whose gestalt personality is formed from the people and yet who rules the people, it also defines the purpose of all conciliators: to enable humanity to accept an authority greater than itself through the mediation of a human figure with which it can identify. In orthodox Christianity, that figure is Christ; in the Commonwealth, it is the Conciliator who performs the mediating function.

Wolfe himself demonstrates the artificiality of the Conciliator legend by revealing the mythic figure to be a time-travelling Severian. The equivocality of Severian's messianic role is underlined by the disclosure, in Chapter L of *The Urth of the New Sun*, that Severian is an aquastor—animated by Tzadkiel—which is 'as solid as most truly false things are' (*Citadel*, p. 251). The metaphorical solidity of Severian's aquastor arises from the faith invested in it by the people of the Commonwealth, all of whom remain ignorant of their 'saviour's' secular nature.

The deployment of a conciliator-figure forms part of the Hierogrammates' exploitation of the human tendency towards mythmaking or myth-accepting. Humanity's predilection for transcendental accounts of existence is shown as an inescapable condition at the conclusion of *The Urth of the New Sun*. On his arrival in the village on the post-diluvian shore of Ushas, Severian discovers 'that the House Absolute and our court had become the frame for a vague picture of the Increate as Autarch. In retrospect, it seemed inevitable', he adds drily, having become a god in yet another mythological system (*Urth*, p. 367).

Hence, The Urth Cycle demonstrates an ultimate kind of sublimation within the fictional environment. On Urth, the uncertainties of humanity are given form and meaning through the incorporation of the species into a cosmological system that implies, however spuriously, a transcendental, spiritual aspect to existence. Fears of isolation, insignificance and dissolution are countered by the assurance that there is a purpose, a metaphysical reason, for human suffering.

The success of the Hierogrammates' clandestine strategies depends on their capacity to convince Severian of his own divinity and on the divine nature of their actions. This seduction is effected by Tzadkiel, who nurtures Severian's faith by assuming the guise of an angel (*Urth*, pp. 151–52) (which the torturer recognises from Melito's story, 'The Cock, the Angel and the Eagle' [see *Citadel*, pp. 67–72]), and who employs suitably inflated, pseudo-religious rhetoric to account for the Hierogrammates' actions. For example, the destruction of Urth's millions, who perish with the arrival of the New Sun, is clothed in mysticism when Tzadkiel tells Severian that, 'The death agonies of your world will be offered to the Increate' (*Urth*, p. 153). While this statement obscures the Hierogrammates' selfish actions behind the implication of a vague higher purpose, the full irony of Tzadkiel's statement only becomes apparent when the reader realises that the Increate, 'that which is not itself the creation of another',[18] is not an omniscient god, but a collective term for those who formed the Hierogrammates. On Yesod, Apheta asks Severian if he knows

'... The meaning of ... Hierogrammate?'
   I told her that someone had once told me it designated those who recorded the rescripts of the Increate.
   'So much is correct.' She paused again. 'Possibly we are too much

in awe. Those whom we do not name, the cognates I spoke of [the Hieros], evoke such feelings still, though of their works only the Hierogrammates remain.' (*Urth*, pp. 137–38)

The New Shorter Oxford English Dictionary defines a rescript as 'Any official edict, decree or announcement ... The action or an act of rewriting something; something rewritten again; a copy.'[19] Despite the polysemy of the word, its definition seems to suggest that the Hierogrammates are those creatures who document, and possibly enact, the orders of the Increate.

However, in the context of Wolfe's narrative, Tzadkiel's race are not the clerics of the Increate, but its authors. They are the mechanism by which the Increate is rewritten; their actions are an evolutionary rescripting of their own lineage. The universe is their palimpsest, a vast document from which the original writing, the old creation and the Increate, have been erased by time. The 'death agonies' of Urth are not a religious offering to the Increate but a necessary sacrifice if the species that evolved into the Increate is to be brought into existence.

Severian's susceptibility to sophistry of this kind is exploited further through the agency of the Claw of the Conciliator, a 'light from outside the universe' (*Sword*, p. 296). Wolfe indicates the importance of the Claw in the Hierogrammates' strategies when Severian postulates:

> I am not the first Severian. Those who walk the Corridors of Time saw him gain the Phoenix Throne, and thus it was that the Autarch, having been told of me, smiled in the House Azure, and the undine thrust me up when it seemed I must drown ... Let me guess now, though it is only a guess, at the story of that first Severian.
>
> He too was reared by the torturers, I think. He too was sent forth to Thrax, and though he did not carry the Claw of the Conciliator, he must have been drawn to the fighting in the north ... How he encountered the Autarch there I cannot say; but encounter him he did, and so, even as I, he (who in the final sense was and is myself) became the Autarch in turn and sailed beyond the candles of night. Then those who walk the corridors walked back to the time when I was young, and my own story ... began. (*Citadel*, p. 310)

The first Severian's potential to enact the part of the Conciliator appears to have been recognised when he arrived on Yesod for the first time, at which point the Hierogrammates and their agents reached back in time to reshape his life, Severian's perceptions of himself, and the mythology of Urth by providing him with the Claw of the Conciliator.

This artefact has a remarkable effect on Severian's psychology. After the Claw is freed from its crystalline sheath in *The Sword of the Lictor*, he becomes ensnared in its symbolism:

I felt profoundly an effect I had never noticed at all during the days before it [the Claw] had been taken from me in the hetman's house. Whenever I looked at it, it seemed to erase thought ... by replacing it with a high state for which I know no name ... Each time I emerged, I felt I had gained some inexpressible insight into immense realities.

At last, after a long series of these bold advances and fearful retreats, I came to understand that I should never reach any real knowledge of the tiny thing I held, and with that thought (for it was a thought) came a third state, one of happy obedience to I knew not what, an obedience without reflection, because there was no longer anything to reflect on, and without the least tincture of rebellion. (*Sword*, pp. 297–98)

Severian's consciousness progresses from thought, considered earlier in the novel as the means by which humans attain their humanity ('to become a human being is an achievement—you have to think about it' [*Sword*, p. 140]), through an indefinable mental state to arrive at a position of powerless obedience. The Claw 'erases thought' (and, by implication, a part of Severian's flawed humanity), disarming the power of cognition Severian once considered intrinsic in human consciousness, and substitutes for it an 'inexpressible insight', wholly unknowable but apparently associated with 'immense realities'. By erasing thought, the Claw dispels the questioning scepticism of the logical mind, and draws Severian towards a point of incomprehending reverence and mental serfdom. Through the focalisation and exacerbation of Severian's superstitious faith, the Claw restructures his consciousness until he believes in the myth-system created by the Hierogrammates. In effect, his own perception of the Claw transforms him into the slave the Hierogrammates require.

The Claw has its origin, in a characteristic inversion, towards the conclusion of *The Citadel of the Autarch*. After Severian is rescued from the Ascians, Master Malrubius's aquastor leaves him on the shore of Ocean, where

A thorn caught in my forearm and broke from its branch, remaining embedded in my skin, with a scarlet drop of blood, no bigger than a grain of millet, at its tip. I plucked it out—then fell to my knees.

It was the Claw.

The Claw perfect, shining black, just as I had placed it under the altar stone of the Pelerines. All that bush and all the other bushes growing with it were covered with white blossoms and these perfect Claws. The one in my hand flamed with transplendent light as I looked at it.

What struck me on the beach ... was that if the Eternal Principle had rested in that curved thorn I had carried ... and if it now rested

> in the new thorn (perhaps the same thorn) ..., then it might rest in
> ... everything, in every thorn on every bush, in every drop of water
> in the sea. The thorn was a sacred Claw because all the thorns were
> sacred Claws; the sand in my boots was sacred sand because it came
> from a beach of sacred sand ... Everything had approached and
> even touched the Pancreator because everything was dropped from
> his hand. Everything was a relic. All the world was a relic. I drew off
> my boots ... that I might not walk shod on holy ground. (*Citadel*, pp.
> 252–53)

Throughout this passage there is a deliberate movement from straightforward description to superstitious assertion provoked by what could be
a chance resemblance. An immense leap of faith signifies Severian's sudden
belief in an obscure Eternal Principle and in the omnipresent Pancreator.

The quotation demonstrates the relative ease with which Wolfe
arranges such transitions using the simplest of all argumentative forms to
add a superficial religiousness to the text and suggest the irrational basis of
Severian's faith to the careful reader. 'If,' Severian observes, '[the Eternal
Principle] now rested in the new thorn ... then it might rest in everything.' This simplicity disguises the extreme jump required to make such a
claim, implying that Severian's religious notions develop logically from
the relationship between one verifiable fact and another. In reality, the
Claw is the hook by which the Hierogrammates snare Severian, and his
acceptance of its symbolism marks his abandonment of the physical, or
the 'practical', in favour of a specious 'higher reality'.

The reader later learns that this Claw may indeed be the Claw of the
Conciliator, encased in sapphire and revered by the Pelerines. Its enclosure
may be symbolic in itself: by sealing the naturally occurring thorn, the
broken fragment of a bush, in minerals, its true nature is physically
altered. The real Claw is perceived as a flaw in the heart of a gem until
Baldanders shatters it to reveal the thorn once more. This encapsulation
symbolises how myth (in the form of the Conciliator legends) can obscure,
or conceal, an old reality and shape something new for the faithful.

Although the Claw deceives Severian into believing that he can perform
miracles, all of the apparently mystical incidents that the artefact propagates
can be accounted for rationally by appealing to the physical and scientific
laws operative in Wolfe's fictional heterocosm. For example, the Claw's
apparent capacity to raise the dead is explained by Dorcas, who realises that

> When you brought the ulhan back to life it was because the Claw
> twisted time for him to a point when he still lived. When you
> healed your friend's wounds, it was because it bent the moment to
> one when they would be nearly healed. (*Sword*, pp. 84–85)

The Claw's reanimatory and curative properties arise from its function as the focal point of a localised time-travel field, directing massive amounts of energy from the White Fountain through Severian. The Claw is, therefore, the locus for a power external to Severian. When Apheta suggests that the Claw's ability to channel energy from the White Fountain arises from its immersion in Severian's blood, which 'contains [his] living cells' (*Urth*, p. 144), there is clearly an equation being drawn between blood and the Claw's potency. Severian's cells contain his unique DNA pattern and it could be conjectured that the Hierogrammates employ this DNA pattern to establish a link between Severian and the White Fountain. Using this connection, the Hierogrammates deploy the White Fountain's trans-temporal powers to convince Severian of his god-like nature and establish the icon's mythogenetic influence. The Claw itself may not possess any intrinsic powers or abilities; rather, it may serve as a positioning device, enabling the otherworldly powers manipulating Severian to locate him and orchestrate suitable 'miracles'.

The influence of the Claw of the Conciliator may not be the only method by which the Hierogrammates monitor Severian's movements and direct his behaviour. In his recent article, 'Masks of the Father: Paternity in Gene Wolfe's *Book of the New Sun*', Robert Borski hypothesises other conspiracies occurring around and acting on Severian. Although parts of Borski's argument are conjectural and sustained by convenient misrepresentations of the text, he does make several credible deductions regarding three key figures in the narrative. By assessing the possible connections between, and obscured identities of, the Hierodule Ossipago, Father Inire, the Autarch's alien vizier, and Palaemon, one of Severian's Masters in the guild, Borski suggests ingeniously that these characters are a single Hierodule playing multiple roles in the shaping and monitoring of Severian's life. For example, he argues that Father Inire is the shaman who steals into the dying Autarch's tent to provide him with the implements essential for Severian to later enact 'the abomination' and assume the autarchy. Palaemon he reads as a Hierodule changeling, set to monitor the apprentice Severian, intercede on his behalf when he allows Thecla to commit suicide, and provide him with the carnificial sword, *Terminus Est*, which he claims contains a tracking device that allows the Hierogrammates to follow Severian's movements.

More significant to the establishment of the Conciliator myth is Borski's contention that this figure is also Ceryx, the young 'miracle-worker' who challenges Severian to a duel of 'magic' on his return to Urth from Yesod. As the Hierodules' 'clocks run widdershins round both' the New Sun and the Old Sun (*Urth*, p. 360), Father Inire, Borski maintains, 'ages oppositely to us, becoming "younger", but geriatrically so—all the while seeming to live as a normal, if extraordinarily long-lived, human does'.[20] In other words, although Inire looks physically younger in the past, he is in fact much older and nearing the end of his natural lifespan. His knowledge of the future is, of course, intact because of his alien perception of temporality. Knowing that the mythology of the Conciliator must be established incontrovertibly, Inire-as-Ceryx, who can raise the dead, sacrifices himself spectacularly 'to consolidate and amplify the legend of the Conciliator' and separate him from the host of charlatans emerging during the time of Typhon's rule.[21] That Borski's conspiracy theory—which also casts the alien Cumaean as Inire's female counterpart—may be inaccurate is not necessarily the most important consideration when reflecting on his article. More significant is the fact that Wolfe's text invites and sustains such an interpretation, which only serves to emphasise the importance of masquerades and Machiavellian intrigues to the Hierogrammates' designs. It seems likely, however, that credible though the majority of Borski's observations are, Father Inire (in all his guises) and the Cumaean are merely agents for the Hierogrammates, enlisted and deployed to ensure the success of their placatory mythogenesis.

Given the tension existing between the Hierogrammates' secular purpose and their spiritual pretences, it seems that, throughout The Urth Cycle, Wolfe is re-addressing an issue that Gay Clifford observes in her study of early allegories, which she sees as 'frequently concerned with the dialectic between rationality and other pre-rational thoughts and beliefs'.[22] While the Hierogrammates' actions suggest a purely rational, biological purpose for human existence, Severian's thought processes, and the Hierogrammates' elaborate masquerade, mobilise the pre-rational beliefs to which humanity has clung throughout its history.

What Wolfe's pentalogy suggests is the impossibility of human freedom, a theme that manifests itself most immediately in the recurring iconography of the cell and in the cyclical motif. While the New Sun provides a new creation, the human psyche remains unchanged. This stasis is personified by Dorcas who, although resurrected, cannot free herself from her past (she remains dead to the present and feels compelled to return to Nessus to recover that past); by Jonas, who departs Urth as a cyborg and returns a human, yet who cannot consummate his love for Jolenta, who has died during his absence; and by Jolenta herself who, despite being transformed into a voluptuous woman by surgery, is incapable of sustaining her beauty without chemical preparations, and who returns to her original form on death.

'That we are capable only of being what we are remains our unforgivable sin', Severian observes at the opening and closure of The Claw of the Conciliator,[23] voicing the lament of The Urth Cycle, which reveals the human race as a helpless, incomprehending species, confused by its own angst and abused by power systems it can neither control nor understand. Like 'Trip, Trap', the novel documents how the psychological processes that shape humanity's perception of the universe oppose the discovery of the system governing that universe.

It is around the essence of this systemic 'whole' that Wolfe constructs his interpretative game with the reader. By suppressing the fact that the mythogenetic elements and religious allusions within The Urth Cycle are broadly sham devices, Wolfe attempts to oppose, quite playfully, the reader's understanding that there are no truly epiphanic, spiritual elements to be found in the text. All the pseudo-mystical aspects of, and incidents within, Severian's memoir-novel are fake, and they should not blind the reader to the knowledge that Wolfe's universe is subject to science-fictionally rational, rather than fantastical, or spiritual, explanations. This appeal to rationalism is largely subtextual, however, and only becomes apparent when the reader begins to understand the intergeneric operations at work within the narrative.

6. 'The Last Thrilling Wonder Story'?
Intergeneric Operations

Designed in part to substantiate Wolfe's definition of science fantasy as 'a science fiction story told with the outlook, the flavour of fantasy',[1] The Urth Cycle is a slyly deceptive conflation of these two frequently discrete genres. While this definition is ambiguous, it seems to suggest that Wolfe is hybridising fantasy's employment of a magical force (as described by Ann Swinfen), which is closed to rational or pseudo-rational explanation, with science fiction's appeal to the rational (observed by, for example, Warren W. Wagar).[2]

Brian Attebery remarks on the integration of the genres' contrary rational and non-rational discourses when he posits:

> In many science fantasies, each of the two forms of discourse attempt[s] to account for the other. Sometimes one side is more convincing. If the favoured pattern is science fictional, the result is not so much science fantasy but rationalised fantasy; the apparent magic is explained away by the end of the story. Or the rhetoric of fantasy may prove stronger ...[3]

In Attebery's terminology, The Urth Cycle is a 'rationalised fantasy', wherein 'the apparent magic is explained away at the end of the story', or can be 'explained away' if the reader apprehends the clues that Wolfe provides.

For example, the feast at which Thecla is consumed by Vodalus's rebels in *The Claw of the Conciliator* seems to mark the point at which her soul is mystically amalgamated with Severian's. However, the banquet initiates something far more mundane. Although the feast shares religious parallels with the Roman Catholic Mass, with Saint Symeon the Younger's observation that 'The One who has become many, remains the One undivided, but each part is all of Christ', and with the apocryphal Gospel of Eve ('I am thou and thou art I; and wheresoever thou mayest be I am there. In all I am scattered, and whensoever thou willest, Thou gatherest me; and gathering me thou gatherest thyself'),[4] such allusions are misleading.

If these connotations are excluded, it becomes clear that Severian's progression from the one into the manifold (the Autarch) is not the result of a series of mystical unions but a consequence of an entirely chemical assimilation. When Thecla's half-sister Thea informs Severian that 'When it [the alzabo, from whose glands the drug which incorporates the memory and personality of Thecla into Severian's own memory is made] has fed on human flesh it knows, at least for a time, the speech and ways of human beings' (Claw, p. 90), any spiritual dimension is thoroughly undermined. Similarly, when the alzabo attacks a peasant family in The Sword of the Lictor (pp. 122–30), it is clear that it is the victim's memories rather than his or her soul that the beast absorbs.

Wolfe alludes to the fact that consciousness and memory are inextricably bonded to flesh when Severian philosophises on the alzabo's characteristics:

> I tried to fix … on … that facet of the nature of the alzabo that permits it to incorporate the memories and wills of human beings into its own …
>
> [The alzabo] might be likened to the absorption by the material world of the thoughts and acts of human beings who, though no longer living, have so imprinted it with activities that, in the wider sense we may call works of art, whether buildings, songs, battles or explorations, that for some time after their demise it may be said to carry forward their lives. (Sword, pp. 217–18)

Severian speaks of memories, wills, ideas, desires, needs, thoughts, activities, and works of art, the conscious and material features of life which at no time suggest the existence of a transcendental soul. Indeed, the incorporation of human personalities into the alzabo's consciousness is effected by hormones from a gland located (like the pituitary) at the base of the creature's skull. Writer and critic Darrell Schweitzer has exposed the secular nature of these unions by observing how the consequences of the cannibalistic actions of Vodalus's outlaws, through which they gain knowledge of the past, closely resemble the results of experiments conducted on planarian, or flatworms.[5]

Despite providing several clues to the physiological nature of the communions facilitated by the alzabo's hormones, Wolfe presents Severian's reunion with Thecla in a manner that implies a spiritual transcendence. Unlike other cannibals, Severian does not forget Thecla's memories or personality. In The Citadel of the Autarch, a Pelerine priestess accounts for this phenomenon by suggesting that the Claw of the Conciliator resurrected Thecla within Severian. This pseudo-mystical explanation, readily accepted by Severian (who has a penchant for metaphysical accounts), is countered when the reader recognises that Severian is a mnemonist: he forgets little and, hence, remembers Thecla's memories with abnormal clarity.

Similarly, there are no seemingly 'magical' incidents within The Urth Cycle that are not subject to such rational explanation. As Carl D. Malmgren observes:

> The source, validity, cogency, or plausibility of that explanation is not at issue; indeed, frequently the explanation draws on questionable analogies, imaginary science, far-fetched gadgets, or counterfactual postulates. Even so, the science fantasy is rooted in a discourse which takes for granted the validity of the scientific reversal of natural law. The 'science' in science fantasy represents 'an attempt to legitimise situations that depend on fantastic assertions.'[6]

Wolfe legitimises numerous 'situations that depend on fantastic assertions' by locating the text's narrative action on a far future world where, as Joan Gordon has observed, (Arthur C.) Clarke's Dictum is believed to apply.[7] However, Clarke's Dictum (also known as Clarke's Third Law), which states that 'any sufficiently advanced science is indistinguishable from magic', requires a degree of qualification if it is to remain valid. As Michael W. McClintock observes:

> The worlds of science fiction admit technology but not magic; the worlds of fantasy admit magic but not usually advanced science. If Clarke's Third Law in fact ruled in this matter, the mutual exclusion would make no difference, for sorcery and technology would inter-change indistinguishably with each other ... But parlance and practice, the labels and signals for generic code, argue that this is not the case for literate science fiction and fantasy.[8]

Overlooking whatever argument may arise from the ambiguous phrase 'literate science fiction and fantasy', McClintock's remarks reveal the flaw in Clarke's reasoning: if sorcery is indistinguishable from science, why draw attention to its indistinguishability with a special law? If Clarke had recognised this non sequitur he might have modified his statement to propose that any sufficiently advanced science may become indistinguishable from magic, but will remain subject to rational or pseudo-rational explanation.

Colin Greenland argues that in *The Book of the New Sun* there

> seems to be sorcery but here Wolfe blurs the definition because like Vance, Moorcock and [M. John] Harrison, he sets his ... society in the remote future, after the rise and fall of a 'high and gleaming' culture [where Clarke's (augmented) Dictum applies].[9]

Greenland's observations demonstrate the importance of considering the outwardly magical elements of The Urth Cycle in their proper context. To the scientifically amnesiac peoples of Urth, including Severian, the effects obtained through advanced or alien science appear magical or mystical. The reader, Wolfe suggests, should not be so easily deceived. 'There is no magic. There is only knowledge, more or less hidden', the witch Merryn counsels (*Claw*, p. 287), an aphorism which confirms that the pentalogy is bound by the (pseudo-)rationalism demanded by SF.

This intrinsic rationalism is obscured, however, behind a façade of fantastic conventions that playfully seduce the reader into formulating an extrinsic, or incorrect, generic reading. At the simplest level, Wolfe invites a fantastic interpretation by imitating the titles of paraliterary fantasy novels. Such imitation can lead, as Clute observes, to the reader believing the text to be 'yet another high-fantasy hyperventilation show'.[10] However, Wolfe's intergeneric masquerade does not simply misguide the incautious reader but also enables the author to produce a text in which 'science fiction constructs interrupt the discourse of fantasy [to make the sceptical reader] think about them and work out their implications'.[11]

The Urth Cycle is a science fantasy about science fantasy. The tension between the science fictional explanations for what occurs on Urth and the apparently fantastic occurrences themselves alerts the reader to the differences between the rational worlds of SF and the non-rational worlds of fantasy, thereby leading to a clearer understanding of Wolfe's text. To create and maintain this tension, Wolfe recontextualises elements from the literary tradition to which The Urth Cycle belongs, fashioning a historical, meta-textual discourse with that tradition.

The concept of a historical meta-text derives from Malmgren's definition of a meta-text as a narrative that investigates the boundaries of the genre from which it draws inspiration.[12] Accordingly, a historical meta-text can be seen as a work that interacts with the generic characteristics present during the historical development of its parent tradition and which re-presents those characteristics in an altered form.

The Book of the New Sun is the apotheosis of a tradition characterised by visions of humanity at the conclusion of the natural history of the solar system when the sun faces extinction. For purposes of distinction and mnemonic integrity, this specific subset of narratives will be termed the 'dying sun tradition', as the image of Earth's failing star forms the group's dominant motif.

The dying sun tradition has its origins in H. G. Wells's *The Time Machine* (1895), and encompasses William Hope Hodgson's *The Night Land* (1912), Clark Ashton Smith's Zothique tales (1932–52), the short stories 'Twilight' and 'Night' (1934) by John W. Campbell, and Jack Vance's *The Dying Earth* (coll. 1950). Michael Moorcock's *Dancers at the End of Time Trilogy* (*An Alien Heat* [1972], *The Hollow Lands* [1974] and *The End of All Songs* [1976]), together with its sequels, *Legends from the End of Time* (1976) and *The Transformation of Miss Mavis Ming* (also known as *A Messiah at the End of Time*) (1977), are firmly situated within this tradition but will not be considered here as Wolfe had no first-hand knowledge of them when writing The Urth Cycle.

Wolfe's pentalogy is more than the summation of this literary heritage, however: it is, as Douglas Barbour suggests, a mosaic of that ancestry:

> Wolfe has not only written a truly marvellous science fantasy set millions of years in our future on a dying 'Urth', he has written the book on such works, a kind of Borgesian sub-textual reference guide where every formal development in this sub-genre is laid out for our interpretation and then done right.[13]

Contrary to Barbour's claim, Wolfe constructs his narrative with intertextual rather than subtextual references to earlier works in the dying sun tradition. Wolfe's self-consciousness here leads him to allude to this intertextuality in the legend Cyriaca relates to Severian in *The Sword of the Lictor* (pp. 51–55). Cyriaca's tale appropriates its dominant theme, rebirth, and its dominant icon, the automated city, from John W. Campbell's 'Twilight'. In each story, the author describes a humanity that has lost a part of itself to machines. The parable that Wolfe provides (which shows how imperialism divests humanity of its compassion—a thematic echo from *The Fifth Head of Cerberus*) casts the machines into the role of guardians and saviours. Similarly, in 'Twilight', the sentient machines that removed the need for work and fostered an enervated human race hold the key to rebirth.

Although Wolfe insists that the similarities between Cyriaca's story and 'Twilight' are not the result of 'conscious imitation', he admits, paradoxically, 'that it was no coincidence. I read "Twilight" as a teenager, and it impressed me greatly.'[14] Wolfe's inclusion of an allusive reference to Campbell's tale is more than just a homage to a writer who impressed him, however. In using 'Twilight' as the basis for a pseudo-historical tale from Urth's past, Wolfe acknowledges his response to a specific literary past.

'Twilight' is a model dying sun narrative, reflecting Wells's theme of evolutionary regression and entropic collapse in its Eloi-like humanity and its vision of Earth's expiring star. These themes, conveyed through the Time Traveller's experience on the 'terminal beach' in Chapter 11 of *The Time Machine*, became subject matter that was to pervade later dying sun fiction.

Wolfe's pentalogy not only provides a continuity with the regression and dissolution captured so effectively in *The Time Machine*, but also establishes a direct dialogue with Wells's novel to substantiate Wolfe's definition of science fantasy and offer a response to the pessimism with which *The Time Machine* concludes. The contrast between the two texts is demonstrated best in the Wellsian sequence in *The Claw of the Conciliator* (pp. 40–63).

Lured into the mine of the man-apes by Agia, Severian, like the Time Traveller, descends into a Morlockian pit to confront degenerate sub-humans. Bernard Bergonzi has proposed that the Time Traveller's exploration of the Morlocks' underworld resembles Christ's Harrowing of Hell,[15] and it seems probable that, given the continual identification of Severian with Christ, Wolfe chose this sequence for its religious connotations.

For his descent into the Morlocks' 'hell', the Time Traveller is armed with a box of matches, which symbolises Wells's belief that

> Science is a match that man has just got alight. He thought he was in a room—in moments of devotion a temple—that his light would be reflected from and display walls inscribed with wonderful secrets and pillars carved with philosophical systems wrought in harmony. It is a curious sensation, now that the preliminary sputter is over, and the flame burns up clear, to see his hand lit and just a glimpse of himself and the patch he stands on visible, and around him, in place of all the human comfort and beauty he anticipated, darkness still.[16]

Wells's observation suggests his lack of faith in science's ability to provide peace of mind for humanity. He recognises that the illumination that science offers reveals nothing more than a greater darkness beyond that which it dispels. By invoking the metaphor of the temple, Wells seems to be alluding to the usurpation of religious belief as science became the dominant ideology, bringing with it a corresponding sense of spiritual void.

Michael Draper remarks that

> When the matches the Traveller strikes reveal horror and cause destruction, he reveals himself to be part of a universe to which ideas of heaven and hell are finally irrelevant; one ... from which human values and aspirations emerge as mere by-products ... Any independence from the material world does not open the way to transcendence, but to a painful and irreconcilable tension between the actual and the ideal.[17]

This 'painful and irreconcilable tension' also exists between what science informs humanity is real and what humanity wishes to believe. The gulf between faith and science, between a belief in a positive human purpose and the chilling knowledge of human insignificance in the face of time and entropy, is what invests *The Time Machine* with its desperate angst and drives the Time Traveller to hurl himself finally into the temporal void.

It is this lack of faith in science's ability to provide solace for humanity that constitutes the background against which Wolfe locates both his text and his own Wellsian episode. Instead of carrying matches on his journey into the subterrene, Severian bears the Claw of the Conciliator. As he retreats from the man-apes with the Claw outstretched, he receives a revelation:

> I began to back away. The man-apes looked up at that, and their faces were the faces of human beings. When I saw them thus, I knew of the eons of struggles in the dark from which their fangs and saucer eyes and flap ears had come to be. We, so the sages say, were apes once, happy apes in forests swallowed by deserts so long ago they have no names. Old men return to childish ways when at last the years cloud their minds. May it not be that mankind will return (as an old man does) to the decaying image of what once was, if at last the old sun dies and we are left scuffling over bones in the dark? I saw our future—one possible future at least—and felt more sorrow for those who had triumphed in the dark battles than for those who had poured out their blood in the endless night. (*Claw*, pp. 53–54)

The different qualities of the lights carried by Severian and the Time Traveller are significant. Wells's protagonist relies on fire, which serves both to dazzle the Morlocks and to remind them, possibly, of their heritage of ancient science and their current degeneracy. Consequently, the matches provoke the Morlocks either into taking flight or into attacking. Conversely, the Claw burns without threat. In its light, Severian perceives the man-apes as more human than ape, in contrast to the Time Traveller, who sees only the Morlocks' bestiality. Rather than alienating Severian from the man-apes, as the matches distance the Time Traveller from the Morlocks, the Claw draws man and man-ape together. Severian's understanding of the creatures moves from the perception of them as anthropomorphic horrors to be slaughtered to an appreciation of the kinship he shares with them.

Their biological relationship is obscured, however, by imagery rich in associations with fantastic literature and art. When Severian first produces the gem, the Claw

> gathered to itself all the corpse light and dyed it with the colour of life ... For one heart beat the man-apes halted as though at the stroke of a gong, and I lifted the gem overhead: what frenzy of terror I hoped for (if I hoped at all) I cannot say now ...
>
> The man-apes neither fled shrieking, nor resumed their attack. Instead they retreated ... and squatted with their faces pressed against the floor of the mine. (*Claw*, p. 53)[18]

In this sequence, Wolfe demonstrates how 'the flavour of fantasy' can be evoked by subordinating the rational explanation for an incident to the fantastical spectacle of the incident itself. While the Claw's effect on the man-apes recalls the talismanic power of the cross when employed against vampires, it seems probable that the man-apes' response is little more than the result of the fascination and terror that purblind creatures feel for light. Although they seem to be paying homage to Severian, they could simply be concealing their bedazzlement.

Just as the man-apes' reaction to the Claw can be explained rationally, so Severian's insight into the nature of the creatures can be explained 'scientifically'. As the Claw is a device used by the Hierogrammates to help secure their own evolution, it is fitting that, in its radiance, Severian's increased sensitivity to the man-apes' degeneracy is an acute appreciation of heredity. Throughout the scene, he philosophises on the force of natural selection, recognising that the man-apes' 'fangs and saucer eyes' are a morphological adaptation to the evolutionary pressures of their 'eons of struggles in the dark'.

The pity that Severian feels for the man-apes is not the product of compassion but a form of fearful empathy arising from the realisation that a similar fate may befall all of humanity should the sun finally die. Such empathic connection is precisely what Wells's Time Traveller lacks.

The Claw 'twists time' (Sword, p. 85) to reconcile 'the actual [the man-apes and Severian] with the ideal [the 'happy ape' from which they both evolved]'. It acts as a conciliating device, drawing Severian's attention to the relationship he shares with the man-apes. This evolutionary kinship, which unites Hierogrammate, human and man-ape, is Wolfe's response to Wells's Huxleyan Cosmic Pessimism, and in its interconnection lies the secular salvation of the human race. Where Wells sees a disunity of species over time, Wolfe concentrates on the continuity that will produce a species not only capable of opposing the force of entropy but also inextricably embroiled in a scheme for ensuring its own evolution.

This conflation of optimism and pessimism, of change and stasis, may have entered The Urth Cycle through William Hope Hodgson's *The Night Land*, a bizarre fantasy that is both an acceptance of Wells's Cosmic Pessimism and a manifesto detailing how the human race might live as though the ultimate futility of all human endeavour were avoidable.

Hodgson's novel begins in a pre-industrial age with the unnamed narrator wooing Mirdath the Beautiful. Eventually, they marry, but their idyllic life together ends when Mirdath dies in childbirth. Devastated by his loss, the protagonist dreams his way into another realm in a manner reminiscent of Edward Bellamy's *Looking Backwards* (1880) and William Morris's *The Dream of John Ball* (coll. 1888).

The narrator, whose soul transmigrates into the body of a younger man, awakes in the far future on a world extrapolated from Wells's vision of the dying earth.[19] In *The Night Land* the sun is dead and the Earth a barren wasteland lit by volcanic fires and gas geysers. Degenerate humans populate its dark recesses and hideous creatures prey on the human survivors. Every battle with these monsters is not merely a physical contest but a struggle against the destruction of the soul; and only human love, Hodgson suggests, provides any escape from, or triumph over, this bleak existence.

On this world, the last remnants of the human race are gathered together in the Great Redoubt, a vast metal pyramid besieged by supernatural, Boschian horrors. Although it is crowned with a tower designed to project and receive telepathic communications from other sanctuaries, the Great Redoubt has received no such messages for millennia. When the narrator 'hears' a telepathic call from Naani, a young woman resident in the Lesser Redoubt, he learns that she is the reincarnated spirit of Mirdath, his lost wife, and eventually he sets out alone to rescue her. The remainder of the book describes, in painstaking detail, his perilous journey through the Night Land, his salvation of Naani, and their return home in eventual triumph.

The Night Land is a pivotal work in the generic transformation of the dying sun tradition from the straight SF of *The Time Machine* to the integrated science fantasy of The Urth Cycle. To Wells's image of a world overcome by biological and societal deterioration, Hodgson brings supernatural manifestations and a hero who, like a medieval knight-errant, departs the Great Redoubt on a quest to rescue an archetypal damsel in distress.

It is possible that Hodgson's idea for *The Night Land* arose as a pun on the phrase 'dark age', since the death of the sun literalises the metaphoric expression. Accordingly, every element of the novel, from its archaic prose to its quest pattern and its idealised (not to mention fetishised and sexist) love story, conspires to create a sense of medieval, romantic chivalry. This '"return to medievalism", in which learning has been lost and the inhabitants are baffled by much of the technology developed by their ancestors, [became] a staple theme in contemporary SF',[20] and a characteristic of science fantasy in general and of dying sun literature in particular.

Although *The Night Land* may have been constructed as a pastiche either of William Morris or of genuine medieval romances, including Malory's *Le Morte D'Arthur*, Hodgson's antiquated prose style is unlike anything 'ever written before or since':[21]

> And because that the Light was vanished, I was the more set that we come speedy out of the Land. And we went forward with a strong speed, and had the Great Red Fire-Pit of the Giants to our

rear and unto our left, and a mighty way off in the night; but yet I
did wish it the further; and before us was a small ridging up of the
dark Land, as I did judge, because that our view of the Light and the
shining was bounded; and to our left at a great way the low
volcanoes, and somewhat to our right, across all that part of the
land went the cold and horrid glare of the Shine.[22]

Despite the censure that this idiosyncratic prose attracted,[23] Hodgson's
style is vitally important in creating the ambience of a world in decline and
one that could, in the throes of its entropic dissolution, be situated just as
easily in the remote past as in the far future, in a dark age that never was.

Wolfe admits that *The Night Land* exerted a formative influence on The
Urth Cycle,[24] which re-presents the 'formal developments' that Hodgson
worked on *The Time Machine* following the conventions of science fantasy
as Wolfe interprets them.

In his pentalogy, Wolfe appropriates the fantastic elements of Hodgson's
novel, its unnatural creatures, its medieval quest pattern and its archaic
prose style, rationalises them and yet preserves the sense of the fantastic
that they evoke. For example, in *The Night Land*, the nature of the entities
besieging the Great Redoubt remains a source of supernatural mystery.
Conversely, in The Urth Cycle, Erebus, Abaia, Arioch and Scylla, the
monstrous Hodgsonian creatures controlling the Ascians and perpetrating
their war of attrition against the Commonwealth, are revealed, with Wolfe's
characteristic indirectness, as beings alien to Urth.

The shift from Hodgson's supernatural denizens to Wolfe's extraterrestrial
forces is small but significant, and one that illustrates the distinction
between SF's inherent rationalism and fantasy's employment of the non-
rational. By providing a pseudo-scientific explanation for the monstrous
forces at work on Urth, Wolfe makes the presence of such creatures
plausible. During this process of rationalisation, Abaia and the rest lose
none of their mystery but obtain an origin which, while it divests them of
their apparent supernaturalism, preserves the novel's fantastic ambience.

The disjunction between the apparent and the real found in the nature
of Wolfe's unearthly creatures reappears on a structural level when he
adopts the mythic/medieval quest pattern employed by Hodgson as the
narrative model for The Urth Cycle. Although Severian's phantasmagoric
wanderings seem to locate Wolfe's text in the realm of paraliterary fantasy
(characterised as it is by formulaic quest narratives), the structure of his
memoir-novel supports a deception. Unlike Hodgson, who employs the
motif of the questing knight in a virtually unmodified form, Wolfe uses
the pattern of the traditional fantasy quest to mislead the unwary reader.
(For a discussion of the interpretative effect of the quest structure of The
Urth Cycle, see Chapter 7.)

Although the form of the quest myth is essential in fostering the sense of the neo-medieval in *The Night Land*, it is Hodgson's archaic style that confirms the sense of a world entering a latterday dark age. It seems certain that while Wolfe appreciated the potential that such language had for creating the sense of the neo-medieval, he also understood that a narrative composed entirely in a dislocated, mock-medieval style was likely to alienate the reader. Accordingly, Wolfe restricts his use of archaisms to the level of diction alone, lacing The Urth Cycle with unfamiliar nouns from the Classical, Roman, medieval and Renaissance periods.

By deploying such terms as 'alcalde', 'claviger', 'gyves' and 'vates' (among many others), Wolfe shifts his text towards generic fantasy, whose authors often borrow historical diction to suggest the pre-technological ambience of their fictional worlds.[25] However, in order to sidestep any charges that his language is temporally discordant with the fictional setting, and to move his text back into the province of science fantasy, Wolfe presents the narrative as a manuscript which came to him across 'so many centuries of futurity' (*Shadow*, p. 303). In his guise as the editor of this manuscript, Wolfe provides an appendix to *The Shadow of the Torturer* and explains:

> In rendering this book—originally composed in a tongue that has not yet achieved existence—into English, I might easily have saved myself a great deal of labour by having recourse to invented terms; in no case have I done so. ... Such words as *peltast, androgyn* and *exultant* are substitutions ... and are intended to be suggestive rather than definitive. (*Shadow*, p. 302)

Clearly, Wolfe has his authorial tongue firmly in his cheek as he confirms the fictional nature of his text by attempting to deny its fictiveness (and making of it an impossible document in the process). His supposed substitution for words 'in a tongue that has not yet achieved existence' enables him to account for his incongruous archaisms by 'having recourse' to the Wellsian device of time travel. Not only has the manuscript entered his possession across the seas of time, but Wolfe, in his role as editor, also suggests that he has travelled, tourist-like, to the 'post-historic' period:

> To those who have preceded me in the study of the posthistoric world, and particularly to those collectors—too numerous to name here—who have permitted me to examine artefacts surviving so many centuries of futurity, and most especially to those who have allowed me to visit and photograph the era's few extant buildings, I am truly grateful. (*Shadow*, p. 303)

While this concluding paragraph provides a subtextual, metafictional acknowledgement of the authors 'who have allowed [Wolfe, as a reader] to visit ... the era', and who have inspired him to write The Urth Cycle, it also shows how Wolfe apparently treats his fictional future as indistinguishable from the historic past. This indistinguishability suggests, albeit falsely, that Urth expresses the same ahistorical qualities as most fantasy worlds. However, this is not the case.

The actual, but obscured, historicity of Urth is revealed when Wolfe's pentalogy is compared with Clark Ashton Smith's Zothique cycle, a series of stories located beneath a dying sun and influenced, at least in part, by Hodgson's *The Night Land*.[26] Originally termed Gyndron, Zothique is

> a continent of the far future, in the South Atlantic, which is more subject to incursions of 'outsideness' than any former terrene realm; and more liable to visitations of beings from galaxies not yet visible; also to shifting admixtures and interchanges with other dimensions or planes of entity.[27]

The reader could be forgiven for thinking that this is a description Wolfe formulated to define conditions on Urth and, indeed, certain similarities exist between The Urth Cycle and Smith's stories. Both authors, for example, share a fascination for 'the line dividing illusion from substance [for] the supreme superstition: Reality',[28] and it seems possible that Smith's 'The Isle of Torturers' (1933) influenced Wolfe's conception of the Guild of Seekers for Truth and Penitence.

Despite these similarities, Wolfe not only subverts the kind of sorcery operative throughout Smith's stories, but also reacts against the ahistoricity of Smith's world and those of other fantasists. Like Hodgson, Smith depicts the fall of civilisation as a descent into a fantastic past which contradicts the linear direction of time implied by the entropic decay that gnaws at Zothique's decadent realms. Wolfe, on the other hand, defines his fictional future in purely historical terms. In an interview with Greenland, Wolfe explains the reasoning behind his reappropriation of societal models from the past:

> First of all, there's a recognition that if you are on a certain economic level you have to have some sort of set-up that will work on that level. I don't really think my world [of Urth] is all that medieval, but a medieval set-up is a way of dealing with that sort of thing. When you have a relatively impoverished country, as the Commonwealth is, you can't educate everyone, you can't teach everyone to read, you can't publish newspapers, and this means that if you're going to have a democracy you have to do it some other way. This is what they [the inhabitants of the Commonwealth]

have done ... They have ... a democratic top [in the composite
personality of the Autarch] with an aristocratic underclass. If you
have the commonality of the poor people and uneducated you have
to have some way of putting people over people who can exact
obedience and keep the thing organised ... Not the only possible
way but one fairly easy way [of achieving this] is with a hereditary
aristocracy ...[29]

Dismissing the 'whiggish' view of history as a narrative of progress,
Wolfe makes it clear that the Commonwealth's decline into a condition
requiring a social system analogous to those of the past is necessitated by
the re-emergence of technological and economic conditions similar to
those that shaped that past. The impoverished economic status of the
Commonwealth, the denuded nature of Urth, and the collapse of indus-
trialised production, all conspire to produce a historically eclectic and
accretive society.

Wolfe's creation of a culture that embraces aspects of the Classical,
medieval and Renaissance periods arises, in part, as a response to his belief
that: 'The challenge to science fiction today is ... to describe a ... real
future—a time radically unlike the present that is nonetheless derived
from it.'[30] Rather than existing in the dislocated temporal limbo occupied
by many fantasies, the dramatic action of The Urth Cycle is situated firmly
in the realm of the historical, assembling a range of allusions to Earth's
past to sustain a sense of temporal continuity with the reader's contemporary environment.

Such continuity is demonstrated in Wolfe's decision to locate the
majority of the pentalogy's narrative events in South America, where the
greatest concentration of sun-worshipping cultures were situated. By
siting the incidents of Severian's odyssey on a continent associated with
sun cults and religions, Wolfe implies a cultural succession that possesses a
degree of historical integrity.[31]

This continuity demonstrates that the narrative reflects SF's awareness of

History, in the guise of analogical historicity, [which] is [a] crucial
step in the understanding of SF: story is always also history, and SF
is always also a certain type of imaginative historical tale ... It is an
escape from constrictive old norms into a different and alternative
time stream, a device for historical estrangement, and an at least
initial readiness for a new norm of reality.[32]

Wolfe disguises the 'analogical historicity' of his world, and achieves
the required 'spirit of fantasy', through the employment of archaic language. However, Wolfe's obsolescent diction is 'intended to be suggestive
rather than definitive' and does not indicate the re-emergence of a society

populated by 'peltasts', 'lictors' and 'portreeves', but a culture that requires individuals to fulfil roles analogous to these once redundant historical occupations. As Greenland observes, the words 'supply the restored antiquity of the "posthistoric world" [showing] us the true perspective of the restoration'.[33]

Unlike other writers working in the dying sun tradition, Wolfe recognises that a sense of history is vital to any far future vision of Earth. By describing his world as 'posthistoric', Wolfe alludes to the vast span of time essential for the credibility of a text whose principal conceit involves the rejuvenation of the sun. To achieve the necessary ambience of antiquity, Wolfe not only relies on the presence of relics, ruins and mysterious technology common to most dying sun fiction, but also incorporates history into landscape, into his rural and urban environment, until Urth is both a culmination and a manifestation of its history.

Wolfe's vision of the archaic Urth was certainly inspired by James Hutton's *Theory of the Earth* (1795), in which Hutton proposed what came to be known as 'deep time'. This eloquent term, coined by geologist John McPhee, describes the incredible depth of history laid down and recorded in the continuum of Earth's geological strata.[34]

Wolfe transforms Hutton's theory of 'deep time' into 'deep history', replacing geological strata with layers of archaeological remains, wherein each stratum represents a previous civilisation, to accentuate the age of Urth. This transformation becomes clear when Severian descends the sheared cliff-side outside Casdoe's home in *The Sword of the Lictor* (pp. 106–107). His journey is a symbolic descent into the past which prefigures his literal movements through time in *The Urth of the New Sun*. As Severian navigates the cliff, the reader encounters allusions to Urth's contact with alien travellers, to a period of human domination, and to millennia of decline during which even human bones have fossilised. In this way, Wolfe conveys the immense history of Urth with startling economy.

To communicate the collapse of Urth's highly mechanised and technological society, Wolfe selects one of SF's most potent icons, the spaceship, and changes its symbolic code by incorporating it into the urban landscape of the Citadel.[35]

From the publication of Yevgeny Zamyatin's *We* (1924), the spaceship has often represented dynamic colonial power. For example, in 'Rocket Summer', Ray Bradbury describes an archetypal, vigorous science fictional vessel.[36] Like a dragon, Bradbury's ship vomits flame, transforming winter into an illusory summer that symbolises the halcyon days of Martian colonisation that Earth enjoys before it is consumed by nuclear war. Bradbury's repetition of 'the rocket' throughout 'Rocket Summer' reinforces the reader's understanding that the change in Earth's climate is the result of the starship's dynamism and humanity's desire to conquer and colonise.

In Wolfe's pentalogy, Urth has enjoyed this summer and now faces a winter of protracted decline. On Urth, the spaceship is no longer a symbol of technological might but of degeneration and stagnancy. 'The Citadel' in which Severian reaches maturity, with its towers and curtain wall, is, in fact, a disused spaceport containing the hulks of spaceships that fulfil the role of medieval bastions. Permanently grounded, Wolfe's vessels have become gothic haunts for Guilds following ancient and often purposeless traditions and rituals. The 'silver locust' that brought Urth its empire has become an embodiment of humanity's paralysis.

In order to sustain a 'spirit of fantasy' and play his game with the reader, Wolfe does not make the precise nature of the Matachin Tower explicitly clear. Indeed, the monastic lifestyle of the torturers' guild that occupies the Matachin Tower serves to conceal the structure's actual nature by fostering the ambience of a medieval religious house tainted with the influence of the Inquisition. However, Severian's occasional references to 'bulkheads', the tower's metal construction and his dreams of seeing the Citadel's corroded hulks leaping into space once more, alert the reader to contrast, rather than compare, the Matachin Tower with the edifices of wood and stone common to fantasy fiction. By revising the icon of the spacecraft backwards until it serves the function of a historic building, Wolfe reveals how rich a territory the posthistoric setting is for an effective exploration of how careful manipulation of the historicity of SF can produce the ahistorical flavour of fantasy.

An awareness of historical process first entered the dying sun tradition through Jack Vance's *The Dying Earth*, a collection of six short stories published in 1950, which became the principal literary motivation behind Wolfe's writing of The Urth Cycle. Wolfe was deeply impressed with Vance's collection and, wanting 'very much to have written *The Dying Earth* ... set out to create a work of my own on the same theme'.[37]

The stories in *The Dying Earth* recount the exploits of various wizards, witches and adventurers on an Earth that has become

> a dim place, ancient beyond knowledge. Once it was a tall world of cloudy mountains and bright rivers, and the sun was a white blazing ball. Ages of rain and wind have beaten and rounded the granite, and the sun is feeble and red. The continents have sunk and risen. A million cities have lifted towers, have fallen to dust. In place of the old peoples a few thousand strange souls live. ... Earth is dying and in its twilight ...[38]

Influenced by Hodgson, Edgar Rice Burroughs and, in particular, Smith,

Vance offers his readers a fantastic society grown decadent on lands littered with faded ruins and infused with sorcery, where human knowledge and dynamism, like those of Urth's imperial past, have been dissipated by time.[39]

SF writer Robert Silverberg sees *The Dying Earth* as an eloquent paradox, finding in its description of decay and decline the sense of a return to a golden age, to an unpolluted world, of wizards and decadent monarchs, of fairy-tale values and the conflict of good and evil.[40] This sense of a return to a fantastical age of sorcerers and magic, of simple morality and heroic struggle, suggests that *The Dying Earth* belongs to the fantasy tradition of Smith's Zothique stories, and an initial reading of Vance's stories invites this supposition. However, such a reception would overlook the subtle structuring of Vance's collection.

The text's narrative patterning charts a generic shift from the ahistorical fantasy of the first tale 'Turjan of Miir', to the integrated science fantasy of the historically oriented final story, 'Ulan Dhor', and the concluding novelette, 'Guyal of Sfere'. This generic movement is arranged in parallel with, and serves to support, a corresponding thematic shift from static equivalence to dynamic change. 'Guyal of Sfere' completes the unifying thematic and generic patterns of the book, the progression from magic to science, from decline and hopelessness to vigour and optimism, from tradition to innovation, and from the prospect of dissolution to the promise of rebirth.[41]

'Guyal of Sfere' disturbs Vance's finely balanced world by introducing an eponymous character driven by an inquisitiveness that reflects Campbell's appeal to the reinvigorating power of curiosity in 'Twilight'. Discontented with his home life, Guyal travels in search of the Museum of Mankind, which alludes to the ruined museum found by Wells's Time Traveller in the Palace of Green Porcelain. When Guyal reaches the museum, he becomes heir to the knowledge of past ages and he and his companion Shierl turn their eyes to the stars, thereby presupposing a technological renaissance for humanity. Symbolically, Guyal's journey is a movement into history. As he enters the museum, he walks a version of Wolfe's Corridors of Time, and begins a reappropriation of the information contained in its halls.

Vance's moral is simple: a rebirth can only be effected when the petty power struggles of the selfish are put aside in favour of a quest for ways to advance knowledge and, therefore, humanity. Guyal recognises that the human race cannot return successfully to the cultural models and traditions of the past and turns his attention to the stars. He upsets the established balance, and his burgeoning relationship with Shierl suggests a fresh potency in humanity in its allusion to a new Adam and Eve.[42] Vance encourages the reader's faith in this rebirth by suggesting that Guyal is an everyman figure, a man whose name can be translated as 'guy all of sphere' or 'all men of Earth'.

Severian, like Guyal, is a catalyst for change, but The Urth Cycle is, at least in part, a reaction to the simplicity of Vance's stories. Wolfe alludes to this complication in *The Sword of the Lictor*, when the Hierodule Famulimus asks Severian: 'Is all the world a war of good and bad? Have you not thought it could be something more?' (p. 273). The ambiguity of her final question, which does not specify whether the world or the war is 'something more', has both a thematic and a metafictional function. In the context of Wolfe's self-consciousness, her words imply an authorial question to the reader: Have you not thought that Urth might be something more than the arena for a conflict between good and evil, between Commonwealth and Ascian Empire, that coincides with events leading to the rejuvenation of Urth?

Of course, Urth is very much more than such an arena, but by posing the question Wolfe not only indicates to the reader that the resolution of his textual puzzle will not be a simple one but also seems to intimate his debt to the motivating force of Vance's uncomplicated vision, with its clear morality, fairy-tale-like oppositions and humanistic conclusion.

In terms of The Urth Cycle functioning as a historical metatext, the most important complication of Vance's vision lies in Wolfe's transformation of the image of rebirth with which *The Dying Earth* concludes. For Vance (as for Walter M. Miller in *A Canticle for Leibowitz* [1960]), humanity's salvation lies among the stars. The rebirth of human culture depends solely on a science fictional conceit: the ability to abandon Earth when conditions are no longer tenable and assume a new home in space. Unfortunately, this option is closed to the inhabitants of Urth. Nevertheless, this is not to say that the vision of deliverance that Wolfe offers is any less science fictional in nature.

SF writer Norman Spinrad observes cogently that

> The 'Coming of the New Sun', with its punning references to the Second Coming of Christ [God's New Son] at the end of time, especially when linked to the eventual raising of its protagonist to Glory, in the end is revealed as nothing more multiresonant than the astrophysical renovation of a dying star.[43]

Like Clark Ashton Smith, whose story 'Phoenix' (1954) describes the rejuvenation of the sun through the explosion of powerful nuclear devices on its cooling surface, Wolfe constructs his narrative on the basis of a need to engineer a single solar event. Unlike Smith, who achieves the rebirth of the sun in the space of a short story, Wolfe takes five volumes and half a million words.

The Urth Cycle is, therefore, in part, a hyperbolic inflation of 'Phoenix' in which 'the spirit of fantasy' is used to dress up the events leading to the redemption of the sun. By presenting the Hierogrammates' rekindling of Urth's star as a fantastic pseudo-religious tale, in which there is more than a suggestion that the New Sun is both a literal star and the resurrection of the human spirit, Wolfe obscures the fact that it is only the sun that enjoys a rebirth: the people of Urth remain incapable of psychological or spiritual growth.

In Wolfe's pentalogy the traditions of fantasy and SF are hybridised to encourage the reader to consider how he or she ascribes meaning to a text by depending on genre conventions. As a result, Wolfe reveals how that process of ascription can be manipulated to elicit conclusions contrary to those pertinent to the narrative. In this way, he awakens the reader to his or her condition as a reader of generic signs.

Wolfe effects something similar in 'The Last Thrilling Wonder Story' (1982) (*Species*, pp. 119–49), a metafiction in which a god-like author writes a pulp SF story whose protagonist gains autonomy to hunt down his vindictive creator, Gene Wolfe.[44] Here, Wolfe not only reveals the traditions of pulp SF, but also uses his protagonist's reactions against the constraints of those traditions to address the themes of manipulation, freedom and faith.

Accordingly, in The Urth Cycle, Wolfe hybridises the practices of fantasy and science fiction to extend and support his thematic concerns. By conflating genre conventions until the reader hesitates between a fantastic and a science fictional reading, Wolfe casts the reader into the role of an inhabitant of the Commonwealth, for whom the effects of an ancient alien technology have become seemingly magical. In provoking this hesitation, Wolfe increases the cautious reader's awareness of the assumptions and biases that affect his or her judgement by establishing a distinction between the apparent and the real on a generic level. Hence, Wolfe's reader is required to master the particular norms of a particular genre. In this instance, the reader must become proficient in the criteria of Wolfe's conception of science fantasy as rationalised fantasy and discover the rational (if improbable) laws governing Wolfe's universe if he or she is to determine the text's story from its plot. In this way, he or she will be able to formulate an intrinsic rather than an extrinsic generic interpretation.

By creating a historical metatext that conceals its own apparent appeal to the rational behind the spectacle of apparently non-rational incidents, Wolfe initiates his interpretative game with the reader, a game he extends and develops with unrelenting mischievousness by continually subverting the reader's previous reading experiences.

7. 'How the Whip Came Back': Directing Reader Response[1]

Having attempted to convince the reader that his pentalogy is a non-rational fantasy, Wolfe complicates his literary game by deploying three motifs which can serve to deactivate interpretative enquiry: a first-person narrator, the autobiographical form, and the structure of the monomythic cycle. If the reader is familiar with these paradigms, he or she may not apprehend the subtle subversions that Wolfe works on their conventions and may, accordingly, be drawn further from the story shaping the action of the novel.

Wolfe's employment of a first-person narrator expedites the reader's trust in the veracity of the document, and in the credibility of the protagonist himself. During the act of reading, Severian's voice becomes, inexorably, that of the reader, until the identification between reader and character becomes so intimate that an autonomous view of Severian's thoughts and actions is subordinate to passive acceptance. Leech and Short observe that a close relationship between reader and character inevitably prejudices the reader in the narrator's favour. Consequently, such bias can lead the reader into adopting opinions that he or she would not normally entertain during the reading process.[2] In the context of The Urth Cycle, this effect assists the reader's acceptance of a torturer as a sympathetic protagonist.

Wolfe makes considerable efforts towards evoking this sympathy by making Severian appear almost benign. For example, when Severian executes Agilus towards the conclusion of *The Shadow of the Torturer*, Wolfe places considerable emphasis on the fact that Agilus has attempted to deceive and murder Severian, has killed innocent bystanders at the Sanguinary Field, and remains unrepentant even when condemned. In his dealings with Agilus, Severian, in his role as headsman, is presented as considerate; he visits Agilus before his execution to ensure that his actions on the scaffold do not disgrace him:

> I said, 'You will die tomorrow. That's what I have come to talk to you about. Do you care how you look on the scaffold?'
> He stared at his hands … 'Yes,' he said. …

I told him then (as I had been taught) to eat little in the morning so that he would not be ill when the time came, and cautioned him to empty his bladder, which relaxes at the stroke. I drilled him too in that false routine we teach all those who must die, so that they will think the moment is not quite come when in fact it has come, the false routine that lets them die with something less of fear. I do not know whether he believed me, though I hope he did; if ever a lie is justified in the sight of the Pancreator, it is that one. (*Shadow*, p. 255)

Severian's counselling is used by Wolfe to suggest that the torturer is a professional, fulfilling his social role. Importantly, though, his position as a state-sanctioned murderer is presented in a manner subordinate to his status as a craftsman skilled in the arts of execution and dispensing pain. The important auxiliary verb 'must' emphasises the impossibility of Agilus's situation: his death is assured, and Severian is present to mitigate its cruelty through his advice and expertise.

Wolfe dispels any doubts or objections that the reader may have concerning Severian's actions by ensuring that Agilus's execution quickly degenerates into farce:

The headless body ... must be taken away in a manner dignified but dishonourable .... The chiliarch ... had solved the problem by ordering that the body should be pulled behind a baggage sumpter. The animal had not been consulted, however, and being more of the labourer than the warrior kind, took fright at the blood and tried to bolt. We had an interesting time of it before we were able to get poor Agilus into a quadrangle from which the crowd could be excluded. (*Shadow*, p. 265)

Clearly, the method of removal is far from dignified but the presence of the adjective implies a reverence for the dead, a reverence strongly undermined by the anecdotal tone that Severian adopts. Severian's concluding ironic recollection effaces any reservations that the reader may feel concerning the events of the narrative as he or she begins to partake of, and even enjoy, the character's rather dark sense of humour. As Wayne Booth observes:

Since we are not in a position to profit or be harmed by a fictional character, our judgement [of him or her] is disinterested, even in a sense irresponsible. We can easily find our interests magnetised by characters who would be intolerable in real life.[3]

Since the reader is in no danger of benefit or harm from Severian, he or she may find his or her imagination captivated by him and, as a consequence, begin to adopt Severian's perspectives.

In *The Claw of the Conciliator*, Wolfe is so confident that he has 'magnetised' the reader into accepting Severian's actions that he feels he can admonish the reader, through the agency of Severian, for experiencing any vicarious pleasure at his descriptions of mutilation:

> I have recounted the execution of Agia's twin brother because of the importance of it to my story, and that of Morwenna [in *The Claw of the Conciliator*] because of the unusual circumstances surrounding it. I will not recount others unless they hold some special interest. If you delight in another's pain and death, you will gain little satisfaction from me. (*Claw*, p. 39)

The implication here is that Severian derives no pleasure in dispensing pain and death, and the reader may begin to see him as an (artificially) moral character. However, while it is quite probable that Severian does not obtain any satisfaction from the executions and suffering for which he is responsible, it is not because of sympathy but a result of Severian's complete lack of empathy for his victims. He does not 'delight in another's pain and death' because he has been trained to view and treat those judged guilty as objects. Hence, identifying with Severian may serve to obviate any compassion that the reader might feel for his victims; he or she may also begin to view them as merely 'those who must die'.

The reader may begin to 'explain [Severian's] behaviour by relating him to his environment, but,' as Booth remarks, 'even to explain away is to admit that something requires excuse'.[4] Clearly, from a modern liberal standpoint, Severian's conduct does demand extenuation, but Wolfe's skill at reducing the emotional distance, at forging an empathic link between protagonist and reader, is such that the reader does not feel compelled to excuse Severian's activities. He is presented, and received, as a necessary and valuable element in the legal system of his society.

The creation of a close relationship between Severian and the reader serves to obscure the fact that, as a first-person narrator, his account is subjective and, therefore, highly focalised. Katie Wales notes how 'readers normally assume that narrators are reliable, especially if they are the implied author, namely [they regard] what is being told [as] the (fictional) truth'.[5] When reading The Urth Cycle, assuming that Severian's observations are a complete and trustworthy account of what is transpiring on Urth automatically prejudices the reader's chances of determining the fictional truth.

Having elicited the reader's trust in Severian's integrity, and in the integrity of his portrayal as a character, Wolfe then misleads the reader by making his protagonist an unreliable narrator. Severian's unreliability manifests itself in a number of ways. Primarily, his inescapable subjectivity renders the accuracy of his observations, suppositions and conclusions questionable. For example, in the ruins of southern Nessus, he feels that

> The Increate was there, a thing beyond the Hierodules and those they serve; even on the river, I could feel his presence as one feels that of the master of a great house ... When we went ashore, it seemed to me that if I were to step through any doorway there, I might surprise some shining figure, and that the commander of all such figures was everywhere invisible only because he was too large to be seen. (*Citadel*, p. 306)

Wolfe's manipulative technique is deceptively simple. The implication of the passage, that there is a god-like being presiding over the universe, is extremely tenuous. Severian's initial declaration is based on a feeling, yet Wolfe seems to qualify Severian's mystical perception by drawing an analogy to 'the master of a great house'. This analogy lowers Severian's overwhelming theological assertion to the level of the commonplace, thereby lending credibility to his claim. However, the analogy is misleading since, while it gives the impression of the existence of a supreme deity, it is nothing more than an example of Severian's burgeoning faith in such a being. His failure to categorise the Increate, which remains a 'thing', not only emphasises his uncertainty, his subjectivity, but also allows for Wolfe's later revelation that the Increate is the Hierogrammates' reverential name for their creators.

After Severian goes ashore, his subjectivity remains intact: 'It seemed to me that if I were to step through any doorway ...,' he remarks, 'I might surprise some shining figure.' This possibility remains suspended with that conditional, but is introduced in such a way that, after the apparently fantastical creatures encountered throughout the preceding chapters of *The Book of the New Sun*, the presence of an angelic entity would not be unlikely.

Severian closes his rhetorical affirmation with an assurance that the Increate was 'everywhere invisible only because he was too large to be seen', a non sequitur that opposes any objections raised against his mystical sensations by providing an assertion whose unprovability renders them irrefutable.

Subjective passages like this, instead of bringing Severian's rationality into doubt, serve to introduce and sustain the sense of religiosity that pervades the narrative.[6] Wolfe's technique of statement, artificial rationalisation and conclusion is accepted by the reader because he or she has established an identifying link with Severian and trusts his credibility to guide him or her conscientiously and objectively through an unfamiliar world. Wolfe uses this trust to assist the reader's acceptance of the narrative's metaphysical concerns as genuine rather than as evidence of Severian's superstitiousness.

Wolfe attempts to disguise Severian's unreliability by providing him with an apparently faultless memory. While Severian's mnemonism seems to compensate him for his subjectivity, enabling him to recount his experiences with a clarity that implies a form of omniscience, his total recall actually intensifies his unreliability.

As Wolfe took 'beginning and advanced courses in Abnormal Psychology' at Miami University in Ohio in the late 1960s, and an introductory course at the University of Houston, it is probable that he was familiar with the clinical studies of the psychology of mnemonists when he began writing *The Book of the New Sun*.[7] It is not surprising, therefore, that Severian is the embodiment of the mnemonist 'S.', who was studied by the Russian psychologist Aleksandr Romanovich Luria.

Both Severian and S. share a 'passive-receptive attitude, almost precluding organised striving', where 'a wealth of thought and imagination were curiously combined with limitations of intellect'.[8] Severian's mnemonism ensures that he is the ideal candidate for the Hierogrammates' conspiracy. He accepts his exile with equanimity, journeys to Thrax because it is expected of him, becomes Autarch through circumstances contrived by the Hierogrammates and their servants, and complies with their plans for the destruction of Urth without objection.

Severian's equation with S. is extended when he admits that

> Two thoughts (that were nearly dreams) obsessed me and made them infinitely precious. The first was that at some not-distant time, time itself would stop ... the sullen sun wink out at last. The second was that there existed somewhere a miraculous light—which I sometimes conceived of as a candle, sometimes a flambeau—that engendered life in whatever objects it fell on. (*Shadow*, p. 22)

Here, Severian, like S., reveals himself as 'a dreamer whose fantasies were embodied in images that were all too vivid, constituting in themselves another world, one through which he transformed the experiences of everyday life'.[9] Severian's images, 'two thoughts (that were nearly dreams)', are exploited by the Hierogrammates, who attire the provision of the New Sun in the trappings of transcendence and ceremony to convince Severian of his vital role in the cosmos. In convincing Severian that he is a messiah, the Hierogrammates stimulate the faith of others, including the reader. Accordingly, Severian's mnemonism has important implications not only for his fictional universe but also for the reader's reception of the text.

In his introduction to Luria's study, Jerome S. Bruner draws attention to the fact that S. is a man whose memory is a memory of particulars, particulars that are rich in imagery, thematic elaboration, and effect. But it is a memory that is particularly lacking in one important feature: the capacity to convert encounters with the particular into instances of the general, enabling one to form general concepts even though the particulars are lost.[10]

While the pentalogy deepens Severian's characterisation by demonstrating a corresponding richness in 'imagery' and 'thematic elaboration', Severian's inability to form general principles out of particular encounters is one of his abiding characteristics. His inability to explain the nature of the cosmos in which he lives, and the interrelationships of the species that inhabit that cosmos, seems to reflect a powerlessness to proceed from the particular to the general. While he can observe that, 'I have found always that the pattern of our guild is repeated mindlessly in the societies of every trade, so that they are all of them torturers, just as we ...' (*Shadow*, pp. 41–42), he is unable to apply this maxim and appreciate the scheme of humanity's metaphorical torturers, the Hierogrammates. This incapacity contributes to his unreliability: Severian cannot learn from his experiences but must face each new encounter with no general principles to guide him. As a consequence, he is continually deceived, surprised and betrayed.

Bruner remarks that in addition to S.'s ineffectiveness in extracting collective principles from particular incidents, 'there is also a non-selectivity about his memory, such that what remains behind is a kind of junk heap of impression'.[11] This 'junk heap' is represented by the universalism of Wolfe's text. Although Joan Gordon has argued that Wolfe's intertextual and extraliterary references add detail to the fictional universe,[12] their sheer number is remarkable. Their deflective qualities ensure that the reader experiences the same difficulty as S. expressed when presented with 'some details in a passage I happened to have read elsewhere. I find then that I start in one place and end up in another—everything gets muddled.'[13]

The intratextuality of The Urth Cycle indicates that Severian suffers a form of confusion analogous to that endured by S., in which an experience provokes the recall of an earlier memory which, in turn, arouses a second memory-image, which elicits a third, and so forth. This aspect of Severian's psychology begins to confuse any reader who follows the often fruitless textual connections established by the narrator's abnormal thought processes (see Chapter 10).

Like S., Severian remembers 'details which other people would overlook, or which would remain on the periphery of awareness [and which take] on independent value in his mind, giving rise to images that tended to scatter meaning'.[14] Severian's memories direct his attention from what is immediate towards a number of associations. Just like S., whose memory-images 'carried him so far adrift that he was forced to go back and rethink the entire passage',[15] Severian must struggle to concentrate on what confronts him at any given moment. Unfortunately, Severian does not possess the faculty required to achieve this mental focus. On several occasions (including his consideration of Ymar, a previous Autarch [*Claw*, pp. 158–59]), his rethinking of an event ends with an inconclusive rhetorical question which both underlines the ambiguity of his anecdote and confirms his maladroitness in handling information and formulating hypotheses.

Luria observes that

> there were many instances ... in which images that came to the surface in S.'s mind steered him away from the subject of a conversation. At such moments his remarks would be cluttered with details and irrelevancies; he would become verbose, digress endlessly and finally have to strain to get back to the subject of the conversation.[16]

An example of Severian's own mental movement from an image to a series of verbose ramblings elicited by that image occurs in *The Sword of the Lictor*. Travelling across the mountains, Severian reflects on how the Pelerine cape he intends to leave as payment for the food he takes from a shepherd's bothy came to be in the stone town described in *The Claw of the Conciliator*. His thoughts form one of the longest digressions in the pentalogy:

> I have never fully understood how it [the cape] came to be where we found it [in the stone town], or even whether the strange individual [Apu Punchau] who called us to him so that he might have that brief period of renewed life had left it behind intentionally or accidentally when the rain dissolved him again to that dust he had been for so long. The ancient sisterhood of priestesses [the Pelerines] beyond question possesses powers it seldom or never uses, and it is not absurd to suppose that such raising of the dead is among them. If that is so he may have called them to him as he called us, and the cape may have been left behind by accident.
>
> Yet even if that is so, some higher authority may have been served. It is in such fashion that most sages explain the apparent paradox that though we freely choose to do this or the other, commit some crime or by altruism steal the sacred distinction of the Empyrian, still the Increate commands the entirety and is served equally (that is, totally) by those who would obey and those who would rebel.

Not only this. Some, whose arguments I have read in the brown book and several times discussed with Thecla, have pointed out that fluttering in the Presence there abide a multitude of beings that though appearing minute—indeed, infinitely small—by comparison are correspondingly vast in the eyes of men, to whom their master is so gigantic to be invisible. (By this unlimited size he is rendered minute, so that we are in relation to him like those who walk upon a continent but see only forests, bogs, hills of sand, and so on, and though feeling, perhaps, some tiny stone in their shoes, never reflect that the land they have overlooked all their lives is there, walking with them.)

There are other sages too, who doubting the existence of that power these beings, who may be called amschaspands, are said to serve, nonetheless assert the fact of their existence. Their assertions are based not on human testimony—of which there is much and to which I add my own, for I saw such a being in the mirror-paged book in the chambers of Father Inire [in the House Absolute]—but rather on irrefutable theory, for they say that if the universe was not created (which they, for reasons not wholly philosophical, find it convenient to disbelieve), then it must have existed forever to this day. And if it has so existed, time itself extends behind this present day without end, and in such a limitless ocean of time, all things conceivable must of necessity have come to pass. Such beings as the amschaspands are conceivable for they, and many others, have conceived of them. But if creatures so mighty once entered existence, how should they be destroyed? Therefore they are still extant.

And as such beings certainly exist, may it not be that they interfere (if it can be called interference) in our affairs by such accidents as that of the scarlet cape I left in the bothy. It does not require illimitable might to interfere with the internal economy of ants—a child can stir it with a stick. I know of no thought more terrible than this ...

Yet there is another explanation: it may be that all those who seek to serve the Theopany, and perhaps even all those who allege to serve him, though they appear to us to wage a species of war on one another, are yet linked, like the marionettes of the boy and the man of wood that I once saw in a dream [*Shadow*, pp. 139–42] and who, although they appeared to combat one another, were nevertheless under the control of an unseen individual who operated the strings of both. If this is the case, then the shaman we saw may have been a friend and ally of those priestesses who range so widely in their civilisation across the same land where he, in primitive savagery, once

sacrificed with liturgical rigidity of drum and crotal in the small
temple of the stone town. (*Sword*, pp. 219–21)

In this passage, the memory of finding the Pelerine cape provokes a series
of images that steer Severian away from the subject of the conversation,
the cape itself, into a philosophical discussion laden with details and
irrelevancies. Like S., he digresses ceaselessly before finally striving to
return his attention to the original subject.

Severian's ruminations are, paradoxically, both revelatory and obfuscatory, demonstrating how Wolfe fashions the text to work actively against
itself. The first paragraph begins to establish the pattern of inconclusive
considerations that will characterise the quotation. Severian wonders
how the cape came to be in the stone town and about the Pelerines'
power to raise the dead. No answers are provided and Wolfe uses this
indefiniteness to launch a verbose philosophical account of the nature of
the universe. Composed of a series of conjectures made by sages, this
discussion heaps meditation on meditation to confound the reader.

These strategically arranged hypotheses include the concept that the
Increate 'commands the entirety', that humanity is surrounded by
infinitely small yet comparatively huge angelic creatures serving God, and
that there is no God but, paradoxically, his servants can be accounted for
by both 'human testimony' and 'irrefutable theory' (a clause which,
importantly, emphasises that the theory may not be true). In the sixth
paragraph, Severian finally returns to the subject of the priestesses and the
assertion that there is an individual controlling the entire cosmos.

This cyclical arrangement (which reflects the principal structural motif
of the pentalogy) foregrounds the fact that Severian's argument does not
progress towards a conclusion and, hence, serves little purpose in advancing
the plot. It does, however, present itself as profound by disguising its own
lack of direction with associational material, obscure diction and the now
familiar technique of analogising metaphysical claims with physical
actions (principally by likening the vast [and invisible] presence of the
supreme being to the huge and unobservable nature of the entire Urth
when perceived from an individual, subjective standpoint).

Conversely, behind Wolfe's 'muddying' discourse, the quotation contains
an implicit revelation concerning the nature of the fictional universe.
Amid Severian's confusing outrush of theories there is the implication
that God's servants (or those purporting to be his servants) are real.
Severian conjectures that they might be interfering (although he immediately questions the validity of describing such contact as interference) in
human affairs. Here, the introduction of a commonplace analogy alludes
to Wolfe's theme of power relationships: the child and its stick represent
the Hierogrammates and their Conciliator, while the ants' nest symbolises

Urth. Severian considers 'no thought more terrible than' the idea of his society being manipulated and, in so doing, reveals the purpose for the Hierogrammates' delusory mythogenesis.

Contained in the final paragraph is the all-important implication that there is a force controlling individuals as if they were puppets in a toy theatre. However, Wolfe disguises this implicit revelation by furnishing the reader with the final impression of the existence of God, or of a similar central figure.

This passage is a representation of Wolfe's entire strategy throughout The Urth Cycle. Mystification abounds but at the core of such inflation and confusion resides the fictional reality, or at least implications of that reality. Severian's inability to grasp these implications results in the reader experiencing his fantasy rather than the reality of his universe. Accordingly, the reader, like Luria, would find it difficult to say which was more real for Severian (and S.): the world of subjective illusion in which he resided, or the real world, in which he was an infrequent and always transient tenant.[17] The reader confronts a puzzle: the notion of a character whose powers of recall are comparatively reliable and yet whose effectiveness at analysing his recollections is dubious.

The first-person narrative not only militates against the reader's effort to comprehend more than the protagonist but also encourages the reader to accept, and in so doing, adopt, Severian's reasoning capacity. If Severian chooses not to, or cannot, explain certain phenomena, then the reader is free to allow the unresolved elements to contribute to establishing the strange ambience of the alien Urth. To this end, the obscure intimations of future events in the sheared cliff beyond Casdoe's home in The Sword of the Lictor are perfunctorily dismissed:

> But though I stopped several times and strove to understand what might be pictured there [in a ruined mosaic] (whether it was writing, a face, or perhaps a mere decorative design of lines and angles, or a pattern of intertwined verdure) I could not; and perhaps it was each of those, or none, depending on the position from which it was seen and the predisposition the viewer brought to it. (Sword, p. 108)

Overlooking its self-conscious allusion to the multiple interpretations invited by The Urth Cycle, the passage implies that Severian is a subjective narrator. Significantly, the incautious reader, convinced of his or her dependence on the protagonist's thought processes, is unlikely to question Severian's credibility. Clearly, if the reader does apprehend this indication of the character's subjectivity, he or she will begin to understand that the account is an extremely focalised perspective on the fictional universe, biased by Severian's burgeoning superstition and limited intellect.

'Playing fair' with the reader, Wolfe provides an additional clue to Severian's unreliability. Towards the conclusion of *The Citadel of the Autarch*, Severian remarks:

> I cannot help but wonder how much any of us see of what is before us. For weeks ... Jonas had seemed to me only a man with a prosthetic hand [and not a robot with a torso and face of flesh], and when I was with Baldanders and Dr. Talos, I had overlooked a hundred clues that should have told me Baldanders was master. (*Citadel*, p. 257)

Coming as it does in the final movement of *The Book of the New Sun*, this paragraph exposes Severian's subjectivity and suggests to the reader that he or she should re-examine the text to determine, from the subtextual evidence provided, the precise nature of the events that Severian misreads.

Having disclosed his protagonist's limited and inaccurate perception, Wolfe reveals that Severian's faith in the reliability of his memory is misplaced. Greenland observes that

> At the very beginning of the second volume he [Severian] recalls an incident from the very beginning of the first, giving us a chance to compare—and yes, there is a slight disparity between the two accounts.[18]

The incident in question occurs in the necropolis of the Citadel when Severian watches Vodalus the outlaw hand a laser pistol to one of his companions. In *The Shadow of the Torturer*, Severian reports the weapon passing to Hildegrin, Vodalus's henchman (*Shadow*, p. 14); yet in *The Claw of the Conciliator*, he remembers Vodalus handing it to his mistress, Thea (*Claw*, p. 13).

Wolfe offers further indications of the fallibility of Severian's memory on each occasion that the torturer recalls what kind of material composes the bag Dorcas makes for the Claw of the Conciliator. In *The Sword of the Lictor*, Severian describes the cloth as 'doeskin' (p. 13); in *The Citadel of the Autarch*, it has become 'leather' (p. 252); while in *The Urth of the New Sun*, it is both 'leathern' (p. 38) and 'manskin' (p. 279).

It seems probable that Wolfe provides these clues not only to reveal Severian's Jamesian 'inconscience', his mistaken faith in his memory, but also to suggest, albeit indirectly, that the abnormality of that memory may be the source of a more extensive and significant unreliability that the reader must uncover for him- or herself. However, discovering these clues requires a degree of concentration that some readers may not wish to sustain and Severian's unreliability may pass (and has passed) largely unnoticed.

Severian is Wolfe's mask, not only in the poetic sense of an assumed persona, but in the very literal definition of a garment designed for concealment. He forms the 'front line' of defence against any reader who seeks to isolate the central issues of the narrative. If the reader succeeds in recognising that Severian is fundamentally untrustworthy, he or she has an opportunity to perceive the textual nuances behind, or beyond, this persona. Yet, Wolfe opposes this perception further by ensuring that the form and structure of the text function as secondary barriers to full comprehension.

The Urth Cycle is contrived as a fictive autobiography, a form that upholds reader identification. In her study of memory, Mary Warnock observes how becoming privy to the inner thoughts of the autobiographer results in the reader identifying him- or herself with the subject. Once this identification is achieved, the reader begins to sense that what the auto-biographer experienced, he or she experienced also.[19] Since 'the keeping of diaries and the writing of autobiographies are two ... related forms of the passion for truth through memory',[20] the reader assumes that Severian is providing a truthful and full account of his journey. This sense of truthfulness arises partly from Severian's disclosure that he wishes no ambiguity to surround his motives or actions: 'Once I referred to a certain incident in the life of Ymar. Now I have spoken with Ymar himself, yet that incident remains ... inexplicable ... I would prefer that similar incidents in my own life not suffer a similar obscurity' (*Urth*, p. 280). Although Wolfe's arch irony resonates through Severian's confession, this passage is significant for insinuating that the protagonist is attempting both to make sense of his life and clarify his status to those who read his autobiography, to state categorically that his account is the 'truth'. Here, Wolfe is toying with the veracity that Warnock argues is inherent in the autobiographical form. If the reader accepts Severian's account as truth, then he or she is unlikely to uncover *the* truth, that is, the factors uniting all the diverse elements of Wolfe's cosmos.

To help the reader recognise that Severian is capable of conscious deception, and thereby call into question the accuracy of his document, Wolfe provides evidence to indicate that his protagonist is lying at various points in the narrative. For example, when Severian first encounters Valeria, an attractive young woman in the Atrium of Time, he denies the existence of a 'Tower of Torment', by answering her question literally (see *Shadow*, p. 45).

On other occasions, Wolfe seems to indicate that Severian is attempting to confer an (artificially) transcendent quality on his consciousness by implying his reception of 'presentiments'. For example, *The Shadow of the*

Torturer begins with a bold and questionable assertion: 'It is possible that I already had some presentiment of my future' (*Shadow*, p. 10). Clearly, the reader should be suspicious of this claim considering that the events of the narrative are recorded after their conclusion, when Severian has gained that ultimate but useless boon, hindsight.

Through the deployment of prescient imagery, Severian purports to have visionary powers that he does not possess. In this way, he suggests that he receives a precognisant symbolic image of Thecla's fate on the Revolutionary (an implement of torture employing electricity to turn the body against itself), when the scent of her prostitute-clone makes him 'think of a rose burning' (*Shadow*, p. 91). Similarly, when he meets Agilus for the first time, the primary image ('a slash of red sunshine ... stood stiff as a blade between us' [*Shadow*, p. 154]) anticipates the moment when Severian will execute him. Later, when Agia takes him to the Botanic Gardens, Severian appears foresighted as he muses: 'I'm almost inclined to think this whole affair is some trick of yours or of your brother's' (*Shadow*, p. 173), which, of course, it is.

This kind of prefiguration also occurs in *The Sword of the Lictor*, when Severian observes, 'and only I [was] unchanged, as it is said the velocity of light is unchanged by mathematical transformations' (*Sword*, p. 42). Here, Severian's analogy alludes to his equation with the New Sun, contributing to the text's deceptive mythogenesis. The misleading aspect of this device is embellished further in *The Citadel of the Autarch*, where Severian describes his fever as so intense that 'the very glaciers of the south would melt if I came among them' (*Citadel*, p. 46). In these latter cases, the rhetoric is hyperbolic, designed (by Wolfe and Severian) to increase Severian's identification with the New Sun.

Accordingly, Severian's act of writing becomes analogous to the Hierogrammates' schemes, in which his personal history is rewritten; both strive to create a fiction from fact in order to gain control over their fictional auditors. Just as the Hierogrammates fabricate a myth to make their selfish actions less apparent, so Severian creates a false image of himself by suggesting that he is more percipient than he really is. The shared qualities of each species gradually become apparent and indicate that the Hierogrammates' capacity for deception lies within the human psyche.

To develop his manipulative control over the reader, Wolfe places a narrative gap between each volume of his pentalogy. Although these gaps preserve a sense of the erratic nature of memory, Severian's near-perfect recall indicates that such ellipses are not forgotten episodes but deliberate omissions that renew the reader's identification with, and dependency on, Severian at the beginning of each new volume. These gaps subjugate the reader to Severian's (and Wolfe's) will, casting him or her adrift until Severian (and Wolfe) decide to reveal the incidents omitted.

Clearly, the controlled, elliptical release of information is necessary if the novels are to possess an element of mystery or suspense. However, by occasionally suppressing Severian's hindsight, Wolfe ensures that The Urth Cycle reads more like a diary than an autobiography, and thereby deepens the text's fantastic ambience. For example, towards the conclusion of *The Shadow of the Torturer*, Severian and Dorcas witness a miraculous apparition:

> Hanging over the city like a flying mountain in a dream was an enormous building—a building with towers and buttresses and an arched roof. Crimson light poured from its windows. I tried to speak, to deny the miracle even as I saw it; but before I could frame a syllable, the building had vanished like a bubble in a fountain, leaving only a cascade of sparks. (*Shadow*, p. 269)

Wolfe establishes the solidity of this floating castle with references to 'a building with towers and buttresses and an arched roof', with 'windows' and illumination. Paradoxically, he then has the building dissolve in a simile of quintessential transience. Only the brief 'dream' suggests that Severian's perception of this so-called 'miracle' may be incorrect. The reader must wait until *The Claw of the Conciliator* to discover that this 'floating castle' was, in fact, the Cathedral of the Claw, fashioned in silk and set alight by the Pelerines after the Claw was stolen:

> 'I said they burned it. They must have set fire to the straw floor.'
> 'That's what I heard too. They just stood back and watched it burn. It went up to the Infinite Meadows of the New Sun, you know.'
> ... I said, 'I know that certain persons claimed to see it rise into the air.'
> 'Oh, it rose alright. When my grandson-in-law heard about it, he was fairly struck flat for a day. Then he pasted up a kind of hat out of paper and held it over my stove, and it went up, and then he thought it was nothing that the cathedral rose, no miracle at all.' (*Claw*, pp. 24–25)

While this 'revelation' underlines Merryn's statement that 'there is no magic. There is only knowledge more or less hidden' (*Claw*, p. 287), the way in which the information is imparted suggests, initially, that there is some strangely miraculous non-rational power operating on Urth. Rather than explaining the mystery immediately, Wolfe delays the disclosure until the point at which Severian learns the truth. Accordingly, the author controls how far and how quickly the reader's understanding progresses by prohibiting him or her from knowing more than Severian at any one time.

Mysteries such as the floating cathedral, which are, for the most part, satisfactorily explained by the conclusion of *The Urth of the New Sun*, are all ephemeral enigmas. The frequency of such puzzles disguises the fact that the novel's central conundrum (the motivation behind the Hierogrammates' actions) remains almost wholly unaddressed. Indeed, as the reader trusts Severian, he or she may never become aware of the text's lack of a resolution.

As its plot develops, it becomes apparent that The Urth Cycle is a narrative of recollection rather than reflection. Severian recounts what he has experienced and discovered without ever directly analysing the implications of these experiences. He is a static character, possessing as little insight into the nature of his universe at the conclusion of *The Urth of the New Sun* as he does at the beginning of *The Shadow of the Torturer* because he is psychologically mature throughout, even when writing of his youth. The reader is unprepared for such stasis since the narrative structure, relating Severian's maturation, implies that the protagonist will undergo psychological development. As a result, increasing knowledge can be misinterpreted as increasing insight, despite the only evidence of Severian's freethinking, of his maturity, being restricted to one statement: 'Now I realised that the House Absolute and our court had become the frame for a vague picture of the Increate as Autarch. In retrospect it seemed inevitable' (*Urth*, p. 367). Severian has suddenly been permitted a psychological development, an awareness of the human tendency for mythogenesis.

Severian's new comprehension, attained (in terms of the fictional chronology) before he writes *The Urth of the New Sun*, is deliberately undeveloped; he fails to employ his understanding when constructing his memoirs. Rather, it functions to alert the reader to Wolfe's calculated lack of exposition. Wolfe himself even telegraphs this by employing the uncharacteristically crude 'in retrospect' to signpost the lack of retrospection throughout the narrative. The attentive reader is likely to be struck by the perspicacity of Severian's recognition that the shore culture's act of mythogenesis 'seemed inevitable'. On this level, Severian's bald comment contrasts with, and helps to reveal, the obfuscation that keeps the human dependence on myth subordinate to the plot. Severian's appreciation of humankind's penchant for myth-making appears at the end of the novel to give the reader one final opportunity to perceive the entire pentalogy as an elaborate masquerade before Wolfe returns to his allusiveness. References to Adam and Eve and the Crucifixion soon follow, symbolic renderings of birth and death, the two fundamental facts of life and evolution that are elaborated on continually throughout the text.

The autobiographical form of the novel prepares the reader for a narrative that will carry him or her forward, in close association with the protagonist, to its completion. From the first chapter of *The Shadow of the Torturer* the reader is aware that Severian has 'backed into the throne' (*Shadow*, p. 18) to become Autarch; and that reader is seemingly merely required to observe how this 'long journey' progresses and is resolved. Such passivity is encouraged further by the structure of the pentalogy.

The Urth Cycle is communicated in a familiar form, adhering closely to Joseph Campbell's structural rendering of the heroic cycle, the formulaic pattern, based on the rites of passage, which is followed by the hero in most mythological adventures. In *The Hero with a Thousand Faces*, Campbell terms the journey of the hero from separation to initiation to return the 'nuclear unit of the monomyth', describing how such heroes depart from the mundane world, encounter fantastical and supernatural forces, and win decisive victories. The hero then returns from his adventure with the ability to confer benefits on his fellows.[21] Clearly, Severian's exile, implied apotheosis and re-emergence as the Conciliator reflect this traditional progression from separation to initiation and return.

When Campbell delineates his thesis into more concise stages, it becomes apparent that Wolfe has appropriated recurrent motifs from the heroic cycles. Even the raddled Urth assumes a mythic presence: 'He [the hero] and/or the world in which he finds himself suffers from a symbolic deficiency ... The physical and spiritual life of the whole earth can be represented as fallen.'[19] Importantly, Urth's fall is the result of entropy rather than sin. Hence, its need for redemption is not spiritual but physical, demonstrating that the central theme of the text, the rebirth of the sun, is based on science rather than metaphysics.

The structuring of the narrative's dramatic action according to the progression of the monomythic cycle automatically suggests that the text is a mythoplasm. Severian experiences the Campbellian 'Call to Adventure' in the form of the 'herald figure' of Thecla. His answer to this call is not, however, the result of his own free will. Rather, he is exiled from his guild in a sequence with metaphorical parallels to the Edenic Fall. Thecla represents both forbidden fruit and the tempting serpent. As a servant of Abaia, her influence is analogous to that of the Old Testament snake; as a well-educated, sexually active woman, she symbolises the tree of both erotic and worldly knowledge. It is Severian's desire for her, his sin of transgression, that results in his being cast out of the safety and comparative innocence of his guild.

Before his exile, Master Palaemon provides Severian with the executioner's sword, *Terminus Est*, in a sequence that demonstrates Wolfe's adherence to Campbell's schema. In the monomyth, the hero's initial encounter is often with a protective character—usually an old man or woman—who supplies the hero with talismans or 'amulets' against the forces that may oppose him.[23] Palaemon, whose name derives from the Greek παλαίος, meaning 'old in years', personifies this essentially helpful figure. Similarly, the lochage who controls a bridge over the Gyoll represents the 'threshold guardian', who signifies the line of division between the known and the unknown.[24] Although Severian overcomes this obstacle without difficulty, its symbolism remains archetypal.

Beyond the bridge, Severian sets his feet on the Campbellian 'Road of Trials', on which he journeys, encountering a series of characters whose identities are as fluid and ambiguous as any described by Campbell. Like many of the myths that Campbell describes, The Urth Cycle deploys fluidity of identity as a sustained formal property, with characters adopting different guises, or revealing contrasting aspects of their personalities, and undertaking subterfuges to accomplish their own objectives. The subplot involving Agia's and Agilus's plan to steal Severian's sword is a case in point (see *Shadow*, pp. 152–266).

The narrative's parallels with Campbell's study continue through 'The Meeting with the Goddess' in the form of Apheta, to the 'Atonement with the Father', in the shifting shape of Tzadkiel, to Severian's supposed apotheosis, his gaining of 'The Ultimate Boon' (the New Sun), 'The Return' to Urth, his 'Magic Flight' and 'The Crossing of the Return Threshold', to his apparent mastery over the power of two worlds.

Severian's ability to travel through time along the Brook Madregot, which flows from the universe of Yesod to the Urthly universe of Briah, recalls Campbell's observation that the hero's

> [f]reedom to pass back and forth across the world division from the perspective of apparitions of time to that of the causal deep and back—not contaminating the principle of the one with those of the other, yet permitting the mind to know the one by the virtue of the other—is the talent of the master.[25]

Urth is such an 'apparition of time', while the Brook Madregot symbolises the energy stream passing from the higher energy state universe of Yesod to the lower, Briahtic universe; it is the 'causal deep', representing the unidirectional flow of energy defined by the Second Law of Thermodynamics. Significantly, Severian's mastery is facilitated and controlled by Tzadkiel, whose advice and power permit Severian to move through time.

Despite the obvious affinities that Wolfe's pentalogy shares with Campbell's schema, The Urth Cycle is not a rite-of-passage tale. While the events of *The Book of the New Sun* could be misinterpreted as such, this is simply not the case. When Severian assimilates the Autarch's multiple personality, his experiences count for little as he internalises all the knowledge he requires to rule the Commonwealth from his predecessor. As Algis Budrys observes:

> When we began with *Torturer*, the main assumption here ... was that we had a rite-of-passage novel. We were getting to know a young man, and following his adventures, in order to see how he grew. This expectation imposed a certain linearity on the story. It gave us a thread to follow while, all around us, Wolfe was exploding bombs, tripping trapdoors, unfurling peacocks' tails and playing counterpoint. But this turns out to be only the most cunning of Wolfe's false trails. I'm not sure that one of the things he most intended doing was to describe a time in which rites-of-passage have no applicability, but that is one of the things he has done.[26]

Whether Wolfe is actually following Campbell's blueprint or re-running the quest myth from his own reading of myths and fantasy novels, including *The Night Land*, is impossible to determine, nor is the discovery as important as an appreciation of the effect gained by the employment of such a format. Budrys's comments reveal that Wolfe is using the quest myth as a *piyout* of the kind described by Brazier. Accordingly, the text's mono-mythic structure is rather more than an organising principle of literary form. It is employed not to mitigate Wolfe's task of structuring a five-volume novel, but to provide the author with a strategy for concealing his ideas in a manner that influences the reader's reception of the text. In this case, the monomythic pattern is deployed as an obfuscatory literary prefiguration.

In *Mythology in the Modern Novel*, John White describes a prefiguration as a literary device that employs both mythological motifs and other patterning in the formulation of character and plot.[27] Hence, any mythic model deployed in a modern novel can prefigure and therefore anticipate the plot. In The Urth Cycle, Wolfe's adoption of the monomyth prepares the reader for a narrative pattern found not only in mythic tales but also in a significant number of literary and paraliterary fantasy novels. The motif of the quest is found in Tolkien's *The Lord of the Rings* (1954–55, rev. 1966); in Stephen Donaldson's *The Chronicles of Thomas Covenant, the Unbeliever* (1977–83), in Raymond E. Feist's *Riftwar Saga* (1983–86), and in innumerable volumes inspired by TSR's *Dungeons and Dragons* role-playing game. As a consequence of a familiarity with this fantasy fiction, the reader may accept the quest structure of Wolfe's pentalogy as confirmation of its fantastic nature. After all, it is a reader's prior reading experiences that anticipate and delimit the routes that his or her consciousness can take.[28]

The prefigurative aspect of the quest myth generates in the reader certain patterns of expectation 'concerning what is going to happen to the fictional characters', leading to 'an unequivocal anticipation of the novel's plot'.[29] If the reader assumes the level of the plot to be the only level at which Wolfe's text can be read, this anticipation may serve to disengage close scrutiny from the narrative.

Wolfe exploits his reader's awareness of the direction of the plot by enlisting his or her powers of recollection (the reader knows Severian is Autarch from the beginning of *The Shadow of the Torturer*) and by employing a prefigurative title for his concluding volume, *The Urth of the New Sun*. As White observes, 'titles remain the most direct narrative device the author can choose to trigger off a prefigurative pattern',[30] and, in this case, the title of *The Urth of the New Sun* serves to remove any indeterminacy concerning the possibility of Severian's success. From the outset, the title of Wolfe's final volume is an implicit comment on the preordained masquerade to which the reader is witness; it is certain that Urth will be granted a New Sun. However, the title may be perceived by the reader not as indicative of the artificiality of Severian's progression from torturer to messiah, but as a thematic element. White accounts for this phenomenon by stating: 'We are accustomed to associate titles with main themes and may be unable to see the modern use of prefigurative titles from the right perspective.'[31] In the case of The Urth Cycle, the right perspective is gained by those readers who recognise that such a prefiguration alludes to the Hierogrammates' schemes.

White notes that

> [a] complete pattern of mythological correspondences covering the whole of a novel is bound to generate a far greater mood of inexorability. Events then appear to be following some preordained course for which a familiar analogy assumes the role almost of an influence, and the prefiguration seems to retain its former religious aura.[32]

The monomythic prefiguration of The Urth Cycle functions precisely in this manner. The reader is seemingly required to follow Severian's tracks somewhat doggedly, recognising analogies to culture heroes and other fictional protagonists, while being encouraged to believe that the narrative is, in some vague way, a religious parable. However, the cautious, reflective reader may recognise such an extensive prefiguration as a structural clue used by Wolfe to indicate how Severian's life is being rescripted by the Hierogrammates, through the agency of the Claw and other celestial sleights of hand. In other words, Severian's life follows a mythic pattern because the Hierogrammates have contrived it to follow that mythic pattern.

Unfortunately, as a consequence of what Campbell sees as the universal status of the monomyth, critics have overlooked Wolfe's ironic recontextualisation, seized on the mythic elements of the narrative and pronounced it a mythoplasm, ignoring the deceptive role that the heroic cycle fulfils. Peter Nicholls, for example, considers Wolfe as

> [the] metaphysical poet of science fiction; he has a great deal in common with Donne or Marvell [and] the references [in *The Urth of the New Sun*] to Dante's great work [*La Commedia*] are appropriate enough, for *The Urth of the New Sun* is as much a description of a spiritual pilgrimage as it is of a physical voyage ... *The Urth of the New Sun* is a vigorous story of a flight through time and space, a judgement, a return to an Urth of an earlier era, a brief period at the end of the world, and finally the beginning of a new world. On the spiritual level the book is quite astonishing ... Lame Severian is not merely the Fisher King, he is the Redeemer, the Christ. Severian, though he may be assisted by the Increate, is his own man. He has Free Will ...[33]

Falling victim to Wolfe's recontextualisation of form and symbol, Nicholls is simply wrong in his reading of the text. Severian is neither the Fisher King nor Christ since, as White observes, 'a character within a novel cannot be a mythological god in the literal sense'.[34] Nicholls's discovery of Severian's Free Will, an astounding achievement considering the puppet/ actor imagery surrounding Wolfe's protagonist, whose actions are, at best, reactions to events instigated by 'powers from above the stage', reduces his argument to the level of assertion.

John Clute is similarly entangled in Wolfe's associational material and the monomythic prefiguration, suggesting that 'Severian is both Apollo and Christ and that the story of his life is a secular rendering of the parousia, the Second Coming. His cruelty ... is the cruelty of the universe itself ...'.[35] Like Nicholls, Clute fails to draw the important distinction between Severian's carefully rendered resemblance to Christ and Apollo and the impossibility of his being either. Together, they accept the pentalogy's symbolism as indicative of its assumed symbolist qualities rather than as a deflective plot in Wolfe's elaborate interpretative game. In asserting that Severian is Christ, Apollo and the Fisher King, Nicholls and Clute ignore the fact that Severian's resemblance to these figures confirms the artificiality of the Hierogrammates' mythogenesis, and suggests, albeit elliptically, that much of human mythology has been constructed using recurrent mythic patterns.

Clute's analysis is, however, more penetrating than Nicholls's appreciation. He recognises Severian's 'parousia' as 'secular', as something worldly rather than spiritual, indirectly expanding on his earlier understanding that 'the miracle' in *The Book of the New Sun* 'is that Severian is allowed to perform a miracle' (*Strokes*, p. 151). Unfortunately, Clute does not capitalise on either of these observations, and his suggestion that Severian's 'cruelty … is the cruelty of the universe itself' is simply ambiguous rhetoric which may, or may not, imply the Darwinian laws governing Severian's cosmos.

In an interview with Wolfe, Darrell Schweitzer seems to stumble on the significant point that Nicholls and Clute overlook:

> It seems to me that the document Severian has produced will be remembered in his world not as an autobiography or historical memoir but as a great myth. It will become like Homer's works and might even be the basis of a religion.[36]

Schweitzer's remarks are important since they draw attention to the way in which 'Severian's autobiography' could affect its own world while suggesting implicitly that the text should be read differently by contemporary readers.

Nicholls and Clute do not make this distinction between the novel as a mythogenetic narrative with ramifications for its own fictional culture and the text as a modern novel constructed to establish an intricate game with the reader. They are beguiled by what are, essentially, the products (Severian as saviour, the heroic adventure, the cosmological act of rebirth) of the themes and notions of the novel, misreading them as if they were the genuine themes of the text. White marks this subtle difference when he states, 'We have … no reason to suppose that a work of literature is necessarily constructed to create or resuscitate myth, just because it includes mythic motifs'; 'the context is more important than the source'.[36]

In The Urth Cycle, the context is obscured by the source material, a fact that leads the reader to perceive what the text resembles rather than what it actually is: Wolfe uses mythology, he does not create it outside the fictional environment. He is, in effect, toying with the reader's susceptibility to the transcendental visions of existence offered by mythical narrative. His employment of the monomyth exploits the primary psychological character of the human species: its need for myth.[38] Wolfe thereby disarms both the reader's desire and his or her ability to uncover the disturbing biological reality described in Chapter 5.

Disentangling context from allusion and recognising the equivocal subjectivity of 'Severian's' narrative remain the two most fundamental requirements in understanding The Urth Cycle and in recognising the nature of Wolfe's interpretative game. Standing sagaciously above the reader, Wolfe demonstrates his skill as a writer by producing a deliberately abstruse novel designed not for readers who will 'read his book, pitch it away and reach for the next'[39] but for those who 'will read and reread, study the cover, perhaps, in search of some clue, shelve the book and later take it down again just to hold'.[40]

This self-conscious, and possibly facetious, narcissism results in a novel whose dizzying rhetoric, deflection and inflation serve to keep the reader in the custody of the text. Wolfe's obscurantist approach can be perceived, therefore, as a technique for attracting and retaining reader interest through outright puzzlement, functioning analogously to the tactics he adopted for *The Fifth Head of Cerberus*.

Finding the solution to Wolfe's literary puzzle depends on the reader recognising that The Urth Cycle cannot be unlocked by applying the kind of knowledge that seems appropriate. Rather, the reader must apprehend the recontextualisations that Wolfe effects on the traditions of the first-person narrative, the autobiographical form and the monomythic structure, and determine the role played by this recontextualised material.

What Wolfe is endeavouring to teach the cautious and reflective reader (who recognises the characteristics of his literary game and hence colludes with the author) is the possibility of the existence of 'realities' beyond the reality that is perceived or learned or institutionalised. As Wolfe implies that blind religious faith may obviate the acceptance of a more scientifically rational explanation for existence—that, although he is a practising Catholic, he is perfectly capable of producing a text that does not rely on a Catholic or even a Christian view of the cosmos—he also indicates that beyond familiar literary forms there exists a huge potential for innovation. He revitalises the reading process in a genre that, in many cases, has become increasingly formulaic; he deconstructs reader expectations and undermines their casual suppositions. He helps the reader to discover, or rediscover, the need for scepticism in its original sense, when sceptics 'were those who thought, not those who scoffed',[41] and issues an unvoiced challenge to apply that scepticism when reading his fiction. In this respect, The Urth Cycle offers an invitation to understand and not merely to observe.

8. 'Cues': The Function of Unfamiliar Diction

The casual reader's potential to grasp the story of The Urth Cycle is reduced further by Wolfe's deployment of esoteric nouns. However, the inclusion of obscure diction is not solely a method for obfuscating the narrative's subtext. Rather, its introduction establishes a shifting kaleidoscope of adumbration and revelation which confronts the reader with the problem of determining when Wolfe's vocabulary serves to reveal and develop the pentalogy's themes and when it functions deflectively.

In *The Castle of the Otter*, Wolfe admits that he has no fondness for 'gibberish' (by which he means neologisms), and his use of archaisms is, fundamentally, an expression of his own aesthetic preferences. He explains that he has 'used odd words to convey the flavour of an odd place at an odd time',[1] and these 'odd words' are, therefore, substitutes for SF's more usual neologistic invention. Nevertheless, somewhat ironically, Wolfe's archaisms function as neologisms, acting as agents of estrangement to render the fictional Urth alien; they may be as much 'gibberish', or nonsense, to the reader, as invented language.[2]

More importantly, in his interview with Larry McCaffery for *Science-Fiction Studies*, Wolfe suggests that the historical nomenclature of Urth provides a sense of continuity with Earth, a sensation of 'where you've been and how far you've travelled …'. He also acknowledges that 'a great deal of knowledge can be intuited if you know something about the words people use',[3] self-consciously hinting at his indirect disclosure of information through the allusive qualities of his language.

Paradoxically, Wolfe's Classico-medieval references function both deflectively and candidly on this intuitive, allusionary level. While they imply that Urth is an ahistorical fantasy world, they also ensure that the Commonwealth resounds with an archaic quality that is appreciable by the reader (indeed the 'Ur-' prefix, which alludes to the primitive, or the earliest, implies a direct association with the past).

Equally, Wolfe's replacement of neologistic experimentation with archaic reappropriations conveys the notion of recycling, of social, linguistic and creative exhaustion. As Severian observes, the stagnation of the Commonwealth, which is manifest in its language, arises in part '[b]ecause the prehistoric cultures endured for so long, [so that] they have shaped our heritage in such a way as to cause us to behave as if their conditions still applied' (*Citadel*, p. 217). This remark alludes to the method by which Wolfe visualised his dying empire. In his interview with McCaffery, Wolfe admits that most of his research for The Urth Cycle involved an examination of 'Byzantium and the Byzantine Empire, which was a stagnant political entity that had outlived its time in much the same way the Urth of the Commonwealth [sic] had'.[4]

The analogue that Wolfe chose for his fictional society is founded on a stern Classico-rationalist version of Byzantine culture of the kind expressed by William Lecky:

> Of that Byzantine Empire the universal verdict of history is that it constitutes without a single exception, the most thoroughly base and despicable form that civilisation has yet assumed ... There has been no other enduring civilisation so absolutely destitute of all the forms and elements of greatness, and none to which the epithet mean may be so emphatically applied ... Its vices were the vices of men who had ceased to be brave without learning to be virtuous. Without patriotism, without the fruition or desire of liberty ... slaves and willing slaves, in both their actions and their thoughts, immersed in sensuality and in the most frivolous pleasures, the people only emerged from their listlessness when some theological subtlety or some chivalry in the chariot races stimulated them to frantic riots ... The history of the empire is a monotonous story of the intrigues of priests, eunuchs and women, of conspiracies, of uniform ingratitude, of perpetual fratricides.[5]

Lecky's criticism reads as an abstract of the Commonwealth's sociopolitical situation; it is a destitute empire in decline, mean, slavish to the historical influences of its past (a fact embodied in the prison community below the House Absolute in *The Claw of the Conciliator*, pp. 122–67), sustaining a series of intrigues masterminded by the Hierogrammates, the neutered Autarch, and his subjects.

Throughout The Urth Cycle, Wolfe's distribution of Latin and Greek reflects a corresponding linguistic division within Byzantine culture itself. Although the bureaucratic/martial system of the Commonwealth is not exclusively characterised by the use of Latin to denote its functionaries, it seems reasonable to assume that Wolfe was influenced by the knowledge that, until the time of Justinian, the Byzantine system preserved a Latin nomenclature of office, which it had inherited directly from Rome, and employed Latin as an official language.[6]

During his journey, Severian encounters *optimates* from Roman aristocracy; a *castellan*, or governor of a castle, from *castellanus*, pertaining to a fortress; and later becomes both the *carnifex*, or executioner, and the *lictor* (a public attendant of the principal Roman magistrates once responsible for carrying out the sentences they pronounced) of Thrax.

The distinction between the bureaucratic and the religious functionaries of the Commonwealth is placed in relief by the almost exclusive use of Greek to describe the latter. The adjectival prefix *hiero-* (from the Greek ἱερός, or divine) occurs throughout the text in various forms, including Hierogrammate, Hierodule, Hierophant (ἱερός, holy, φαντασία, the force by which an object is presented to the mind), one who teaches the rules of worship, and hierarch (ἱερός, holy, αρχος, ruler), or priests of high order. Similarly, Severian refers to *epopts* (from the Greek ἐπόπτης, meaning those individuals admitted to the highest theological or philosophical mysteries), or acolytes, and *psychopomps* (ψυχή, life or spirit, and πομπός, a guide), the conductors of souls.

Urth's stagnation, suggested by the Byzantine analogue, is not restricted to human culture. Indeed, the entire planet lacks fecundity and the ability to provoke evolutionary succession. Wolfe introduces this notion by suggesting that several extinct species have reasserted themselves on Urth, 'a phenomenon Severian himself sometimes assumes to have occurred' (*Shadow*, p. 302). Wolfe's decision to effect the apparent re-emergence of such creatures may have been prompted by a theory advanced by Charles Lyell in his *Principles of Geology* (1830–33):

> We may see ... an advance in design from fish to ichthyosaur to whale, but we view only the rising arc of a great circle that will come round again, not a linear path to progress. We are now ... in the winter of the 'great year', or geological cycle of climates. Tougher environments demand hardier, warm-blooded creatures. But the summer of time's cycle will come around again ...[7]

Should this occur,

> then might those genera of animals return, of which the memorials are preserved in the ancient rocks of our continents. The huge iguanadon might reappear in the wood, and the ichthyosaur in the sea, while the pterodactyl flit again through umbrageous groves of fir trees.[8]

While the extinct forms found in The Urth Cycle sustain the text's cyclical motif, it should be stressed that, although Lyell's returning ichthyosaurs would be sufficiently similar to their Jurassic counterparts for taxonomists to classify them as belonging to the same genus, they would not be morphologically identical to their prehistoric antecedents.[9]

If the extinct species found in The Urth Cycle are tabulated according to their distribution throughout Earth's prehistory, additional phenomena become observable. Table 1 illustrates the major geological periods of Earth: the first column shows the macro-periods, the Caenozoic, the Mesozoic, and the Palaeozoic; the second contains the subdivisions that are found within the macro-periods; the third provides the approximate age and duration of each era in millions (m) of years; and the fourth column gives groupings of the extinct species to which Severian refers.

What Table 1 highlights is the increasing frequency with which Wolfe selects species from the more recent geological periods, principally the Pleistocene and the Pliocene or, temporally, from the last 5.5 million years. Although Wolfe's borrowings from prehistory do not express a strictly uniform increase towards these epochs, there seems to be a pre-conceived strategy of placing a greater number of recent forms within the text, rather than appropriating more ancient types. The only appearance of a pre-Mesozoic species occurs when Severian and Agia encounter a pelycosaur (probably an edaphosaurus from the brief description offered in Chapter XX of *The Shadow of the Torturer*, p. 181 and p. 206), in the Jungle Garden of the Botanic Gardens in Nessus.

From what little information Wolfe provides, the reader can deduce that the captive biospheres that constitute the Botanic Gardens are temporal ecosystems, isolated bubbles of earlier (or later, or possibly both) time periods in which a circuitous pathway retreats (or advances) through time before turning forward (or back) to bring the visitor to his or her point of arrival (and departure). The pelycosaur exists in an earlier (or later) period of history, in which the sun is bright, where Severian and Agia discover pseudo-Christian missionaries converting the natives to God, and where aeroplanes bring in mail to airstrips cleared in the vegetation.

Wolfe underlines this temporal shift by locating a more archaic species of dinosaur in this (probably) earlier period of history—by using the pelycosaur as a temporal marker. This notion can be extended to the species chosen from the Pleistocene and Pliocene eras which seem to allude to a new phase of human evolution, prefiguring the solar rebirth and the beginning of a new creation in *The Urth of the New Sun*.

The Pleistocene and Pliocene were periods in which the ancestors of modern *Homo sapiens* began to emerge. Don Johanson, a palaeontologist working at Hadar in Ethiopia, has noted that, 'It's clear that upright walking happened long before brain expansion. Hominid brains don't show any striking signs of getting particularly big until two and a half million years ago, and yet these creatures were bipedal at least two million years before that.'[11]

Table 1 *Extinct species occurring in The Urth Cycle*[10]

Macro-period	Era	Age in Years (m)	Species
Caenozoic	Pleistocene	1.8	Mammoth
			Smilodon
			Teratornis
			Megatheria
			Cynocephalus
			Cathartidae
	Pliocene	5.5	Glyptodon
			Thylacosmil(us)
			Platybelodon
			Aelurodon
			Merychip(pus)
			Oreodonta
	Miocene	22.5	Baluchitherium
			Trilophodon
			Phorusrhacos
	Oligocene	36.0	Metamynodon
			Arsinother
	Eocene	58.0	Basilosaurs
			Uintathers
			Phenocod(us)
			Coryphodon
			Diatrymae
	Palaeocene	65.0	Barylambdas
			Arctother
			Thylacodon
Mesozoic	Cretaceous	135	Tyrannosaur
			Hesperorn
			Kronosaur
	Jurassic	200	
	Triassic	240	
Palaeozoic	Permian	280	Pelycosaur
	Carboniferous	370	
	Devonian	415	
	Silurian	445	
	Ordovician	515	
	Cambrian	590	

Clearly, there is a temptation to read what Johanson means literally as a metaphor for humanity's apparent situation in The Urth Cycle. The insertion of species from the Pleistocene and the Pliocene implies that, on Urth, humanity has metaphorically learned to walk, yet the brain has not expanded sufficiently for the human race to be accepted with equanimity among the alien peoples of the cosmos and so humankind must endure its 'penance'. Such an assertion recalls Cyriaca's remark in The Sword of the Lictor: 'The past cannot be found in the future where it is not—not until the metaphysical world, which is so much larger and so much slower than the physical world, completes its revolution and the New Sun comes' (p. 55).

Cyriaca and Johanson both draw a distinction between the physical and the metaphysical/mental. They recognise that Urth's humanity and the early hominids could walk, figuratively and literally, before their conscious or metaphysical development was under way. Consequently, in The Urth Cycle, the increasing number of extinct forms from the more recent past implies that Cyriaca's 'metaphysical' cycle is nearing its completion, that a new stage of human development (represented by the shore culture at the conclusion of The Urth of the New Sun) is about to begin. Of course, in the context of Wolfe's novel, the metaphysics of humanity's penance are fabrications of the Hierogrammates; the evolutionary step to be taken by humanity will be purely biological.

In addition to their role as temporal markers, Wolfe's extinct species also reveal how the author creates a fictional world that is geographically, as well as temporally, eclectic. Table 2 demonstrates this eclecticism by showing the geographical distribution of the prehistoric forms encountered in the text.

Wolfe confirms that his far future South America has become a culmination, or an aggregation, of Earth's/Urth's history by borrowing from a variety of lexical sets. For example, during his odyssey, Severian refers to, among other creatures, the thyacine (from thylacine), the Tasmanian zebra-wolf; jennets, small Spanish horses; the fennec (*Vulpes zerda*), an African fox-like mammal; the margay, a Central or South American felid (*Felis wiedii*); dholes (*Cuon alpinus*), the wild dogs of India; the capybara (*Hydrochoerus hydrochaeris*), a South American guinea pig and the largest rodent in the world; and the agouti (*Dasyprocta agouti*), a rodent found in Western Indian and South American areas.

The armies of the Autarch are similarly eclectic. From the Classical period Wolfe imports the hipparch (Greek: ἱππαρχος), a general of cavalry, and the chiliarch (Greek: χιλιάρχος), the commander of a thousand men. The reader also discovers the Parthian cataphracts, cavalry troops in full-scale mail dating from the first century BC. Similarly, Septentrions, derived from the Latin *septemptrionalis*, pertaining to the northern regions;

Table 2 *The Geographical Distribution of Extinct Species found in The Urth Cycle*

Species	Range
Mammoth	Europe, Asia, East Indies, Africa, North America
Smilodon	The Americas and Asia
Teratornis	North America
Megatheria (Megatherium)	The Americas
Cynocephalus (Papio)	Southern Asia and Africa
Cathartidae (Cathartes)	The Americas
Glyptodon (Glyptodontoidea)	The Americas
Thylacosmilus	South America
Platybelodon	Asia in U. Miocene, N. America during Pliocene
Aelurodon	North America
Merychippus (Protohippus)	North America
Oreodonta	North America
Baluchitherium	Asia
Trilophodon (Gompotherium)	Eurasia and Africa, North America
Phorusrhacos	South America, particularly Patagonia
Metamynodon	North America: L.–M. Oligocene
	East Asia: U. Eocene–L. Oligocene
Arsinother	North Africa, principally Egypt
Basilosaurs	North America and North Africa
Uintathers	North America
Phenocodus	North America
Coryphodon	North America: U. Palaeocene–L. Eocene
	Europe: L. Eocene
Diatrymae	North America and Europe
Barylambdas	North America
Arctother (Arctoycon)	North America
Thylacodon	North America
Tyrannosaur (T. Rex)	North America
Hesperorn	North America
Kronosaur	Australia
Pelycosaur	North America

praetorians, the bodyguards of the Roman generals; clavigers, or club-bearers, from the epithet of Hercules; and hastarii, from the Latin *hasta*, a spear, pike or javelin fitted with a thong to assist in its throwing, are all extracted from their historical settings to serve the Autarch. From other eras and geographical locations Wolfe selects uhlans, the Polish and German cavalry lancers; spahis, members of the cavalry corps within the Ottoman Turkish army; and an *estafette*, a French term for a mounted military courier.

The weapons carried by these troops are no less obscure. From the fourteenth and fifteenth centuries Wolfe appropriates the misericorde, the Anglo-French dagger carried by knights, whose name derived from a corruption of the plea for mercy, *misericordia*, that wounded combatants would ask of their would-be slayers; from the fourteenth century comes the estoc, or tuck, a thrusting sword used by cavalry as an auxiliary sidearm; and from the fourteenth and fifteenth centuries Wolfe selects the light spear or lancegay. The Russian berdiche (or berdysh), a narrow-headed axe, was used by Muskovy's infantry in the sixteenth and seventeenth centuries; the ransieur, or rawcon, was a staff with a three-pronged head of the same period; the English caliver, a firearm larger than an arquebus but smaller than a musket, orginates in the sixteenth century; the hanger, a slightly curved hunting sword, comes from the seventeenth and eighteenth centuries; and the spadroon, or simplified broadsword, was the eighteenth- and nineteenth-century German and East European sabre.[12] The temporal range covered by these weapons is reflected in a corresponding geographical diversity which ranges from the shotel, the Abyssinian sickle-shaped edged weapon, to the jezail, the Afghani long-rifle, and the achico, or South American bolus.[13]

Wolfe's eclecticism results in an image of South America, once considered as the New World, as the last refuge of the old. The extinct forms, suggesting biological regression, and the defamiliarised contemporary species, which imply evolutionary stagnation, seem to have migrated to South America's continental sand trap. Coexisting with military ranks and weaponry from across the globe, these creatures function collectively to establish the peculiar ambience of Wolfe's denuded fictional world.

Clearly, it is unnecessary for the reader to uncover the meaning of each obscure word for this atmosphere to be created. The historical associations register on one level or another to consolidate the text's themes and motifs of decay, inertia and temporal cyclicity. Any reader who fails to recognise the origins of baluchither, for example, will certainly understand the nature of tyrannosaur, mammoth or smilodon, and the same can be said for other lexical sets. Conversely, many of these nouns dangle invitingly before the reader, their unfamiliarity possessing the potential to induce efforts towards clarification. It is at this most elementary level that Wolfe's diction betrays its dual nature, its interpretatively obfuscatory and thematically revelatory qualities.

The eccentricity of Wolfe's diction, much of which enjoys no expository material in the text, may induce the reader into physically withdrawing from the narrative in an attempt to render it intelligible. The reader's scrutiny and deductive capacities are diverted to dictionaries or specialist encyclopaedias, further removing attention from the text itself. Wolfe himself encouraged this abstraction when he published *The Castle of the Otter* (1983), his book about *The Book of the New Sun*, which included a lexicon of obscure (and not so obscure) words from *The Shadow of the*

Torturer. The recent success of Michael Andre-Driussi's *Lexicon Urthus* seems to confirm that Wolfe's readers still feel a need for linguistic clarification.

It is probable that the reader may be displaced further from the text's story when his or her extratextual investigations yield apparently valuable information. Wolfe assists this displacement by embedding intimations within the text, which can only be revealed when his diction is either handled analogously to scientific data (as in the case of the extinct species and their allusions to a new phase of evolution), or has its connotations resolved through cross-referencing.

Several of Wolfe's proper names provide this kind of artificial reader reward. For example, the river Cephissus, which runs beyond the gardens of the House Absolute, enjoys certain mythical associations. Historically, Cephissus rose at Lilaea in Phocis, where it was the favoured place of the Graces, the goddesses who bestowed beauty and charm.[14] In *The Claw of the Conciliator*, the monstrous undine Juturna, a perversion of the Graces, tempts Severian on the bank of the fictional Cephissus with promises of an underwater kingdom and her companions as concubines. Juturna is named after Iuturna, the sister of Turnus, King of the Rutuli, who scorned Jupiter's affection but who, 'according to others, would not have been unfavourable to his passion'.[15]

Dubious parallels exist between the mythic Iuturna and Jupiter and the fictive Juturna and Severian. The reader comprehends that Severian's role as the New Sun identifies him with Jupiter, the supreme god of the Romans, whom they regarded as 'acquainted with everything, past, present and future', and whose 'worship was universal: he was the Ammon of the Africans, the Belus of Babylon, the Osiris of Egypt, etc.', all of whom were sun-figures of one form or another.[16]

Accordingly, Juturna's name generates a whirl of associational material that sustains the illusion that Severian is a genuine mythic figure, diverting the reader's attention from his status as the Hierogrammates' pawn. The reader feels that he or she has extracted a vital clue to Severian's nature when, in fact, the allusiveness of Wolfe's diction contributes to, and reinforces, the illusory nature of the pentalogy.

On other occasions, Wolfe's proper names contain elliptical indications of the operations being conducted on the level of the subtext. Several place names, when their meanings are deduced, prefigure events within the narrative, insinuating that future incidents have made themselves known in the past and thereby supporting the notion of 'reflective time' posited by Dr Talos in his allusion to Mary Shelley's *Frankenstein* (1818) (see *Sword*, p. 277). For example, the village name of Vici, from *vicis*, meaning change or alteration, or 'I conquered', indicates Severian's triumph when, returning from Yesod, he corrects a young girl's withered arm and begins to establish the myth of the Conciliator. Similarly, Liti, from *litigo*, a quarrel or contentious incident, alludes to Severian's betrayal and capture after he assumes his messianic role. Such prefigurations suggest that Severian's journey as the Conciliator has been carefully mapped out for him. Place names become indicators of the actions he will perform according to the Hierogrammates' plan, and vigorously undercut any suggestion that he possesses autonomy or free will.

The conflation of genuine but suppressed clues to the Hierogrammates' schemes and the obfuscatory effects of other associations ensures that the reader must make a constant effort to determine when examinations of Wolfe's language provide insights into the text and when he or she is being led astray either by disingenuous allusions or fruitless abstraction.

Wolfe attempts to prevent the reader from reaching this awareness by ensuring that his diction produces '[m]ythical, biblical, numerical, geographical, physical and metaphysical explanations [that] break down into a total overdetermination of meaning, which therefore become meaningless', but whose presence suggests the existence of a reducible meaning existing 'just over one's shoulder', beyond perception.[17] This apparently infinite regression of meaning is symbolised in the House Absolute's Hall of Meaning, where

> [t]here are two mirrors. Each is three or four ells wide, and each extends to the ceiling. There's nothing between the two except a few dozen strides of marble floor. In other words, anyone who walks down the Hall of Meaning sees himself infinitely multiplied there. Each mirror reflects the images of its twin. (*Shadow*, p. 181)

However, the presence of this hall does not indicate, as C. N. Manlove suggests, the constant deferral of any identifiable meaning in the text (which becomes clear once the story of The Urth Cycle is understood), but alludes to the dilatory operations occurring at the level of the individual signifier.

Wolfe invites the reader to assume that the meaning of his pentalogy is as unapprehendable as all the mythic, historic and metaphoric nuances of his obscure diction by equating his fictional cosmos with language. The Pancreator, he informs the reader through Severian, spoke 'the long word that is our universe' (*Sword*, p. 150), an image he develops into a further metaphor for 'a living vapour that seethed as I might have imagined the logos to writhe as it left the mouth of the Pancreator' (*Sword*, p. 280). The allusion to the Christian concept of the Logos, the Word of God and the Second Person of the Trinity, notwithstanding, Wolfe's refusal to capitalise *logos* invites a more secular reading of the Greek λόγος, in terms of 'the word by which the inward thought is expressed'.[18] Severian imagines this word to 'writhe' on utterance, undergoing a linguistic convulsion as it leaves 'the mouth of the Pancreator' that implies the tacit distortions that Wolfe (the Pancreator of the text) works on the relationship between signifier and signified.

Wolfe ensures that his referents writhe by investing them with an enforced polysemy, achieved through the appendix to *The Shadow of the Torturer* where he explains that the obscure nouns found in his 'translation' of The Urth Cycle are 'intended to be suggestive rather than definitive' (*Shadow*, p. 302). In this appendix, which, in a typical inversion, reads more like an introduction, Wolfe destabilises the status of his language; previously concrete nouns have their unequivocal meaning subverted by his 'translation'; they become indeterminate 'substitutions'.

This indeterminacy is thematised when the alien Cumaean observes: 'Death is nothing and for that reason you must fear it. What more is to be feared?' (*Claw*, p. 283). Her words stress the ambiguity of 'nothing' in a shift of emphasis that moves from representing 'nothing' as a dismissive adjective in 'death is nothing', to become that which signifies non-existence. By implication, this transition also underlines the equivocal nature of 'death' by suggesting the existence of two contrary philosophical stances that are represented by the changing connotations of 'nothing'. At first, death is rendered insignificant by the seeming repudiational power of 'nothing', which alludes, perhaps, to a transcendental view of death as transformation. Almost immediately, the Cumaean qualifies her statement, dispelling the transcendental vision by suggesting an atheistic view of death as the point at which existence and consciousness cease.

This linguistic uncertainty is constantly re-emphasised by Wolfe's puns on the vagueness of the meaning of everyday words: on 'present' in time and 'present' meaning gift (*Claw*, p. 33); on 'be-headed', suggesting both an act of execution and two-headedness (*Sword*, p. 202); and on 'waves of gravitation', pertaining, in context, to gravitational effects, but misapprehended by Severian's ageing autarchia, Valeria, as 'waves of dignity' (*Urth*, p. 271). At one point, Wolfe seems compelled to clarify his stressed homonymy in order to corroborate his point: 'My guards had become my guards, my jailers' (*Urth*, p. 271). Through the employment of these puns, Wolfe is not merely echoing Wittgenstein's observation that '[w]hen something seems queer about the grammar of our words, it is because we are alternately tempted to use a word in several different ways',[19] he is using his ambiguous diction to emblematise the slipperiness of form and symbol in the text.

By destabilising the meaning of his signifiers, Wolfe also ensures that his narrative can be perceived as a 'writerly' text in the Barthesian sense of containing linguistic deviations and indeterminacy of meaning.

Accordingly, The Urth Cycle may appeal to a post-structuralist reading since it displays a

> shift from meaning to staging, or from the signified to the signifier ... Broadly [it follows post-structuralism's] critique of ... the theory of the sign [as] post-structuralism fractures the serene unity of the stable sign and the unified subject.[20]

Equally, the text's obscure diction invites any deconstruction-oriented approach by showing

> the possibilities of writing no longer as a representation of something else but as the limitlessness of its own play. To deconstruct a text is not to search for its 'meaning', but to follow paths by which writing both sets up and transgresses its own terms, producing a semantic drift (dérive) of meaning.[21]

The Urth Cycle seems deliberately contrived to facilitate this kind of critical approach. Wolfe himself fosters a sense of play in his literary game with the reader, and his allusiveness not only entices a vision of limitlessness but also makes manifest a semantic drift generated by the plasticity of previously concrete nouns.

It could be argued that Wolfe is acting similarly to James Joyce (who once admitted of *Ulysses*: 'I have put in so many enigmas and puzzles that it will keep professors busy for centuries over what I meant, and that's the only way of ensuring one's immortality'[22]), by making his text capable of sustaining practicable post-structuralist and deconstructionist approaches, critical methods that remained in vogue during the writing of *The Book of the New Sun*. While this may seem improbable, Wolfe's appendix to *The Shadow of the Torturer* opens his text to such readings with a conciseness that seems unlikely to be coincidental.

Although Frank Kermode suggests that Joyce's strategy 'makes the surface of the narrative more like the surface of life', and would consequently support Robert Young's view of deconstruction as not removing 'the "world" but [demanding] that we rethink the terms in which we formulate it', it is possible that Wolfe is also making his text available to criticism to achieve exactly what Joyce suggested.[23] Indeed, Wolfe's attention to linguistic indeterminism ensures that his novel is particularly well suited to analyses based on the theory of the text advanced by Roland Barthes in his article, 'From Work to Text'. In this essay, Barthes sets out a series of conditions for differentiating between work and text. He posits that 'the work is concrete, occupying a portion of book space (in a library for example); the text, on the other hand, is a methodological field'. 'The work,' he suggests, 'is held in the hand, the text is held in language: it exists only as discourse ... *The text is experienced only in an activity, a production.*'[24]

This production is made conspicuous by Wolfe's use of archaic and unfamiliar diction. The reader's activity arises as a result of the gaps between the sense, or linguistic meanings, of the words in the context of the novel, and their referential meaning, namely what those words signify in the extra-literary world. When Wolfe suggests that his 'translation' is an approximation, his language generates a text that is

> not coexistence of meaning but passage, traversal; thus it answers ... to an explosion, a dissemination. The text's plurality does not depend on the ambiguity of the contents, but rather on what could be called the stereographical plurality of the signifiers that weave it (etymologically the text is a cloth, *textus*, from which the text derives, means 'woven').[25]

Wolfe's eclectic signifiers both fuel this explosion and establish a 'stereographical plurality' within the text (in a general sense) by their appearance out of context. For example, the peltast, or peltasti (from the Greek πελταστής), were lightly armed troops of the ancient world who derived their name from the small shield or pelta (Greek πέλτη) they carried. Wolfe adopts this noun to refer (and here the term is employed cautiously) to a soldier 'dressed in half armour, bearing a transparent shield [and carrying a] blazing spear'(*Shadow*, p. 132).

The reader experiences a temporally discordant noun which, despite reaching back into the Classical past, has been projected into the 'post-historic' future. The disparity between the reader's image of the Classical *peltasti* and the indistinct nature of the fictional peltast, or peltast-analogue, results in a gap that opposes a concise apprehension of what the word signifies. The reader is left with words as free substitutions that are already redundant in the English language of the early twenty-first century.

However, the phonetic connotations of 'peltast' succeed in prompting the reader to undertake, possibly subconsciously, a degree of activity and production. The first element of peltast, 'pelt-', nurtures a vague image of a warrior who throws a weapon (from pelt, the verb meaning to deliver blows or strike repeatedly with small missiles) and who may be attired in animal skins (from pelt, the noun for an animal skin with the wool, fur or hair attached). Consequently, the reader is confronted with the possibility of only partial interpretation. At the moment of estrangement, when the reader encounters an unfamiliar word, the Barthesian process of production begins.

On many occasions, this process of image-building remains unaided by such connotations and the intensity of the indeterminism is extreme. For example, Wolfe's extinct species are rarely described in detail:

As it was I had not seen a living animal, not so much as a garbage-eating thylacodon ... (*Shadow*, p. 38)

Hulking barylambdas, arctothers, the monarchs of bears, glyptodons, smilodons with fangs like glaives ... (*Shadow*, p. 43)

Around us swirled traffic of every sort: ... riders on the backs of dromedaries, oxen, metamynodons ... (*Shadow*, p. 164)

Recalling Patrick Parrinder's observation that 'where we perceive no grounds for analogy with the familiar we can perceive no meaning either', these nouns are barely comprehensible.[26] The reader is directed to reference works for clarification or else is distracted into producing an image of what is signified to fill the gap in the text's informational content.

Citing Vereker and Corvick, Wolfgang Iser, a German theoretician who specialises in the procedures and techniques of reading, remarks how '[t]he formulated text ... presents a pattern, a meaning [which] can only be grasped as an image. The image provides the filling for what the textual pattern structures but leaves out. Such a 'filling' represents a basic condition of communication.'[27]

In The Urth Cycle, Wolfe's reader can only associate the extinct creatures with a non-specific image of some form of animal within his or her imagination. This image can never be clarified due to the lack of a frame of reference and remains indistinct: 'the image itself cannot be related to any such frame, for it does not represent something that exists; on the contrary, it brings into existence something that is to be found neither outside the book nor on its printed page'.[28] In the case of Wolfe's prehistoric species, the beasts signified exist neither in the reader's contemporary realm nor in the text because their signifiers are only 'suggestive'.

The incorporation of Wolfe's reader into the process of production, of re-creation, arises from the asymmetry between the knowledge of the author/narrator and that of the reader. By denying many concrete nouns a definitive meaning, Wolfe creates outbreaks of indeterminacy which 'enable the text to "communicate" with the reader, in the sense that they induce him to participate both in the production and the comprehension' of the work.[29] Ironically, in The Urth Cycle, when the reader becomes involved in the production of linguistic meaning, the comprehension of what has been termed the text's 'shareable meaning'[30] (the vision of humanity as a deluded and manipulated species) is opposed.

Iser suggests that, in general, readers are drawn '[i]nto the events and [are encouraged to supply] what is meant by what is not said. What is said only appears to take on significance as a reference to what is not said; it is the implications and the statements that give shape and weight to the meaning.'[31] In The Urth Cycle, this encouragement functions to distract the reader's attention from the story driving the novel. With his usual sense of fair play, Wolfe covertly warns the reader against becoming lost in the creation of linguistic meaning when Severian remarks:

> The speaking of a word is futile unless there are other words. Words that are not spoken ... The powers we call dark seem to me to be the words the Increate did not speak, if the Increate exists at all; and these words must be maintained in a quasi-existence, if the other word, the spoken word, is to be distinguished. What is not said can be important—but what is said is more important. (*Sword*, p. 182)

Wolfe provides the reader with an ensconced clue not to be deceived by his 'stereographical plurality', his multiple allusions that are largely external to the text and of little use to an understanding of the narrative. On one level at least, Wolfe's 'dark powers' are the adumbrative effects of the author's obscure diction, which are experienced by any reader enticed into making connections between the text, the extraliterary realms of history, popular science, cosmology, and so on, and the critical theories to which Wolfe opens his text.

While Barthes's considerations of the text and Iser's gap theory seem to provide useful critical tools for analysing The Urth Cycle, they constitute an additional form of misdirection. Wolfe's narrative appears contrived to appeal to such approaches to conceal further the Hierogrammates' mythogenesis, the 'truth' inherent in the book, by suggesting that the pentalogy is part of a post-structuralist's philosophical quest for a 'perpetual detour towards a truth that has lost any status or finality'.[32]

More importantly, the text's Iserian gaps elicit a subjective vision of Urth from the reader. Each reader will, inevitably, construct a different mental image of a baluchither, or a peltast, or the diatrymae, and the unique nature of the images formed to fill the informational gaps in the text extends Wolfe's thematic concerns with subjectivity. Indeed, Wolfe suggests a connection between language and subjectivity when Severian visits the House Azure, a brothel in Nessus administered by the Autarch in one of his various guises. Here, Thecla's khaibit, or prostitute-clone, suggests that 'the Chatelaine Thecla is not the Chatelaine Thecla. Not the Chatelaine Thecla of your mind, which is the only one you care about. Neither am I. What, then, is the difference between us?' (*Shadow*, p. 94).

Aside from the khaibit's word game, in which she implies that two different objects, equally different from something else, are in fact the same, her repetition of 'Chatelaine Thecla' emphasises the 'existence' of four aspects of the character: the real Thecla, her khaibit, and their corresponding images in Severian's mind. The signifier 'Chatelaine Thecla' is a noun group whose psychological image is subjective and related to the Iserian images that the reader produces when confronted with an unfamiliar word.

'All of us, I suppose, when we think we are talking most intimately to someone else, are actually addressing an image we have of the person to whom we believe we speak' (*Sword*, pp. 77–78), Severian observes, his postulation on subjectivity an allusion to Proust's *Swann's Way*, which Wolfe has described as 'one of the best' psychological novels he has read:[33]

> None of us can be said to constitute a material whole, which is identical for everyone, and need only be turned up like a page in an account book or the record of a will; our social personality is created by thoughts of other people. Even the simple act which we describe as 'seeing someone we know' is, to some extent, an intellectual process. We pack the physical outline of the creature we see with all the ideas we have already formed about him … so that each time we see the face or hear the voice it is our own ideas of him we recognise and to which we listen.[34]

This thematic echo of an interpretative ploy is extended further when Severian suggests that the subjective nature of perceived reality is constructed through language. At the beginning of *The Shadow of the Torturer*, he remarks that 'Certain mystes aver that the real world has been constructed by the human mind, since our ways are governed by the artificial categories into which we place essentially undifferentiated things, things weaker than our words for them' (*Shadow*, pp. 11–12). Of course, Severian's 'real world', the world of fiction, has been constructed by the author's 'human mind'. Hence, Severian's comment reminds the reader that the text is a fiction and its philosophical quality is, therefore, inextricably linked with the narrative's playful metafictiveness.

The relationship of language to reality is a theme that Wolfe develops to formulate a series of thematic-interpretative echoes. Through the surreptitiously metalinguistic description of the white statue in the gardens of the House Absolute (*Claw*, pp. 116–17), Wolfe reminds the reader that he or she is 'in the realm of discourse, of the perception and interpretation of reality through language … "We only think the thoughts we have the words to express." Language structures and orders our perceptions.'[35]

Severian cannot describe the white statue adequately because he lacks a frame of reference, a vocabulary, which will order the 'reality' that confronts him. Like the reader, he finds himself faced by 'an ancient and terrible alphabet' (*Claw*, p. 116) he does not understand. Severian's inability to discover a coherent analogy means that he cannot 'convey the essence of the thing' and that the precise nature of the white statue remains as indeterminate to Severian (and, hence, the reader), as peltast or chiliarch or barylambdas do to the reader.

This indeterminism reflects Wittgenstein's notion that:

> We are tempted to think that the action of language consists of two parts; an inorganic part, the handling of signs, and an organic part, which we may call the understanding of these signs, meaning them, interpreting them, thinking. These latter activities seem to take place in a queer kind of medium, the mind; and the mechanism of the mind … can bring about effects which no material mechanism could. Thus e.g. a thought (which is such a mental process) can agree or disagree with reality.[36]

Wolfe dramatises this kind of communication theory when prisoners are brought to the torturers for punishment:

> Each client carried a copper cylinder supposedly containing his or her *papers* and thus his or her *fate*. All of them had read those *papers*, of course; and some had destroyed them or exchanged them for another's. Those who arrived without *papers* would be held until some further *word* concerning their disposition was received— probably for the remainder of their *lives*. Those who had exchanged *papers* with someone else had exchanged *fates*; they would be held or released, tortured or executed in another's stead. (*Shadow*, p. 35, with additional emphasis)

Throughout the passage, Wolfe associates the written word with fate. The prisoners' papers form an analogue of the inorganic element of Wittgenstein's hypothesis. When the orders are opened, destroyed or exchanged, the 'signs' are handled, quite literally, and the inorganic process is concluded. When the torturers receive their clients, the organic aspect begins as the orders are understood, interpreted, and start to shape the prisoners' realities, or lives, accordingly. In the case of those captives 'who had exchanged papers', and who had thereby 'exchanged fates', or realities, the actions of the torturers may not correspond with the punishment decreed originally by the judges. As a result, the torturers' thoughts 'can agree or disagree with reality'. This dramatisation implies that a linguistic exchange (here symbolised by the sealed orders) between two communicants may, by the indeterminism present in the exchange, result in two different perceptions of reality: one belonging to the judges, the other to the torturers. It is significant that those prisoners who arrive with no orders have their lives suspended, and their abstraction from the fictive world is terminated only when 'some further word' is received.

Wolfe's emphasis on how language can determine reality indicates his awareness of how his sleight of hand functions in the text's interaction with the reader. Juggling with analogies, it is possible to identify Wolfe with the prisoners' judges, the senders of a statement, the text with the sealed orders, and the reader with the torturers, the receivers of language. The duplicity of the prisoners who exchange or destroy their sentences (a pun, perhaps, on the grammatical 'sentence'?) represents the playful indeterminism present in the narrative's vocabulary.

The torturers do not concern themselves with the possibility of interpretation in their reception of the prisoners' sentences but follow their written instructions literally. In their literalness lies a clue as to how the reader can overcome the discursive effect of Wolfe's obscure diction, which can only be countered if the reader reads Wolfe's signifiers with a corresponding literalism.

In Shoshana Felman's opinion:

> The literal is 'vulgar' because it stops the movement constitutive of meaning, because it blocks and interrupts the endless process of metaphorical substitution. The vulgar is anything which misses, or falls short of, the dimension of the symbolic, anything which rules out, or excludes, meaning as a loss and as a flight—anything which strives to eliminate its inherent silence.[37]

It is the literal that is destabilised by Wolfe, who breaks down the relationship between signifier and signified, and lets the reader wander in the echoing silences, those areas of 'loss and flight', of indeterminate meaning.

Wolfe's signifieds 'writhe' because their signifiers are invested with a polysemy that expands Felman's 'silences'. Typically, this unvoiced but intrinsic equivocality is alluded to in Severian's conversation with the hetman of the floating islands, in which '[t]he words he said and the words I heard were quite different ... There was in his speech a hoard of hints, clues and implications as invisible to me as his breath' (Sword, p. 249). While this observation stresses Wolfe's thematic preoccupation with the subjective nature of perception, it also serves as a self-conscious suggestion of 'the hoard of hints, clues and implications' with which the author invests the text.

The *sub silentio* information contained in Wolfe's allusive language must be treated prudently, however. In The Claw of the Conciliator, Dorcas warns Severian against any 'dangerous, bad metaphor [that is] aimed at you like a lie' (Claw, p. 201), and the reader benefits from accepting her words as wise counsel against the duplicity of Wolfe's 'metaphors', his linguistic approximations and their implications. Many of Wolfe's allusions are dubious metaphors, aimed (like lies) to stimulate the reader into often fruitless research. An escape from this influence can only be effected if the reader withdraws slightly from the text, reacts unwillingly to the Barthesian 'dilatory' effect and withstands the temptation to become lost in the manifold silences of implication. By contextualising the superficial properties of Wolfe's unfamiliar language, the reader can determine the nondeflective, cumulative thematic effect of the author's diction, and free him- or herself from the invitation to explore an encyclopaedia of allusions external to, and often irrelevant to, an understanding of the text's metaphorical significance. Indeed, it is advantageous to recall that 'rational people know that things act of themselves or not at all' (*Shadow*, p. 17), that is, they act in context, in harmony with their own nature, regardless of their name.

9. 'There Are Doors': Memory and Textual Structure

The deflective effect of Wolfe's allusive diction is an essential element in the textual memory system that the author constructs using the dramatic action of his pentalogy. By recognising how Wolfe structures The Urth Cycle to produce this memory system, and by understanding how it functions, the reader learns how the text is designed to aid the recollection of its plot and of a range of extraliterary and intertextual information. Accordingly, the reader will also appreciate how the plot's patterning can oppose the recall of the novel's thematic nuances, how Wolfe creates a text planned (with perhaps little concern for success) to perpetuate his name, and how the author uses esoteric means to further convince the reader that Severian is a saviour invested with genuine holy power.

In the organisation of this memory system, as in *Peace*, Wolfe follows the principles of the Classical art of memory. As Frances Yates documents in her study *The Art of Memory* (1966), Classical mnemonic strategies

> imprint on the memory a series of loci or places ... The clearest description of this process is that given by Quintilian. In order to form a series of places in memory, he says, a building is to be remembered, as spacious and varied a one as possible, the forecourt, the living rooms, bedrooms, and parlours, not omitting statues and other ornaments with which the rooms are decorated. The images by which the speech [for example] is to be remembered ... are then placed in imagination on the places which have been memorised in the building. This done, as soon as the memory of the facts requires to be revived, all these places are visited in turn and the various deposits demanded of their custodians.[1]

Like the Classical orators, who used such mentally constructed architectural locations to site their mnemonic images, Wolfe arranges the narrative events of The Urth Cycle to form the architecture of a written memory system.

The *Ad C. Herennium libri IV*, an anonymous work on the art of memory, advises that the locations, or loci, in which the orator situates his mnemonic images, should be varied, since any resemblance between them will lead inevitably to confusion.[2] This counsel provides a possible explanation for the diversity of fictional settings that Severian encounters during his odyssey. In many of Wolfe's other texts, particularly the mid-western novels (*Free Live Free*, *There Are Doors* and *Castleview*), the fictional locations are not greatly differentiated; they are nondescript streets or dreary tenements, grey cities or patches of countryside. Conversely, in The Urth Cycle, Severian is constantly moving from one contrasting location to the next, from the monastic Matachin Tower to the varied streets of the city beyond, from the rag shop to the Sanguinary Field, from the city wall to the wider Commonwealth.

The correlation of the dramatic incidents that transpire in each of these contrasting locations partakes of Aristotle's principles of association and, hence, order through similarity, dissimilarity and contiguity. Through these laws, Aristotle describes how, by starting from something similar, contrary or related to the information an individual wishes to remember, he or she will recall it without difficulty.[3]

Wolfe appropriates these Aristotelian principles in his deployment of the similarities, counterpoints and contiguities that coordinate mnemonically the events of each successive chapter of The Urth Cycle. While the application of these rules reflects the associational qualities of Severian's memory, identifying him with clinically examined mnemonists (including Luria's S.), it also facilitates the reader's recollection of the narrative's plot.

The inversions, parallels, repeated motifs and juxtapositions that characterise The Urth Cycle are most apparent in *The Shadow of the Torturer*. The novel begins and ends with Severian at the threshold of a gate, a feature to which Wolfe draws attention when his narrator observes: 'Here I pause, having carried you, reader, from gate to gate—from the locked and fog-shrouded gate of our necropolis to this gate with its curling wisps of smoke …' (p. 301). This image recalls the 'wisps of river fog threading [the spikes of the gate into the necropolis] like mountain paths …' (p. 9), which, in turn, alludes to the route that Severian will follow in *The Sword of the Lictor*.

This pattern is repeated in each volume of *The Book of the New Sun*: *The Claw of the Conciliator* begins and ends in a stone town; the events recounted in *The Sword of the Lictor* are contained between Severian's presence in two fortresses which are, in effect, symbolic gateways; and *The Citadel of the Autarch* concludes the design 'having carried [the reader] from gate to gate—from the locked and fog-shrouded gate of the necropolis to that cloud-racked gate we call the sky …' (*Citadel*, p. 313). The image of the gate at the beginning of *The Shadow of the Torturer* provides a logical point of entry into the text since the image of a gate or portal is often associated with passage into a realm of great significance.[4] Accordingly, the necropolis gate has the important mnemonic function of aiding the reader's recollection of how the pentalogy begins.

Having provided the reader with a symbol sufficiently potent to keep the opening sequence of the novel clear in his or her mind, Wolfe then patterns the novel's chapter sequence using Aristotle's laws of association to enable the reader to recall the narrative from memory. For example, Severian's position at the gate in Chapter I prompts the reader's recollection of the events that brought him to that portal, which are the subject of Chapter II. The reader will remember the incidents of the second chapter as a result of bringing the first to mind, but may reorient them chronologically in his or her imagination. Chapter II relates how Severian was saved, 'resurrected', after almost drowning in the river Gyoll. This Jungian image of rebirth (emphasised by the difficulty Severian experiences in reentering the nurturing 'womb' of the Matachin Tower), when recalled sequentially, prefigures the concluding events of Chapter I, 'Resurrection and Death'.

These events invert the details of Severian's watery rebirth as Vodalus the outlaw disinters, or raises from the earth, the dead woman he intends to cannibalise. Severian's encounter with Vodalus also establishes what becomes a recurrent (and therefore mnemonic) numerical motif in the tetralogy, that of a group of two women (Thea and the corpse) and three men (Severian, Vodalus and Hildegrin).

In Chapter III, Wolfe inverts the image of a woman being disentombed by describing the imprisonment, the symbolic entombment, of Thecla's maid, Hunna, below the Matachin Tower. The description of Hunna's flayed leg functions mnemonically to provoke the reader's recollection of Severian's subsequent discovery, in Chapter IV, of the punningly named Triskele, the injured fighting dog whose shattered leg Severian removes and sutures in an operation antithetical to the torturers' infliction of a related injury on Hunna.

When the reader remembers Severian's discovery of Triskele, the animal's general symbolic function as a traditional guiding figure prompts the reader's recall of how Triskele abandons his rescuer and inadvertently leads him to the Atrium of Time and Valeria at the conclusion of Chapter IV.[5] Wolfe contrasts the unsolicited journey that Severian makes in pursuit of Triskele with the assigned duty he must perform for Master Gurloes in Chapter V. Gurloes sends Severian to the Library of Nessus to borrow books from Thecla. Recalling this venture to the library not only provides a framework on which Severian's encounters with Sieur Racho and Rudesind the Picture-Cleaner can be located but also prepares the reader for his meeting with Thecla in Chapter VII.

Wolfe's employment of similarity, counterpoint, and logical and chronological contiguity persists through *The Shadow of the Torturer* and the remaining volumes of The Urth Cycle, producing a narrative that can be reconstructed, with comparative ease, almost entirely from memory. This reconstruction is assisted by the deployment of Wolfe's dramatis personae, which does not depend on the introduction of new characters but on the constant reintroduction of the same characters who reveal different aspects of their personalities. While this technique sustains continuity, it also serves a mnemonic function: the reappearance of familiar characters provides a series of loci around which the events of the narrative can be gathered and reappropriated from memory.

This reappropriation is assisted by the embedded stories, 'The Tale of the Student and His Son' (*Claw*, pp. 142–59) and 'The Tale of a Boy Called Frog' (*Sword*, pp. 146–57) which, together with the play 'Eschatology and Genesis', serve as abstracts of the text's plot, abetting its recall by providing parallels with its development.

Into this carefully patterned narrative 'architecture' Wolfe inserts his images, his allusive words, intertextual references and so forth. He provides a variety of short asides to topics including evolution (*Claw*, pp. 53–54), the nature of courage (*Claw*, pp. 56–59), and the difficulties of siting prisons effectively (*Sword*, pp. 10–11), all of which are introduced at suitable points in the narrative. Severian's thoughts on evolution occur as he struggles with the degenerate man-apes; his analysis of courage appears when he is outnumbered by the creatures; and his examination of the problems of incarceration are provided shortly after he has taken charge of the vincula in Thrax. By situating these discursive thoughts at points where Severian's physical location and experiences are likely to arouse such contemplations, Wolfe ensures that his text encompasses a variety of extraliterary considerations in a logical manner.

In addition to these more substantial asides, every place name, character appellation, word and deed in The Urth Cycle is associated with an event or element that exists, or has existed, in the non-fictional world. Each has, therefore, the potential to function as a mnemonic image. This encyclopaedism reflects how Wolfe, when writing the novel, sought to 'encompass the entire universe'.[6]

If the reader is prepared to pursue Wolfe's references to evolution, Greco-Roman social and military history, the Byzantine Empire, Victorian geological theory and twentieth-century physics, he or she will find his or her knowledge of these subjects increased remarkably. Similarly, through the deployment of intertexts, Wolfe encourages the reader to revisit, or recall, the work of Mary Shelley, Lewis Carroll, H. G. Wells, Jack Vance, Rudyard Kipling, Marcel Proust, Jorge Luis Borges, Charles Dickens and many others.

Hence, within The Urth Cycle, 'so strong is the power of association' (*Claw*, p. 30) that a single word, or image, might carry 'the meaning of ten thousand' (*Urth*, p. 173). By cross-referencing each allusion, by uncovering the resonances of every word and name, the reader understands that Wolfe's text constitutes a library of images that serves as a means of remembering a significant portion of the extraliterary world.

Severian, for example, is one of the most potent mnemonic images found in the narrative. As the Conciliator and the New Sun he embodies the characteristics of a variety of religious and mythological sun/son figures including the Sky Father, Oshatsh the Sun, of the Pueblo Indians; the Egyptian Aten, the physical manifestation of the power and being of the stars; the Unique Inca, Intip Cori, the son of the Sun; the Mayan Ahau, or Sun God who, like Severian, was identified as much with darkness as with light; the Indian sun god Surya, the husband of Ushas, the Dawn (which Wolfe makes more explicit by naming the reborn Urth Ushas); Helios and Apollo; Christ, whose birth is commemorated near the winter solstice when the Brumalia, the feast of the birth of the unconquered sun, was celebrated; and, perhaps, most importantly, Lucifer, the Bringer of Light and the Morning Star, an association that implies the duality of Severian's character: is he humanity's saviour, or its devil?[7] When the reader uncovers these connections, Severian stands at the hub of a vast web of information relating to humanity's mythical/spiritual relationship with the sun, and comes to serve as an image through which this information can be retrieved.

Wolfe's memory system becomes complete with the interaction of the structured narrative and the images it incorporates. As a pattern, the text provides a series of loci that preserve the order of the information to be recalled while Wolfe's allusions designate the information itself.

It seems probable that this memory system was conceived with a number of related purposes in mind. Primarily, it demonstrates Severian's associative thinking, which the text's allusiveness encourages the reader to adopt until he or she, like Severian, perceives a wealth of superfluous detail rather than the Hierogrammates' selfish motives. Similarly, the narrative's patterned progression, the parallels and contrasts which aid the recollection of its plot, further diffuses the reader's attempts to reflect on the implications of that plot by forever slipping from one narrative incident to the next. As one fictional encounter is recalled, its association with a subsequent or a preceding event leads to its replacement in the reader's memory with another episode which, in turn, provokes further images. Eventually, unless the reader concentrates determinedly, a point is reached where the associative images begin to guide a reader's thought processes (just as they guide those of a mnemonist), actually replacing thought as the governing cognitive element.

By constructing a mnemonically patterned, encyclopaedic text, Wolfe not only seeks to restructure the reader's thought processes until he or she adopts (or appreciates) the psychological characteristics of a mnemonist but also attempts to guarantee that The Urth Cycle endures in the reader's memory. Wolfe's allusions, like all intertextual and extraliterary references, exist in a dual relationship with their source material. Just as the narrative embraces elements from the Bible, Hindu mythology and Borges's stories, so the Bible, Hindu mythology and Borges's stories all reflect facets of The Urth Cycle. All intertextual references, as Michael Riffaterre points out, 'belong equally in text and intertext, linking the two, and signalling to each the presence of their mutually complementary traits'. The quotations and allusions found in Wolfe's pentalogy are no exception. They are, in Riffaterre's terms, 'signposts' or 'connectives', which are mutually reflective.[8]

Through the intensity of his allusive references, Wolfe ensures that his text is inescapable; wherever the reader turns he or she is constantly reminded of Severian's odyssey because, just as the novel alludes to the 'universe', so the 'universe' alludes back to Severian's odyssey. For example, when Jonas remarks, 'The White Knight is sliding down the poker. He balances very badly, as the King's notebook told him' (*Claw*, p. 137), Wolfe makes an intertextual reference to Chapter 1 of Carroll's *Through the Looking Glass and What Alice Found There* (1872). Accordingly, if the reader of Carroll is familiar with Wolfe's pentalogy, Chapter 1 of *Through the Looking Glass* will, inevitably, contain an allusion to *The Claw of the Conciliator*. This mutual connectivity works for every intertextual and extraliterary reference that Wolfe weaves into The Urth Cycle; and when the reader's attention is guided back to Wolfe's text by such a reference, the mnemonic patterning of the narrative can prompt the recall of the entire pentalogy.

Wolfe seems to want his novel remembered, asking his readers, implicitly, as Fiola asks Severian in *The Citadel of the Autarch*, to remember: 'The rest [of the storytellers and their audience] are dead', Fiola explains on her deathbed. 'You will be the only one who remembers Severian ... I want you to tell other people' (*Citadel*, p. 145).

In a sequence of novels that seemingly deal with transcendence, Wolfe is apparently seeking his own kind of immortality through the intermediary of art. While this may seem unlikely, Severian's observations concerning the 'higher truth' of the alzabo affirm the supposition:

> At last I decided that it [the alzabo] might be likened to the absorption by the material world of the thoughts and acts of human beings who, though no longer living, have so imprinted it with activities that in the wider sense we may call works of art, ... that for some time after their demise it may be said to carry forward their lives. (*Sword*, p. 216)

Considering Severian's speculation from this perspective, it seems that the reader is cast into the role of the alzabo, consuming Wolfe's work just as the creature consumes Casdoe's family, until the text resides irremovably within the reader's memory, even beyond Wolfe's own physical death.

Wolfe's memory system does not, however, operate solely as a means by which the author can satisfy, or perhaps, pacify, himself with thoughts of having 'imprinted' the world with a work that will 'carry forward' his life. The narrative structure of The Urth Cycle appears mapped on, while inverting, the symbolism of the pre-existing memory system devised by the sixteenth-century Italian scholar Giulio Camillo, and this has important, although abstruse, implications for Severian's characterisation.

John Clute first made this connection when he remarked that, 'Like Funes the Memorious in Borges' story, Severian cannot forget anything ... so The Book [of the New Sun] which tells his life is like a Theatre of Memory, where everything stands for something else, where everything is a relic' (Strokes, p. 152). Although Clute may have employed the 'Theatre of Memory' analogy as a convenient metaphor without realising its implications, his comment stresses the abiding allusiveness that associates the text with Camillo's own Memory Theatre.

Inverting the structure of the semicircular Vitruvian theatre, Camillo's memory system rose from a small stage in seven grades or steps, divided by seven gangways representing the seven planets. On each of the seven gangways were seven gates, and on each gate were located a series of mnemonic images. The theatre was not designed for an audience; rather, the solitary observer would stand on the 'stage', looking up at the 49 gates rising on the seven tiers. These gates are the mnemonic loci for the memory images perceivable from the stage.[9]

Resting on the Seven Pillars of Solomon's House of Wisdom, and uniting the 'three worlds of the Cabalists, as Pico Della Mirandolla had expounded them; the supercelestial world of the Sephiroth, or divine emanations, the middle celestial world of the stars; [and] the subcelestial or the elemental world', the purpose of Camillo's theatre was to represent 'the order of eternal truth; in it the universe will be remembered through the organic association of all its parts with their underlying eternal order'.[10]

Hence, Camillo's theatre

> represents the universe expanding from First Causes through the stages of creation. First is the appearance of the simple elements from the waters of the Banquet grade; then the mixture of the elements in the Cave; then the creation of man's *mens* in the image of God in the grade of the Gorgon Sisters; then the union of man's soul and body on the grade of Pasiphe and the Bull; then the whole world of man's activities on the grade of the Sandals of Mercury; his

arts and sciences, religion and laws on the Prometheus grade.
Though there are unorthodox elements ... in Camillo's system, his
grades contain obvious reminiscences of the orthodox days of
creation.[11]

Since Wolfe, like Camillo, wished to 'encompass the entire universe', it is,
perhaps, not surprising that there are significant overlaps between the
narrative events of The Urth Cycle and the symbolism of Camillo's
theatre, as depicted in Frances Yates's translation in *The Art of Memory*.
Although Wolfe suggests, with his usual irony, that he 'cannot remember'
reading Yates's work,[12] The Urth Cycle reverses the theatre's development
outward from First Causes to the complexities of the Prometheus grade
during Severian's exile, and his adoption of the role of the Conciliator,
with surprising consistency.

Tables 3 to 7 reproduce the symbolism of the 49 gates on the seven tiers
of Camillo's theatre and add, in italics, the narrative events of The Urth
Cycle that mirror these symbols either literally or metaphorically. For
example, the outermost, or Prometheus grade, encompasses a selection of
equivalents to features from Chapter I through Chapter X of *The Shadow of
the Torturer*. The symbol of the elephant, representing religion, myth, rites
and ceremonies, suggests the monastic life of the Matachin Tower.
Severian's relationship with Thecla is implied in the image of the hymen,
signifying weddings and relationships. More explicitly, the minotaur, which
emblematises the vicious arts, brothels and the sensual arts of the prostitute,
seems to anticipate not only the torturers' 'art' but also Severian's visit to
the House Azure in Nessus. Even Master Ultan's wry comment concerning
Severian's poor grammar (p. 56) appears anticipated by the image of the
boy with the alphabet, signifying the art of grammar in Camillo's system.
Correspondences such as these can be traced through the grades. The
Sandals of Mercury tier corresponds to *The Shadow of the Torturer*, Chapters
XI to XIV; the grade of Pasiphe and the Bull reflects Severian's adventures
from *The Shadow of the Torturer*, Chapter XV to *The Citadel of the Autarch*,
Chapter XXXVIII; the level of the Gorgon Sisters parallels the first 27
chapters of *The Urth of the New Sun*; the symbolism of the Cave grade
resembles the events of Chapters XXVIII to XLIII; the Banquet tier approxi-
mates to Chapters XLIV through L; and the reversed Banquet section in
the central aisle of the theatre compares favourably with the concluding
fifty-first chapter of *The Urth of the New Sun*.

The juxtaposing of the Banquet grade with that of the planets is
accounted for by Yates, who explains:

the planet images, and the characters of the planets, which are placed
on the first grade are to be understood, not as termini beyond which

we cannot rise, but as also representing, as they do in the minds of the wise, the seven celestial measures above them. [Accordingly in Yates's translation, this idea is indicated] by showing on the gates of the first or lowest grade, the characters of the planets, their names (standing for their images) and then the names of the Sephiroth and the angels which Camillo associates with each planet. To bring out the importance of Sol, he varies the arrangement in this case by representing the sun on the first grade ... placing the image of the planet, an Apollo, above this on the second grade.[13]

The plot development of The Urth Cycle parallels Camillo's inversion. The sun imagery within the Apollo section fits comfortably with the surrounding six segments of the Banquet tier, which form metaphorical equivalents to the events related in Chapters XLIV to L of *The Urth of the New Sun*, including the deluge that destroys Urth, Severian's retelling of his tale to Eata, and the near-idyllic life he finds in the Inca village, where he dwells as Apu Punchau. The image of Vulcan corresponds to the New Sun, while the simple element of earth is a metaphorical allusion to the less complex past in which Severian finds himself, where the planet's landscape and cultures have not been shaped by a long succession of human civilisations.

The dislocated central gate of the Banquet level, positioned in the first grade of the theatre, with its inclusion of Cause, Beginning and End, symbolises, respectively, Severian as the Hierogrammates' representative—the cause of the change—the birth of Ushas, the end of Urth, and the close of the narrative.

Wolfe's apparent inversion of the theatre's expansion from First Causes represents an undoing of creation. Severian's movement from the strict order of his guild to his eventual trial, the granting of the New Sun, his metaphoric 'star-soul', and the rebirth of Ushas, all mark a gradual dismantling of the old creation, a return to the simple elements of fire (the New Sun), water (the flood), and earth (the re-emergent fertile land of Ushas) in preparation for the new.

The affinity between The Urth Cycle and Camillo's Memory Theatre suggests that Wolfe may have used the theatre as a blueprint for his plotting. However, the similarity of the two systems may arise not from any conscious appropriation by Wolfe but from the fact that the creators of these systems share a familiarity with archetypes, cosmologies, mythologies and symbolism.

The parallels that do exist may be nothing more than coincidences developing from this eclecticism and the importance of the sun to each construction. For example, in the central aisle on the Cave grade of his theatre, Camillo places '[t]he Cock and the Lion—the Solar Virtue possessed

Table 3 The correspondences between the symbolism of the Prometheus grade of Camillo's Memory Theatre and the narrative events of Chapters I–X of The Shadow of the Torturer

Prometheus	Prometheus	Prometheus	Prometheus	Prometheus	Prometheus	Prometheus
Diana and the Garment – the months and their parts: *the 'garden' of the necropolis in Nessus* (p. 21). Hymen – weddings and relationships: *Severian's relationship with Thecla* (pp. 69–103).	Elephant – religion, its myths, rites and ceremonies: *the monastic life of the Matachin Tower* (pp. 10–103). Hercules shooting arrow with three points – libraries: *Severian's visit to the library of the Citadel* (pp. 56–67). Iris and Mercury – letter writing: *Gurloe's letter to Ultan* (pp. 56–57). Three Pallases – painting and perspective: *Severian's encounter with Rudesind and his perspective on the astronaut* (pp. 50–53).	Hercules cleaning the Aegian stables – arts of cleaning and bathing: *Severian's swim in the Gyoll* (pp. 24–27) *and the Bell Keep* (pp. 22–23). Minotaur – vicious arts, ruffianism, brothels, arts of prostitutes: *'art' of torture* (pp. 29–30), *the House Azure and Thecla's khaibit* (pp. 87–94).	Geryon killed by Hercules – minutes, hours, years, art of clock-making: *Severian's visit to the Atrium of Time* (pp. 42–46). The Cock and the Lion – rule, government and its appurtenances: *function of the torturers in the Autarchial system.* Apollo and the Muses – Poetry: *Severian's rhyme of concealment* (p. 32). Apollo and the Python – the whole art of medicine: *Severian's rescue and salvation of Triskele* (pp. 37–42).	Rhadamanthus – criminal law: *the torturers as arm of the law.* The Furies – prisons, tortures, punishments: *the Matachin Tower and the excruciation of Thecla's Maid, Hunna* (pp. 29–30).	Europa on the Bull – conversion, consent, holiness, humility, religion: *life in the Matachin Tower.* Judgement of Paris – civil law: *the torturers as a cornerstone of the law.*	Boy with alphabet – grammar: *Ultan's comment to Severian on his poor grammar* (p. 56). Ass – animal of Saturn – porterage: *Severian's life as a young apprentice.*

Table 4 *The correspondences between the symbolism of the Sandals of Mercury grade of Camillo's Memory Theatre and the narrative events of Chapters XI –XIV of* The Shadow of the Torturer

Sandals of Mercury	Sandals of Mercury	Sandals of Mercury	Sandals of Mercury	Sandals of Mercury	Sandals of Mercury	Sandals of Mercury
Neptune – crossing water: *Severian crossing the Gyoll (pp. 31–35).* Diana and the Garment – changing things: *Severian departing the Guild (pp. 120–31).* Juno in the Clouds – hiding things: *Severian concealing the knife for Thecla (p. 118).* Prometheus with the Ring – gratitude: *Severian's thankfulness for his salvation (pp. 120–27)*	Atoms – diminishing, dissolving, discontinuing: *Severian's exile (pp. 104–10) and exile.* Pyramid – raising, lowering: *Severian's elevation (pp. 104–10) and exile.* Juno as Cloud – deceiving: *Severian's deception of the Guild by permitting Thecla to die (pp. 118–19).*	Cerberus – eating, drinking, sleeping: *the Feast of St. Katherine (pp. 104–10).* Tantalus Under the Rock – to vacillate: *the Guild's indecision over Severian's fate (pp. 121–23).* Minotaur – vicious operations: *Thecla's excruciation on the Revolutionary (pp. 117–18).*	Golden Chain – stretching out towards the sun: *the beginning of Severian's exile.* Cock and Lion – giving place to: *Severian made Lictor of Thrax (pp. 123–26).* The Fates – causing, beginning, ending: *Severian's exile as beginning and ending.* Apollo shooting at Juno in the Clouds – manifestation and bringing to light of persons or things: *the beginning of Severian's role as the Conciliator.*	Mars on a Dragon – hurting, being cruel: *Thecla on the Revolutionary (pp. 116-8).* Vulcan Strking Fire: *the Revolutionary itself.*	Minotaur Killed by Theseus – exercising virtue: *Severian's gift of the knife to Thecla (p. 119).* The Graces – exercising beneficence: *Severian permitting Thecla to die quickly (p. 119).*	Proteus Bound – making immobile: *Severian's imprisonment (pp. 120–21).* Solitary Sparrow: *abandoning – exile.* Pandora – causing tribulation: *Severian's fear of execution.*

Table 5 *The correspondences between the symbolism of the Pasiphe and the Bull Grade of Camillo's Memory Theatre and the narrative events of* The Book of the New Sun *from Chapter XV of* The Shadow of the Torturer *to Chapter XXXVIII of* The Citadel of the Autarch

Pasiphe and the Bull	*Pasiphe and the Bull*	*Pasiphe and the Bull*	*Pasiphe and the Bull*	*Pasiphe and the Bull*	*Pasiphe and the Bull*	*Pasiphe and the Bull*
Girl descending through Cancer – descent of soul into body: *Severian's ingestion of Thecla's and the Autarch's memories* (Claw, pp. 98–100 *and* Citadel, pp. 234–36). Diana and the Garment – mutation in man: *the man-apes* (Claw, pp. 48–55). Juno in the Clouds – hidden things in man: *Severian destined to be Autarch.*	Atoms – discrete quality in man: *Severian as Autarch.* Juno as Cloud: false, dissimulating character: *Agia, Agilus, Jolenta, Dr Talos, Baldanders, Dorcas and Severian himself.* Ixion on the Wheel – moral cares, labours: *Severian's exile.*	Cerberus – hunger, thirst, sleep: *Severian's hardships during exile.* Narcissus – beauty of the body, love, desire: *Agia, Jolenta, Dorcas and (especially) Jolenta.* Minotaur – nature inclined to vice: *Dr Talos and Baldanders.* Tantalus – timid nature: *Dorcas.*	Geryon killed by Hercules – Age of Man: *Severian's journey and presentation as Man* (Sword, p. 223). Cock and Lion – excellence, superiority, dignity, dominion of man: *Severian as Lictor and Autarch.* Apollo Shooting at Juno in the Clouds – bringing to light of man: *Severian's 'growth' or movement towards the Autarchy.*	Headless Man: mad, furious nature: *Baldanders and Typhon.* Two Fighting Serpents – contentious nature: *Agilus and Severian, and Ascia and the Commonwealth at war.*	Caduceus – friendly nature, including to care for the family: *Severian's attempt to protect Casdoe's family* (Sword, pp. 110–96).	Heads of Wolf, Lion and Dog – man under time: *old Urth.* Endymion Kissed by Diana – mystical union, death and funerals: *Severian's unions with Thecla and the Autarch and his encounter with Apu Punchau in the Stone Town.*

Table 6 *The correspondences between the symbolism of Gorgon Sisters grade of Camillo's Memory Theatre and the narrative events of Chapters I–XXVII of* The Urth of the New Sun

Gorgon Sisters	Gorgon Sisters	Gorgon Sisters	Gorgon Sisters	Gorgon Sisters	Gorgon Sisters	Gorgon Sisters
Girl drinking from the cup of Bacchus – human oblivion, ignorance, stupidity: *Severian's acceptance of the Hierogrammates' apparent holiness – his inability to grasp the truth.*	Torch of Prometheus – human intellect, ability in learning: *Hierogrammates as the product of human ingenuity and intellect.*	Eurydice Stung on the Foot by a Serpent – human will, affectations, governed by the will: *Severian's affection for Urth which aids his faith in the Hierogrammates' schemes.*	Golden Bough – the Intellectus Agens: Nessamah, or the highest part of the soul, the rational soul; spirit and life: *Severian's discovery of his role as 'the New Sun' as a 'saviour' with a 'star soul'.*	Dido with unshod foot – hasty and rash decisions: *Severian's impulsive response to his show-trial on Yesod: his total faith in the Hierogrammates.*	Stork Flying Heavenward with Caduceus in Beak: heavenward flight of the tranquil soul – choice, judgement, counsel: *Severian's journey to, and experiences on, Yesod (Urth, pp. 1-176).*	Hercules raising Antheus – struggle between human spirit and human body: *battle between Severian's memories and the sailors (Urth, pp. 154–55).* Girl Rising Through Capricorn – ascent of the soul towards Heaven: *flight to Yesod.*

Table 7 The correspondences between the symbolism of The Cave, Banquet and First Cause grades of Camillo's Memory Theatre and the narrative events of Chapters XXVIII–LI of The Urth of the New Sun

The Cave	The Cave	The Cave	The Cave	The Cave	The Cave	The Cave
Neptune and Water as mixed element: *the Flood* (pp. 309–42). Aegian Stables – imperfection in the world: *Urth 'corrupted' by time* (pp. 209–81).	Pyramid – continuous quality in things: *Urth's renewal.* Juna as Cloud – false appearances: *Severian and Ceryx as false prophets.*	Hercules Cleaning Aegian Stables – things clean by nature: *Urth cleansed.* Tantalus under the rock – impending things: *the Flood.*	Argus – whole world vivified by the stars: *The New Sun and the Flood.* Cock and Lion – Camillo's solar virtue shown by his power over a lion: *Severian's power over a smilodon* (pp. 276–80).	Two fighting serpents – discord, difference: *Severian and the Commonwealth's authorities* (pp. 245–81).	Horns of the Lyre – sound carried on air: *flood warning and flood* (pp. 295–308). Caduceus: serpents united – *unity of destruction in flood.*	Heads of Wolf, Lion, Dog – Past, Present and Future: *Severian's time travelling.* Pandora – Affliction of Things: *the 'sickness' of Urth.*

Banquet	Banquet	Banquet	Banquet	Banquet	Banquet	Banquet
Proteus – materia prima or chaos: *Ocean as symbol of chaos.* Neptune: water as simple element: *post-deluge Ocean.*	Elephant – fables of the gods: *Severian tells his story to Eata* (p. 329); *his role as Apu Punchau.*	Sphere with Ten Circles – Paradise: *the Inca Village* (pp. 343-51).	Apollo, the Sun, Anima Mundi, Spiritus Mundi: *Severian as the New Sun and Apu Punchau.*	Vulcan – fire as simple element: *the New Sun.* Mouth of Tartarus – Purgatory: *Severian's guilt* (Urth, p. 331).	Europa and the Bull – body and soul: *Severian as Apu Punchau and as an aquastor.*	Earth as simple element: *the less complex past.*

			Banquet			
Diana Margut Gabriel	Mercury Iesod Michael	Venus Hodnisach Honiel	Pan: the three worlds: *Urth, Yesod, Ushas.*	Mars Gabiarah Camael	Jupiter Chesed Zadkiel	Saturn Bina Zaphchiel

by the author of the Theatre shown by his power over a lion', an authority reflected in Severian's mastery over a smilodon, a sabre-toothed cat, in *The Urth of the New Sun* (pp. 276–80). Wolfe need not have encountered Camillo's theatre to know that Leo, the lion of astrology, has as its planet the sun to incorporate such an allusion into his text to suggest Severian's own 'solar virtue'.

However coincidental the connections between these two systems may be, the purpose of Camillo's theatre provides a further insight into Wolfe's decision to make Severian a mnemonist. Despite appearing as a 'highly ornate filing system' with drawers crammed with symbols, the theatre encompasses the notion of organically uniting an individual's memory with the cosmos as a whole.[14]

Infused with the Renaissance's 'occult philosophy', Camillo integrated his beliefs with the principles of the Classical art of memory to claim that he was capable of remembering the structure of the universe. Accordingly, the human individual, the microcosm, could fully recall the macrocosm.[15] By achieving this, Camillo believed that he could gain divine powers as '[t]he magic of celestial proportion flows from his world memory into the magical words of his oratory and poetry'.[16]

Unlike Camillo and Wolfe, who both have a clear objective in mind, Severian creates his memory system unconsciously as a result of his encyclopaedic memory and his tendency to think associatively. The existence of this memory system in The Urth Cycle does not, therefore, indicate that Severian has divine powers, achieved through a conscious effort to grasp 'the world'. Rather, it is Wolfe who creates the memory system to suggest, albeit esoterically, that Severian can both fully understand and fully remember the macrocosm, holding it within his 'divine' memory.

Towards the conclusion of *The Urth of the New Sun*, Severian is resurrected (reconstituted, the reader is told, from memories lying latent in his dying mind) for a second time, and speaks to his Hierodule advisers Ossipago, Barbatus and Famulimus in the tomb constructed for Apu Punchau:

> Barbatus' pleasant baritone flouted the gloom. 'You're conscious. What do you remember?'
> 'Everything,' I said. 'I've always remembered everything.'
> Dissolution was in the air, the fetor of rotting flesh.
> Famulimus sang. 'For that were you chosen, Severian. You and you alone to save your race from Lethe.' (*Urth*, p. 353)

Famulimus's explanation for Severian's selection contradicts that offered earlier by Apheta, who suggests that he was chosen 'to save the world' because he was a torturer and would, therefore, not flinch from being party to a scheme that meted out the harshest justice and destroyed Urth (see *Urth*, p. 161). Famulimus's comments encourage the reader to believe that Severian's mnemonism was instrumental in his recruitment by the Hierogrammates, not because it rendered him incapable of deducing what was actually occurring around him but because it conferred on him some mystical importance. Although she does not explain what it is that Severian should remind humanity of, her statement seems to imply that he was chosen because he could internalise the universe, could reconcile the microcosm with the macrocosm through his status as a solar magus. In effect, he is shown reforging the links between the individual and the cosmos, bringing his species out of its millennial 'penance' into a new age. He is, after all, the 'Conciliator'.

Wolfe invites such a reading by presenting the recollections of Severian, the microcosm, in patterns that correspond to and mimic the two metaphors of time that characterise his fictional macrocosm: the arrow and the cycle. The unidirectional passage of time (time's arrow) is manifest in the dying sun's loss of energy to the universal void. Time's cycle is represented by the Hierogrammates' ability to bring a white hole ('the time reverse of a black hole ... in which infinitely dense matter would explode into life along with a blinding release of light'[17]) into the heart of Urth's old sun and thereby produce new cycles of creation and evolution.

The existence of such cycles is conjectured in *The Citadel of the Autarch* when Severian recounts what Master Malrubius's aquastor revealed to him on the shore of Ocean:

> Just as a flower blooms, throws down its seed, dies, and rises from its seed to bloom again, so the universe we know diffuses itself to nullity in the infinitude of space, gathers its fragments ... and from that seed blooms again ... As the flower that comes is like the flower from which it came, so the universe that comes repeats the one whose ruin was its origin ... though just as the flower evolves from summer to summer, all things advance by some minute step. (*Citadel*, p. 278)

Wolfe's evolving flower emblematises the human race, which undergoes a series of painfully slow 'minute steps', or developmental stages, in its transformation into the Increate. These steps unite time's arrow with time's cycle in a series of evolving cycles that are represented diagrammatically in Figure 1.

This universal progression is paralleled by the cyclical patterns found in Severian's recollections. While The Urth Cycle is broadly linear in its progression, there are two non-sequential episodes in *The Book of the New Sun*: in *The Shadow of the Torturer*, the events of Chapter II precede those related in Chapter I; and in *The Sword of the Lictor*, the action of the first

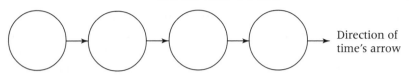

Figure 1 *The resolution of time's arrow and time's cycle as a sequence of evolving temporal cycles*

four pages of Chapter XII occurs before that of Chapters VIII–XI.

If Wolfe's narrative is conceived of as a line whose unidirectional development represents Severian's passage from birth to death, its affinity with time's arrow becomes clear.[18] Located along this line is a series of allusions (which also suggest Severian's precognition) and flashbacks that establish a sequence of 'memory cycles', or non-chronological recollections. For example, if Severian's journey from the necropolis gate to the Piteous Gate in the wall of Nessus in *The Shadow of the Torturer* is envisaged as a line, the non-sequential events of Chapter II produce a memory cycle. Figure 2 illustrates this phenomenon, together with the corresponding restructuring required to arrange Severian's account sequentially.

In Figure 2, point A corresponds to Chapter I of *The Shadow of the Torturer*; point Z to the closing page of the book; points B and C to Chapters II and III respectively; and B ➤ D ➤ E to the mental movement that the reader must make to restructure the narrative into chronological order. Antecedent to Chapter I, line E ➤ A describes the information supplied in Chapter II, which provides details of Severian's early life from his memory of 'piling pebbles in the Old Yard' (p. 19), to the point when he 'had so nearly drowned' (p. 9), before reaching the gate to the necropolis. Accordingly, the reader creates a mental cycle that reaches back to events preceding Chapter I, before having to 'skip' mentally forward 'over' the events of Chapter I, as indicated by A ➤ F ➤ C, to the start of Chapter III. The non-sequential episode in *The Sword of the Lictor* works in a comparable manner.

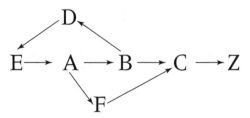

Figure 2 *A diagrammatic representation of the cyclical motif achieved by a non-sequential event in* The Shadow of the Torturer

More commonly, the cyclical patterns in the text are achieved on the more modest level of allusion. At numerous points, Severian refers to events he has experienced but which he has yet to describe. When the reader has completed the narrative, he or she recognises these mysterious references as intimations of the future. For example, Severian alludes to his approaching act of cannibalism, in which Thecla's memories become his own, when he looks romantically on Dorcas, seeing her as 'another self (as Thecla was yet to become in a fashion as terrible as the other was beautiful) ...' (p. 270). Similarly, after his battle with the man-apes in *The Claw of the Conciliator*, Severian admits:

> Not long ago, when the Samru was near the mouth of the Gyoll, I looked over the sternrail by night; there I saw each dipping of the oars as a spot of phosphorescent fire, and for a moment I imagined that those from under the hill had come for me at last. (*Claw*, p. 49)

The reader may be puzzled by Severian's reference to 'the Samru' which, although recognisable as a ship from his remark concerning 'the sternrail' and 'oars', does not enter the narrative until Chapter XXXII of *The Citadel of the Autarch*.

These pre-emptive disclosures, in which Severian alludes to some future event before returning to the point in the text where he made the allusion, also form temporal cycles. Figure 3 represents this textual feature diagrammatically.

In Figure 3 the narrative is again depicted as an A–Z line; point B marks an arbitrary location where Severian introduces an allusion to a later incident; point C shows the position at which that event actually occurs. Lines B ➤ D ➤ C and C ➤ E ➤ B demonstrate the temporal movement that Severian's memory makes when incorporating those references into his account.

This pattern recurs throughout The Urth Cycle, mimicking the succession of universal cycles strung together on the thread of progression suggested by Malrubius.[19] By ensuring that the 'microcosmic' structure of

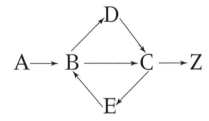

Figure 3 *A diagrammatic representation of the cyclical motif achieved by Wolfe's introduction of intratextual allusions to events occurring later in the narrative*

Severian's recollections reflects the 'macrocosmic' temporal patterns of the fictional universe, Wolfe assists the reader's belief in the importance of the character's memory to his potential as a messiah.

In her study of the art of memory, Frances Yates explains that Camillo's hermetic philosophy embraced the idea that if an individual's *mens*, his or her reasoning or intellect, is divine, then the correspondingly divine structure of the universe lies within it. Hence, an art, or system, that reproduces this divine organisation in the memory will draw on the powers of the macrocosm which are to be found in proportion within the individual.[20] Wolfe perpetrates his textual masquerade by apparently conferring this divine quality on Severian and by suggesting that the New Sun is the external expression of Severian's own inner divinity or light. He sustains the reader's belief in Severian's divine nature by having his protagonist return to Urth and adopt the messianic role with enthusiasm.

Preaching liberalism and environmentalism ('We must be one .... We must tell only the truth, that our promises may be relied on. We must care for Urth as you care for your fields' [*Urth*, p. 207]), Severian's words resound with hypocrisy. He is, himself, a liar, and his acceptance of the part of the Conciliator contrasts sharply with his willingness to torture and execute individuals throughout the text. Severian's words demonstrate all the emotional conviction of a rehearsed platitude, lacking any heartfelt passion.

When he heals Herena's arm by re-channelling 'Urth's energies' (*Urth*, pp. 200–201), smoothes away Declan's tumour (*Urth*, p. 205) and raises Zama from the dead (*Urth*, pp. 218–19), Severian is convinced of his identification with the New Sun:

> I knew myself the star, a beacon at the frontier of Yesod and Briah, coursing through the night ... The fatigue I felt after I restored him [Zama] to life had been sponged away by a sensation I am not tempted to call unreality—the exultation of knowing that my being no longer resided in the marionette of flesh people were accustomed to call Severian, but in a distant star shining with energy enough to bring a thousand worlds to flower. (*Urth*, pp. 220–21)

Severian is 'not tempted to call' his thoughts and emotions 'unreality' because he has been convinced that he is the living embodiment of the New Sun. From his birth among the torturers to his sexual union with Apheta (*Urth*, p. 145), in which he hyperbolically likens his ejaculation to a burst of stars, Severian has been groomed for his part in the Hierogrammates' drama, and his mnemonism contributes to his self-deception.

The Hierogrammates' 'granting' of the New Sun to Severian, and the supposedly higher consciousness he gains as a result, parallels the introduction of the individual's *mens* in Camillo's theatre. As Yates documents,

'Created divine and having the powers of the star-rulers, [which] on falling into the body comes under the dominion of the stars, [the *mens*] affirms the divinity of man, and that he belongs to the same race as the creative star-demons.'[21] Consequently, the impression that Severian has of his consciousness residing not 'in the marionette of flesh ... but in a distant shining star' seems to suggest that he has received his *mens* and is progressing towards divinity. However, while Severian is an indirect ancestor of, and therefore belongs partly to, the same race as the star-demons, the impression he has of possessing a star-soul arises not from the receipt of his *mens* but from the peculiarities of his memory.

Severian is not recruited by the Hierogrammates merely because his associative thinking prevents him from forming general principles and from determining the reality of his situation, he is also chosen for his tendency to distance his consciousness from his corporeal form. Severian thinks analogously to the mnemonist S., who informed Luria that he could ease the pain caused by having his teeth drilled by imagining that it was someone else receiving dental work. He would simply observe 'the other' in the dentist's chair, impervious to pain since it was 'he' and not S. being worked on.[21]

After his beating by the Autarch's soldiers on his return to Urth, Severian shows the same ability to abstract his consciousness from his body. Badly injured, Severian feels himself riding

> the horizon, futilely directing my vitality towards the broken figure sprawled so far away ... The void put it at naught, and I channelled Urth's energies instead. His bones knit, and his wounds healed ...
> (*Urth*, p. 248)

The sense that Severian has of being estranged from his body, of being able to channel power from 'his' star, or from Urth, into his physical form, is probably attributable to a mnemonist's capacity for considering his body as belonging to another, for converting the first person to the third, rather than to some mystical relationship between his consciousness and the New Sun.

While Severian's recovery appears to be miraculous, it seems likely that his ability to heal rapidly (like his failure to get wet during a storm [*Urth*, p. 241] and his survival after being struck by a heavy calibre weapon [*Urth*, p. 255]), can be rationalised by recognising his status as an aquastor, an entity reconstructed from its own memories and gradually gaining material form. Severian cannot drown on the post-deluge Ushas (*Urth*, pp. 331–35) because he has not amassed enough corporeality to die; it is only later, in his role as Apu Punchau, the Head of Day, that he has gained sufficient substantiality to be killed and resurrected once more (see *Urth*, pp. 351–62).

Severian does not realise the implications of his status as an aquastor because he cannot dissociate himself from his own psychological processes. Like S., he is convinced that he can cure himself if he can imagine the process clearly enough and, like S., he is convinced that he can heal other people.[22] As the Conciliator, Severian is similarly certain of his power to heal and yet the sense he has of this power, solicited as it is by the Hierogrammates, is merely the result of his abnormal memory.

Severian's mnemonism is both the source of, and the excuse for, several aspects of the interpretative game that Wolfe plays: the text's allusive diction arises from Severian's capacity to remember his experiences in detail; its patterned structure from his associative thinking; and the entire memory system that suggests his divinity from a combination of these two tendencies. It could be argued, therefore, that The Urth Cycle contains and reflects one of the most intricate characterisations found in SF.

However, to explain such features as solely the result of Wolfe's considerable skill at characterisation is to lose sight of the shaper behind what is shaped. Wolfe stands behind Severian, structuring the text to prompt us into remembering the narrative's surface texture (while overlooking its implications) and into accepting his protagonist as a solar magus. Unless the reader can counter these strategies, the narrative will remain consistently misunderstood.

10. 'A Solar Labyrinth': Metafictional Devices and Textual Complexity

By changing generic codes, subverting traditional literary conventions, employing an unreliable narrator and exploiting the deflective effect of unfamiliar diction, Wolfe creates a text organised specifically to be understood, or at least appreciated, only by those readers who are willing to question their own literary assumptions, pause, reflect and reread.

As a result, The Urth Cycle shares its systematised oracularity with the parable stories, which were constructed 'with the express purpose of concealing a mystery that was to be understood only by insiders'.[1] In effect, Wolfe is behaving in the manner of Mark's Christ, who explains to his disciples:

> To you has been given the secret of the Kingdom of God, but for those outside everything is in parables; so that they may indeed see but not perceive, and may indeed hear but not understand; lest they should turn again, and be forgiven. (Mark 4:11–12)

Although Wolfe is not attempting to propound a religious doctrine, his adoption of the parable form's surreptitiousness results in the pentalogy constituting an intellectual and interpretative labyrinth, a term often applied by critics and reviewers of the text. He can, therefore, be seen as an analogue of the Borgesian character Bioy Cesares, who

> talked to us at length about a great scheme for writing a novel in the first person, using a narrator who omitted or corrupted what happened and who ran into various contradictions, so that only a handful of readers, a very small handful, would be able to decipher the horrible or banal reality behind the novel.[2]

Severian is just such a narrator: unreliable, intensely subjective and seemingly incapable of analysing his experiences. Equally, The Urth Cycle is, itself, the product of Wolfe's 'great scheme for writing a novel [which] only a handful of readers ... would be able to decipher'.

Many of the difficulties that the reader experiences in deciphering the text arise from Wolfe's appropriation of traditional metafictional strategies. These devices are used to create a confusing series of connections between the text itself and what can be termed its 'hermeneutic circle', 'which represents the dynamic process of interpretation in terms of a continual interplay of interpreter and the text, of whole context and individual parts',[3] and between the action of its heavily intertextual embedded stories and that of the main narrative.

Critics have largely overlooked such metafictional aspects and the purpose they serve in The Urth Cycle. This oversight, which would have exposed the text's self-reflexive preoccupation, arises from the fact that Wolfe and his commentators have their creative and analytical powers concentrated in opposite directions. Where Wolfe turns his attention inward to fabricate a lengthy and involved educational puzzle for the reader, his critics have peered outwards from the text, searching for a point where the novels correlate with life itself. Accordingly, they have failed to appreciate that the metaphorical significance of The Urth Cycle (its examination of faith, deception and manipulation) lies in, and is sustained and deepened by, the game that Wolfe initiates with the reader. It is only by observing how he or she has been deceived and cajoled that the reader comes to appreciate more fully Wolfe's vision of humanity as a helplessly subjective species dependent on the whim of manipulatory forces. That reader, in turn, may then recognise his or her position in an analogous system.

Wolfe alludes to the beguiling qualities of The Book of the New Sun in 'A Solar Labyrinth' (1983), a short metafiction whose figurative title implies the tetralogy's contrived structuring and whose subject matter suggests, albeit indirectly, the nature and effects of Wolfe's artifice.[4] First published in The Magazine of Fantasy and Science Fiction shortly after The Citadel of the Autarch, and reprinted in Storeys from the Old Hotel, 'A Solar Labyrinth' tells the story of 'Mr Smith', Wolfe's fictional alter ego, who has 'invented a new kind of maze'. His labyrinth is formed from

> a collection of charming if improbable objects. There are various obelisks, lampposts from Vienna, Paris, and London, as well as New York; a pillar box, also from London; fountains that plash for a time and then subside; a retired yawl, canted now on the reef of grass but with its masts still intact; the standing trunk of a dead tree overgrown with roses; many more. The shadows of these objects form the walls of an elaborate and sophisticated maze. (Storeys, p. 197)

Mr Smith's temporally and spatially eclectic artefacts, which cast their shadows on his lawn, seem likely to be a metaphorical representation of the allusive mythological, historical, scientific and literary material that Wolfe incorporates into The Urth Cycle. Since these allusions work deflectively in the novel, they form the misleading avenues of Wolfe's textual maze.

In Severian's odyssey, the explosive effect of Wolfe's deployment of archetypes, Jungian and religious symbols and mythic allusions, ensures that this 'maze [also] changes from hour to hour, and indeed from minute to minute' (*Storeys*, p. 197). Hence, the shifting patterns of Mr Smith's labyrinth can be seen as a figurative expression of the apparent interpretative plasticity of The Urth Cycle.

Although Wolfe's textual maze is one 'from which the explorer can walk free whenever he chooses' (*Storeys*, p. 198), its abstruseness engenders a notion that a reducible meaning, a specific truth, can be found somewhere within the text, and to depart without uncovering that truth, without solving the riddle of the labyrinth, would be to admit defeat. Consequently, the reader, like 'most adults' who enter Mr Smith's garden, is unlikely to abandon Wolfe's narrative without first becoming lost in its wheeling patterns as he or she searches, not for a way out, but for a way *in*, for a means of determining what is transpiring in Severian's universe.

Wolfe alludes to the interpretative game he plays with the reader who seeks the solution to his textual conundrum in the guidance that Mr Smith offers those guests who enter his labyrinth:

> Mr. Smith begins to tread his maze, but he invites his guest to discover paths of his own. The guest does so, amused at first, then more serious. Imperceptibly, the shadows move. New corridors appear; old ones close, sometimes with surprising speed. Soon Mr. Smith's path joins that of his guest (for Mr. Smith knows his maze well), and the two proceed together, the guest leading the way. Mr. Smith speaks of his statue of Diana, a copy of the one in the Louvre; the image of Tezcatlipaca, the Toltec sun-god is authentic, having been excavated at Teotihuacan. As he talks, the shadows shift, seeming almost to writhe like feathered Quezalcoatl, with the slight rolling of the lawn. Mr. Smith steps away, but for a time his path nearly parallels his guest's. (*Storeys*, p. 198)

In The Urth Cycle, Wolfe encourages the reader to follow his or her own path by presenting allusions that draw the reader along digressive avenues and into blind passages. These extraliterary and intertextual references may appear, initially, to be no more than decorative additions used to create the ambience of Wolfe's fictional world, but in time the reader begins to look for a deeper relevance in their connections. As he or she does so, 'the shadows move', and the reader suspects that the text is open to all manner of interpretations.

'New corridors appear; old ones close' as features of the novel shift and change. Things are consistently not what they seem in Wolfe's pentalogy: Dorcas is initially a beautiful young woman who rescues Severian from drowning, and yet, in reality, she is a corpse restored to life by the Claw's apparent ability to bend time. Later, Wolfe reveals that she is none other than Severian's paternal grandmother. However, the clues to her status as a revivified cadaver are already in place before Dorcas enters the narrative. Her husband, the aged and Charonic boatman poling his skiff across the Lake of Birds in the Garden of Endless Sleep, introduced early in *The Shadow of the Torturer* (p. 27), is searching for his wife Cas (*Shadow*, pp. 195–200). Cas and Dorcas are one and the same person, identified by the similarity of their names and their blue eyes. Wolfe exploits this nomenclatory link between Cas and Dorcas when he introduces Casdoe, a woman whose name may encourage the reader to search for an absent set of liaisons between her and Cas/Dorcas.

Where Mr Smith's 'path joins that of his guest', the guest apparently leads the way. The guest's anteriority may be a physical manifestation of the notion of the reader 'getting ahead' of the author, where he or she presupposes developments or connections in the manner of the Cas–Dorcas–Casdoe relationship. However, Mr Smith 'knows his maze well' and the lead that the guest enjoys is illusory: he or she is always following Mr Smith's grand design.

Meanwhile, the host himself is speaking of 'his statue of Diana ... Tezcatlipaca ... Teotihuacan', constantly diverting the guest's attention from the labyrinth moving all around. His path 'nearly parallels his guest's' to facilitate this diversion. A corresponding parallel is achieved in The Urth Cycle when Wolfe's persona, Severian, addresses the reader directly in the tone of a confidant: 'Allow me to pause here and speak to you as one mind to another ...' (*Claw*, p. 39), Severian says, at which point he becomes a conversationalist, dependent on the reader for identity and sympathy. This conversationalism fosters an empathy between character and reader that further substantiates Severian's assumed candidness.

In this way, Severian gives the reader the confidence he or she requires to believe that he or she can comprehend the narrative fully by simply trusting his or her recollections. This misreading of Severian's veracity is reflected in the misconceptions of Mr Smith's guest:

> 'Do you see that one [a shadow] there?' says the guest. 'In another minute or two, when it's shorter, I'll be able to get through there.'
>
> Mr. Smith nods and smiles.
>
> The guest waits, confidently now surveying the wonderful pattern of dark green and bright. The shadow he had indicated—that of a Corinthian column, perhaps—indeed diminishes; but as it does another, wheeling with the wheeling sun, falls across the desired path. Most adult guests do not escape until they are rescued by a passing cloud. Some, indeed, refuse such rescue. (Storeys, p. 198.)

Wolfe seems to be cautioning the reader here against presupposing a way through his maze, which, with its recontextualisations and its subversions, is sufficiently unpredictable to invalidate any prejudgements.

The suspension of the labyrinth's existence by a passing cloud can be seen as a metaphor for a lacuna in the reading process which rescues the reader from Wolfe's puzzling narrative. Readers who ignore any interruption in their reception of the text, or who struggle stalwartly to unravel its mysteries, are those that 'refuse such rescue'.

At the centre of the solar labyrinth,

> [i]nlaid on a section of crumbling wall that at least *appears* ancient, he [Mr Smith] points out the frowning figure of the Minotaur, a monster that, as he explains, haunts the shadows. From far away … the deep bellowing of a bull interrupts him. (Perhaps a straying guest might discover stereospeakers hidden in the boughs of certain trees; perhaps not.) (*Storeys*, p. 198)

The centre of the maze is a sham display. The wall only '*appears* ancient'; the Minotaur has been deprived of its dynamism and has become a decoration: it no longer haunts this or any other maze, and its implied presence is the product of clandestine technology used to countenance an illusion. This is the symbolic expression of what lies at the heart of The Urth Cycle: a story obscured by the artifice of Wolfe's (and the Hierogrammates') plot and by the shifting shadows of the author's allusiveness.

Wolfe defends his duplicity by proposing that Mr Smith

> is fair to all the children, giving each the same instructions, the same encouragement. Some reject his maze out of hand, wandering off to examine the tilted crucifix or the blue-dyed water of the towering Torricelli barometer, or to try (always without success) to draw Arthur's sword from its stone. Others persevere longer, threading their way between invisible walls for an hour or more. (Storeys, p. 199)

Every reader receives the same printed text but Wolfe recognises that each individual will react slightly differently to the whole. Some will focus on the narrative's recontextualised religious motifs (represented by the 'tilted crucifix'); others will examine its attractive embellishment, its 'baroque' qualities symbolised by 'the blue-dyed water of the towering Torricelli barometer'; still others will try to uncover the story and the metaphorical significance of the text, 'to draw Arthur's sword from its stone'.

Wolfe constructs The Urth Cycle to make the task of drawing 'Arthur's sword from its stone' particularly difficult. However, while the pentalogy is deliberately contrived to appeal to multifarious readings, 'the notion of a text absolutely free, absolutely open to us, in which we "produce" meaning at will is—as most of its proponents allow—a utopian fiction. There are constraints that shadow interpretation.'[5] In Wolfe's pentalogy, these constraints are manifest in the author's obliqueness, in his subversions, in his abstruse methods of imparting significant information, and in the text's often gratuitous complexity. Such features, like the shadows of Mr Smith's solar labyrinth, conspire to oppose the reader's efforts to gain the 'centre' of the text, to uncover the solution that Wolfe prepares for the cautious and reflective reader who bypasses his deflective paths to uncover his artifice, the 'stereospeakers hidden in the boughs of certain trees'.

Like Mr Smith, Wolfe is a Daedalian artificer. Accordingly, his narratives, especially The Urth Cycle, display a remarkable delight in design. With its carefully structured patterning, its similarities, counterpoints and contiguities, The Urth Cycle asserts the authority of the author. It is this authority over the reader's reception of the text that Wolfe never relinquishes, choosing to encourage his reader to believe that the novel possesses some obscure mystical or metaphysical truth beyond its overtly complex design. Given the susceptibility of humans to mythic explanations for existence, the reader is likely to find this belief reassuring, although, in a sense, it is the opponent of 'truth' since it stifles critical enquiry. The reader must always be cautious if he or she is to see through the shifting shadows of Wolfe's design.

Still playing fair with the reader, Wolfe provides clues to his grand scheme for deception at various points in the text. In *The Claw of the Conciliator*, for example, Severian is tricked into perceiving a contrived room in the House Absolute as a painting, leaving the Autarch to explain that

> The room is shallow ..., indeed it is shallower than you perceive even now ... The eye is *deceived* in a picture by ... converging lines ... So that when it encounters them in reality, with little actual depth and the *additional artificiality* of monochromatic lighting, it believes it sees another picture—*particularly when it has been conditioned by a long succession of true ones*. (*Claw*, p. 182, with additional emphasis)

Wolfe's self-conscious stress on deceit and artificiality alludes to his misleading of the reader. The Urth Cycle is analogous to the Autarch's 'shallow room' inasmuch as it describes a universe lacking a spiritually transcendental dimension. Like the stereospeakers, which suggest the proximity of the Minotaur in Mr Smith's solar labyrinth, the monochromatic lighting (another form of technical trickery) that transforms a contrivance into a work of art symbolises the literary tricks that Wolfe plays on the reader. Clearly, the effectiveness of these ploys is increased if the reader has been conditioned by a long succession of 'true' texts, that is, narratives that do not attempt to delude their recipients.

Wolfe is facing something of a dilemma, however. While he seems to express a desire to beguile the reader, he also appears to want that reader to observe the craftsmanship with which the text was produced—without revealing the answer to his central conundrum. In order to apparently satisfy both inclinations, Wolfe disguises his artfulness by proposing that his pentalogy explores a 'theory of fiction through the practice of fiction'.[6] By having the narrative masquerade as a metafiction, Wolfe emphasises the conscious and intricate design of the whole while retarding the reader's recognition of the Borgesian 'horrible or banal reality behind the novel'.

Wolfe encourages the reader to accept the text as a metafiction in a number of ways. His self-consciousness manifests itself, primarily, in Severian's observations, which include: 'Such a mighty structure was the Wall [of Nessus] that it divided the world as the mere line between their covers does two books' (*Claw*, p. 7). Occurring on the opening page of *The Claw of the Conciliator*, the imagery highlights the existence of Wolfe's text as separate volumes, and affirms the physical gap between *The Shadow of the Torturer* and *The Claw of the Conciliator* with a corresponding narrative gap. Wolfe's metaphor makes the reader aware that the world of Urth is encountered within a book, that he or she is separated from the fictional world just as Nessus is isolated from the Commonwealth by its immense curtain wall. The reader and the world of the text are only united when the book cover is opened and the reading process is begun.

This self-consciousness is expressed more covertly in images ('I seemed a man of paper' [*Urth*, p. 3]); in pseudo-philosophy ('We are but dreams, and dreams possess no life by their own right' [*Claw*, p. 223]); in ironic statements ('In books, this sort of stalemate never seems to occur …' [*Sword*, p. 30]); and in Severian's encounters with other characters. For example, when Severian is brought before a lochage commanding a bridge over the river Gyoll, the officer's 'quill, which had skated along steadily before, paused. "I had never thought to encounter such a thing [a torturer] outside the pages of some book, but I daresay he speaks no more than the truth"', the lochage remarks (*Shadow*, p. 133). This meeting results in a disjunction between the awareness of the reader and that of the lochage. As the lochage stops writing, he becomes a reader-figure, literally and figuratively receiving Severian, and realising that such a person can exist in his own (fictional) reality. Severian becomes less fictional to the lochage as he enters the same fiction with his first speech act. Conversely, the reader becomes more aware that Severian is a character encountered in 'the pages of some book'.

In each of these examples, Wolfe demonstrates that his text, like any other, is being contrived by an author figure. According to Thomas D. Clareson, it is through this self-consciousness that Wolfe 'reminds the reader that these narratives are fictional constructs and should be read as fiction'.[7] However, by reminding the reader of this, Wolfe initiates that reader into a system of inter- and intratextual connections which obscure the text's all-important story further by suggesting that The Urth Cycle is an ingenuous, straightforward metafiction.

These conjunctions are readily observable in the fabric of the novel. Wolfe's self-consciousness, or self-reflection, is punningly thematised in Severian's own self-reflections (described more accurately as recollections because of his lack of insight); his acts of remembering give rise to a self-reflexive text. His memory not only constitutes the contents of the book, it also dictates the structure of the text and itself functions like a book. This analogy is exposed when Severian observes: 'When I think back on that time [his youth], it is that moment [his elevation to journeyman] I recall first; to remember more I must work forward or backward from that' (*Shadow*, p. 107). Like a scholar searching for an apt quotation, he must find a well-remembered entry point, for, 'As I have said, I remember everything; but often can find a fact, face or feeling only after a long search' (*Shadow*, p. 213).

Similarly, his memory, like the narrative itself, becomes increasingly 'intertextual' as his odyssey progresses. His incorporation of Thecla's memories (*Claw*, pp. 94–98) and those of the previous autarchs (*Citadel*, pp. 234–38) appear as thematic parallels to the breaking of the one into the manifold achieved on the textual level through the deployment of intertexts. Nevertheless, identifying the existence of such parallels is often of little benefit to the reader who will quickly find him- or herself enmeshed in a network of such analogies. This network overloads the reader's senses with a series of reflections, similarities and echoes that could possess some obscure significance for the whole.

The presence of these multiple connections is carefully mitigated, and apparently explained, by Wolfe's incorporation of a theory of fiction in *The Shadow of the Torturer* (pp. 281–82). Although the presence of this hypothesis invites a more literary reading, a recognition of literary codes, by making such an invitation Wolfe assists the reader's acceptance of an explanation for his duplicity contrary to that suggested by the manipulative properties of the narrative. Essentially, Wolfe excuses his wily artfulness by suggesting that his texts are primarily educational.

In 'his' theory of fiction, Severian confesses, 'If I were writing this history to entertain or instruct, I would not digress here ...' (*Shadow*, p. 281). Of course, Wolfe is writing Severian's history to entertain, yet, more importantly, by its proximity to the veracious 'entertain', 'instruct' gains a degree of substantiality. The purpose of Severian's digression is, seemingly, principally instructive; he is propounding his subscription to the notion that the act of writing is equivalent to an act of public execution. However, the theory's instructive or educational properties are only valid if the reader has first solved The Urth Cycle's literary puzzle and recognises Severian's theory for what it is: yet another duplicitous counter in Wolfe's textual game.

For example, while Wolfe's subversions of the traditions of the mono-mythic structure and the autobiographical form may help the reader to recognise how literary conventions 'provide a frame of reference for the reader, helping him orient himself [while providing] material for parodic or ironic scrutiny by the author who manipulates the conventions',[8] this recognition is only achieved after the reader has determined what is occurring in Wolfe's fictional heterocosm. The subverted properties of Wolfe's appropriations are always subordinate to their similarities to the original material. Accordingly, the text's perceptible affinities to the monomythic progression from initiation to separation and return adumbrate Wolfe's extirpation of the mythic hero's traditional spiritual development.

Wolfe knows that his subversions will, in some cases, be apprehended and thereby bring to the reader's attention conventions of fiction of which, through over-familiarisation, he or she has become unaware. He also understands that, in many instances, the reader's comfort and familiarity with such conventions will sustain his literary masquerade. Naturally, if the reader perceives Wolfe's recontextualisations, the inclusion of 'Severian's' hypothesis of textual construction confirms that his intention was, in reality, to obfuscate information in a manner that reveals it to be obfuscated.

However, for those readers who do not apprehend the rules and dimensions of Wolfe's interpretative game, the theory of fiction presented in *The Shadow of the Torturer* constitutes a further set of deceptive moves in that game. If the reader becomes convinced that The Urth Cycle is a metafiction, diligently exploring a theory of fiction through the practice of fiction, he or she may not recognise Wolfe's recontextualisations of traditional metafictional devices and may, thereby, misapprehend the role played by these devices within the context of the narrative.

Wolfe conceals this recontextualisation by implying that his text can be received in two distinct ways: by those who read it as fantasy; and by those more informed readers who understand the metafictional qualities of his work. This bipolar separation of the readership is suggested by Severian's observation that 'the contending parties of tradition pull at the writers of histories ... One desires ease; the other, richness of experience in the execution ... of the writing' (*Shadow*, p. 282). Wolfe apparently gratifies both 'parties' through his skill as a metafictionist and by his ability to produce an enjoyable and imaginative adventure: 'by positioning one party on the right side of the block and the other on the left, by his great skill [he] made it appear to each that the result was entirely satisfactory' (*Shadow*, p. 281).

Perhaps predictably, such a theoretical distinction, proposed by the author himself, is fraught with irony. The supposedly literate reader who perceives the metafictional qualities of The Urth Cycle and accepts them at face value is as much a victim of Wolfe's manipulations as the reader who remains oblivious to the author's self-consciousness. Faith in the primary metafictiveness of Wolfe's narrative obscures this additional set of deflective ploys with an unhelpful and false literary concern. For example, Wolfe, through the agency of Severian, suggests that 'for him to perform his function' as a writer, he must do so 'in keeping with the teachings of his masters and the ancient traditions' (*Shadow*, p. 282). These 'ancient traditions' are the genre conventions, the monomythic cycle, the autobiographical form and the first-person narrative that Wolfe subverts throughout the pentalogy. The reader's recognition of these subversions (achieved only when the text's story has been determined) is, however, discouraged by the suggestion that the author is acting 'in keeping with ... the ancient traditions'. Nowhere in his theory of literature does Wolfe allude to the recontextualisation of such traditions and, therefore, Severian's comment works to sustain the reader's faith in the apparently conventional qualities of the text. Wolfe's 'masters', the reader might suppose, are his sources of inspiration, among them Borges, Proust, Kipling and Dickens. His intertextual borrowings from these and other writers are introduced into the text on two distinct levels: that of the main narrative, where elements from anterior texts form part of Severian's universe; and that of the embedded tale.

Wolfe's reference to Mary Shelley's *Frankenstein* (1818) is explicit when the islanders storm Baldanders's castle in *The Sword of the Lictor*. Moments before Severian and Baldanders do battle, Dr Talos regards the scene before him and asks:

> Look about you, don't you recognise this? ... The castle? The Monster? The man of learning? Surely you know that just as the momentous events of the past cast their shadows down the ages, so now, when the sun is drawing towards the dark, our own shadows race into the past to trouble mankind's dreams. (*Sword*, p. 277)

Talos's interjection (which recalls his instruction for a tableau during the performance of his play 'Eschatology and Genesis' in *The Shadow of the Torturer* [p. 275] and establishes a link between play and text) is an odd conflation of the cinematic and the literary. The three iconic elements of 'the castle ... the Monster ... the man of learning' are more suggestive of James Whale's 1931 Expressionist filmic treatment of *Frankenstein* than of the novel itself. Conversely Talos's reference to dreams recalls Mary Shelley's preface to the 1831 edition of her novel (in which she attributes the inspiration of her story to a dream-vision), while condensing the duration of Urth's existence to one day and advancing the peculiar notion of history as the shadow of light. By deploying both cinematic and literary references to the *Frankenstein* tradition, Wolfe ensures that his readers apprehend the intertextual allusion. Those readers unfamiliar with Mary Shelley's original story are likely to recognise the cinematic imagery and, like those acquainted with the novel, will have their attention directed away from The Urth Cycle along this intertextual pathway. Equally, the curious representation of time poses a small puzzle that will, almost inevitably, diffuse the reader's concentration.

The 'shadows [cast] down the ages' symbolise a thematic and inter-pretative aspect of Wolfe's pentalogy. It is, in part, representative of the author's supposed inheritance from 'his masters', yet it also stresses the long history of Urth. This history is represented by the millions of books housed in the Library of the Citadel in Nessus which, fairly obviously, derives from Borges's 'Library of Babel'. Acknowledging this connection, Wolfe suggests that 'the library is larger than the world that contains it', for 'the library of Master Ultan is in *The Book of the New Sun*, and *The Book of the New Sun* is in the library'.[9] There is no real paradox in this statement; its apparent contradiction arises from little more than a manipulation of language. *The Book of the New Sun* does not contain the library in the literal sense, it merely describes the building during Severian's visit (*Shadow*, pp. 54–67) and internalises aspects of the library in the stories that Severian recounts from the book of legends he carries. Wolfe's indebtedness to Borges is total, as he allusively directs the reader to Borges's text and relies on the complexity of that work to reflect back on his own writing and confer its merits on *The Book of the New Sun*. Put simply, Wolfe lets Borges do his work for him. Wolfe's library possesses none of the labyrinthine and repetitive complexity of Borges's edifice. The Library of Babel returns again and again to its fictional beginning; it 'is infinite and periodic ... The same volumes are repeated in the same disorder (which, repeated, would constitute an order: Order itself'),[10] whereas Wolfe's library is merely a large building playing host to a vast collection of books and other recording devices.

Wolfe's intertextuality is more overt in the embedded tales reproduced from Severian's Brown Book, which Wolfe describes as 'a future Bullfinch's Age of Fable'.[11] The book contains legends that form a library of allusions ranging from works by Borges and Kipling, to US history, Classical and Roman mythology, and the Old Testament.[12]

In writing the legends [Wolfe begins innocently], I have supposed facts and old stories to have become confused with others, a rascally technique that has earned me at least one vehement accusation of plagiarism. Thus, for example, the custom of the academic thesis is confounded with the legend of Theseus in 'The Tale of the Student and His Son' [and with Borges's 'The Circular Ruins'].[13]

Thematically, Wolfe seems to be echoing a logical supposition advanced by Borges, who proposed that, with time, the individual identity of authors and their work would disappear:

I think they [Wells's stories, *The Time Machine*, *The Island of Dr Moreau*, *The Plattner Story* and *The First Men in the Moon*] will be incorporated, like the fables of Theseus or Ahasuerus, into the general memory of the language into which they were written.[14]

Although Wolfe's eclectic recombinations suggest the age of Urth, their apparent metafictional role calls attention to the myth of originality. Rather than writing, Wolfe is, in many instances, rewriting. However, in the context of the pentalogy, these tales are less involved with subverting the notion of originality than with directing the reader's attention from the narrative's story in three distinct ways. Primarily, they interrupt the progression of the narrative, diverting attention from clues embedded in the plot; second, their allusiveness guides the reader to other texts; and third, they establish a series of thematic and conceptual intratextual echoes which can serve to confound the reader.

For example, in 'The Tale of the Student and His Son', Wolfe engenders a series of fictional frames in which Wolfe is 'dreaming' Severian, Severian is 'dreaming' the student as he reads, and the student is 'dreaming' his son, a Theseus figure, in the manner of Borges's unnamed protagonist from 'The Circular Ruins'. Like Severian, the student's son embarks on a quest to slay a monster: in *The Book of the New Sun* it is the metaphorically monstrous black hole at the heart of the old sun; in the embedded tale, it is a Naviscaput, Wolfe's hybridised personification of the Cretan King Minos and his Minotaur. Theseus, the student's son and Severian all encounter creatures who exact a tribute from a subjugated people: King Minos demands seven youths and seven maids every nine years for the death of his son Androgeus; the Naviscaput takes the Corn Maidens (their name suggestive of the yearly crop they represent) and, when Severian reanimates Typhon, the giant offers him mastery over Urth for which he will exact a 'tribute of fair women and boys' (*Sword*, p. 213). A less explicit allusion to this motif is Baldanders's theft of the Shore People's children (*Sword*, p. 248).[15] Wolfe's version of the Cretan maze appears in the story as a tortuous waterway modelled on the fingerprint of the Naviscaput.

The student navigates his way out of the maze by flaying the tip from this digit on the instructions of the Naviscaput's daughter, Noctua, whose actions recall those of Minos's daughter Ariadne, who provides Theseus with his all-important ball of thread.

Intratextual connections are established with the main narrative when Severian, struggling to control his multiple personality, realises that his mind is 'a maze, but I was the owner and builder of the maze, with the print of my thumb on every passageway' (*Citadel*, p. 243). This image undermines Severian's status as a hero figure by suggesting that he is an oppressive subjugator akin to the Naviscaput. As the Hierogrammates' unwitting agent, Severian fulfils this role completely by ensuring that the future of humanity will, eventually, form a tribute to the Hierogrammates.

The conflation of Kipling's *The Jungle Book* with the legends of Moses and Romulus and Remus in 'The Tale of a Boy Called Frog' (*Sword*, pp. 147–57) creates connections that are, in this case, more figurative, opening a Pandora's box of metaphorical and symbolic readings based on Jungian psychology (indeed, Jungian motifs appear throughout).

While these embedded tales perform a mnemonic function within The Urth Cycle, facilitating the reader's recall of the narrative's plot, the increasingly complex system of relationships between the text and its stories is designed to imprison that reader in a mirror hall of textual reflections.

If the connections between the dramatic action of the pentalogy and the stories it includes were not confusing enough, Wolfe then thematises the entire notion of rewriting when Severian conjectures that he is 'not the first Severian' but a man whose 'story' has been rewritten by the Hierogrammates. This thematic rendering of Wolfe's rewriting is developed further when he reveals that the Hierogrammates are also rescripting the Increate. This system of conjoined associations—one of many occurring in the text—undermines the reader's efforts to isolate individual elements of the text as these elements are forever combining and recombining with other inter- and intratextual material. However, one such series of connections does provide an important insight into Wolfe's scheme.

The Urth Cycle contains a horizontal *mise en abîme*, a series of apparently endless inclusive duplications 'on the level of the "fiction" [which not only] calls attention to the "unlifelike nature of the plot"' but also indicates, somewhat obliquely, the circuitous effect of Wolfe's textual strategies.[16]

When Severian first recounts Dr Talos's play, 'Eschatology and Genesis' (*Claw*, pp. 211–36), the drama is described as 'a dramatisation ... of certain parts of the lost Book of the New Sun' (*Claw*, p. 211). Later, in *The Citadel of the Autarch*, Severian explains that, when he is bound for Yesod, he will recopy his manuscript, 'every word, just as I have written it here. I shall call it *The Book of the New Sun*, for that book, lost now for many ages, is said to have predicted his [the Conciliator's] coming' (*Citadel*, p. 309).

In *The Urth of the New Sun*, Severian returns to Urth millennia before his own birth and is incarcerated in the Matachin Tower where his 'disciples' visit him:

> Declan wished to know how Urth would fare when the New Sun came; and I, understanding little more than he did himself, drew on Dr. Talos' play, never thinking that in a time yet to come Dr. Talos' play would be drawn from my words. (*Urth*, p. 266)

Severian's words become *The Book of the New Sun*, recorded by Canog, a prisoner in an adjacent cell. 'That was a fine tale', he observes. 'I took notes as fast as I could, and it should make a capital little book whenever I'm released' (*Urth*, p. 266). The original, lost version of *The Book of the New Sun* is recreated from its own half-remembered fragments and will go on to form the inspiration for Talos's 'Eschatology and Genesis'.

This continuous propagation of fiction from fiction, from drama to book to drama, alludes to the progression of influences from, for example, Borges to Wolfe. Lucien Dallenbach describes such *mises en abîme* as simple reduplication, 'in which the mirroring fragment [in this case 'Eschatology and Genesis'] has a relationship of similitude to the whole [The Urth Cycle] that contains it'.[17] The text also expresses an implied *aphoristique*, such that 'the fragment [Canog's notes for *The Book of the New Sun*] is supposed to include the work in which itself is included'.[18]

Wolfe's *mise en abîme* seems to suggest that the relationship between the writer figures (Talos, Severian and Canog) is analogous to the process carried out by the author and reader of a text. Severian becomes the reader of Talos's play, recreating the drama in his own mind, while Canog becomes Severian's reader, recopying Severian's story onto paper. Although this dramatisation of the reading process seems to represent Wolfe's production, and the reader's reproduction, of The Urth Cycle, such a reading overlooks the most important feature of Wolfe's *mise en abîme*: the symbolism of its cyclical stucture. The propagation of one fiction from another is a closed circle. This pattern emblematises the way in which Wolfe opposes enquiry by generating convoluted associations that disguise the stable story and the intended interpretation at the heart of the text (see Fig. 4). Hence, Wolfe's deployment of a *mise en abîme* marks a curious fusion of the obfuscatory and the revelatory. Its significance depends not on a serious literary awareness of the kind the reader might suppose to be required, but on a recognition of Wolfe's abstruse way of providing clues to an accurate reading of the narrative.

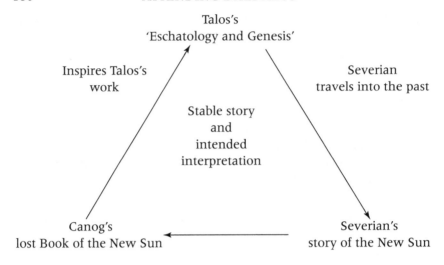

Figure 4 *The cyclical structure of Wolfe's* mise en abîme

Similarly, the novel's self-conscious intertextuality is a playful conceit rather than a straightforward attempt to formulate a theory concerning literary influence. Indeed, Wolfe's management of his source material reveals how writers feed on the work of other writers; he shows plagiarism to be inevitable and that originality can be found in the recontextualis- ation of existing forms and conventions deployed to fulfil new or innova- tive functions. Wolfe clearly enjoys his plagiarism, possibly on the assumption that his reader will be beguiled by his textual bricolage into following, at least for a time, an additional set of digressions.

When Severian concludes his theory of fiction, he further complicates attempts to interpret the narrative by remarking:

> There remains the carnifex himself; I am he. It is not enough for him to earn praise from all. It is not enough, even, for him to perform his function in a way entirely creditable and in keeping with the teaching of his masters and the ancient traditions. In addition to this … he must add to the execution some feature however small that is entirely his own and that he will never repeat. Only thus can he call himself a free artist. (*Shadow*, p. 282)

Any reader who has already recovered the story of The Urth Cycle, and recognised the interpretative game that Wolfe masterminds to oppose such a recovery, is likely to see this passage as a sizeable clue to the existence of Wolfe's 'original' story and the game that conceals it.

For those readers who have not discovered the Hierogrammates' evolutionary and mythogenetic strategies, Severian's thoughts encourage them to search for the elusive spark of originality that enables Wolfe to 'call himself a free artist'. As a result of this encouragement, it seems likely that some readers will 'refuse ... rescue' from Wolfe's solar labyrinth as they attempt to identify that small feature that the author 'will never repeat'.

How, then, should The Urth Cycle be read? Wolfe may provide a clue in the final paragraph of 'A Solar Labyrinth':

> But always, as the shadow of the great gnomon creeps towards the sandstone XII set in the lawn, the too-old, too-young, insufficiently serious and too-serious drift away, leaving only Mr. Smith and one solitary child playing in the sun. (*Storeys*, p. 199)

The maze 'is insoluble at noon, when the shadows are shortest' (*Storeys*, pp. 197–98) and it is this apparent insolubility that drives the majority of Mr Smith's guests away. The 'one solitary child' who remains is probably the personification of Wolfe's ideal reader, the inducted 'disciple' who enjoys playing Wolfe's game as much as Wolfe appears to relish its creation.

In the arena of this game, the reader derives satisfaction from reaching a point where he or she can collude with the author, from comprehending the interpretation that Wolfe intends and, from this comprehension, gaining an insight into his or her own subjectivity and vulnerability to deceit. Wolfe expects his readers to stand somewhere between the 'insufficiently serious' and the 'too-serious', to be prepared to apprehend and enjoy the literary pranks he performs on them and to remain 'playing in the sun'.

Part III
Conclusions

... the thoughtful reader will find little difficulty in advancing at least one plausible speculation.

—Gene Wolfe, *The Urth of the New Sun* (1987)

Part III
Conclusions

11. 'The Map': The Multi-volume Novels and Metafictional Cartography[1]

Since the publication of *The Citadel of the Autarch*, Wolfe has attempted to guide his reader to the interpretation of The Urth Cycle offered in the preceding section by providing a series of parallels and clues to the narrative's hidden subtexts in his subsequent fiction. Although this process began when *The Book of the New Sun* was still in its draft stages with the dramatisation of a simple reception theory in 'The God and His Man', and continued with 'A Solar Labyrinth', it was not until the appearance of *Soldier of the Mist* in 1986 that Wolfe's intentions became clear.

John Clute has already acknowledged how Wolfe's

> stories and novels reflect one another; how 'The Eyeflash Miracles' is a stab at the story of Severian; how Little Tib in 'Eyeflash' is 'really' Ozma in the way that Severian is 'really' Thecla ... But there's something more than repetition going on here. (*Strokes*, p. 160)

Although Clute believes that the repetitions found in Wolfe's oeuvre represent a 'pattern of responses to the chance of escaping from ... the prison of the self' (*Strokes*, p. 161), it is more judicious to argue that this pattern arises as a consequence of Wolfe's continued interest in the workings of the mind as such, and in the effects that can be gained during the reading process through the deployment of intratextual and intertextual allusions. Taking Clute's example, it is clear from textual evidence that Severian recalls Little Tib from 'The Eyeflash Miracles' (1978) not only because Wolfe was having a 'stab' at a narrative with similar themes but also so that the habitual Wolfe reader could gain further insights into Severian's character through his similarity to Little Tib. While Severian's blindness is metaphorical where Little Tib's is literal, Wolfe uses the same intergeneric hybridisation of SF and fantasy in The Urth Cycle as he does in 'The Eyeflash Miracles'; both narratives employ comparable mask imagery and follow the experiences of artificial messiah-figures who perform rationally explicable miracles.

During the years from 1986 to 1996 this interconnectedness has evolved from being an often oblique sequence of intertextual echoes to become a piece of 'metafictional cartography', a deliberate 'mapping' of the subtexts

of The Urth Cycle designed to lead the reader to the specific interpretation
Wolfe intends and prescribes. This latter part of Wolfe's career can,
therefore, be considered as a revisionist period in which the author has
sought to expose and clarify the obfuscated aspects of Severian's odyssey.
Just as the title of Wolfe's short story, 'Ain't You "Most Done"?' forms a
metafictional comment on his 'lack of progress on *Exodus from the Long
Sun*',[2] so *Soldier of the Mist*, *Soldier of Arete* and *The Book of the Long Sun* offer
a detailed exegesis of The Urth Cycle.

Set in Greece towards the conclusion of the Persian Wars, *Soldier of the Mist*
opens in 479 BC, after the defeat of Xerxes's army by the Greeks at the Battle
of Platæa. During the fighting, Wolfe's narrator, a Roman mercenary enlisted
with the Persians, suffers a head wound that disables his long-term memory.
Unable to remember his own name, he is called *Latro*, the Latin for a hired
servant or mercenary, by his healer, who also provides him with a scroll on
which to record his experiences. Every morning, Latro must reread this
scroll, which forms the fabric of the novel, to discover his identity, his
purpose, and the relationships he shares with the people who accompany
him as his social status changes from refugee, to prisoner, to slave.

As compensation for his loss of memory, Latro discovers that he can
communicate with the gods. After he has fled the Spartan forces con-
verging on Platæa, this dubious blessing brings him into contact with 'the
Swift God', Asopus, and then 'the Shining God', Apollo, who appears to
him at his temple in Thebes. Apollo informs Latro that his wound was
inflicted near a shrine of 'the Great Mother' and, if he is ever to regain
knowledge of his past, to a 'shrine of hers [he] must return' (*S. Mist*, p. 12).
He learns that by some previous action, now forgotten, he has offended
her and must seek her 'forgiveness for the injury [he] did her that caused
her to injure [him]' (*S. Mist*, p. 17).

In the company of Io, a slave girl who claims to have been given to him
by Apollo, and the poet Pindaros (who is none other than the Theban poet
Pindar), Latro begins a journey that takes him from Thebes to Corinth,
from Salamis to the ruins of Athens and to the temple of Demeter in Eleusis.
He visits Acheron and Thermopylae, and takes part in the siege of Sestos.
During this dual quest for identity and redemption, Latro is constantly
helped and hindered by the intervention of the gods: he meets Hades on
the shore of the Peloponnese, Aphrodite makes love to him in a brothel in
Athens, and Persephone takes him to a vestibule beneath her mother's
temple. Gradually, Latro is drawn into a feud between Demeter (also
identified with Gæa and Cybele) and the Triple Goddess, whose aspects
include Selene, the Huntress (known as Auge, Orthia, Artemis and Diana)
and the Dark Mother, Enodia, or Hecate.

The precise nature of these encounters is not, however, readily apparent, not least because Wolfe realises that every god had 'a name suitable for the tongue of each nation' (*S. Mist*, p. 23), and employs this multitude of names and epithets to refer to any one god or goddess. Accordingly, Dionysis becomes 'the king of Nysa', 'the God in the Tree' and 'the Kid' (*S. Mist*, p. 23). Zeus is referred to as 'the Thunderer' (*S. Mist*, p. 33), and Persephone is presented as Kore, or 'the Maiden' (*S. Mist*, p. 146). While this kind of multiple denomination is explained in the text as an effort towards historical veracity, Wolfe's strategy also deconstructs the reader's familiarity with the Greek world.

This deconstruction is extended by the employment of a Roman first-person narrator who writes no Greek and who mistranslates many Greek nouns according to their phonetic similarities to other words. In Latro's scroll, Spartans become 'rope-makers' as he confuses Sparta with σπάρτον, the Greek word for a rope or cable. Similarly, the town of Eleusis is mistaken for ἔλευσις, meaning the advent of the Lord, and named Advent, while Platæa is termed Clay as Latro fails to distinguish between Πλάταια and πλαστός, meaning something moulded in clay or wax.

Algis Budrys remarks that 'to call a Spartan a "rope maker" is to demythologise him instantly, make him accessible as a realistic character',[3] but in making such a statement he overlooks how Wolfe's refusal to utilise recognisable historical nouns defamiliarises the reader from the Classical period. By adopting this strategy of estrangement, Wolfe forces the reader to experience the same sense of dislocation felt by Latro as a world with which they were both once familiar is recreated as an almost wholly alien environment. Where Latro's defamiliarisation arises from his faulty memory, the sense of estrangement experienced by the reader is the result of Wolfe's effort to describe the society and mythology of ancient Greece, familiar to many readers from its cinematic treatments in *Jason and the Argonauts* (1963) and *Clash of the Titans* (1981), in a manner more historically accurate, and consequently more strange, than Hollywood's.

Throughout *Soldier of the Mist*, Wolfe invites the reader to make comparisons between Latro's narrative and that of Severian. Baird Searles, for example, recognises how, '[l]ike the component "novels" of the "*Book of the New Sun*", *Soldier of the Mist* is obviously only a part of the whole ...'.[4] While this analogy may seem mundane, the publication of *Soldier of the Mist* marked only the second occasion on which Wolfe chose to write a multi-volume narrative, a fact that establishes an obvious link between Latro's odyssey and Severian's journey across Urth. Although the validity of Searles's claim for a textual association is not in doubt, it does not adequately represent how extensively *Soldier of the Mist* reflects on The Urth Cycle.

Wolfe explicitly identifies Latro's account with that of Severian when he adopts the persona of an editor who tenders both narratives as transla-tions from historical accounts.[5] Where Severian's memoir comes to Wolfe, in his guise as editor, along the fictional corridors of Time, he receives Latro's dislocated notations, more feasibly, from a 'Mr. D_____ A_____ ... a dealer and collector in Detroit [who] knowing my interest in dead languages ... asked me to provide [a] translation' after a number of Latro's scrolls were 'found behind a collection of Roman lyres in the basement of the British Museum' (*S. Mist*, p. xi). It seems probable here that Wolfe is punning on 'lyre' and 'liar', self-consciously acknowledging the falseness of his claim for the scroll's veracity and Latro's unreliability: Latro is, albeit unwittingly, a Roman liar.

Latro, Wolfe explains in the preface to *Soldier of the Mist*, expresses a 'disastrous penchant for abbreviation' (*S. Mist*, p. xii) and, as a consequence, Wolfe the editor has been 'forced' to add 'details merely implied in the text in some instances and [give] in full some conversations given in summary' (*S. Mist*, p. xii). Such expansion corresponds to the 'substitutions' that Wolfe makes in his 'translation' of Severian's narrative in which linguistic rather than narratorial, dialogic or grammatical approximations are provided for the reader. In each instance, he emphasises the inherent fictionality of the narrative by endowing it with an ironic pseudo-veracity.

Wolfe extends these fictional associations further by drawing an explicit equation between the 'substitutions' operating in *The Book of the New Sun* and Latro's mistranslations of common Greek nouns, which arise from the character's inability to read Greek. Although these linguistic approxima-tions develop from different sources, with one set furnished by a fictional editor and the other by a fictional protagonist, and serve particular thematic and interpretative functions in their respective novels, both have their origin in Wolfe the author, who draws attention to the gap between the signifier and what is signified to show how the diction of each text is 'suggestive rather than definitive'.

The presentation of *Soldier of the Mist* and *The Book of the New Sun* as imprecise renderings of actual manuscripts provides the foundation for the more complex, and more significant, relationship that Wolfe constructs between Latro and Severian. As Jenny Blackford remarks:

> Latro ... shows an odd similarity with a familiar torturer [Severian], questing with a small changing band of people in a magic-charged and dangerous landscape. Severian talks with the cacogens and the ultimate (?) deity, Latro with Mediterranean gods and goddesses.[6]

While the reader could disagree with Blackford's assertion that Severian quests across a 'magic-charged ... landscape', the comparison she draws is a valid one. Each narrator is accompanied by a group of characters whose composition shifts constantly as the narrator progresses from one encounter to the next. Observing this connection, Robert Killheffer has argued that the members of Latro's group equate broadly to those who associate with Severian:

> Eurykles the Necromancer, who slowly changes sex and becomes Drakaina, is like Dr Talos and Baldanders (as a man) and like Jolenta as a woman. As Eurykles he follows the same Faustian quest for forbidden knowledge ... As Drakaina, she, like Jolenta, is irresistible in her beauty, seeking power over men ... unswerving in her pursuit of her own self-interest ...
>
> Io ... is like Dorcas. She attaches herself to Latro ... and she too is the embodiment of innocence.
>
> The Black Man [Seven Lions] is comparable to Jonas though the relationship between him and Latro is the reverse of that between Jonas and Severian. Seven Lions cares for Latro after the battle where he is wounded, as Severian cares for Jonas in the forgotten prison room in the House Absolute ... Severian helps Jonas return to his lost past, and Seven Lions is trying to help Latro back to his.[7]

In describing these connections, Killheffer overlooks the fact that Pindaros, who befriends Latro and who seeks constantly to free him from slavery, is also a candidate for an equation with Jonas. Apart from this oversight, Killheffer's observations expose an uncomplicated affinity between the two narrators which Wolfe develops through the plotting of *Soldier of the Mist*.

Like Severian, Latro is in exile: where Severian is literally expelled from his Guild, Latro's banishment is an 'eviction' from his past. The fate of each narrator is the result of an action found to be unacceptable by those in positions of power: Severian is despatched by his Masters for aiding Thecla while Latro is afflicted with amnesia for defiling the temple of Demeter at Platæa (something to which Wolfe alludes in his quotation from Herodotus [see *S. Mist*, p. vii]).

In time, Severian and Latro become conciliators. As Severian reconciles the Hierogrammates with humanity by securing the success of the former's evolutionary plans, so Latro, somewhat more modestly, makes the gods and goddesses who appear to him manifest to others simply by touching them (for example, see *S. Mist*, pp. 29 and 234). In each case, the character forms a bridge between the natural and supranatural worlds.

Wolfe explicitly confirms Latro's identification with Severian in *Soldier of Arete*. When Latro encounters the wood nymph, Elata, in a stand of pine trees, she remarks, 'Most who come to my wood sacrifice to me, and I wondered why you—who are so many—did not.'[8] Elata's parenthetical clause, emphasised as it is by its position, seems to have little direct relevance in the context of the *Soldier* novels except, perhaps, for suggesting the numerous roles that Latro is encouraged to play in the scheme of various gods and goddesses. However, this clause serves a more important intertextual function, establishing an unambiguous link between Latro and Severian who, as Autarch, embodies the personalities and memories of a succession of previous rulers.

Most critics have overlooked these similarities in favour of emphasising the apparent differences between the two protagonists. Working from a review of Latro's narrative by Dennis Callegari, Van Ikin insists that *Soldier of the Mist* 'is in many ways a "mirror image" of aspects of *The Book of the New Sun*; Severian relied on a trustworthy memory, whereas Latro's "memory" [his scrolls] is artificial and questionable'.[9] Despite observing a number of parallels shared by the texts, Killheffer concurs: 'The *Soldier* series is a "mirror image" of *The Book of the New Sun*: Severian relied on a trustworthy memory, and only misses the events of his earliest youth; Latro has almost complete amnesia ...'.[10] By concentrating on the differences between Wolfe's characters, Ikin and Killheffer accept Latro's unreliability as a simple inversion of Severian's evident reliability. This assumption prevents them from recognising that Latro's fallibility actually represents an exaggerated expression of Severian's own unreliability.

Wolfe's penchant for enfolding significant intertextual analogies within ostensibly insignificant contrasts first became apparent when he acknowledged that, in one way at least, *Soldier of the Mist* was a response to *The Book of the New Sun*. In his interview with Elliot Swanson, Wolfe observes how '[a] dozen reviewers have said Severian has a magic sword. It isn't magic, he doesn't think it's magic. In *Soldier of the Mist* I gave up and gave the hero ... a magic sword—it cuts things.'[11] Wolfe's response to his inattentive reviewers borders on the sardonic. In his artificial, despondent 'surrender' to such commentators he does not simply invert the nonmagical status of *Terminus Est* to provide Latro with a magic weapon, but exaggerates the ordinary qualities of Severian's sword to give the impression that Latro's blade embodies such an inversion.

For all his protestations, Wolfe is not surrendering to his critics by providing them with what they expect. Rather, he is continuing the game that reflects his fascination for the distinction between the apparent and the real. 'I ... gave the hero ... a magic sword—it cuts things', he remarks, and his contemptuous bathos undermines the observable difference between *Terminus Est* and Latro's *Falcata* by emphasising the formidable sharpness shared by each blade. What appears initially as Wolfe's compromise with those reviewers who wished to find magical swords in his fiction is, on closer examination, merely the illusion of a compromise: *Falcata*, although blessed by 'the Swift God', is akin to *Terminus Est*; it simply 'cuts things'.

Wolfe's affection for parallels and inversions (and parallels in inversions) is also manifest in the relationship between Latro and Severian. Although Latro's amnesia is a seemingly obvious inversion of Severian's mnemonism, this inversion conceals a basic similarity: both protagonists have an abnormal memory capacity. In this context, Latro exists, primarily, to destabilise the reader's faith in Severian's credibility. By exaggerating Latro's focalisation, Wolfe undermines whatever confidence the reader has in the ability of a first-person narrator to produce a veracious autobiography. Having subverted this narrative form generally, Wolfe directs the reader to his specific subversion of Severian's account by ensuring that the reader apprehends the parallels—discussed previously—that identify Latro's memoir with that of Severian.

In *Soldier of the Mist*, Wolfe refutes the reader's trust in the accuracy of first-person accounts by allowing the reader to understand more than the protagonist. Unlike Latro, who neglects to reread his scroll, and thereby misinterprets the political and social situations he encounters, the reader is capable of recalling the incidents that Latro has recorded. As the fantasy writer and reviewer Craig Shaw Gardner observes, 'When a serpent-demon possesses the body of a necromancer ... Latro perceives the necromancer's true nature immediately, but forgets it over and over again. Of course, we remember it.'[12]

In *Soldier of the Mist*, the fictional 'I' is never assimilated into the actual 'I' because of this asymmetrical distribution of knowledge. As Killheffer remarks, Latro 'can only read as we read, and while this brings us closer to him in one sense, it prevents the same kind of understanding and identification [found] in *The Book of the New Sun*'.[13] By retarding the kind of intimate reader–character relationship found in Severian's account, Wolfe encourages the reader to view Latro's observations objectively and then apply that objectivism to The Urth Cycle.

Once Wolfe has disturbed the reader's confidence in the probity of Severian's memoir-novel, he is free to signal that Severian is both intentionally perfidious and unintentionally deceived. For example, when Latro forgets, or chooses not to record his experiences, lacunae break the novel into dislocated sections which the reader must unite using the non-sequential accounts of other characters to preserve a sense of continuity. This fragmented record, as Budrys observes, reflects back on Severian's memoir: 'As in *The Book of the New Sun*, some events are omitted, to be picked up in subsequent volumes, and some may prove to have been mistakenly described by persons with an interest in those descriptions.'[14]

In *Soldier of the Mist*, the lacunae that fracture Latro's record arise from his incapacity to remember that he must write in his scroll every day: he is an unwittingly unreliable narrator. Conversely, the gaps occurring between each volume of The Urth Cycle are the result of Severian consciously omitting certain details: he is, therefore, in part, an intentionally unreliable narrator.

By juxtaposing the accidental lacunae present in Latro's scroll with the omissions that divide Severian's text, Wolfe is again attempting to dispel the myth that when reading The Urth Cycle, 'the reader must be as patient as if he or she were truly a passive observer of a living mind'[15] by showing that 'living mind' to possess a disingenuous artfulness.

Latro's amnesia also alludes to the source of Severian's own involuntary unreliability. When Latro elects to trust the will and guidance of Apollo, Pindaros asks him, somewhat rhetorically: 'Is it because you can't remember the past that you're so wise, Latro?' (*S. Mist*, p. 104). This question provides a conspicuous juncture between Latro's narrative and *The Book of the New Sun* by implying that because Severian can remember the past with abnormal clarity he lacks the wisdom that Pindaros observes in Latro.

Clearly, wisdom can be viewed as either a personal quality derived from experience and knowledge or as an individual proclivity, autonomous from previous experience, and possibly pertaining to a perception of arcane or recondite matters. It is this latter form of wisdom that Pindaros sees in Latro who, although capable of misinterpreting his situation, is remarkably perspicacious in his understanding of the mechanics of his universe within the frame of his socio-cultural references.

As he forgets the secular events and relationships he endures, Latro is deprived of the experiential prejudices and associations that would otherwise colour his observations. As a result of his amnesia he is able to offer clear, commonsensical, philosophical commentaries on the Olympian-governed life of Classical humanity. In *Soldier of Arete*, for example, he realises:

> The gods own this world, not we. We are but landless men, even the most powerful king. The gods permit us to till their fields, then take our crop. We meet and love, someone builds a tomb for us, perhaps. It does not matter—someone else will rob it, and the winds puff away our dust; we shall be forgotten. For me it is no different, only faster; but I have written in my scroll how Pharetra [an Amazon] smiled at me. For as long as the papyrus is preserved she will be here, though even little Io is only brown dust sobbing down the night wind with all the rest. (*S. Arete*, p. 166)

Latro's wisdom—in this case his understanding of the irrelevance of the individual in the face of time—exists as a sharp contrast to Severian's verbose, and often irrelevant, pseudo-philosophical digressions. Unlike Latro, Severian remembers a wealth of colourful but largely extraneous information that opposes any chance he has of determining the 'reality' of his Hierogrammate-governed universe.

For all the meandering exegeses that Severian offers to account for what he witnesses on Yesod and Urth, he lacks Latro's talent for recognising the relationship between the metaphysical, or suprareal world, and the realm of humanity. When Latro asks himself, and the reader, 'How can a man draw conclusions from what he does not comprehend?' (*S. Mist*, p. 145), the question reflects back on the invalidity of Severian's own conclusions.

In his role as a 'meta-character', Latro also reveals how fruitlessly deflective The Urth Cycle actually is. By confronting the reader with a character who is ignorant of the identities of the Immortals and the events unfolding around him, yet who provides sufficient clues for the reader to ascertain such information, Wolfe encourages the reader to clarify the details of the *Soldier* novels through cross-referencing. Blackford, for example, notes how *Soldier of the Mist* sent her 'to Mircea Eliade's *Zalmoxis: The Vanishing God* ... then ... to *The Penguin Atlas of Ancient History* ...'.[16] While this response implies that *Soldier of the Mist* is as unrelentingly digressive as The Urth Cycle, such a suggestion would overlook a fundamental difference between the narratives. Unlike the deflective allusions found in Severian's account, the mythical and historical references in *Soldier of the Mist* provide points from where the reader can seek clarification of the book's events. In this case, it appears that Wolfe has written *Soldier of the Mist* to demonstrate, by contrast, the unproductive digressive influence of The Urth Cycle.

Having used *Soldier of the Mist* to reveal the existence and source of Severian's unreliability and to show The Urth Cycle as often being unprofitably dilatory, Wolfe employs its sequel, *Soldier of Arete*, to disclose how Severian's text functions as a memory system inspired by the Classical art of memory.

In *Soldier of Arete*, Wolfe transports Latro to the Pythian Games at Delphi, having embroiled him in the pursuit of Oeobazus, the engineer responsible for splicing the huge ropes that held Xerxes's bridge of boats intact across the Hellespont. After a number of interconnected adventures, Latro is introduced to the poet Simonides, now reputed to have been the originator of the principles of the Classical art of memory.[17]

When Simonides learns of Latro's amnesia, he resolves to give him 'a lesson in the art of memory' (*S. Arete*, p. 225) in an attempt to alleviate some of Latro's difficulties. During this lesson, Simonides instructs Latro to erect a large 'memory palace' in his mind, to imagine its location, and the very stones of its walls, in absolute detail:

> 'Now you must lay your foundation ... Then you're ready to lay the floor. It must be of smooth marble, white, but veined brown and black. Into each slab some glyph has been cut, and no glyph is like any other ... Look back at your palace. It's very high, isn't it?'
> It was, with a hundred lofty arches and airy galleries, and course on course of pillars, each towering colonnade thrusting a hundred carved capital above the last ...
> 'What do you see ... before you?'
> An avenue lined with statues.
> 'What are the statues? Describe them.'
> Lions with the faces of men.
> 'No, only the one nearest you is a lion with a man's face—that's what's deceived you ... Describe the statue facing the one you've already described.'
> A winged lion, with the head and breasts of a woman ...
> *'Look back now at the lion with a man's face. Study it carefully. It shall be the conservator of your name. The stone is soft. Take out your knife and carve your name ... in the right foreleg of this statue.'* (*S. Arete*, pp. 226–30)

While this sequence identifies Latro with the sphinx, thereby implying that his life and his narrative are a riddle to be solved through interpretation, Latro's meeting with Simonides allows Wolfe to provide the reader with the principles of the Classical art of memory. Using Simonides's lesson, Wolfe illustrates how the ancients believed that the memory could be artificially enhanced by imagining a series of locations (in Latro's case the floor slabs and statues of his palace) on which mnemonic images or memory prompts could be inscribed.

Imagined stone by stone, Latro builds his memory palace at the border of a desert: to the north is nothing but '[d]esert. Yellow sand and red stones'; to the east, '[m]ore desert. Rocky hills ... that climb higher and higher. The sun peeps above them'; to the south, 'yellow sand lying in waves like the sea'; and to the west, '[f]ields of barley and millet, and the mud huts of peasants. Beyond is the river, and beyond the river the setting sun' (*S. Arete*, pp. 227–28). By situating the palace in an arid land where it is flanked by the rising and setting sun, Wolfe emphasises the importance of an image of the sun to Latro's memory system. In fact, Wolfe makes a considerable effort to draw the reader's attention to the presence of the sun by compressing time until Latro witnesses both sunrise and sunset in a matter of moments. The diurnal arc described by the sun as Latro looks south not only symbolises his day-long memory but also represents how his memory palace exists, quite literally, under the sun.

For Wolfe, a writer with an undeniable penchant for metaphor and symbol and renown for linguistic puns, such a location is unlikely to be coincidental. Indeed, by positioning the building under the sun he seems to be directing the reader, albeit elliptically, to the existence of the similar system implicit within, that is metaphorically 'lying beneath', the structure of Severian's narrative.

To confirm the basic principles of the Classical art of memory for the reader, Wolfe describes Simonides's technique a second time when Latro needs to recall the proceedings of a banquet he is to attend:

> In my avenue of statues there stands one of the Hydra; it has seven heads and four feet. I cut an event into each: *the first sacrifices, the speeches, Themistocles' own speech, the presentations of the gifts to him, his offerings, our march, my offering, the ceremony of manumission, and the drowning of the torches.* (*S. Arete*, pp. 281–82)

At this point in the narrative, the italicised passage collates with the similarly highlighted paragraph in Simonides's original explanation to reinforce the reader's understanding of how a memory system functions. Having delineated the conventions of the Classical art of memory, Wolfe leaves the reader to apprehend the connection between the memory system described in *Soldier of Arete* and that which is implicit in The Urth Cycle. Appreciating this juncture depends on the reader recognising the possibility that if an amnesiac must construct a memory palace to improve his memory, then a mnemonist like Severian is capable of producing a similar system subconsciously, a system that will be perceptible in the memoir he produces.

Clearly, Wolfe does not make the association between Latro's memory palace and Severian's mnemotechnically arranged text explicit. However, he does provide sufficiently comprehensive details of the *ars memoriae* for the reader to begin to understand how the narrative patterning of Severian's account might constitute the elementary 'architecture' of a memory system.

Such a reading seems to be entirely in keeping with Wolfe's desires, as the advice Latro receives from Apollo shortly after the battle of Platæa suggests. 'Look beneath the sun' (*S. Mist*, p. 16), the god counsels, an instruction Pindaros believes to indicate 'that the light of understanding [will come] from' Apollo (*S. Mist*, p. 16). The god's words, and Pindaros's interpretation, not only allude to the guidance that Apollo could offer Latro during his quest but also represent important recommendations to the reader of The Urth Cycle.

By re-examining Wolfe's pentalogy in the light of the *Soldier* novels, that is, by metaphorically looking 'beneath the sun' at the subtexts revealed in Latro's account, 'the light of understanding' shines on the reader, who begins to realise the interpretation Wolfe intends for the text. 'Those who stare at the sun go blind' (*S. Arete*, p. 8), Latro warns, and his words imply that if the reader wishes to understand Severian's story fully then he or she must look beneath its surface features or risk being dazzled by its extravagant complexity.

Wolfe endeavours to help the reader to overcome the intricacy of The Urth Cycle by paralleling its most significant subtext, Severian's manipulation by the Hierogrammates, in the *Soldier* novels. To ensure that the unveiling of this subtext is palpable, Wolfe establishes analogies between the socio-political situation of the Greek city states in the fifth century BC and that of the Commonwealth of Urth. In *Soldier of the Mist*, Greece is, as Algis Budrys explains, 'locked in combat with Persia, and riven internally by aggravated forms of its customary warfare between the city states, all of which expresses itself with what we today would call Byzantine complexity'.[18]

The unstable political situation of the Hellenic world recalls conditions in Severian's Commonwealth. Both societies have been invaded by an empire with superior military power: in *Soldier of the Mist* the empire is Persia; in The Urth Cycle, it is Ascia's forces that have ravaged the Commonwealth's northern lands. In Greece, the intrigue between Athens and Sparta, which led to the Peloponnesian War, mirrors the unrest in the Commonwealth, reflecting the division between Vodalus's radicals, who wish to restore Urth to its former imperial glory, and the Autarch's conservatism, which holds society in stasis for the coming of the New Sun. Standing above the petty affairs of humankind are the gods and goddesses of the Greek pantheon and the Hierogrammates, both of whom interfere constantly with the course of human history.

By invoking the name of Byzantium, Budrys draws, apparently by chance, an unconscious but significant analogy with observations made by Faren Miller concerning life on Urth. Miller considers Severian to be 'enmeshed in a metaphysics of Byzantine ... complexity',[19] a metaphor that underlines the resemblance between Classical Greece and the post-historic Urth.

Into these complex worlds, Wolfe introduces narrators who become inextricably entangled in the machinations of political groups and non-human entities who manipulate them for their own purposes. In contrast to Severian's recruitment by the otherworldly forces that shape human destiny, which has passed largely unacknowledged by critics, Latro's enlistment has been reported in a number of reviews. Robert Reilly, for example, notes how Latro 'is the focal point for a struggle between Cynthia and Gaea, constantly manipulated by the men and women around him, who want to use his heroic military capabilities to advance their own ends'.[20] Blackford agrees: 'Latro and his companions are pawns in the politics of the Greek city states and their northern neighbours in the turmoil of the Persian war. At a deeper level, however, they are also the playthings of the gods.'[21]

It is surprising that no critic has remarked how Latro's exploitation by Demeter and the Triple Goddess is a duplication of Severian's employment by the Hierogrammates, particularly when Wolfe makes considerable efforts to identify Latro with Severian, and the Greek gods with the governors of his cosmos. Indeed, Wolfe facilitates the comparison between Classical deity and myth-making alien further by demonstrating how the gods and goddesses of ancient Greece can manifest themselves in a number of different aspects or guises: like the Hierogrammates, they are, in a sense, metamorphs or shape-shifters.

For any reader who overlooks the kinship between these plastic creatures, Wolfe furnishes a key metaphor that unambiguously unites god with Hierogrammate. In *Soldier of Arete*, Wolfe informs the reader that two of the goddesses from the Greek pantheon, '[t]he Lady of Thought [Demeter] and the Huntress [Diana], were playing draughts, which means that each will use [Latro] in the game if she can' (*S. Arete*, p. 79). The metaphor of the game of draughts recalls Apheta's description of the Hierogrammates' actions against entropy as a game of 'shah mat'—an early form of chess (see *Urth*, p. 135). Clearly, the Greek gods and the Hierogrammates both play games with humanity to satisfy their desires. For Demeter and Diana, Latro is a pawn in a feud over land and worship; for the Hierogrammates, Severian is the key actor in the masquerade that enables them to obviate a rebellion on Urth.

Perhaps uncertain that his readers would register this comparison, Wolfe identifies himself with Demeter just as he associates himself with the Hierogrammates. 'The wolf is one of the badges of the Great Mother [Demeter or Ceres]' (*S. Mist*, p. 133), Pindaros explains in the company of Latro, who bears 'the wolf's tooth' (*S. Mist*, p. 147), the wound that enabled Demeter to steal his memory. While Demeter does not quite become synonymous with Wolf(e), the references made to her association with wolves leave the reader in no doubt that the goddess is an analogue of a manipulative author figure.

Using these analogies and relationships, Wolfe seeks to expose Severian's manipulation to help the reader to apprehend the story that accounts for the textual strategies and conceits he employs throughout The Urth Cycle. If he succeeds in alerting his readers to Severian's recruitment by the Hierogrammates, they are likely to ask: What prevents Severian, and the reader, from recognising his seduction into the Hierogrammates' schemes? What is the purpose of the masquerade perpetrated by the Hierogrammates? And, if the Hierogrammates can engineer their own solar systems, why do they need Severian to rejuvenate the old sun? Each of these enquiries brings the reader closer to the interpretation that Wolfe intends for his pentalogy, an interpretation he continues to direct the reader towards in the four-volume *The Book of the Long Sun*.

It seems probable that the reluctance of critics and reviewers to observe the commentary offered on The Urth Cycle by the *Soldier* novels was at least partly responsible for Wolfe's decision to make a second, less equivocal attempt to reconstruct the reader's understanding of Severian's account. No longer trusting the effectiveness of elliptical parallels embedded within apparent inversions to chart the subtexts of Severian's narrative, Wolfe constructed *The Book of the Long Sun* to expose the subterfuge at the heart of The Urth Cycle once and for all.

Wolfe makes the intertextual correlation between these two multi-volume texts explicit by imitating the title and four-volume structure of *The Book of the New Sun* in *The Book of the Long Sun*. *The Book of the Short Sun* trilogy (*On Blue's Waters*, *In Green's Jungles* and *Return to the Whorl*), like *The Urth of the New Sun*, forms a coda to its four-volume forerunner, establishing a further relationship between the two series. In order to extend this connection further, Wolfe locates the dramatic action of *The Book of the Long Sun* aboard *The Whorl*, a vast generation starship launched by the Urthly dictator Typhon the First.

When the first volume, *Nightside the Long Sun* (1993), begins, *The Whorl* has been travelling for 300 years. Like Urth, the vessel is succumbing to entropy and supports a number of cultures in which advanced technology is becoming scarcer every year; the androids or 'chems' aboard are malfunctioning and irreparably archaic; children use slates rather than keyboards; and mechanised transportation is retained only by rich criminals, corrupt politicians, or the military. Even the nine major gods who once presided over life aboard the ship seem to have withdrawn themselves from the affairs of humanity and retired to their Olympian realm of 'Mainframe', unwilling to manifest themselves in their 'sacred windows'.

Nightside the Long Sun opens in the city of Viron as Patera Silk, the young augur of the Sun Street manteion, or church school, and Wolfe's protagonist, receives enlightenment—a momentary flash of insight into the workings of *The Whorl* and the universe—from the Outsider, a minor god in the ship's pantheon who seems to correspond particularly to the Christian

Trinity. After his enlightenment, Silk becomes embroiled in a series of typically labyrinthine Wolfeian intrigues that force him to develop from an uncertain though perspicacious priest into a reluctant thief and an errant political leader in less than a fortnight. Bribed into becoming a thief for Blood, a criminal who purchases the manteion from Silk's holy chapter, Silk is, both literally and figuratively, 'the tool of Blood'.[22] In this new role, he unwittingly prompts a rebellion against the corrupt Ayunta-miento, or city council, which has retained absolute and illegal power since the old caldé, or mayor, died without nominating a clear successor.

Silk, like Latro, is a protagonist who demonstrates a remarkable affinity with Severian. However, unlike the characteristics that Latro shares with Severian, which are obfuscated by tortuous inversions, the similarities that unite Silk with Severian are simple, readily observable, and often dependent on details of physical appearance. Both characters, for example, are raised in a monastic environment and wear black robes; both follow rigid traditions and rites; and both, in their own way, are executioners. Although Silk's victims are animals, he, like Severian, 'butchers' creatures in his power as part of his duty to an organisation whose code of practice was prescribed centuries before. It is even possible that Silk's chapter may have been based on the Order of Seekers for Truth and Penitence just as its religion is based on a perversion of the state religion of Typhon's era.

As *The Book of the Long Sun* develops, it becomes increasingly apparent that Wolfe wants the reader to make these connections as his inter-character analogy becomes more explicit. At the conclusion of *Nightside the Long Sun*, Silk realises:

> The Outsider had not only spoken to him, but had somehow split him in two: the Patera Silk who lived here [at the manteion] and he, himself, the failed thief … Patera Silk and Silk nightside. He found that he, the latter, was contemptuous of the former, though envious, too. (*Nightside*, pp. 331–32)

Silk is divided into a literal and a metaphorical light and dark aspect, a 'dayside' and a 'nightside' existence that recalls Severian's seemingly opposite, though ultimately convergent, roles as torturer and 'saviour', as a personification of darkness and a symbol of light.

Wolfe confirms this identification in *Lake of the Long Sun* when Mamelta, a woman newly awakened from suspended animation in the chambers beneath Viron, tells Silk: 'You have a bruise on your face, and you're lame' (p. 247). Mamelta's reference to Silk's lameness (a consequence of a broken ankle) and his facial contusions immediately recalls the injuries that Severian receives to his leg and face in *The Citadel of the Autarch*, which leave him limping and badly scarred. The contrast between Silk's injuries, which will eventually heal, and Severian's permanent scars, which reassert themselves even after his resurrection in *The Urth of the New Sun*, serves to separate Silk, who can transform himself from priest to thief to political leader as the secular and religious conditions around him change, from Severian, whose personality remains largely static.

Despite the disparity of their reactions to changes in their personal and social circumstances, Silk and Severian find themselves in situations that are not altogether dissimilar. Both characters are born into worlds in the throes of entropic decline, divided by political instability and threatened by a sun that has begun to falter. On Urth, the sun is gradually cooling; within *The Whorl*, the Long Sun is overheating, suffering from an imbalance that has probably arisen as a result of the erasure of a core program from the supercomputer regulating life aboard the vessel.

As *The Book of the Long Sun* and The Urth Cycle progress, Wolfe's protagonists rise from obscurity to positions of political or religious prominence after having their lives 'rewritten' by external forces. In *The Book of the New Sun* this rewriting is achieved by the Hierogrammates through the agency of the Claw of the Conciliator. In *The Book of the Long Sun* a comparable influence is effected over Silk when he receives enlightenment from the Outsider. Whether this experience is a religious one or, as Blood's doctor, Crane, suggests, a psychological phenomenon prompted by the bursting of a blood vessel in Silk's brain, is of secondary importance to the effect Silk's 'enlightenment' has on his life.[23] The incident arouses Silk's faith in the Outsider, and this faith, like Severian's belief in the religious power of the Claw of the Conciliator and his own divinity, allows Silk to justify his own willingness to be subjected to the desires of others: he is convinced that his trials are the result of the Outsider's undisclosed plan and suffers his hardships and pain with a kind of joyous fatalism until the final volume when he almost succumbs to despair.

Silk believes that the Outsider has recruited him to save the manteion on Sun Street from destruction. To facilitate this salvation, he becomes an agent of Blood, is embroiled in a plot by the city of Trivigaunte to restore Viron's caldé and control the expansionist policies of its Ayuntamiento, finds himself at the heart of an intrigue within his own chapter of augurs, is caught in a dispute between the major gods and goddesses of *The Whorl* and the minor goddess, Kypris, and submits to the will of the people by becoming caldé. He meets one of the ship's crew, travels to Mainframe and sees the first lander leave *The Whorl* bound for the colony world Blue. Like Severian and Latro, Silk is engaged by various factions as they struggle to further their own specific personal or political agenda. Indeed, the very fact that Silk is so obviously the puppet of numerous god-like, political and religious groups suggests a certain desperation in Wolfe, who may have begun to doubt that any reader of The Urth Cycle would recognise Severian as a lay figure in the Hierogrammates' plans.

However, *The Book of the Long Sun* is much more than a further attempt by Wolfe to awaken the reader to Severian's manipulation within systems over which he has no control. Rather, Wolfe has created *The Whorl* and its conflated religion to reveal, through analogy, how the Hierogrammates control the responses of the Commonwealth's population subliminally by exploiting the human need for myth and worship using the contrived legend of the Conciliator.

Wandering the subterranean corridors under Viron with two chemico-mechanical soldiers in *Lake of the Long Sun*, Silk draws the reader's attention to this human requirement when he acknowledges that

> [a] need to worship is [one] of those standing orders. It is innate in man that he cannot help wanting to thank the immortal gods, who give him all he possesses, even life. You and your sergeant saw fit to disparage our sacrifices, and I will very willingly grant that they're pitifully inadequate. Yet they satisfy, to a considerable degree, that otherwise unmet need, for the community as well as for many individuals. (*Lake*, pp. 223–24)

This need, which is intrinsic in the people of Severian's Commonwealth, was recognised and exploited by Typhon, the monarch who oversaw the construction and launch of *The Whorl*. Later, in *Lake of the Long Sun*, one of the councillors on Viron's Ayuntamiento explains to Silk:

> The monarch's doctors tinkered with the minds of the men and women he put into the Whorl [skilfully] erasing as much as he dared of their personal lives.
>
> … The surgeons found, however, that their patients' memories of their ruler, his family, and some of his officials were too deeply entrenched to be eliminated altogether. To obscure the record, they renamed them. Their ruler … became Pas, the shrew he married, Echidna, and so on. She had borne him seven children. We call them Scylla, Molpe, Tartaros, Hierax, Thelxiepeia, Phaea, and Sphigx.
>
> … Scylla was as strong-willed as the monarch himself [and] her father allowed her to found our city [Viron] and many others. She founded your chapter as well, a parody of the state religion of her own whorl. She was hardly more than a child, you understand, and the rest younger than even she. (*Lake*, p. 299)

The state religion that Scylla parodied was Roman Catholicism, evidenced by the reappearance of exorcism (*Nightside*, pp. 282–93), the recurrent use of the sign of the cross as 'the sign of addition' (*Nightside*, p. 20), the last rites as 'the Pardon of Pas' (*Nightside*, pp. 74–75), and, most obviously, confession, absolution, and penance, or forgiveness, which re-emerge as the shriving of sin from individuals who can redeem themselves through 'meritorious acts' (see *Nightside*, pp. 80–87) rather than through additional rosaries.

Wolfe's willingness to pervert his own religion, as he does other mythological systems, for the creation of a fictional faith should indicate to the reader that the Christian echoes found in The Urth Cycle must be examined in their context rather than being accepted simply as an indication that the text is some form of obscure Christian allegory. Indeed, *The Book of the Long Sun* reads very much as a renunciation of the orthodoxy and paraphernalia of Roman Catholic worship in favour of the less formulated Christianity of the Apostolic Era.

Aware of the human need for myth and religious practice described by Silk, 'Pas' and his family were loaded into 'Mainframe' (a place considered synonymous with Heaven by Silk and his fellow augurs but really the supercomputer controlling *The Whorl*) as 'patterns' (*Lake*, p. 115), where they assumed the status of gods to the conditioned colonists—the 'cargo'—on board. These 'patterns' are artificially intelligent computer programs capable of evolving, 'learning and growing' (*Lake*, p. 115), but held in Mainframe as binary code (see *Lake*, p. 116).

After their introduction into the ship's computer systems, Typhon and his family retained their psychologically disturbed personalities (see *Lake*, p. 299–300). In a parody of Genesis, Scylla reveals how these warped individuals

> [in] the beginning ... chose up, with Daddy to be god of everything ...
> ... Mama got to pick next, and she grabbed the whole inner surface.
> ... What none of us knew was that he'd let *her* choose, too. So she picked love, what a surprise. And got sex and everything dirty with it. (*Lake*, pp. 274–75)

The 'her' to whom Scylla refers with childish petulance is Kypris, Pas/Typhon's mistress and a pattern that has been a fugitive in the ship's computer systems ever since Pas/Typhon was 'wiped ... out of core' 30 years earlier by members of his own family (see *Lake*, p. 274).

Pas/Typhon's erasure not only forced Kypris to flee from his angered wife and homicidal daughter Scylla but also resulted in a shift in the form of freedom experienced by the inhabitants of *The Whorl*. As Patera Quetzal, the Prolocutor of Silk's chapter, notes: 'There are people who love birds so much they free them. There are others who love them so much they cage them. Pas's love of us was of the first kind. Echidna's and the Seven's is of the other.'[24] Quetzal's remark reveals the difference between Pas, who sent his subjects into the void in order to free them from the denuded Urth, and Echidna, Scylla and the rest, who desire to keep humanity locked within *The Whorl* to force them to participate in their god-games and idolatrous worship. It is reasonable to assume that Pas was erased in an attempt to prevent *The Whorl* from reaching its destination and thereby provide Echidna and her family, who failed to appreciate the dangers of destroying a program vital to the ship's survival, with a captive audience.

Having disclosed this information, Wolfe leaves the reader to observe the parallels between the god-game occurring in *The Whorl* and that played out on Urth by the Hierogrammates. However, the reader is now likely to recognise that the Hierogrammates, like Scylla and Echidna, are false gods, selfish and dictatorial, and only humanity's penchant for service and obedience to apparently metaphysical powers greater than itself enables these forces to masquerade as omnipotent gods. As Silk remarks, some-what fatalistically, 'the gods are our superiors and may act towards us as they see fit' (*Nightside*, p. 177); 'We are subject to them, not they to us, and so it shall forever be' (*Lake*, p. 39).

The contrast between Silk's direct and highly relevant observations and Severian's convoluted digressions is reflected in the striking difference between the heavily ornamented, 'Baroque' style of The Urth Cycle and the spare, unadorned writing of *The Book of the Long Sun*. This stylistic variety emblematises how Silk's story clarifies Severian's own adventures. Lacking the deflective embellishments of Wolfe's earlier pentalogy, *The Book of the Long Sun* offers a more ingenuous study of the themes of faith and delusion, of manipulation and servitude.

For those readers who fail to apprehend the metafictional nuances of *The Book of the Long Sun*, Wolfe offers one unequivocal clue to the connection between the two sequences. The manteion that Silk feels compelled to save is built on Sun Street, an avenue that runs parallel to the Long Sun. This orientation signposts the parallels between *The Book of the Long Sun* and The Urth Cycle, between Silk and Severian, *The Whorl* and the Commonwealth, and the nine artificial gods and the Hierogrammates. Sun Street also recalls Iubar Street, an avenue outside the Citadel in Nessus where Severian grows to manhood. '*Iubar*' translates from the Latin as 'a beaming light, radiance ...; the light of the sun ...'[25] and, consequently, forms an intertextual pairing with the Sun Street of *The Book of the Long Sun*.

Together, the science fantasy of *The Book of the Long Sun* and the historical fantasy of the *Soldier* novels provide a series of keys designed to unlock the subtexts of The Urth Cycle and allow something close to an authoritative understanding of its thematic concerns and textual strategies. This meta-phor is by no means inappropriate since Wolfe deploys identical symbolism in *Pandora by Holly Hollander* (1990), a self-reflexive murder mystery characterised by the consistent deployment of lock and key iconography.

Pandora by Holly Hollander is set in Barton, a small town outside Chicago and an elided form of Barrington, the Chicago suburb where Wolfe and his wife Rosemary currently live; their neighbouring town of Palatine reappears as Palestine, and David Hartwell, Wolfe's editor at Tor, is cited in passing as the man who encouraged Holly, the novel's narrator, to write her story. The reader is, consequently, involved with a fiction that plays with Wolfe's own suburban and literary environment.

If the *Soldier* novels and *The Book of the Long Sun* allude to the subtexts of The Urth Cycle, then *Pandora by Holly Hollander* serves to confirm that such oblique intertextual metafictions exist within Wolfe's oeuvre. *Pandora's* self-consciousness and its barely fictionalised rendering of Wolfe's residential area awaken the reader to the knowledge that he or she is being admitted into 'Wolfe territory'. To the cautious reader, the conspicuous lock and key iconography suggests that the novel itself is a key to understanding Wolfe's work; that the author is unlocking, or making overt, strategies he has employed more covertly in earlier fiction.

Significantly, the text's half-disclosures and endless conjectures reveal how Wolfe creates ambiguity in his fiction. When Wolfe's protagonist, Holly Hollander, meets the punningly named Aladdin Blue, an ex-con turned criminologist, Blue observes: 'An exhaustive list of my acquaintances ... would do you no good, only confuse you. If you can't guess [how he knows Holly's uncle, who is in an asylum] without that sort of information, you couldn't possibly guess if you were burdened with it.'[26] Here, and at several points within the novel, Blue and Holly are symbols for Wolfe and his reader. In this instance, Blue is offering advice not only to Holly but also to the reader of Wolfe's fiction as Wolfe often relies on a form of informational overload to confound interpretation. Such avalanches of detail, most noticeable in *The Book of the New Sun*, where an often insignificant event is used to initiate a confusing digression, burden the reader, diffusing concentration along digressive speculative paths.

Similarly, *Pandora's* conclusion, which exposes the murderess and resolves the mystery in true generic style after a welter of protracted and intricate hypotheses, implies that many of Wolfe's narratives have unequivocal solutions concealed behind a network of possible, though incorrect, interpretations.

A further insight into Wolfe's authorial strategies is provided when Holly begins to understand Blue's wily character and realises that: 'I'd told him [Blue] all the stuff I'd figured out but he hadn't told me any of his—just showed me how something I said could be wrong' (*Pandora*, p. 105). Wolfe works in precisely this manner. In The Urth Cycle, the reader is encouraged to conjecture what is occurring on Urth, to respond to the text's symbolism, its allusions, intertexts and generic characteristics, only to have Wolfe disprove or invalidate these theories later in the narrative without directly resolving the puzzles he creates. Like Blue, he holds the key to the mystery, but he does not simply hand this key to the reader, preferring to encourage 'plausible but false assumptions that [tend to] confuse things' (*Pandora*, p. 186). Behind the mask of his artful criminologist, Wolfe discloses that he knows 'a few tricks and occasionally [invents] a new one' (*Pandora*, p. 85), a self-conscious reference to the theory of fiction given in *The Shadow of the Torturer* which reveals, indirectly, the nature of these tricks to the reader.

The relationship between Blue and Holly, like that existing between Mr Smith and his solitary child, that of guide and initiate, is one that Wolfe has attempted to construct between himself and the reader throughout his intertextual metafictions. The need he sees among his readers for oblique clarifications, for a process of indirect initiation into his techniques in general and the subtexts of The Urth Cycle in particular, arises from his desire to produce narratives that are both understandable and abstruse. Wolfe wants The Urth Cycle to be understood, if only by an initiated minority, since he believes that, 'In the end … it's important for … the reader not to be confused' by what has occurred. However, he does not wish the reader to achieve this familiarity easily, partly because he enjoys literary games-playing, believing that 'part of the fun [of reading his work] is supposed to be figuring out what's happened'[27] and partly because he wishes to enlighten the reader, just as the Outsider—itself a Wolfe figure—enlightens Silk.

When critics have failed to deduce what is happening in his fiction, Wolfe has solved, either explicitly or implicitly, some of the puzzles he creates. For example, when every reviewer of *Peace* overlooked that Weer was a ghost, Wolfe explained the character's condition with surprising frankness in several subsequent interviews.[28] Wolfe's uncharacteristic candidness in these interviews can be seen as his frustrated response to critics incapable of meeting the challenges he sets, and emphasises, somewhat starkly, his desire for his work, and his concerns as a writer, to be apprehended.

For Wolfe, an author with an undeniable tendency towards indirectness, feeling compelled by reviewers incapable of recognising the subtle nuances of *Peace* to provide a bald revelatory statement could hardly have been satisfactory recompense for the effort involved in creating such a structurally and thematically complex novel. Indeed, it seems probable that Wolfe experienced a sense of regret or self-reproach for revealing the fantastical conceit at the heart of *Peace* for, when *The Book of the New Sun* met with similar critical confusion, his reaction was markedly different. During an interview with Michael Bishop, for example, Wolfe exhibited his more usual non-committal self when questioned about the enigmas of *The Shadow of the Torturer*:

> 'Will we,' [asked Bishop] 'during the course of the tetralogy, discover the identity of Severian's parents?'
> 'Only if you pay attention.'
> 'Will Thecla undergo a resurrection or metamorphosis in a subsequent book? Has she perhaps done so already?'
> 'That depends on how you define those terms.'[29]

Wolfe's deliberately laconic responses place the onus on the reader to solve the puzzles he sets: to discover who Severian's parents are, deduce what form of 'resurrection' Thecla experiences, and so forth.

It is clear that Wolfe will no longer be drawn into acts of direct clarification or demystification. Indeed, recent evidence suggests that Wolfe's attitude towards his questioners remains unchanged. When Michael Andre-Driussi compiled a list of questions from bemused readers contributing to *Whorl*, the e-mail discussion list dedicated to *The Book of the Long Sun*, Wolfe's responses were no less brusque.[30] However, as this conclusion has sought to reveal, despite remaining averse to supplying the reader with straightforward indications of how The Urth Cycle should be read, Wolfe does not abandon those readers who have found the involutions of Severian's life story too baffling to interpret. Wolfe's sense of 'fair play' manifests itself, on one level at least, in the metafictions he produces to assist a more complete reading of Severian's odyssey.

The intricacy of Wolfe's fiction, and the provision of clues designed to help the reader overcome such intricacy, reveal that Wolfe's writing is the product of two powerful, associated impulses. On the one hand, he possesses a tremendous urge to play literary games, to write complex, demanding narratives and thereby produce what he considers to be 'literary writing';[31] on the other, he wants his readers to be illuminated through the reading process, to grow and understand more of his work, of themselves, and of the world at large. The dynamic tension existing between these inclinations forms the engine that drives Wolfe to produce tortuous but ultimately solvable and satisfying textual puzzles. Like the resonantly named Mr Smith, Gene Wolfe is a Daedalian artificer of formidable skill, who, nevertheless, seems determined to encourage the reader to fly metaphorically beyond his or her own initial limits. Lest that reader suffer the fate of Icarus, though, he or she must attend Wolfe well and follow the guidance he provides.

Notes

Chapter 1

1. John Clute, 'Gene Wolfe', in John Clute and Peter Nicholls, eds, *The Encyclopedia of Science Fiction*, 2nd edn (London: Orbit, 1993), pp. 1338–40, esp. p. 1338.

2. See Malcolm Edwards, 'Gene Wolfe: An Interview', *Vector: The Critical Journal of The British Science Fiction Association*, May/June 1973, p. 7.

3. See Larry McCaffery, 'On Encompassing the Entire Universe: An Interview with Gene Wolfe', *Science-Fiction Studies*, 15, 1988, p. 349.

4. Ibid., p. 338. See also Robert Frazier, 'Gene Wolfe: The Legerdemain of the Wolfe', *Thrust: Science Fiction in Review*, Winter/Spring 1983, p. 5.

5. Gene Wolfe, in a private conversation with the author, 16 April 1997.

6. Joanna Russ, review of *Operation Ares*, *The Magazine of Fantasy and Science Fiction*, April 1971, p. 69. See also Paul Kincaid's review of *Operation Ares*, *Vector*, January/ February 1978, pp. 34–38.

7. Joan Gordon, *Starmont Reader's Guide 29: Gene Wolfe* (Washington: Starmont House, 1986), p. 17. All future references to this edition are given after quotations in the form: (*Guide*, p. xx).

8. See Michael Bishop, review of *The Fifth Head of Cerberus*, *Delap's Fantasy and Science Fiction Review*, November 1976, pp. 26–27; Pamela Sargent's review, 'Lost Peoples', *Vector*, May/June 1973, pp. 17–19; and P. Schuyler-Miller's review, *Analog Science Fiction/Science Fact*, December 1972, p. 171.

9. Thomas Monteleone, review of *The Fifth Head of Cerberus*, *Amazing Science Fiction Stories*, November 1972, p. 124.

10. Ibid., p. 129.

11. George Turner, review of *The Fifth Head of Cerberus*, *Science Fiction Commentary*, November 1973, p. 4.

12. Ibid., p. 6.

13. Ibid.

14. Albert Wendland, *Science, Myth and the Fictional Creation of Alien Worlds* (Michigan: UMI Research Press, 1985), p. 139. For Wendland's discussion of *The Fifth Head of Cerberus*, see pp. 130–39.

15. See Martin Last, review of *Peace*, *Science Fiction Review*, May 1975, p. 30; Richard Lupoff's comments in *Algol: The Magazine About Science Fiction*, Winter 1976, p. 41; and Colin Greenland's review in *TLS*, 15 March 1985, p. 284.

16. Steve Carper, review of *Peace*, *Delap's*, April 1976, p. 11.

17. George Turner, review of *Peace*, *Science Fiction Commentary*, December 1975, p. 32.

18. Ibid., p. 30.

19. Ibid., p. 31.

20. Threads of this fabric have been explored by William M. Schuyler in his review of *Peace* for *The New York Review of Science Fiction*, January 1996, pp. 19–21 and by Damien Broderick in 'Thoughts on Gene Wolfe's *Peace*', *The New York Review of Science Fiction*, March 1996, pp. 16–17.

21. Carper, review of *Peace*, p. 11.

22. Beverly Friend, review of *The Devil in a Forest*, *Delap's*, March 1977, p. 22.

23. Compare Darrell Schweitzer's review of *The Devil in a Forest*, *Science Fiction Review*, May 1977, p. 75, with Susan Wood's review in *Locus: The Newspaper of the Science Fiction Field*, April 1978, p. 13.

24. For a detailed discussion of Gene Wolfe's Catholicism in relation to 'Seven American Nights' (1978) and 'The Detective of Dreams' (1980), see Kathryn Locey, 'Three Dreams, Seven Nights, and Gene Wolfe's Catholicism', *The New York Review of Science Fiction*, July 1996, pp. 1, 8–12.

25. Gene Wolfe, cited in Joan Gordon, 'An Interview with Gene Wolfe', *Science Fiction Review*, Summer 1981, p. 18.

26. Last, review of *Peace*, p. 30.

27. See, for example, Michael Bishop's 'Pitching Pennies Against the Starboard Bulkhead: "Gene Wolfe as Hero"', *Thrust: Science Fiction in Review*, Fall 1980, pp. 10–12; Baird Searles's review of *The Shadow of the Torturer*, *Isaac Asimov's Science Fiction Magazine*, October 1980, pp. 12–15; and the late Thomas D. Clareson's comments in *Extrapolation*, 21, 1980, pp. 388–89.

28. Bishop, 'Pitching Pennies', p. 12.

29. Richard E. Geis, review of *The Shadow of the Torturer*, *Science Fiction Review*, August 1980, p. 40.

30. Colin Greenland, review of *The Shadow of the Torturer* and *The Claw of the Conciliator*, *Foundation: The International Review of Science Fiction*, 24, 1982, p. 85.

31. Algis Budrys, review of *The Claw of the Conciliator*, *The Magazine of Fantasy and Science Fiction*, June 1981, p. 49.

32. Baird Searles, review of *The Citadel of the Autarch*, *Isaac Asimov's Science Fiction Magazine*, May 1983, p. 167.

33. Colin Greenland, 'Wolfe in Sheep's Clothing', *City Limits*, 21–27 October 1983, p. 18.

34. Steve Palmer, 'Looking Behind the Sun', *Vector*, August/September 1991, p. 10.

35. Searles, review of *The Citadel of the Autarch*, p. 167.

36. See Robert Borski's 'Thinking About the Mandragora in Wolfe's *Citadel*', *The New York Review of Science Fiction*, July 1999, pp. 16–18; and 'Masks of the Father: Paternity in Gene Wolfe's *Book of the New Sun*', *The New York Review of Science Fiction*, February 2000, pp. 1, 8–16.

37. See C. N. Manlove, 'Terminus Non Est: Gene Wolfe's *The Book of the New Sun*', *Kansas Quarterly*, Summer 1984, pp. 7–20.

38. Peter Malekin, 'Remembering the Future: Gene Wolfe's *The Book of the New Sun*, in Donald Morse, ed., *The Fantastic in World Literature and the Arts: Selected Essays from the Fifth International Conference on the Fantastic in the Arts* (Westport: Greenwood Press, 1987), p. 56.

39. Ibid., p. 49.

40. Compare Colin Greenland's review of *The Urth of the New Sun*, *TLS*, 15–21 January 1988, p. 69 and Peter Nicholls's review, *Foundation*, 41, 1987, pp. 92–97, with Martin Taylor's and Paul Kincaid's reviews, *Vector*, April/May 1988, p. 28.

41. Gene Wolfe cited in Elliot Swanson's 'Interview: Gene Wolfe', *Interzone*, Autumn 1986, p. 39.

42. See Gene Wolfe, *Free Live Free* (New York: Tor, 1986), p. 403.

43. John Clute, *Strokes: Essays and Reviews 1966–1986* (Seattle: Serconia Press, 1988), p. 162. All further references to this text are given after quotations in the form: (*Strokes*, p. xx).

44. See Fernando Quadros Gouvêa's review of *Soldier of the Mist*, *Fantasy Review*, September 1986, p. 33.

45. See, for example, Van Ikin's review of *Soldier of the Mist*, *Science Fiction: A Review of Speculative Literature*, 25 (n.d.), pp. 22–23; and Robert Kilheffer's review of *Soldier of Arete*, *The New York Review of Science Fiction*, November 1989, pp. 6–7.

46. Joan Gordon, review of *There Are Doors*, *The New York Review of Science Fiction*, April 1989, p. 16.

47. See John Clute, review of *There Are Doors*, *Interzone*, July/August 1989, p. 61. Clute also observes Wolfe's indebtedness to Kafka and the myth of Atys and Cybele.

48. John Clute, review of *Castleview*, *The New York Review of Science Fiction*, August 1990, p. 6.

49. Drake Asbury III, review of *Castleview*, *Science Fiction Research Association Review*, January/February 1992, p. 98.

50. Gene Wolfe, *Castleview* (London: New English Library, 1991), p. 99.

51. Editor's note to Asbury's review of *Castleview*, p. 98.

52. Faren Miller, review of *Pandora by Holly Hollander*, *Locus*, November 1990, pp. 62–63.

53. This connection is also made by Paul Di Filippo in 'Long Night of the Wolfe', his review of *The Book of the Long Sun*, *Isaac Asimov's Science Fiction Magazine*, December 1997, pp. 154–57.

54. See, for example, Paul Park, review of *Nightside the Long Sun* and *Lake of the Long Sun*, *Foundation*, 61, 1994, pp. 97–99; and David Langford, review of *Nightside the Long Sun* and *Lake of the Long Sun*, *Vector*, February/March 1994, pp. 27–28.

Chapter 2

1. Michael Bishop, 'Pitching Pennies', p. 12.

2. Wolfe, cited in Gordon, 'An Interview with Gene Wolfe', p. 18.

3. Wolfe, cited in Melissa Mia Hall, 'An Interview with Gene Wolfe', *Amazing Science Fiction Stories*, September 1981, p. 126.

4. Both 'The Dead Man' and 'The Grave Secret' were reprinted in Wolfe's small press anthology, *Young Wolfe* (Ontario: U. M. Press, 1992), pp. 12–15 and pp. 8–10.

5. 'The Packerhous Method' and 'Checking Out' were first collected in Wolfe's anthology, *Storeys from the Old Hotel* (Worcester Park, Surrey: Kerosina Publications, 1988), pp. 99–104 and pp. 204–206. 'The Other Dead Man' was reprinted in *Endangered Species* (London: Orbit, 1990), pp. 377–99. All future references to these anthologies will be given after quotations in the text in the form: (*Storeys*, pp. xx) and (*Species*, pp. xx).

6. Bertrand Russell, *History of Western Philosophy*, 2nd edn (London: George Allen & Unwin, 1961; repr. Routledge, 1991), p. 151.

7. Ibid., p. 701.

8. Ibid., p. 702.

9. Richard L. Gregory, 'Perception' in Richard L. Gregory, ed., *The Oxford Companion to the Mind* (Oxford: Oxford University Press, 1987), p. 599.

10. Ibid.

11. Thomas D. Clareson, 'Gene Wolfe' in David Cowart and Thomas Wymer, eds, *The Dictionary of Literary Biography: Twentieth Century Science Fiction Writers*, 8 vols (Detroit: Gale Research Company, 1981), VIII, Part 2, p. 207.

12. Katie Wales, *A Dictionary of Stylistics* (London: Longman, 1989; repr. 1990), p. 179.

13. 'Feather Tigers' was reprinted in Wolfe's first anthology, *The Island of Doctor Death and Other Stories and Other Stories* (London: Arrow Books, 1981), pp. 132–39. All further references to this edition are given after quotations in the text in the form: (*Island*, pp. xx).

14. Wolfe, cited in McCaffery, 'On Encompassing the Entire Universe', p. 343.

15. Gene Wolfe in a personal conversation with the author, 16 April 1997.

16. Ibid.

17. See, for example, Edwards, 'Gene Wolfe: An Interview', p. 11.

18. Mary Warnock, *Memory* (London: Faber & Faber, 1987; repr. 1989), p. 54.

19. Ibid., pp. 54–56.

20. For a concise discussion of the respective stances of these philosophers, see Warnock, *Memory*, pp. 57–64.

21. See Gordon, *Guide*, p. 59.

22. Joan Gordon discusses Wolfe's preoccupation with isolation and isolates in *Guide*, pp, 35–36 and pp. 58–64.

23. See Gordon, *Guide*, p. 60.

24. Frances A. Yates, *The Art of Memory* (London: Pimlico, 1992), p. 11. The importance of the Classical art of memory to Wolfe's fiction is discussed in Chapters 9 and 11.

25. The sense the reader has of the text-as-puzzle compels that reader to investigate the narrative as a detective would a mystery.

26. Wolfe, cited in Gordon, 'An Interview', p. 19.

27. Gene Wolfe in a personal conversation with the author, 16 April 1997.

28. 'The Blue Mouse' was collected in *Gene Wolfe's Book of Days* (London: Arrow Books, 1985), pp. 74–88. All further references to this edition are given after quotations in the form: (*GW Days*, pp. xx).

29. 'Thou Spark of Blood' was first published in *Worlds of IF*, May 1970, pp. 105–109 and p. 157.

30. Wolfe, cited in Gordon, 'An Interview', p. 18. See also McCaffery, 'On Encompassing the Entire Universe', p. 342.

31. Gene Wolfe, *Operation Ares* (London: Fontana Books, 1978), p. 131.

32. Gene Wolfe in a personal conversation with the author, 16 April 1997.

Chapter 3

1. For an expression of Wolfe's belief in the importance of possessing an understanding of a reader's possible reactions to any given text during the writing process, see *Endangered Species*, pp. 1–2.

2. Wayne C. Booth, *The Rhetoric of Fiction* (Chicago: University of Chicago Press, 1961), p. 159.

3. Ibid., p. 324.

4. George Aichele, 'Self-reflexivity in Gene Wolfe's "Seven American Nights"', *The Journal of the Fantastic in the Arts*, 2, 1991, p. 38. See also Gordon, *Guide*, pp. 67–72.

5. Michael Bishop, 'Pitching Pennies', p. 12.

6. Booth, *The Rhetoric of Fiction*, p. 304.

7. Ibid.

8. Bruce Gillespie, 'Gene Wolfe's Sleight of Hand', *The Australian Science Fiction Review*, March 1986, p. 12.

9. Michael Bishop, review of *The Fifth Head of Cerberus*, p. 26.

10. Gillespie, 'Gene Wolfe's Sleight of Hand', p. 15.

11. Ibid.

12. Wolfe, cited in Gordon, 'An Interview', p. 20.

13. Booth, *The Rhetoric of Fiction*, p. 125.

14. Gene Wolfe in a personal conversation with the author, 16 April 1997.

15. See Darko Suvin, *The Metamorphoses of Science Fiction* (London: Yale University Press, 1979), passim.

16. Booth, *The Rhetoric of Fiction*, p. 302.

17. Michael Worton and Judith Still, eds, 'Introduction', in *Intertextuality: Theories and Practices* (Manchester: Manchester University Press, 1990), p. 2.

18. Ibid., p. 11.

19. Ibid., p. 12.

20. Wendy Bradley, review of *Castleview*, *Interzone*, April 1991, p. 66.

21. Michael Riffaterre, 'Compulsory Reader Response: The Intertextual Drive' in Worton and Still, eds, *Intertextuality*, p. 58.

22. Ibid., p. 68.

23. See Chapter 10, 'A Solar Labyrinth', for a discussion of this effect in The Urth Cycle.

24. Wolfe, cited in Edwards, 'Gene Wolfe: An Interview', p. 11.

25. Ibid.

26. Wolfe, cited in Hall, 'An Interview with Gene Wolfe', p. 126.

27. Wolfe, cited in McCaffery, 'On Encompassing the Entire Universe', p. 337.

28. Riffaterre, 'Compulsory Reader Response', p. 57.

29. For a summary of this discussion see Damien Broderick, 'In Search of Lost Suzanne: A Lupine Collage', *The New York Review of Science Fiction*, December 1998, pp. 11–16.

30. Riffaterre, 'Compulsory Reader Response', p. 77.

31. Jonathan Culler, 'Literary Competence' in Jane P. Tompkins, ed., *Reader Response Criticism from Formalism to Post-Structuralism* (Baltimore: Johns Hopkins University Press, 1980), p. 102.

32. See Chapter 2, pp. 25–26.

33. E. D. Hirsch, *Validity in Interpretation* (London: Yale University Press, 1967), p. 74.

34. Ibid., p. 88.

35. Stanley Fish, 'Is There a Text in this Class?', *Is There a Text in this Class: The Authority of Interpretative Communities* (London: Harvard University Press, 1980), p. 316.

36. Wolfgang Iser, 'The Reading Process: A Phenomenological Approach', *The Implied Reader: Patterns of Communication in Prose Fiction from Bunyan to Beckett* (Baltimore: Johns Hopkins University Press, 1974), p. 290.

37. Culler, 'Literary Competence', p. 116.

38. Ibid., p. 117.

39. Paul McAuley, review of *Storeys from the Old Hotel*, *Interzone*, May/June 1989, p. 64.

Chapter 4

1. Gene Wolfe, *The Shadow of the Torturer* (London: Arrow Books, 1981; repr. 1982), p. 226. All further references to this edition are given after quotations in the text in the form: (*Shadow*, p. xx).

2. Gene Wolfe, *The Citadel of the Autarch* (London: Arrow Books, 1983), p. 235. All further references to this edition are given after quotations in the text in the form: (*Citadel*, p. xx).

3. See Clute, *Strokes*, pp. 164–72.

4. Gene Wolfe, *The Urth of the New Sun* (London: Orbit, 1988), pp. 361–62.

5. For an example, compare Darrell Schweitzer's pro-fantasy review of *The Citadel of the Autarch*, *Science Fiction Review*, Spring 1983, p. 41, with Algis Budrys's science fictional reading of *The Sword of the Lictor*, *The Magazine of Fantasy and Science Fiction*, April 1982, pp. 25–29.

6. Paul Kincaid, review of *The Shadow of the Torturer*, *Vector*, June 1981, p. 32.

7. See Frazier, 'Interview: Gene Wolfe', p. 7.

8. Schweitzer, review of *The Sword of the Lictor*, *Science Fiction Review*, May 1982, p. 26. See also Faren Miller, review of *The Citadel of the Autarch*, *Locus*, January 1983, p. 26; and Taylor, review of *The Urth of the New Sun*, p. 28.

9. Frank Catalano, review of *The Book of the New Sun*, *Amazing Science Fiction Stories*, January 1983, p. 9. See also Algis Budrys, review of *The Citadel of the Autarch*, *The Magazine of Fantasy and Science Fiction*, April 1983, pp. 43–46.

10. Chris Baldick, *The Concise Oxford Dictionary of Literary Terms* (Oxford: Oxford University Press, 1990), pp. 170 and 211.

11. Susan Wood, review of *The Shadow of the Torturer*, *Starship*, Spring 1981, p. 40.

12. See, for example, Chris Barker, 'The Citadel of the Autarch and the New Sun', *Vector*, April 1984, pp. 35–37; Nicholls, review of *The Urth of the New Sun*, pp. 95–96 and Gordon, *Guide*, pp. 92 and 96.

13. Kincaid, review of *The Urth of the New Sun*, p. 28.

14. See Gordon, *Guide*, p. 92.

15. Faren Miller, review of *The Urth of the New Sun*, *Locus*, August 1987, p. 13. See also Gordon, *Guide*, p. 96.

16. For descriptions of these parallels, see Manlove, 'Terminus Non Est', pp. 7–20 and Gordon, *Guide*, p. 96.

17. See, for example, Roz Kaveney, review of C. N. Manlove's *Science Fiction: Ten Explorations*, *Foundation* 39, 1987, p. 96; Greenland, review of *The Shadow of the Torturer* and *The Claw of the Conciliator*, p. 82; and Nicholls, review of *The Urth of the New Sun*, pp. 94 and 96.

18. Paul Brazier, 'I Feel More Like I Did ... Three Incomprehensions and a Resolution of Gene Wolfe's *The Book of the New Sun*', *The Apple*, March/April 1990, p. 2.

19. Ibid., p. 5.

20. See M. C. Escher, *The Graphic Work* (Berlin: Taschen Verlag, 1990), particularly Plate 66, 'House of Stairs'; Plate 67, 'Relativity'; Plate 75, 'Ascending and Descending' and Plate 76, 'Waterfall'.

21. Brazier, 'I Feel More Like I Did ...', p. 6.

22. Ibid.

23. For example, Baird Searles examines Wolfe's 'baroque' style in his review of *The Shadow of the Torturer*, pp. 12–15; and the late Thomas D. Clareson remarks on the richness of Wolfe's fictional society and the complexity of Severian's characterisation in his review of *The Shadow of the Torturer*, pp. 388–89.

24. See, for example, Baird Searles, review of *The Claw of the Conciliator*, *Isaac Asimov's Science Fiction Magazine*, June 1981, p. 14.

25. See Schweitzer, review of *The Sword of the Lictor*, p. 26.

26. See, for example, Rod French, 'Gene Wolfe and the Tale of Wonder: The End of the Apprenticeship', *Science Fiction: A Review of Speculative Literature*, June 1983, p. 46; Clute, *Strokes*, p. 171; and Mike Dickinson, 'Why They're All Crying Wolfe: A Few Thoughts on *The Book of the New Sun*', *Vector*, February 1984, p. 18.

27. Bishop, 'Pitching Pennies', p. 11.

28. Kaveney, 'Review', p. 96.

29. Gene Wolfe, 'The God and His Man', *Endangered Species* (London: Orbit, 1990), p. 203. All further references to this story are given after quotations in the text in the form: (*Species*, p. xx).

30. For an account of Wolfe's rather low opinion of academics, see Gordon, 'An Interview with Gene Wolfe', pp. 20–21.

31. Gregory, 'Id', *The Oxford Companion to the Mind*, p. 336.

Chapter 5

1. Parts of this chapter appeared in a slightly different form in *Foundation*, 66 (1996), under the title 'God-Games: Cosmic Conspiracies and Narrative Sleights in Gene Wolfe's The Fictions of the New Sun', pp. 13–39.

2. Joe Sanders, review of *Free Live Free*, *Fantasy Review*, May 1985, p. 18.

3. Gene Wolfe, 'The Toy Theatre' in *The Island of Doctor Death and Other Stories and Other Stories* (London: Arrow Books, 1981), p. 243.

4. Gene Wolfe, *The Urth of the New Sun*, pp. 159–60. All further references to this edition are given in the text in the form: (*Urth*, p. xx).

5. Richard Dawkins, *The Selfish Gene*, rev. edn (Oxford: Oxford University Press, 1989), p. 44.

6. Ibid., p. 36.

7. Ibid., p. 4.

8. Ibid., p. 2.

9. Gene Wolfe, *The Sword of the Lictor* (London: Arrow Books, 1982, repr. 1984), p. 205. All further references to this edition are given in the text in the form: (*Sword*, p. xx).

10. Wolfe disclosed this information in two personal letters dated 14 May 1993 and 6 August 1992 respectively.

11. Wolfe also puns on his own name in the short story, 'Procreation' (1985), where the biblical Genesis becomes a series of accounts related by 'Gene', a universe-building physicist, and his sister, 'Sis'.

12. Dawkins, *The Selfish Gene*, p. 8.

13. Ibid., p. 1.

14. See ibid., p. 267.

15. See Richard Leakey's comments in Richard Leakey and Roger Lewin, *Origins Reconsidered: In Search of What Makes Us Human* (London: Little, Brown & Co., 1992), p. xvi.

16. Rollo May, *The Cry for Myth* (London: Souvenir Press, 1993), p. 15. See also Leakey and Lewin, *Origins Reconsidered*, pp. 307–11.

17. C. G. Jung, *The Collected Works of C. G. Jung*, trans. R. F. C. Hull, 2nd edn, 20 vols (London: Routledge and Kegan Paul, 1968), V, p. 231.

18. A definition offered by Wolfe in 'Books in *"The Book of the New Sun"*', in *Plan[e]t Engineering* (Cambridge, MA: NESFA Press, 1984), p. 4.

19. See Lesley Brown, ed., *The New Shorter Oxford English Dictionary*, 2 vols (Oxford: Clarendon Press, 1993), p. 2558.

20. Borski, 'Masks of the Father', p. 14.

21. Ibid., p. 16.

22. Gay Clifford, *The Transformations of Allegory* (London: Routledge and Kegan Paul, 1974), p. 66.

23. Gene Wolfe, *The Claw of the Conciliator* (London: Arrow Books, 1982; repr. 1983), pp. 13 and 295. All further references to this edition are given after quotations in the text in the form: (*Claw*, p. xx).

Chapter 6

1. Wolfe, cited in Frazier, 'Interview', p. 7.

2. For concise genre descriptions, see Ann Swinfen, *In Defence of Fantasy* (London: Routledge and Kegan Paul, 1984), p. 5; and Warren W. Wagar's definition, cited in Gary K. Wolfe, *Critical Terms for Science Fiction and Fantasy: A Glossary and Guide to Scholarship* (New York: Greenwood Press, 1986), p. 39.

3. Brian Attebery, *Strategies of Fantasy* (Bloomington: Indiana University Press, 1992), p. 106.

4. Both sources are cited in Joseph Campbell, *The Hero with a Thousand Faces* (London: Paladin, 1988), pp. 39–40.

5. See Schweitzer, review of *The Sword of the Lictor*, p. 26. Experiments have shown that when flatworms that have been conditioned to respond to certain sense stimuli are dissected and fed to unconditioned flatworms, these latter subjects receive the former's conditioning and react to the same sense stimuli even though they, themselves, have not been conditioned. See G. J. Whitrow, *What is Time?* (London: Thames and Hudson, 1972), p. 36.

6. Carl D. Malmgren, 'Towards a Definition of Science Fantasy', *Science-Fiction Studies*, 15, 1988, p. 261.

7. See Gordon, *Guide*, p. 88.

8. Michael W. McClintock, 'High Tech and High Sorcery: Some Discriminations Between Science Fiction and Fantasy', in George E. Slusser and Eric S. Rabkin, eds, *Intersections: Fantasy and Science Fiction—Essays Presented at the Seventh Eaton Conference* (Carbondale and Edwardsville: Southern Illinois University Press, 1987), p. 33.

9. Greenland, review of *The Shadow of the Torturer* and *The Claw of the Conciliator*, p. 83.

10. See Clute, *Strokes*, p. 149.

11. Greenland, review of *The Shadow of the Torturer* and *The Claw of the Conciliator*, p. 83.

12. Malmgren, 'Towards a Definition of Science Fantasy', p. 261.

13. Douglas Barbour, review of *The Sword of the Lictor*, *Foundation*, 26, 1982, p. 95.

14. Gene Wolfe, in a personal correspondence dated 4 January 1994.

15. See Bernard Bergonzi, *The Early H. G. Wells: A Study of the Scientific Romances* (Manchester: Manchester University Press, 1961), pp. 52–53.

16. H. G. Wells, *The Rediscovery of the Unique*, cited in Michael Draper, *H. G. Wells* (London: Macmillan, 1987), p. 38.

17. Draper, *H. G. Wells*, pp. 38–39.

18. Since *The Book of the New Sun* was marketed largely as a fantasy, it is interesting to note that this sequence was chosen by Don Maitz, the illustrator of the US first edition of the tetralogy, as the cover for *The Claw of the Conciliator*.

19. It is apparent from the transcendental time-travelling sequence in William Hope Hodgson's earlier novel, *The House on the Borderland* (London: Evelyn Nash, 1908), that he was familiar with *The Time Machine*.

20. Roger Dobson, 'Tales of Remote Futures' in Ian Bell, ed., *William Hope Hodgson: Voyages and Visions* (Oxford: Ian Bell and Sons, 1987), p. 53.

21. Andy Sawyer, 'A Writer on the Borderland' in Bell, ed., *William Hope Hodgson*, p. 49.

22. William Hope Hodgson, *The Nightland* (London: Grafton Books, 1990), p. 298.

23. See H. P. Lovecraft's comments in 'Supernatural Horror in Literature', *Dagon and Other Macabre Tales* (London: Granada Books, 1985), pp. 432–520, esp. p. 490; Brian Aldiss's and David Wingrove's remarks in *Trillion Year Spree: The History of Science Fiction* (London: Victor Gollancz, 1986), p. 167; and C. S. Lewis's criticism in Franz Rottensteiner, *The Fantasy Book* (London: Thames and Hudson, 1978), p. 65.

24. An admission Wolfe makes in a personal correspondence dated 6 August 1992.

25. An observation made by Greenland, review of *The Shadow of the Torturer* and *The Claw of the Conciliator*, p. 82.

26. Although Steve Behrends argues that Smith did not read *The Night Land* until 1934, when about a third of the Zothique tales were complete, it is perfectly possible that Smith had encountered Hodgson's work before this date. See Steve Behrends, *Starmont Reader's Guide: Clark Ashton Smith* (Washington: Starmont House, 1990), p. 25. Smith himself described *The Night Land* as 'the ultimate saga of a perishing cosmos, the last epic of a world beleaguered by night and the uninvisigable spawn of darkness' (see Behrends, *Starmont Reader's Guide*, p. 25).

27. Clark Ashton Smith, a synopsis for 'A Tale of Gyndron', cited in Behrends, *Starmont Reader's Guide*, p. 24.

28. Behrends, *Starmont Reader's Guide*, p. 17.

29. Wolfe, cited in Colin Greenland, 'Riding a Bicycle Backwards: An Interview with Gene Wolfe', *Foundation*, 31, 1984, p. 38.

30. Gene Wolfe, 'Helioscope', in *Castle of Days* (New York: Tor, 1992), p. 221.

31. For an account of the geographical distribution of sun cults, see Jacquetta Hawkes, *Man and the Sun* (London: The Cresset Press, 1963), passim.

32. Darko Suvin, *Metamorphoses of Science Fiction* (London: Yale University Press, 1979), pp. 83–84.

33. Greenland, review of *The Shadow of the Torturer* and *The Claw of the Conciliator*, p. 83.

34. For a detailed discussion of Hutton's theories and deep time, see Stephen Jay Gould, *Time's Arrow, Time's Cycle* (London: Penguin Books, 1990), pp. 1–8 and 62–80.

35. 'Icon' is used here according to Gary Wolfe's definition of the term as a 'message in code to the initiated reader and an emblem of dissociation to the uninitiated'. See Gary K. Wolfe, *The Known and the Unknown: The Iconography of Science Fiction* (Ohio: Kent State University Press, 1979), p. 27.

36. See Ray Bradbury, 'Rocket Summer', *The Martian Chronicles* (London: Granada Books, 1977, repr. 1981), p. 13.

37. Gene Wolfe, in a personal correspondence dated 6 August 1992.

38. Vance, 'T'sais', *The Dying Earth* (repr. 1986), p. 42.

39. For a discussion of Vance's literary inspiration for *The Dying Earth*, see Richard Tiedman, 'Jack Vance: Science Fiction Stylist', in Tim Underwood and Chuck Miller, eds, *Jack Vance* (New York: Taplinger Publishing Co., 1980), pp. 179–222, esp. p. 192; and Don Herron, 'The Double Shadow: The Influence of Clark Ashton Smith', in Underwood and Miller, eds, *Jack Vance*, pp. 87–102.

40. See Robert Silverberg, '*The Eyes of the Overworld* and *The Dying Earth*', in Underwood and Miller, eds, *Jack Vance*, pp. 117–30, esp. p. 121.

41. Michael Dirda makes a similar observation in his entry on Jack Vance in E. F. Bleiler, ed., *Supernatural Fiction Writers*, 2 vols (New York: Charles Scribner's Sons, 1985), II, pp. 1105–11, esp. p. 1108.

42. An observation made by Dirda, 'Jack Vance', p. 1108.

43. Norman Spinrad, review of *The Citadel of the Autarch*, *Isaac Asimov's Science Fiction Magazine*, July 1983, p. 171.

44. *Thrilling Wonder Stories* was a US pulp magazine which ran for 111 issues from August 1936 to Winter 1955.

Chapter 7

1. Parts of this chapter also appeared as 'God-Games: Cosmic Conspiracies and Narrative Sleights in Gene Wolfe's The Urth Cycle' in *Foundation*, 66, 1996, pp. 39–59.

2. See Geoffrey N. Leech and Michael H. Short, *Style in Fiction* (London: Longman Publications, 1981), p. 265.

3. See Booth, *The Rhetoric of Fiction*, pp. 130–31.

4. Ibid., p. 131.

5. Wales, *A Dictionary of Stylistics*, p. 317.

6. For further examples of this kind of religionisation, see *Sword*, p. 251, *Citadel*, p. 82, and *Urth*, pp. 321–22.

7. Gene Wolfe, in a personal correspondence dated 5 August 1994.

8. See Jerome S. Bruner, 'Introduction', in A. R. Luria, *The Mind of a Mnemonist*, trans. Lynn Solotaroff (London: Jonathan Cape, 1969), p. x; and Luria, *The Mind of a Mnemonist*, p. 96.

9. See Luria, *The Mind of a Mnemonist*, pp. 151–52.

10. Bruner, 'Introduction', p. viii.

11. Ibid.

12. See Gordon, *Guide*, p. 76.

13. Luria, *The Mind of a Mnemonist*, p. 113. See Chapter 8 for a discussion of the deflective effect of Wolfe's eclectic diction.

14. Ibid., p. 130.

15. Ibid., p. 113.

16. Ibid., p. 155.

17. Ibid., p. 159.

18. Greenland, review of *The Shadow of the Torturer* and *The Claw of the Conciliator*, p. 84.

19. See Warnock, *Memory*, p. 155.

20. Ibid., p. 103.

21. See Campbell, *The Hero with a Thousand Faces*, p. 30.

22. Ibid., p. 37.

23. Ibid., p. 69.

24. Ibid., p. 77.

25. Ibid., p. 229.

26. Budrys, review of *The Citadel of the Autarch*, p. 45.

27. See John White, *Mythology in the Modern Novel* (Princeton: Princeton University Press, 1971), p. 11.

28. See Fish, *Is There a Text in This Class*, p. 320.

29. White, *Mythology in the Modern Novel*, pp. 119 and 125.

30. Ibid., pp. 127–28.

31. Ibid., p. 128.

32. Ibid., p. 151.

33. Nicholls, review of *The Urth of the New Sun*, pp. 95–96.

34. White, *Mythology in the Modern Novel*, p. 98.

35. Clute, 'Gene Wolfe', in *The Encyclopedia of Science Fiction*, p. 1228.

36. Darrell Schweitzer, 'Weird Tales Talks to Gene Wolfe', *Weird Tales*, Spring 1988, p. 24.

37. See White, *Mythology in the Modern Novel*, pp. 8 and 23.

38. See Joseph Campbell, *Myths to Live By* (London: Souvenir Press, 1991), p. 22.

39. Gene Wolfe, 'The Feast of Saint Catherine', *Castle of Days*, p. 211.

40. Ibid.

41. Gene Wolfe, *Soldier of the Mist* (London: Orbit, 1987), p. xiv. All further references to this edition are given after quotations in the form: (*S. Mist*, p. xx).

Chapter 8

1. Gene Wolfe, 'Words Weird and Wonderful', *Castle of Days*, p. 234.

2. For a discussion of the theoretical concept of estrangement, see Suvin, *The Metamorphoses of Science Fiction*, passim.

3. Wolfe, cited in McCaffery, 'On Encompassing the Entire Universe', p. 350.

4. Ibid. The quotation should read: 'the Commonwealth of Urth'.

5. William Lecky, cited in Robert Byron, *The Byzantine Achievement: An Historical Perspective A.D. 330–1453* (London: Routledge and Kegan Paul, 1927; repr. 1987), p. xxxi.

6. See Byron, *The Byzantine Achievement*, p. 122.

7. Cited in Gould, *Time's Arrow, Time's Cycle*, p. 104.

8. Ibid., pp. 101–102.

9. See ibid., p. 166.

10. All information concerning extinct species originates from Alfred Sherwood Romer, *Vertebrate Palaeontology*, 3rd edn (London: University of Chicago Press, 1974), pp. 374–96.

11. Don Johanson, cited in Richard E. Leakey, *The Making of Mankind* (New York: Elsevier-Dutton, 1981), pp. 63–64.

12. See Leonid Tarassuk and Claude Blair, *The Complete Encyclopedia of Arms and Weapons* (New York: Simon & Schuster, 1982), pp. 344, 491, 309, 82, 403, 110, 249 and 444–45.

13. See Robert Wilkinson-Lathom, *Swords* (London: Blandford Press, 1977), p. 128; and Tarassuk and Blair, *The Complete Encyclopedia of Arms and Weapons*, pp. 285–86 and 17.

14. See J. Lempriere, *Lempriere's Classical Dictionary* (London: Bracken Books, 1984), p. 521.

15. Ibid., p. 341.

16. Ibid., p. 340.

17. Manlove, 'Terminus Non Est', p. 18.

18. See Lesley Brown, *The New Shorter Oxford English Dictionary*, 2 vols (Oxford: Clarendon Press), p. 1621; and H. G. Liddell and R. Scott, *An Intermediate Greek–English Lexicon* (Oxford: Oxford University Press, 1889; repr. 1991), pp. 476–77.

19. Ludwig Wittgenstein, *The Blue and the Brown Books: Preliminary Studies for the 'Philosophical Investigations'*, 2nd edn (London: Blackwell Publishers, 1969, repr. 1992), p. 56.

20. See Robert Young, ed., 'Post-Structuralism: An Introduction', *Untying the Text: A Post-Structuralist Reader* (London: Routledge and Kegan Paul, 1981), p. 8.

21. Ibid., p. 18.

22. James Joyce, cited in Frank Kermode, *The Genesis of Secrecy* (Harvard: Harvard University Press, 1980), p. 64.

23. Kermode, *The Genesis of Secrecy*, p. 64 and Young, ed., *Untying the Text*, p. 19.

24. See Roland Barthes, 'From Work to Text' in Josué V. Harari, ed., *Textual Strategies: Perspectives in Post-Structuralist Criticism* (New York: Cornell University Press, 1979), p. 74.

25. Ibid., p. 76.

26. See Patrick Parrinder, *Science Fiction: Its Criticism and Teaching* (London: Methuen, 1980), p. 75.

27. See Wolfgang Iser, *The Act of Reading: A Theory of Aesthetic Response*, trans. The Johns Hopkins University Press (London: Routledge and Kegan Paul, 1978), p. 9.

28. Ibid.

29. Ibid., p. 24.

30. See Hirsch, *Validity in Interpretation*, p. 18.

31. Iser, *The Act of Reading*, p. 168.

32. Young, ed., *Untying the Text*, p. 6.

33. See Gordon, 'An Interview with Gene Wolfe', p. 21.

34. Marcel Proust, cited in Robert Scholes, *Fabulation and Metafiction* (London: University of Illinois Press, 1979), p. 31.

35. Linda Hutcheon, *Narcissistic Narrative: The Metafictional Paradox* (London: Methuen, 1984), p. xiv.

36. Wittgenstein, *The Blue and the Brown Books*, pp. 3–4.

37. Shoshana Felman, 'Turning the Screw of Interpretation', cited in Young, ed., *Untying the Text*, p. 14.

Chapter 9

1. For a further description of the Classical art of memory, see Yates, *The Art of Memory*, p. 18.

2. Ibid., p. 23.

3. Ibid., p. 48.

4. See Hans Biedermann, 'Gates', *The Dictionary of Symbolism: Cultural Icons and the Meanings Behind Them*, trans. James Hulbert (New York: Facts on File, 1992), p. 150.

5. For a discussion of the symbolism of dogs, see Biedermann, *The Dictionary of Symbolism*, pp. 97–99.

6. Wolfe, cited in McCaffery, 'On Encompassing the Entire Universe', p. 336.

7. For a more detailed discussion of these sun figures, see Hawkes, *Man and the Sun*, pp. 62, 90, 128, 143, 172 and 202–203.

8. See Riffaterre, 'Compulsory Reader Response', p. 58.

9. For a detailed description and discussion of Camillo's Theatre of Memory, see Yates, *The Art of Memory*, pp. 135–62.

10. Ibid., p. 142.

11. Ibid., pp. 145–46.

12. Gene Wolfe, in a personal correspondence dated 26 March 1993.

13. Yates, *The Art of Memory*, pp. 142–43.

14. Ibid., p. 149.

15. Ibid., pp. 151–52.

16. Ibid., p. 174.

17. Peter Coveney and Roger Highfield, *The Arrow of Time* (London: W. H. Allen, 1990), pp. 101–102.

18. It must be stressed that every sequential narrative, by definition, follows time's arrow and that this observation alone does not make the arrangement of Wolfe's text unique.

19. For examples of this kind of patterning, see *Shadow*, pp. 45, 67, 78, 234, 281; *Claw*, pp. 13 and 116; *Sword*, pp. 63, 95 (which involves a double cycle in its allusions to the past and the future), 161 and 222; *Citadel*, pp. 20, 188 and 260, where Severian self-consciously admits that, 'I have gotten ahead of my story.' It should be noted that this list is by no means exhaustive.

20. See Yates, *The Art of Memory*, p. 250.

21. Ibid., p. 151.

22. See Luria, *The Mind of a Mnemonist*, pp. 144–45.

Chapter 10

1. Kermode, *The Genesis of Secrecy*, p. 2.

2. Jorge Luis Borges, 'Tlön, Uqbar, Orbis Tertius', in Anthony Kerrigan, ed., *Fictions*, trans. Alastair Read (London: Calder Publications, 1985), p. 17.

3. Wales, *A Dictionary of Stylistics*, p. 216.

4. The metafictiveness of Wolfe's short story was suggested by John Clute in his entry on the author in *The Encyclopedia of Science Fiction*, p. 1339.

5. Kermode, *The Genesis of Secrecy*, p. 18.

6. Patricia Waugh, *Metafiction: The Theory and Practice of Self Conscious Fiction* (London: Methuen, 1984), p. 2.

7. Thomas D. Clareson, review of '"The Book of Gold": Gene Wolfe's *Book of the New Sun*', *Extrapolation* 23, 1982, p. 273.

8. Scholes, *Fabulation and Metafiction*, p. 59.

9. Wolfe, 'Books in *"The Book of the New Sun"*', pp. 4 and 15–16.

10. Borges, 'The Library of Babel', *Fictions*, p. 80.

11. Gene Wolfe, 'Books in *"The Book of the New Sun"*', p. 15.

12. For a detailed discussion of Wolfe's sources for the stories in the Brown Book, see Michael Andre-Driussi, 'A Closer Look at the Brown Book: Gene Wolfe's Five-Faceted Myth', *The New York Review of Science Fiction*, February 1993, pp. 14–19.

13. Wolfe, 'Books in *"The Book of the New Sun"*', p. 15. Wolfe's conflation also depends on a pun on Minotaur and Monitor; see Andre-Driussi, 'A Closer Look at the Brown Book', p. 14. 'The Circular Ruins', trans. Anthony Bonner, is collected in Borges, *Fictions*, pp. 52–58.

14. Jorge Luis Borges, 'The First Wells', *Other Inquisitions 1937–1952*, trans. L. G. Ruth (London: Souvenir Press, 1973), p. 88. Ahasuerus was the name of the Wandering Jew.

15. For a detailed account of the Theseus legend, see Robert Graves, *The Greek Myths*, complete edn (London: Penguin Books, 1992), pp. 323–70.

16. Hutcheon, *Narcissistic Narrative*, p. 54.

17. Lucien Dallenbach, *La Recit Speculaire*, cited in Hutcheon, *Narcissistic Narrative*, p. 56.

18. Hutcheon, *Narcissistic Narrative*, p. 56.

Chapter 11

1. A version of this chapter first appeared in *Foundation*, 66, 1996, under the title 'Grasping the God-Games: Metafictional Keys to the Interpretation of Gene Wolfe's Fictions of the New Sun', pp. 39–59.

2. Gene Wolfe, in a personal correspondence dated 9 September 1994.

3. Algis Budrys, review of *Soldier of the Mist, The Magazine of Fantasy and Science Fiction*, January 1987, p. 66.

4. Baird Searles, review of *Soldier of the Mist, Isaac Asimov's Science Fiction Magazine*, May 1987, p. 185.

5. It is interesting to note how the post-historic nature of Urth is emblematised by the 'post-textual' position of Wolfe's expository appendices, while the comparatively (pre-)historic status of Latro's Greek city states is represented in the 'pre-textual' preface to *Soldier of the Mist*.

6. Jenny Blackford, review of *Soldier of Arete, Australian Science Fiction Review*, Vol. 5, No. 2, Winter 1990, p. 19.

7. Killheffer, review of *Soldier of Arete*, p. 6.

8. Gene Wolfe, *Soldier of Arete* (London: New English Library, 1990), p. 36. All future references to this edition are given in the text in the form: (*S. Arete*, p. xx).

9. Iken, review of *Soldier of the Mist*, p. 23.

10. Killheffer, review of *Soldier of Arete*, p. 6.

11. Wolfe, cited in Swanson, 'Interview: Gene Wolfe', p. 40.

12. Craig Shaw Gardner, review of *Soldier of the Mist, The Plain Dealer*, 14 January 1987, n.p.

13. Killheffer, review of *Soldier of Arete*, p. 6.

14. Budrys, review of *Soldier of the Mist*, p. 66.

15. Tom Easton, review of *The Sword of the Lictor, Analog Science Fiction/Science Fact*, May 1982, p. 168.

16. Blackford, review of *Soldier of the Mist*, p. 19.

17. See Yates, *The Art of Memory*, p. 17.

18. Budrys, review of *Soldier of the Mist*, p. 65.

19. Miller, review of *The Urth of the New Sun*, p. 13.

20. Robert Reilly, review of *Soldier of Arete, SFRA Newsletter*, January/February 1990, pp. 36–37.

21. Blackford,, review of *Soldier of the Mist*, p. 19.

22. Gene Wolfe, *Nightside the Long Sun* (New York: Tor, 1993), p. 331. All further references to this text are given after quotations in the form: (*Nightside*, p. xx).

23. For Crane's comments, see Gene Wolfe, *Lake of the Long Sun* (New York: Tor, 1994), p. 292. All further references to this text are given after quotations in the form: (*Lake*, p. xx).

24. Gene Wolfe, *Caldé of the Long Sun* (New York: Tor, 1994), p. 158.

25. D. P. Simpson, *Cassell's Latin–English, English–Latin Dictionary*, 5th edn (London: Cassell, 1987, repr. 1990), p. 329.

26. Gene Wolfe, *Pandora by Holly Hollander* (London: New English Library, 1991), p. 16. All further references to this edition are given in the text in the form: (*Pandora*, p. xx).

27. Wolfe cited in McCaffery, 'On Encompassing the Entire Universe', p. 345.

28. See, for example, Hall, 'An Interview with Gene Wolfe', p. 129; and Frazier, 'Interview: Gene Wolfe', p. 7.

29. Bishop, 'Pitching Pennies', p. 12.

30. See David Langford, 'The Wolfean Oracle Speaks', 1997. http://www.ansible. demon.co.uk/cc/cc77.html#wolfe (8 September, 2000).

31. Wolfe, cited in Hall, 'An Interview with Gene Wolfe', p. 125.

Bibliography

NB: Where the editions used are not the original publication, the place, publisher and date are listed after the details of the first publication.

Primary Sources

Novels

Operation Ares (New York: Berkley Books, 1970; repr. London: Fontana Books, 1978).

The Fifth Head of Cerberus: Three Novellas (New York: Scribners, 1972; repr. London: Quartet Books, 1975).

Peace (New York: Harper & Row, 1975; repr. London: New English Library, 1989).

The Devil in a Forest (Chicago: Follett Publishing, 1976; repr. London: Grafton Books, 1985).

The Shadow of the Torturer (New York: Timescape, 1980; repr. London: Arrow Books, 1981, repr. 1982).

The Claw of the Conciliator (New York: Timescape, 1981; repr. London: Arrow Books, 1982).

The Sword of the Lictor (New York: Timescape, 1981; repr. London: Arrow Books, 1982).

The Citadel of the Autarch (New York: Timescape, 1983; repr. London: Arrow Books, 1983).

Free Live Free (London: Victor Gollancz, 1985; repr. New York: Tor, 1986; repr. London: Legend, 1989).

Soldier of the Mist (London: Victor Gollancz, 1986; repr. London: Orbit, 1987).

The Urth of the New Sun (London: Victor Gollancz, 1987; repr. London: Orbit, 1988).

There Are Doors (New York: Tor, 1988; repr. London: Orbit, 1990).

Soldier of Arete (New York: Tor, 1989; repr. London: New English Library, 1990).

Castleview (New York: Tor, 1990; repr. London: New English Library, 1991).

Pandora by Holly Hollander (New York: Tor, 1990; repr. London: New English Library, 1991).

Nightside the Long Sun (New York: Tor, 1993).

Lake of the Long Sun (New York: Tor, 1994).

Caldé of the Long Sun (New York: Tor, 1994).

Exodus from the Long Sun (New York: Tor, 1996).

On Blue's Waters (New York: Tor, 1999).

In Green's Jungles (New York: Tor, 2000).

Return to the Whorl (New York: Tor, 2001).

Anthologies

The Island of Doctor Death and Other Stories and Other Stories (New York: Pocket Books, 1980; repr. London: Arrow Books, 1981).

Gene Wolfe's Book of Days (New York: Doubleday, 1981; repr. London: Arrow Books, 1985).

Plan[e]t Engineering (Cambridge, MA: NESFA Press, 1984).

Storeys from the Old Hotel (Worcester Park, Surrey: Kerosina Publications, 1988).

Endangered Species (New York: Tor, 1989; repr. London: Orbit, 1990).

Castle of Days (New York: Tor, 1992).

Young Wolfe (Ontario: U. M. Press, 1992).

Strange Travelers (New York: Tor, 2000).

Uncollected Short Fiction

'Thou Spark of Blood', *Worlds of If Science Fiction*, May 1970, pp. 105–109, 157.

'King Under the Mountain', *Worlds of If Science Fiction*, November/December 1970, pp. 86–90.

'Tarzan of the Grapes', *The Magazine of Fantasy and Science Fiction*, June 1972, pp. 123–29.

'Going to the Beach', in Roger Elwood, ed., *Showcase* (New York: Harper & Row, 1973), pp. 165–72.

'Mathoms from the Time Closet', *Again, Dangerous Visions*, 2 vols (New York: Doubleday, 1972; abr. repr. London: Pan Books, 1977), I, pp. 145–56.

'Four Wolves', *Amazing Science Fiction Stories*, May 1983, pp. 79–84.

At the Point of Capricorn (New Castle, VA: Cheap Street, 1983).

Empires of Foliage and Flower (New Castle, VA: Cheap Street, 1987; repr. *Crank! Science Fiction and Fantasy*, Winter 1993, pp. 15–39).

'Game in the Pope's Head', in Gardner Dozois and Susan Carper, eds, *Ripper* (New York: Tor, 1988).

'The Boy Who Hooked the Sun', *Weird Tales*, Spring 1988, pp. 21–22.

'How the Bishop Sailed to Inniskeen', *Isaac Asimov's Science Fiction Magazine*, December 1989, pp. 69–75.

'The Haunted Boardinghouse', in Kathryn Cramer, ed., *The Walls of Fear* (New York: William Morrow & Co., 1990), pp. 175–204.

'The Monday Man', in Bryan Cholfin, ed., *Monochrone: The Readercon Anthology* (Cambridge, MA: Broken Mirrors Press, 1990), pp. 23–30.

The Old Woman Whose Rolling Pin is the Sun (New Castle, VA: Cheap Street, 1991).

'And When They Appear', in David G. Hartwell, ed., *Christmas Forever* (New York: Tor, 1993), pp. 96–117.

Poetry

For Rosemary (Worcester Park, Surrey: Kerosina Publications, 1988).

Collected Letters

Letters Home (Ontario: U. M. Press, 1991).

Personal Correspondences

Letter dated 6 August 1992.
Letter dated 26 March 1993.
Letter dated 14 May 1993.
Letter dated 4 January 1994.
Letter dated 5 August 1994.
Letter dated 9 September 1994.

Interviews

Baber, Brendan, 'Who's Afraid of Gene Wolfe?', *The Third Word*, June/July 1994, pp. 48–49.
——, 'Gene Wolfe Interview', 20 March 1994, http://world.std.com/~ pduggan/ wolfeint.html.
Edwards, Malcolm, 'Gene Wolfe: An Interview', *Vector*, May/June 1973, pp. 7–15.
Frazier, Robert, 'Gene Wolfe: The Legerdemain of the Wolfe', *Thrust: Science Fiction in Review*, Winter/Spring, 1983, pp. 5–9.
Gordon, Joan, 'An Interview with Gene Wolfe', *Science Fiction Review*, Summer 1981, pp. 18–22.
Greenland, Colin, 'Riding a Bicycle Backwards: An Interview with Gene Wolfe', *Foundation: The International Review of Science Fiction*, 31, 1984, pp. 37–44.
Hall, Melissa Mia, 'An Interview with Gene Wolfe', *Amazing Science Fiction Stories*, September 1981, pp. 125–30.
Hannah, Judith and Nichols, Joseph, 'Two Foot Square of Gene Wolfe', *Vector*, February 1984, pp. 5–12.
Kress, Nancy, 'A Conversation with Gene Wolfe', *Australian Science Fiction Review*, November 1985, pp. 12–22.
Langford, David, 'The Wolfean Oracle Speaks', 1997. http://www.ansible. demon. co.uk/cc/cc77.html#wolfe (8 September 2000).
McCaffery, Larry, 'On Encompassing the Entire Universe: An Interview with Gene Wolfe', *Science-Fiction Studies*, 15, 1988, pp. 334–55.
Schweitzer, Darrell, 'Weird Tales Talks to Gene Wolfe', *Weird Tales*, Spring 1988, pp. 23–29.
Swanson, Elliot, 'Interview: Gene Wolfe', *Interzone*, Autumn 1986, pp. 38–40.
Wright, Peter, 'Peter and the Wolfe', unpublished interview conducted 16 April, 1997.

Secondary Sources

Aichele, George, 'Self-reflexivity in Gene Wolfe's "Seven American Nights"', *The Journal of the Fantastic in the Arts*, 2, 1991, pp. 37–47.
Andre-Driussi, Michael, 'A Closer Look at the Brown Book: Gene Wolfe's Five Faceted Myth', *The New York Review of Science Fiction*, February 1993, pp. 14–19.
——, *Lexicon Urthus: A Dictionary for the Urth Cycle* (San Francisco: Sirius Fiction, 1994).
——, 'Gene Wolfe at the Lake of Birds', *Foundation*, 66, 1996, pp. 5–12.
——, 'Posthistory 101', *Extrapolation*, 37, 1996, pp. 127–38.

Asbury, Drake, III, review of *Castleview*, *Science Fiction Research Association Review*, January/February 1992, pp. 97–98.

Barbour, Douglas, review of *The Fifth Head of Cerberus*, *Riverside Quarterly*, August 1973, pp. 81–82.

——, review of *The Sword of the Lictor*, *Foundation*, 26, 1982, pp. 94–96.

Barker, Chris, 'The Citadel of the Autarch and the New Sun', *Vector*, April 1984, pp. 35–37.

Bertrand, Frank C., 'Late Night Thoughts on Reading Gene Wolfe's *The Devil in a Forest*', *Science Fiction: A Review of Speculative Literature*, July 1985, pp. 12–14.

Bishop, Michael, review of *The Fifth Head of Cerberus*, *Delap's Fantasy and Science Fiction Review*, November 1976, pp. 26–27.

——, 'Pitching Pennies Against the Starboard Bulkhead: "Gene Wolfe as Hero"', *Thrust: Science Fiction in Review*, Fall 1980, pp. 10–13.

Blackford, Jenny, review of *Soldier of the Mist*, *Australian Science Fiction Review*, March 1989, pp. 19–20.

——, review of *Soldier of Arete*, *Australian Science Fiction Review*, Winter 1990, pp. 18–19.

——, review of *The Island of Doctor Death and Other Stories and Other Stories*, *The New York Review of Science Fiction*, February 2000, pp. 17–19.

Borski, Robert, 'Thinking about the Mandragora in Wolfe's *Citadel*', *The New York Review of Science Fiction*, July 1999, pp. 16–18.

——, 'Masks of the Father: Paternity in Gene Wolfe's *Book of the New Sun*', *The New York Review of Science Fiction*, February 2000, pp. 1 and 8–16.

Bradley, Wendy, review of *Castleview*, *Interzone*, April 1991, p. 66.

Brazier, Paul, 'I Feel More Like I Did … Three Incomprehensions and a Resolution of Gene Wolfe's *The Book of the New Sun*', *The Apple*, March/April 1990, pp. 1–10.

Broderick, Damien, review of *The Island of Doctor Death and Other Stories and Other Stories*, *Science Fiction Commentary*, June 1981, pp. 31–32.

——, review of *The Shadow of the Torturer*, *Science Fiction Commentary*, June 1981, pp. 34–35.

——, 'Thoughts on Gene Wolfe's *Peace*', *The New York Review of Science Fiction*, March 1996, pp. 16–17.

——, 'In Search of Lost Suzanne: A Lupine Collage', *The New York Review of Science Fiction*, December 1998, pp. 11–16.

Budrys, Algis, review of *The Devil in a Forest*, *The Magazine of Fantasy and Science Fiction*, May 1978.

——, review of *The Shadow of the Torturer*, *The Magazine of Fantasy and Science Fiction*, May 1980, pp. 26–27.

——, review of *The Claw of the Conciliator*, *The Magazine of Fantasy and Science Fiction*, June 1981, pp. 48–51.

——, review of *The Sword of the Lictor*, *The Magazine of Fantasy and Science Fiction*, April 1982, pp. 25–29.

——, review of *The Citadel of the Autarch*, *The Magazine of Fantasy and Science Fiction*, April 1983, pp. 43–46.

——, review of *The Castle of the Otter*, *The Magazine of Fantasy and Science Fiction*, January 1984, pp. 25–27.

——, review of *Soldier of the Mist*, *The Magazine of Fantasy and Science Fiction*, January 1987, pp. 64–67.

Carper, Steve, review of *Peace*, *Delap's Fantasy and Science Fiction Review*, April 1976, p. 11.

Catalano, Frank, review of *The Book of the New Sun*, *Amazing Science Fiction Stories*, January 1983, pp. 8–10.

Chapman, Edgar L., review of *Storeys from the Old Hotel*, *Science Fiction Research Association Review*, October 1992, p. 50.

Clareson, Thomas D., review of *The Shadow of the Torturer*, *Extrapolation*, 21, 1980, pp. 388–89.

——, 'Gene Wolfe' in David Cowart and Thomas Wymer, eds, *The Dictionary of Literary Biography: Twentieth Century Science Fiction Writers* (Detroit: Gale Research Company, 1981), VIII, Part 2, pp. 207–209.

——, review of *The Claw of the Conciliator*, *Extrapolation*, 22, 1981, pp. 196–97.

——, review of '"The Book of Gold": Gene Wolfe's *The Book of the New Sun*', *Extrapolation*, 23, 1982, pp. 270–75.

——, review of *The Castle of the Otter*, *Extrapolation*, 23, 1983, pp. 392–93.

——, 'Variations and Design: The Fiction of Gene Wolfe', in Thomas Clareson and Thomas Wymer, eds, *Voices of the Future Vol. III* (Bowling Green, Ohio: Bowling Green University Popular Press, 1984), pp. 1–33.

——, review of *Bibliomen: Twenty Characters Waiting for a Book*, *Extrapolation*, 26, 1985, pp. 171–72.

Clute, John, *Strokes: Essays and Reviews 1966–1986* (Seattle: Serconia Press, 1988).

——, review of *There Are Doors*, *Interzone*, July/August 1989, p. 61.

——, review of *Castleview*, *The New York Review of Science Fiction*, August 1990, pp. 6–7.

Coulson, Robert, review of *The Castle of the Otter*, *Amazing Science Fiction Stories*, September 1983, pp. 14–15.

——, review of *Plan[e]t Engineering*, *Amazing Science Fiction Stories*, November 1984, p. 11.

D'Ammassa, Don, review of *Plan[e]t Engineering*, *Science Fiction Chronicle*, July 1984, p. 35.

Di Filippo, Paul, 'Long Night of the Wolfe', *Isaac Asimov's Science Fiction Magazine*, December 1997, pp. 154–57.

Dickinson, Mike, 'A Beast but a Just Beast: A Review of *The Shadow of the Torturer* and *The Claw of the Conciliator*', *Arena Science Fiction*, 13, 1982, pp. 22–24.

——, 'Why They're All Crying Wolfe': A Few Thoughts on *The Book of the New Sun*', *Vector*, February 1984, pp. 13–20.

Dirda, Michael, 'Provocations', *Washington Post Book World*, 21 February 1993.

Easton, Tom, review of *The Island of Doctor Death and Other Stories and Other Stories*, *Analog Science Fiction/Science Fact*, November 1980, pp. 169–70.

——, review of *Gene Wolfe's Book of Days*, *Analog Science Fiction/Science Fact*, October 1981, p. 168.

——, review of *The Sword of the Lictor*, *Analog Science Fiction/Science Fact*, May 1982, p. 168.

——, review of *Peace*, *Analog Science Fiction/Science Fact*, October 1982, p. 166.

Feeley, Gregory, review of *Soldier of the Mist*, *Foundation*, 37, 1986, pp. 69–71.

Frane, Jeff, review of *The Sword of the Lictor*, *Locus*, February 1982, p. 10.

——, review of *The Sword of the Lictor*, *Analog Science Fiction/Science Fact*, May 1982, p. 168.

French, Rod, 'Gene Wolfe and the Tale of Wonder: The End of the Apprenticeship',

Science Fiction: A Review of Speculative Literature, June 1983, pp. 43–47.

Friend, Beverly, review of *The Devil in a Forest, Delap's Fantasy and Science Fiction Review*, March 1977, pp. 21–22.

Gardner, Craig Shaw, review of *Soldier of the Mist, The Plain Dealer*, 14 January 1987, p. 17.

Geis, Richard E., review of *The Shadow of the Torturer, Science Fiction Review*, August 1980, pp. 40–41.

——, review of *The Claw of the Conciliator, Science Fiction Review*, August 1981, pp. 10–11.

Gentle, Mary, review of *Peace, Interzone*, Summer 1985, p. 44.

Gerlach, John, 'The Rhetoric of the Impossible Object: Gods, Chems and Science Fantasy in Gene Wolfe's *Book of the Long Sun*', *Extrapolation*, 40, 1999, pp. 153–61.

Gillespie, Bruce, 'Gene Wolfe's Sleight of Hand', *Australian Science Fiction Review*, March 1986, pp. 12–17.

Gordon, Joan, *Starmont Reader's Guide 29: Gene Wolfe* (Washington: Starmont House, 1986).

——, review of *The Urth of the New Sun, Science Fiction Research Association Newsletter*, October 1987, pp. 37–38.

——, review of *There Are Doors, Science Fiction Research Association Newsletter*, December 1988, pp. 41–42.

——, review of *There Are Doors, The New York Review of Science Fiction*, April 1989, pp. 15–16.

——, review of *Endangered Species, Science Fiction Research Association Newsletter*, July/August 1989, pp. 51–52.

——, review of *Caldé of the Long Sun, Science Fiction Research Association Review*, January/February 1995, p. 60–61.

Gouvêa, Fernando Quadros, review of *Soldier of the Mist, Fantasy Review*, September 1986, p. 33.

——, review of *Endangered Species, The New York Review of Science Fiction*, January 1990, p. 20.

Greenland, Colin, review of *The Shadow of the Torturer* and *The Claw of the Conciliator*, *Foundation*, 24, 1982, pp. 82–85.

——, review of *The Citadel of the Autarch, Foundation: The International Review of Science Fiction*, 28, 1983, pp. 89–91.

——, review of *Plan[e]t Engineering, Foundation*, 32, 1984, pp. 97–98.

——, review of *Peace, TLS*, 15 March 1985, p. 284.

——, 'Wolfe in Sheep's Clothing', *City Limits*, 21–27 October 1983, p. 18.

——, review of *The Urth of the New Sun, TLS*, 15–21 January 1988, p. 69.

Gregg, David W., 'Gene Wolfe: Understanding the Overworld', *The Mage*, Summer 1988, pp. 21–22.

Ikin, Van, review of *Soldier of the Mist, Science Fiction: A Review of Speculative Literature*, 25, n.d., pp. 22–23.

Jeffery, Steve, review of *The Fifth Head of Cerberus, Vector*, July/August 1999, pp. 21–22.

Kaveney, Roz, review of *The Island of Doctor Death and Other Stories and Other Stories*, *Foundation*, 21, 1981, pp. 79–83.

Killheffer, Robert, review of *Soldier of Arete, The New York Review of Science Fiction*, November 1989, pp. 6–7.

——, review of *Lake of the Long Sun*, *The Magazine of Fantasy and Science Fiction*, September 1994, pp. 19–21.

Kincaid, Paul, review of *Operation Ares*, *Vector*, January/February 1978, pp. 34–38.

——, review of *The Shadow of the Torturer*, *Vector*, June 1981, pp. 32–33.

——, review of *The Claw of the Conciliator*, *Vector*, August 1981, pp. 25–27.

——, review of *The Sword of the Lictor*, *Vector*, 108, n.d.,1982, pp. 38–39.

——, review of *The Citadel of the Autarch*, *Vector*, 114, n.d., 1983, pp. 37–38.

——, review of *The Urth of the New Sun*, *Vector*, April/May 1988, p. 28.

Langford, David, review of *Nightside the Long Sun* and *Lake of the Long Sun*, *Vector*, February/March 1994, pp. 27–28.

——, review of *Caldé of the Long Sun*, *Vector*, July/August 1995, p. 24.

——, review of *Exodus from the Long Sun*, *Vector*, July/August 1997, pp. 33–34.

Last, Martin, review of *Peace*, *Science Fiction Review*, May 1975, pp. 30–31.

Locey, Kathryn, 'Three Dreams, Seven Nights, and Gene Wolfe's Catholicism', *The New York Review of Science Fiction*, July 1996, pp. 1 and 8–12.

Lupoff, Richard, review of *Peace*, *Algol: The Magazine About Science Fiction*, Winter 1976, pp. 40–41.

Malekin, Peter, 'Remembering the Future: Gene Wolfe's *The Book of the New Sun*', in *The Fantastic in World Literature and the Arts: Selected Essays from the Fifth International Conference on the Fantastic in the Arts* (Westport: Greenwood Press, 1987), pp. 47–57.

Malzberg, Barry, 'An Imaginary Interview on Gene Wolfe's "Cues"', *Algol: A Magazine About Science Fiction*, May 1974, pp. 29–31.

Manlove, C. N., 'Terminus Non Est: Gene Wolfe's *The Book of the New Sun*', *Kansas Quarterly*, Summer 1984, pp. 7–20.

McAuley, Paul J., review of *Storeys from the Old Hotel*, *Interzone*, May/June 1989, p. 64.

Miller, Faren, review of *The Citadel of the Autarch*, *Locus*, January 1983, p. 26.

——, review of *The Urth of the New Sun*, *Locus*, August 1987, p. 13.

——, review of *Soldier of Arete*, *Locus*, December 1989, p. 17.

——, review of *Pandora by Holly Hollander*, *Locus*, November 1990, pp. 62–63.

——, review of *Nightside the Long Sun*, *Locus*, January 1993, p. 17.

——, review of *Caldé of the Long Sun*, *Locus*, August 1994, pp. 21–22.

Monteleone, Thomas, review of *The Fifth Head of Cerberus*, *Amazing Science Fiction Stories*, November 1972, pp. 123–24 and 129.

——, review of *The Urth of the New Sun*, *Locus*, August 1987, p. 13.

Nicholls, Peter, review of *The Urth of the New Sun*, *Foundation*, 41, 1987, pp. 92–97.

Owen, Ray, review of *The Island of Doctor Death and Other Stories and Other Stories*, *Vector*, February 1982, pp. 24–25.

Palmer, Steve, 'Looking Behind the Sun: Religious Implications of Gene Wolfe's Classic Novels', *Vector*, August/September 1991, pp. 10–11.

Park, Paul, review of *Nightside the Long Sun* and *Lake of the Long Sun*, *Foundation*, 61, 1994, pp. 97–99.

Pollack, Rachel, review of *Free Live Free*, *Foundation*, 35, 1985/6, pp. 99–102.

Reilly, Robert, review of *Soldier of Arete*, *Science Fiction Research Association Newsletter*, January/February 1990, pp. 36–37.

Russ, Joanna, review of *Operation Ares*, *The Magazine of Fantasy and Science Fiction*, April 1971, p. 69.

Sanders, Joe, review of *Free Live Free*, *Fantasy Review*, May 1985, p. 18.

Sargent, Pamela, 'Lost Peoples: A Review of *The Fifth Head of Cerberus*', *Vector*, May/June 1973, pp. 17–19.

Schuyler, William M., review of *The Wolfe Archipelago*, *Fantasy Review*, August 1984, p. 32.

——, review of *Peace*, *The New York Review of Science Fiction*, January 1996, pp. 19–21.

Schuyler-Miller, P., review of *The Fifth Head of Cerberus*, *Analog Science Fiction/Science Fact*, December 1972, pp. 170–71.

Schweitzer, Darrell, review of *The Devil in a Forest*, *Science Fiction Review*, May 1977, p. 75.

——, review of *The Sword of the Lictor*, *Science Fiction Review*, May 1982, pp. 25–27.

——, review of *The Citadel of the Autarch*, *Science Fiction Review*, Spring 1983, p. 41.

Searles, Baird, review of *The Shadow of the Torturer*, *Isaac Asimov's Science Fiction Magazine*, October 1980, pp. 12–15.

——, review of *The Claw of the Conciliator*, *Isaac Asimov's Science Fiction Magazine*, June 1981, pp. 12–15.

——, review of *The Sword of the Lictor*, *Isaac Asimov's Science Fiction Magazine*, April 1982, p. 16.

——, review of *The Citadel of the Autarch*, *Isaac Asimov's Science Fiction Magazine*, May 1983, pp. 167–68.

——, review of *Soldier of the Mist*, *Isaac Asimov's Science Fiction Magazine*, May 1987, pp. 184–85.

——, review of *Castleview*, *Isaac Asimov's Science Fiction Magazine*, August 1990, pp. 187–88.

Spinrad, Norman, review of *The Citadel of the Autarch*, *Isaac Asimov's Science Fiction Magazine*, July 1983, pp. 170–71.

Stephensen-Payne, Phil and Benson, Gordon, *Gene Wolfe: A Working Bibliography* (Leeds: Galactic Central, 1991).

Taylor, Martin, review of *The Urth of the New Sun*, *Vector*, April/May 1988, p. 28.

Turner, George, review of *The Fifth Head of Cerberus*, *Science Fiction Commentary*, November 1973, pp. 4–7.

——, review of *Peace*, *Science Fiction Commentary*, December 1975, pp. 29–32.

——, review of *Storeys from the Old Hotel*, *Science Fiction Commentary*, October 1993, p. 44.

Wilson, James, J. J., review of *Gene Wolfe's Book of Days*, *Science Fiction Review*, Winter 1981, p. 56.

Wood, Susan, review of *The Devil in a Forest*, *Locus*, April 1978, p. 13.

——, review of *The Shadow of the Torturer*, *Starship*, Spring 1981, pp. 40–41.

——, review of *The Island of Doctor Death and Other Stories and Other Stories*, *Starship*, Fall 1990, p. 17.

Wright, Peter, 'God-Games: Cosmic Conspiracies and Narrative Sleights in Gene Wolfe's the Fictions of the New Sun', *Foundation*, 66, 1996, pp. 13–39.

——, 'Grasping the God-Games: Metafictional Keys to the Interpretation of Gene Wolfe's The Fictions of the New Sun', *Foundation*, 66, 1996, pp. 39–59.

General Works

Aldiss, Brian (with Wingrove, David), *Trillion Year Spree: The History of Science Fiction* (London: Victor Gollancz, 1986).

Arnheim, Rudolf, *Entropy and Art: An Essay on Disorder and Order* (Berkeley: University of California Press, 1971).

Ash, Brian, *Faces of the Future* (London: Elek Books, 1975).

Attebery, Brian, *Strategies of Fantasy* (Bloomington: Indiana University Press, 1992).

Baldick, Chris, *The Concise Oxford Dictionary of Literary Terms* (Oxford: Oxford University Press, 1990).

Behrends, Steve, *Starmont Reader's Guide: Clark Ashton Smith* (Washington: Starmont House, 1990).

Bell, Ian, ed., *William Hope Hodgson: Voyages and Visions* (Oxford: Ian Bell and Sons, 1987).

Bergonzi, Bernard, *The Early H. G. Wells: A Study of the Scientific Romances* (Manchester: Manchester University Press, 1961).

Biedermann, Hans, *The Dictionary of Symbolism: Cultural Icons and the Meanings Behind Them*, trans. James Hulbert (New York: Facts on File, 1992).

Bleiler, E. F., ed., *Supernatural Fiction Writers*, 2 vols (New York: Charles Scribner's Sons, 1985).

Booth, Wayne C., *The Rhetoric of Fiction* (Chicago: University of Chicago Press, 1961).

Borges, Jorge Luis, *The Book of Imaginary Beings*, rev. and trans. Norman Thomas di Giovanni (London: Penguin Books, 1974).

——, *Fictions*, ed. Anthony Kerrigan, trans. Alastair Read (London: Calder Publications, 1965, repr. 1985).

——, *Other Inquisitions 1937–1952*, trans. Ruth L. C. Simms (London: Souvenir Press, 1973), pp. 86–89.

Bradbury, Ray, *The Martian Chronicles* (London: Rupert Hart-Davis, 1951; repr. London: Granada Books, 1977, repr. 1981).

Brown, Lesley, ed., *The New Shorter Oxford English Dictionary*, 2 vols (Oxford: Clarendon Press, 1993).

Byron, Robert, *The Byzantine Achievement: An Historical Perspective A.D. 330–1453* (London: Routledge and Kegan Paul, 1927, repr. 1987).

Campbell, John W., *The Thing from Outer Space* (Chicago: Shasta Publishing, 1951; repr. London: Tandem Books, 1966).

Campbell, Joseph, *The Hero with a Thousand Faces* (Princeton: Princeton University Press, 1949; repr. London: Paladin [Grafton Books], 1988).

——, *Myths to Live By* (New York: The Viking Press, 1972; repr. London: Souvenir Press, 1991).

Carroll, Lewis, *Alice's Adventures in Wonderland and Through the Looking Glass*, rev. edn (Oxford: Oxford University Press, 1982, repr. 1991).

Clifford, Gay, *The Transformations of Allegory* (London: Routledge and Kegan Paul, 1974).

Clute, John and Nicholls, Peter, *The Encyclopedia of Science Fiction*, rev. edn (London: Orbit, 1993).

Coveney, Peter and Highfield, Roger, *The Arrow of Time* (London: W. H. Allen, 1990).

Dawkins, Richard, *The Selfish Gene*, rev. edn (Oxford: Oxford University Press, 1989).

Draper, Michael, *H. G. Wells* (London: Macmillan, 1987).

Escher, M. C., *The Graphic Work* (Berlin: Taschen Verlag, 1990).

Evans, Ivor H., ed., *Brewer's Dictionary of Phrase and Fable* (London: Cassell, 1959, repr. 1985).

Finch, Peter, ed., *The New Elizabethan Reference Dictionary* (London: George Newnes, n.d.).

Fish, Stanley, *Is There a Text in This Class?: The Authority of Interpretative Communities* (London: Harvard University Press, 1980).

Fortune, Dion, *The Mystical Qabalah* (1935; repr. London: Aquarian Press, 1987).

Frye, Northrop, *Anatomy of Criticism: Four Essays* (Princeton: Princeton University Press, 1957).

Gould, Stephen Jay, *Time's Arrow, Time's Cycle* (London: Penguin Books, 1990).

Graves, Robert, *The Greek Myths*, complete edn (London: Penguin Books, 1992).

Gregory, Richard L., ed., *The Oxford Companion to the Mind* (Oxford: Oxford University Press, 1987).

Harari, Josué V., ed., *Textual Strategies: Perspectives in Post-Structuralist Criticism* (New York: Cornell University Press, 1979).

Hawkes, Jacquetta, *Man and the Sun* (London: The Cresset Press, 1963).

Haynes, R. D., *H. G. Wells: Discoverer of the Future* (London: Macmillan, 1980).

Hirsch, E. D., *Validity in Interpretation* (London: Yale University Press, 1967).

Hodgson, William Hope, *The House on the Borderland* (London: Evelyn Nash, 1908; repr. London: Panther Books, 1969).

——, *The Night Land* (London: Evelyn Nash, 1912; repr. London: Grafton Books, 1990).

Hutcheon, Linda, *Narcissistic Narrative: The Metafictional Paradox* (London: Methuen, 1984).

Iser, Wolfgang, *The Implied Reader: Patterns of Communication in Prose Fiction from Bunyan to Beckett* (Baltimore: Johns Hopkins University Press, 1974).

——, *The Act of Reading: A Theory of Aesthetic Response* (London: Routledge and Kegan Paul, 1978).

Jarman, Beatriz Galimberti and Russell, Roy, *The Oxford Spanish Dictionary* (Oxford: Oxford University Press, 1994).

Juhl, P. D., *Interpretations: An Essay in the Philosophy of Literary Criticism* (Princeton: Princeton University Press, 1980).

Jung, C. G., *The Collected Works of C. G. Jung*, trans. R. F. C. Hull, 2nd edn, 20 vols (London: Routledge and Kegan Paul, 1968).

Kaveney, Roz, review of C. N. Manlove's *Science Fiction: Ten Explorations*, *Foundation*, 39, 1987, pp. 93–97.

Kermode, Frank, *The Genesis of Secrecy* (Harvard: Harvard University Press, 1980).

Kipling, Rudyard, *The Jungle Book* (London: Pan Books, 1967, repr. 1971).

Leakey, Richard E., *The Making of Mankind* (New York: Elsevier-Dutton, 1981).

Leakey, Richard and Lewin, Roger, *Origins Reconsidered: In Search of What Makes Us Human* (London: Little, Brown & Co., 1992).

Leech, Geoffrey N. and Short, Michael H., *Style in Fiction* (London: Longman Publications, 1981).

Lempriere, J., *Lempriere's Classical Dictionary*, rev. edn (London: Bracken Books, 1984).

Liddell, H. G. and Scott, R., *An Intermediate Greek–English Lexicon* (Oxford: Oxford University Press, 1889, repr. 1991).

Lovecraft, H. P., *Dagon and Other Macabre Tales* (London: Granada Books, 1985).

Luria, A. R., *The Mind of a Mnemonist*, trans. Lynn Solotaroff (London: Jonathan Cape, 1969).

Malmgren, Carl D., 'Towards a Definition of Science Fantasy', *Science-Fiction Studies*, 15, 1988, pp. 259–81.

May, Rollo, *The Cry for Myth* (New York: W. W. Norton & Co., 1991; repr. London: Souvenir Press, 1993).

Miller, Walter M., *A Canticle for Leibowitz* (London: Weidenfeld and Nicolson, 1960; repr. London: Corgi Books, 1974).

Moorcock, Michael, *An Alien Heat* (London: MacGibbon and Kee, 1972; repr. London: Granada Publishing, 1982).

——, *The Hollow Lands* (London: Mayflower Books, 1975; repr. London: Granada Publishing, 1979).

——, *The End of All Songs* (London: Hart-Davis MacGibbon, 1976; repr. London: Granada Publishing, 1984).

——, *Legends from the End of Time* (London: W. H. Allen & Co., 1976; repr. London: Star, 1979).

——, *The Transformation of Miss Mavis Ming* (London: W. H. Allen & Co., 1977; repr. London: Star, 1980).

Moore, R. I., ed., *The Newnes Historical Atlas*, rev. edn (London: Newnes Books, 1983).

Parrinder, Patrick, *Science Fiction: Its Criticism and Teaching* (London: Methuen, 1980).

Romer, Alfred Sherwood, *Vertebrate Palaeontology*, 3rd edn (London: University of Chicago Press, 1974).

Rottensteiner, Franz, *The Fantasy Book* (London: Thames and Hudson, 1978).

Russell, Bertrand, *History of Western Philosophy*, 2nd edn (London: George Allen and Unwin, 1961; repr. London: Routledge, 1991).

Scholes, Robert, *Fabulation and Metafiction* (London: University of Illinois Press, 1979).

Simpson, D. P., *Cassell's Latin–English English–Latin Dictionary*, 5th edn (London: Cassell, 1987, repr. 1990).

Slusser, George E. and Rabkin, Eric S., eds, *Intersections: Fantasy and Science Fiction— Essays Presented at the Seventh Eaton Conference* (Carbondale and Edwardsville: Southern Illinois University Press, 1987), pp. 26–35.

Smith, Clark Ashton, *Zothique* (New York: Ballantine Books, 1970).

Suvin, Darko, *Metamorphoses of Science Fiction* (London: Yale University Press, 1979).

Swinfen, Anne, *In Defence of Fantasy* (London: Routledge and Kegan Paul, 1984).

Tarassuk, Leonid and Blair, Claude, *The Complete Encyclopedia of Arms and Weapons* (New York: Simon & Schuster, 1982).

Tompkins, Jane, ed., *Reader Response Criticism from Formalism to Post-Structuralism* (Baltimore: Johns Hopkins University Press, 1980).

Underwood, Tim and Miller, Chuck, eds, *Jack Vance* (New York: Taplinger Publishing Co., 1980).

Vance, Jack, *The Dying Earth* (1950; repr. London: Grafton Books, 1972, repr. 1986).

Wagar, Warren W., *Terminal Visions* (Bloomington: University of Indiana Press, 1982).

Waite, A. E., *The Holy Kabbalah* (New York: Carol Publishing Group, 1990).

Wales, Katie, *A Dictionary of Stylistics* (London: Longman, 1989, repr. 1990).

Warnock, Mary, *Memory* (London: Faber & Faber, 1987, repr. 1989).

Warry, John, *Warfare in the Classical World* (London: Salamander Books, 1980).

Waugh, Patricia, *Metafiction: The Theory and Practice of Self Conscious Fiction* (London: Methuen, 1984).

Wells, H. G., *The Time Machine* (1895; repr. London: J. M. Dent, 1993).

Wendland, Albert, *Science, Myth, and the Fictional Creation of Alien Worlds* (Ann Arbour, Michigan: UMI Research Press, 1985).

White, John J., *Mythology in the Modern Novel* (Princeton: Princeton University Press, 1971).

Whitrow, G. J., *What is Time?* (London: Thames and Hudson, 1972).

Wilkinson-Lathom, Robert, *Swords* (London: Blandford Press, 1977).

Wittgenstein, Ludwig, *The Blue and the Brown Books: Preliminary Studies for the 'Philosophical Investigations'*, 2nd edn (Oxford: Blackwell, 1969, repr. 1992).

Wolfe, Gary K., *The Known and the Unknown: The Iconography of Science Fiction* (Kent, OH: Kent State University Press, 1979).

——, *Critical Terms for Science Fiction and Fantasy: A Glossary and Guide to Scholarship* (New York: Greenwood Press, 1986).

Worton, Michael and Still, Judith, eds, *Intertextuality: Theories and Practices* (Manchester: Manchester University Press, 1990), pp. 1–44.

Yates, Frances A., *The Art of Memory* (1966; repr. London: Pimlico, 1992).

Young, Robert, ed., *Untying the Text: A Post-Structuralist Reader* (London: Routledge and Kegan Paul, 1981).

Zamyatin, Yevgeny, *We*, trans. Bernard Guilbert Guerney (London: Jonathan Cape, 1970; repr. London: Penguin Books, 1980).

Index